THE GREY LIST

CHEMISTRY

"THE CHEMIST"

Copyright 2024 Grey Huffington

All Rights reserved

GREY HUFFINGTON

Instagram.com/greyhuffington

TRIGGER WARNING

PLEASE READ THIS SECTION!

Seeing this note means the book you are about to read could contain triggering situations or actions. This book is subject to one or more of the triggers listed below.

Please note that this a universal trigger warning page that is included in Grey Huffington books and is not specified for any particular set of characters, book, couple, etc.
This book does not contain all the warnings listed. It is simply a way to warn you that this particular book contains things/a thing that may be triggering for some.

This is my way of recognizing the reality and life experiences of my Romance friends and making sure I

properly prepare you for what is to unfold within the
pages of this book.

violence
sexual assault
drug addiction
suicide
homicide
miscarriage/child loss
child abuse
emotional abuse
mental illness
infidelity
infertility
cancer
criminal activity

CONTENTS

Chemistry   vii

Prologue   1
Chemistry   91
Note.   93
Chemistry   95
Chapter 1   97
Chapter 2   123
Chapter 3   141
Chapter 4   161
Chapter 5   175
Chapter 6   199
Chapter 7   215
Chapter 8   231
Chapter 9   249
Chapter 10   275
Chapter 11   289
Chapter 12   313
Chapter 13   341
Chapter 14   363
Chapter 15   391
Chapter 16   413
Chapter 17   429
Chapter 18   443
Epilogue   467

Next...   475
ghuffington.com   479
More from Grey Huffington   481

THE GREY LIST

CHEMISTRY

"THE CHEMIST"

GREY**HUFFINGTON**

Chemistry

"I am not a drug dealer."

The words I'd spoken time and time again rolled effortlessly off my tongue. Unbuttoning the last button on my right sleeve, I prepared to roll it up slightly. The one on my left wrist and the two closest to my neck had already been undone.

If I needed more reach, *more room*, to get active, I didn't need the twelve-hundred dollar shirt becoming a hindrance. Burning bread was never on my list of things to do, but if the top got in the way of my progression, I'd gladly toss it in a tin of flames.

"I am not a seller. I am not a handler. I am not an abuser. I am not a promoter. I am not a smuggler."

Carefully, I observed the mannerisms of each man who sat before me. Though their faces were concealed, I knew every detail about each of them. Their identity wasn't the mystery. Mine was. So was our location and the meeting in session.

Within twenty minutes, which was the time it would take anyone to reach the address that wasn't available on any mapping system or satellite, they'd be dismissed. However, they wouldn't be the same men who sat down before me. They'd be a lot richer. A lot smarter. More valuable. Highly sought after. Fully protected.

"Nonetheless, I understand I cannot save the world or the people who have chosen those paths. So, making substances safer, grander, and extremely unique is my life's work. What I have created can't be duplicated, stepped on, or mistaken for anything else.

"I've curated one thousand eight hundred twenty-seven strands of the purest, rarest white on the market. I am not interested in or addicted to even one of them. Your clients, nevertheless, are. That is why you are here and that is why your budding empire needs me."

Straightening my slightly misaligned posture, I relieved my spine and squared my shoulders. Taking one step at a time, I treaded the concrete flooring that had been cleaned a hundred times or more. Splattered brains and puddled blood were fed to the hard surface almost as much as forbidden food was spoon-fed to a baby who wasn't quite ready to stomach solids, *according to physicians.*

"I am a Chemist. I am *The Chemist.*"

One by one, I removed the jute bags from the heads of three men. Immediately, visions of their scattered craniums flashed before my eyes. Exposed lobes appeared just as I began to wiggle through the creases of my own. Seconds passed us by until I was able to shake the thought of brain matter and dislodged hearts.

Thanks, Catherine.

Blinking away the bloodshed and tapping back into the moment, I continued my stride. Only this time, I was no longer in front of the men. I remained behind them, daring either of them to attempt to turn. The wrong movement could be their last.

"I am a single element that will take your business to heights you haven't considered in the time my product can make it happen. If you're here, it means you've passed every test and without a doubt in my mind, you belong here.

"Not because I said so but because two of the most important people in my life said so. I trust their word over my very own. Being here is not a privilege you should take lightly. It is an opportunity of a lifetime."

Pausing briefly, I took a good look at the new squad. Each represented a few million in my account. Simultaneously, they could also represent the downfall of my empire. That was always the risk taken when recruiting, but we'd done the homework. Extensive homework. Everyone seated was legit.

"Underneath your chairs, you'll find documentation with a few steps for you to execute to put the plan in motion. When you reach for your file, do not get curious.

Turning around, at any point, could mean the end for you."

Slowly, cautiously, each man reached underneath their seat to obtain the file that had been tailored to their hustle. A standard business model didn't fit everyone who walked through my door, so we created a different one for each person according to their current revenue, location, customers, and proximity to danger.

I observed the trio intensely, keeping my eyes trained on their bodies as I studied their movements. To my dismay, I locked eyes with the man in the middle. Quickly, he turned his head in the opposite direction, but he wasn't quick enough.

Disobeying orders was the quickest way to get buried in my line of business. He'd just tested the theory. Without a doubt, I knew it would be his last time testing anything. It was a fucking shame.

BLOW.

"Che–"

Expanded nostrils and a hiked eyebrow quieted her before she could complete her thought. I pushed forward, out of earshot, to address the woman staring at me with conflict.

"He turned," I explained to one of the few people in my life I felt I owed an explanation.

She and six others who were almost identical were the only women in my world who could get a word, rise, or dime out of me.

Seven, the consuming voice in my head corrected.

Seven. The woman who'd birthed them couldn't be forgotten.

"Fuck," she mumbled, already calculating the time it would take her to clean the mess I'd made.

It wasn't the task or my actions that had her biting her tongue and shaking her head. Those pretty eyes were remorseful. That pretty heart was hurting. Tilting my head, I smiled.

Oh, baby.

I swiped my nose with the back of my hand, still holding the hot tool as I did so.

"You'll find another one."

With a roll of her eyes, she nodded. The gnawing of her bottom lip was evidence of her flared emotions and tampered feelings. There was no place for them here.

"Pull it together." I snapped two fingers.

She nodded again.

"I have."

In an instant, Range was void of emotions and ready for the task ahead of her. Rolling the nigga she was fucking in a body bag wasn't on her schedule this evening, but shit had changed.

"And, avoid fucking the help, baby, so you won't have these types of problems."

With the butt of the gun, I tapped her temple.

"Bosses. Bosses. Ummkay? Bosses. The biggest or no one at all, baby. The best or no one at all, baby. The b–"

"Okay."

I'd tried countless times to program it in their heads.

Certain niggas didn't deserve their presence. The nigga sitting – *that was sitting* – before me was one of them.

Fucking a nigga on the rise was the quickest downfall of a woman who was already seated on her throne. I'd seen it too many times before. It was rare, very rare, a queen entertained a peasant and it turned out in her favor.

"Do better, baby."

I left her where she stood, returning to the men who knew how to follow directions. Diverting my attention was not a smart move; neither was attempting to put a face to my voice. It was pointless because the second you became a liability was the last one you'd breathe.

"Personalized formulas have been distributed. Please remove the solution from the bag inside of the folder you retrieved."

Carefully, each man removed the vial from the small bag before sealing it and closing the folder. I gave them time to observe the amber-colored glass that held the key to their future inside.

"Before your kilos are bricked and sold, increase your profits and its potency by incorporating this very strategically formulated solution. This will give you a safer strand that is undeniably solid, pure, and unique."

Nods from the duo let me know they both understood exactly what was being explained.

"More instructions will come. Take it to the field. Track its performance. That will last you a full week. There's no need to give us a call. We'll always reach out to you. This meeting has concluded. Your vehicles are waiting."

The brown fabric would cover their faces before they had a chance to identify much of anything or anyone in the empty space. However, I allowed them to stretch their legs and prepare for the journey ahead. Unfortunately, shaking the hand or looking in the eyes of the man who would be responsible for their rapid success still wasn't an option.

"There are only two rules."

Their bodies halted right in front of their chairs as if the music had stopped during a game of musical chairs.

"Keep your mouth closed and never... I mean *never*... cut my shit."

Without another second wasted, I pushed through the double doors that led to more emptiness and light. The shell of a building had its purposes and comfort wasn't one of them. I tossed the jute bags into the burning fire. New ones would be distributed. Those, however, carried identifying elements that were to be discarded.

"Pop." A gentleness I was all too familiar with released with a sigh.

"Rome."

Without readjusting my line of vision or position in front of the fire, I breathed the name of my youngest sibling. Though not much changed visibly, parts of me softened that only she had access to. And, my heart, the rate sped as it became increasingly heavy.

Fucking girls. I gritted.

They were reminders I did have a heart and that motherfucker was functional.

"What are you doing here?"

"My lesson was canceled. My profes–"

"That doesn't answer my question, baby."

"I–" she mumbled.

Head down. Hands in front of her. Fingers fondling each other. Eyes low. Heart heavy. I didn't need to see Rome to feel Rome... *to know Rome*. She wore her big feelings on her sleeve, a trait I despised in humans. No one needed to know what you were feeling, what was on your heart that easily.

One should always have the right to choose what information others were privy to. Rome didn't have that privilege. That was why she was the center of my world. Because we were so many years apart, she felt more like a child I shared with my father and stepmother than a sister.

"Rome."

Turning, I found her standing behind me with weary eyes and anxious hands.

"I won't beg you to express yourself."

"I haven't seen you in a few days and haven't had the chance to tell you I'm auditioning for The Black–"

"Swan," I finished.

"Of course, you already knew." Sucking her teeth, she rolled those big, doe-like eyes that were mirrors to her soul.

"It's my job to know, Rome. You've stayed late for the last week. I needed to know why."

"You could've asked."

"I didn't think you were ready for me to know."

"I wasn't. In case I didn't get the part."

"That's impossible." I scoffed.

"Without your help."

"I–"

"Or Royce's."

Chuckling, I nodded. "Okay, I get it, baby."

"I'm serious, Pop. I don't want any of you getting involved. I want to earn this."

"You've earned everything you've been involved in, baby. I don't understand."

"Influence feels like the driving force behind some of the accolades in my life thus far."

"I have never allowed my influence to serve your passion. Neither have I ever lied to you. So hear me very clearly when I tell you it has always been all you. You're the best there is and will ever be.

"You're a natural, baby. Accept it and never credit me for anything other than your discipline and determination. I've done nothing more than push you to heights that were always attainable for you, even when you didn't believe it."

"Thank you."

The longing in her stare made my lips curl and my head shake from one side to the other. She was yearning for something–*someone*. It happened to be me. Physical touch was her greatest love language. It wasn't mine.

I observed as her brows raised on her forehead. Dark skin covered every inch of her except the spot underneath her right arm where her mark of birth rested. With a round head and wondrous eyes, Rome was incredibly beautiful. She shared identical features with at least two of the women she shared blood with and called her sister.

"I'm leaving," I announced.

Before I could fall victim to her antics, I pushed past her toward the door that would lead to the roof where a windy chopper was landing and waiting to airlift me to my next destination. I could feel the effects of the blades as I neared the exit. Just as I thought I'd managed to set myself free, umber-colored skin that resembled mine wrapped around me, stopping me in my tracks.

"Just accept it," Rome demanded.

As cold as she portrayed herself in public, she was almost the warmest. Roaman, the oldest of the bunch, was the epitome of warmth. Her facade was easily tarnished when among the people she loved most. That was when her sleeves were covered with her true feelings, thoughts, desires, and emotions.

"Just accept it, Chem. Don't fight it."

The chuckle I harbored began to slip from my lips. Baby was full of love and containing it was too much of a task. She needed to release it every chance she had. Everyone in our circle had been victimized by her bullshit, but we'd dare dismiss her or avoid the very thing that gave us all something to look forward to.

"Are you done now?"

"Not quite."

She squeezed tighter.

"It's been days since I hugged you, Teddy."

Pop. Teddy. Chem. She rotated the three without issue.

"I'd like to leave now," I expressed.

Turning in her arms, I grabbed the sides of her face and lowered my lips to her forehead. I buried her face in my chest and released everything conflicting with me. Her hugs were healing.

"Okay. See you later?"

"You won't, but I will see you after your audition to congratulate you on another job well done."

"Thanks for the vote of confidence."

"You don't need it. Head up."

Rome backed away as she nodded, understanding every word I'd spoken.

"I love you." She sighed.

"In this lifetime and the others."

Beyond this world's realm, I had a heart for my people. My love wasn't conditional. It was relentless and had no limits. In every lifetime, in every world, it was made for Roulette, Roaman, Rome, Rugger, Royce, Rather, Range, Malachi, Mercer, Milo, and Makai.

"I'll find you there, too."

"I'll wait."

With two fingers, I tapped my chest, finalizing my goodbye. With leaden steps, I ascended the stairs to reach the door where I exited and found a loud, obnoxious helicopter waiting.

"Chemist," Jason acknowledged me with a head nod as the door of the chopper swung open.

A mirrored response sufficed as I climbed into the

rather spacious pit and slid the headphones over my ears. Jason sat beside me, taking on the role of co-pilot after my split decision led my fingers across the motherboard. Waiting as I was airlifted across the city was the initial plan. That quickly changed.

Soundlessly, I began checking off tasks from the list, preparing the aircraft for takeoff. There wasn't much that hadn't already been done.

Within seconds we were back in the air, and I was turning out every anxious word Jason spat in order to take a second to admire the beauty of Clarke. It was nearly the largest city in Huffington. It was, most certainly, the wealthiest with Channing placing second.

Sixteen minutes later, I was whisked away from the noisy piece of machinery, cleaning the traces of uncleanliness from underneath my manicured nails as the tires rotated on the city's paved roads. Once satisfied with my efforts, I gathered my eyelids and explored the folds of my mind.

The sound of crashing waves lulled me. The feeling of cold, aggressive waves pulling me deeper into the ocean's arms caused my skin to grow thicker, producing small, fine bumps all over.

Patiently, I waited for the recurring vision to produce evidence it was real. Because it felt like it. But, just like every other time, nothing more than a few waves, evidence of excellent lung capacity, and commendable endurance revealed themselves.

The persistence of the darkness carried on until the

vehicle came to a complete stop. The engine of the Escalade quieted. So did my mind.

"Chemist." Aden beckoned for my attention.

"I'm aware."

I separated my lids from one another, basking in the silence that preceded what was to come. Sunlight peered down into the backseat as the door widened, waiting to greet me, again. It wasn't for long.

One.

Two.

Three.

Four swift steps led me into darkness again, freeing me from the brightness and risk of public consumption. It was two steps too many. The breezeway that led to the lecture hall was long, but not quite long enough. Exposure was forbidden under any circumstances to maintain the integrity of the quarterly meetings. Someone hadn't gotten the memo.

Stretched legs pushed through the nippy space. I buttoned the single button of the finely pressed jacket Aden handed me as I stepped out of the vehicle. It was a perfect match for the pants that had been designed to complement it.

The vibration of my phone reminded me to silence my notifications. All calls would have to wait. What I was walking into was far more important than whatever was waiting to be divulged to me on the other line.

Fine, small bumps peaked at the expense of my smooth, unblemished skin as I turned the corner and entered the nearly empty room with only a table and three useless chairs.

No one was sitting and I wouldn't be the first. Relaxing my limbs left too much at stake.

Slowed my movement tremendously. Gave me unnecessary resistance when releasing my weapon. And, adding two seconds too many to the escape route was always, *always* prepared in my head. Sitting was not an option. It was never an option.

Valentine. I nodded toward the host of the quarter.

Tension, as thick as a well-done steak at the finest steakhouse, thickened a bit more as my presence was added to the stirring pot.

There was *no beef*.

There was *no competition*.

There were *no ill feelings*.

There were only rules and regulations neither of the families within The Triad cared to abide by. But, to maintain peace and order within the city of Clarke, we had no choice.

If order was ever lost, empires would burn and so would the city we cherished. To evenly distribute the land so the three most powerful families could remain in control without bumping heads, The Triad of Ara was formed.

The first letter from the wives of the leaders' names was combined to identify the triad and solidify its presence in Clarke. Though ghostly in nature, there wasn't a soul in the underbelly that didn't know of its existence.

Ashland. The wife of Kalvin Valentine.

Rhea. My father's wife, *my stepmother*.

Angela. The wife of Henry Baptiste.

"Four steps too many," I informed.

"Noted," Priest responded with a nod. "Pardon my– *misalignment*."

"Shall we get down to business?" Honor cleared his throat, unable to stand still longer than a few seconds. The youngest of the bunch, his head was the hottest.

THE GREY LIST

Situated in the back of the truck with the meeting behind me and a missed call from my father staring back at me, I contemplated dialing him back before allowing everything that transpired to register. It was business as usual, but the presence of a few cats from Perry had ruffled a few of The Triad's feathers.

Nothing had come of their presence yet but could change at any given second. When it did, *if it did*, peace wouldn't be possible in Clarke.

I'd comb every cranny to dead every nigga with a Perry stench so Rugger wouldn't have to. Some shit was below her pay grade and Perry niggas were at the top of the list. Her attention was better elsewhere.

"Rhea," with difficulty, I sputtered.

I expected my father's baritone on the opposite end of the line. Her silky, feminine resolve caught me off guard.

"Yes, son."

"I received a call from my father."

"He's been napping for a while now. By the time you arrive, he will be awake."

"I didn't insinuate my–"

"There aren't many reasons he'd call, Chem. He's requesting you."

"Then, I'm en route."

Wordlessly, I ended the call. The altering of direction made it clear Aden had gotten the memo and knew my father's compound was the new destination.

Knots gathered in a central location, twisting my stomach to the point of discomfort. Coiled and contorted, it increased the saliva in the pit of my mouth.

Weekly, I shook my father's hand and sat at his table. Often, I joined him on the golf course. Spring, early fall, and particular days in the summer when the weather permitted and the winds were low, our shoes treaded the artificial greenery for hours as our bellies grew hungry and we'd quenched our thirst a hundred times or more.

In forty-eight minutes, exactly, we arrived at the gates. Our entry was granted immediately. They were waiting. They always were.

A semi-loop around the fountain in the center of the estate led to the double doors of my family's home. A perfectly manicured yard would impress his neighbors if they lived close enough or could see over the brick. My father valued his privacy. He didn't care if anyone ever knew who was behind the walls he'd built, as long as he was living comfortably behind them, then all was well.

I entered the familiar space. The comfort that usually wrapped me in its arms was replaced with a cold stillness I quickly learned I wasn't fond of. Nothing felt right. Everything was displaced.

I stopped, momentarily, hiking my nose in the air. There was a stench, a repulsive one that began to drain the blood from me without considering the failure of my organs, including the large one that was surrounded by vessels that kept me alive.

Death. It was potent. The smell of it was one I was far too familiar with to dismiss. Flared nostrils and a panged heart led me toward the dining hall where I could feel my father's presence. It pulled me deeper into his home until I reached him.

Quickly repulsed, I slid my back teeth across each other, applying pressure. Naturally, my hands drew inward, fingers curling to accommodate my palms.

Unkempt.

Unwell.

Unrecognizable.

My father sat before me without the beaming smile one would miss if they blinked or the stern gaze he wore most often accompanying him. Confusion gripped me by the neck, threatening to end every single thing right then and there. I tugged the fabric around the button closest to the top.

Finally, once I'd freed the small, round piece of plastic, did I feel my lungs refill with oxygen. There wasn't a day, not one, I recall seeing my father anything other than at his best.

The finest threads covered his body, daily. A gold tooth covered each tooth next to the largest in the front of his mouth. A toothpick rolled between them nearly every waking hour of his life.

Crisp.

Though one word, it described everything about him. Everything about his appearance.

Hairline.

Pant crease.

Shoes.

Jacket.

Coat.

Shirt.

Whip.

He'd been that nigga since I could remember what a real nigga was. He'd been at the top of his game since I'd noticed as a boy there was one. But, this man... the one before me... was a mere shell of the man I knew up until this moment.

"Richie," I muttered, still trying to digest the disruptiveness of his appearance.

"I harbor no apologies for my–" he coughed out, grabbing the glass of room-temperature water in front of him.

By the time he'd finished nourishing the dryness of his throat, words still failed him. Me, however, there were a few at the tip of my tongue. I waited, impatiently, as he regained his composure. And, after a silent battle within, I released them with worry.

"Are you dying?"

Tipping around the matter had never served a purpose, in my opinion. Head on, that was how I preferred facing anything that came my way in life, including death.

It was as sure as birth. Whether we believed it or not, we all had a designated hour to leave Earthside. It was the only sure thing in life. You couldn't cheat it. You couldn't outrun it.

With a nod, my father wiped the residue from his lips with a white cloth I'd seen countless times before. However, it was the pink stain he left on it that I had never bore witness to. His failure to conceal it was due to another coughing fit he quickly fell victim to.

Blood.

Victim?

Weak. Unfit. Sheeply.

Things I'd never mentioned in the same sentence with my father had come to mind. The strength for standing was no longer within my grasp. I slid the chair from underneath the table and had a seat.

My eyes never left the man who had remained a lone figure in my childhood until along came Rhea and created structure and balance in our world. Before her, it was him and I during my frequent visits and lengthy stays at his home. Things changed from the moment she introduced herself at the dining table in front of a full spread of food she'd prepared. Rhea gave us something pretty to see because all we'd seen was each other and the black-and-white world we'd created to live in. She was color in our colorless sphere.

"How long?" I asked when he was able to speak again.

"Hard to say. The shit is everywhere. Could be six months. Could be a year. Could be two years."

Two years, the lengthiest mentioned, and it was still not enough time to prepare me to be fatherless. *Motherless*. An orphan of sorts.

"Don't spare me."

"A year. At best." He shrugged.

I stood, hands and mind anxious.

"Put yourself together, Richie. Get your shit together, you hear? You don't get to die. Not yet."

"I don't plan on it."

"Good."

"But, it will happen."

Nodding, I agreed. The intensity of the moment, the reality of the moment, became too much to bear. I needed fresh air. I needed community. I needed my girls.

One foot in front of the other, I tried putting as much distance between me and the pungent smell. But, it followed me. It followed me until I heard him struggle to call my name.

"Chem!"

The pain in his voice wasn't from the same pain in my chest. It was from the level of difficulty speaking caused.

"Yes."

"I don't want to leave the earth without knowing you've done your part."

History, it was made to be repeated and then

perfected. That was my father's memo and he'd nailed it in my skull as a boy. I was the better version of him. He'd made sure of it. My turn had come. He wanted the same for me. He *needed* the same from me.

An heir.

Questioning his resolve wasn't necessary. It had been discussed time and time again.

It wasn't a request. It was a demand, one he'd given me at the tender age of twenty-two. At thirty-six, it was the only demand he'd ever given that I hadn't fallen through with.

"Understood."

Without another word, I exited his home, leaving my heart right where he'd broken it.

"You know, I've seen so much in my lifetime. So much. But, the one thing I desire I haven't quite gotten the chance to experience has been sitting with me. Heavy on me, one would say. There, every time I lay down for bed the world is finally silenced. There."

"Yeah?" I asked as I lined the ball with the hole I was aiming for.

"Yes."

"What's that?"

I smacked the small white ball, landing it right where I wanted it.

We gathered our things, ready to move to the next hole, but not before my father's words continued.

"My son sharing his heart with someone other than the

girls I gave him or the woman I brought into his life. Other than Malachi's wife, Anna, or his mother."

"You speak about me as if I'm not the one you're speaking to."

"Mmm."

"You said you wanted a grandson. I'll give you that much. Giving pieces of a heart that isn't mine to share, I can't make a promise."

"Your mother." He chuckled. "She was a ball of fire tucked away in the most gentle being one could ever encounter. That's what I loved about her. That's what Maurice loved about her. May his soul rest in peace."

"May it."

"I loved that woman. But, my God. He loved that woman."

"To his detriment," I reminded him.

"Til his death."

"Is that supposed to convince me to fall in love?" Scoffing, I stopped to grab the ball that was in the hole. "If love will be the death of me, then I don't want any parts of it."

"As if your love for your sisters or your brothers wouldn't result in death." He tittered with a shake of the head. My twenty-eight-year-old brain still couldn't wrap my head around the fact Maurice's love for my mother had been as beautiful as it was tragic.

"He loved her to death."

"And that's exactly how it was supposed to be. When you love someone, you don't only love the pretty parts of them. You love the ugly, too."

"Sounds more like a curse to me than a gift."

"Your anger won't let you see past your own feelings."

"Anger?"

"Yeah, that emotion every thought of your mother fuels you with. The reason you look the other way when any woman of your caliber is looking your way. The reason you get your dick wet without giving a name or any indication you truly exist other than a clogged toilet from a flushed condom.

"The reason you don't have a single number in your phone that will lead to a night of unrestricted, unintentional fun. The reason your love has been distributed, in unhealthy amounts, to your sisters. The reason you bury your emotions and pile their gravesite with business dealings, meetings, and whatever else will make you forget they exist.

"The reason you spend more time lapping the pool and in that fucking lab than you do with yourself. You're running from something that will outrun your smart ass every fucking time. You and that damn Milo.

"Books are no substitute for grief. It will hunt you down and gut you like a fish, eventually. And when the time comes, you'll need more than your sisters' love to revive you, stuff you, and stitch your wounds."

"A grandson. I can give you that, Richie. A partner, a wife, I make no promises."

"I'm not asking, Chemistry."

My eyes cut in his direction, and for the first time, I made it clear his order held no relevance in my world.

"An heir, you'll have, Richie. My heart is not part of a business arrangement. It's off-limits. No business of yours.

Your request, it won't hold space in my court. I'm dismissing it. Just so you know."

With a grunt, he dipped his chin to meet his chest, peering up at me. I was four inches taller than him. His six-foot-one frame was no match for my near six-foot-six resolve.

"Your mother," he repeated as he sucked the skin of his teeth, completely disregarding everything I'd said. "She was a ball of fire tucked away in the most gentle being one could ever encounter. That's what I loved about her. That's what makes it so difficult for you to justify the anger you feel for her. That's why you have such a disdain for women. You can't trust them. Just as you couldn't trust your mother. As beautiful, as gentle as she was... she was troubled. Inside, that pretty brain of hers was tarnished. You couldn't see it. Her illness wasn't visible, but it was there. You see her in every woman you encounter. For good reason. But, let yourself grieve, son, so you can free yourself of the shackles her death has–"

Stopping briefly, he sipped from the bottle of water in his hand.

"The fire."

"What fire?"

"The fire within your mother, it will be the characteristic that leads you to choose your mate. Your wife will be beautiful, but she will be hell. There will not be much that is gentle or sheepish about her. She'll be a force to be reckoned with and you'll love her beyond your understanding.

"Beyond anyone's understanding. She'll be the first and she'll be the only woman you'll ever love more than

your sisters. More than your brothers. More than... even more than your mother. She'll be yours. And, you'll know it the second you see her.

"Without a doubt, if death becomes the result of loving her, you'll leave Earth a happy man. Just like me. Just like him. Just like your stepfather. Just like Maurice."

"Richie-" I paused to look him square in the eyes. "I never knew you to have such a vivid imagination."

"I never did."

He responded, taking off ahead of me and leaving me to think about all he'd just said.

"Hmph."

A frustrated grunt rocked my body.

Foolishness, I concluded.

Years had consumed me and so had my journey toward healing. I hadn't yet mastered it, but I was making strides, no matter how small the steps were.

Rather's degree was to credit. Therapy once a month was as much as I could stomach. Though it wasn't nearly enough to unpack the weight of my mind, it made the load lighter.

Schizophrenia

Noun.

A mentality or approach characterized by inconsistent or contradictory elements.

. . .

"Don't bullshit me, Rather."

"Chemistry. Don't insult me."

"As if that's not what you're doing he–" Pausing to collect my thoughts and silence the words swarming my brain, I chuckled. *"Fuck it. There has been a mistake of some kind."*

"Three tests, Chem. We've taken three tests. They all make it clear that the visions, the voices, the disorganized thoughts, delusions, sleeplessness, lack of connections, it all points towar–"

"There's also sanity, education... to the highest degree, orderly thoughts, outstanding hygiene, routine grooming, utter motivation, high spirits, self-sufficient–Rather, baby, come on. This is me. Nothing about me says I'm losing my shit. Nothing about me–"

"Says her. Nothing but this, Chemistry. And it means almost nothing. You're right. You're not losing your shit. You're just being... you. Don't look at it as a bad thing. You're stable. Very. I doubt this will progress, though it is known to. I can't say anything about you has changed in the last six years. That's good news."

"None of this is good news, baby."

"I've already told the others."

"Good. Just keep my brothers out of this."

"Good? Are you afraid?"

"I'm not afraid of shit, Rather, but becoming the woman I called Mother." With a shake of the head, I paced her office. *"Now that my only fear has come to fruition, my list is empty."*

"I love you, Chemistry."

"You never had a choice, baby."

Genetics. They were a motherfucker.

Bipolar disorder. It was the split personalities my mother suffered from each day.

Schizophrenia. It was the invisible illness that I wholeheartedly knew convinced her to kill the man she loved and then herself because she couldn't bear life without him.

That part of her condition was often overlooked and underestimated because it was hardly scribbled across her medical records and barely spoken of during her treatment.

"One thing at a time," her physician requested, though they were both killing her, simultaneously.

Blowing out warm air in frustration, I planted my index fingers in my freshly faded hair and rolled them slowly to relieve the pressure building in my head.

Catherine.

Catherine.

Catherine.

Catherine.

Her name rang out. Over. Over. And over.

Catherine.

Catherine.

Catherine.

Catherine.

"Shhhhhh."

"Say something, Chemist?"

Aden's eyes met mine in the rearview. A shake of the head assured him there was nothing I had to offer.

Catherine.

Catherine.

Catherine.

Catherine.

"Music."

Cathe–

Slow, melodic sounds filled the vehicle, tackling the disorganization of my thoughts. My posture was hardly ever compromised but sometimes it was inevitable.

I slid down the leather of the seat until my neck rested against the coolness and my head dangled behind it. With closed eyes, I drowned in the chords played by the jazz band as darkness and water surrounded me, again.

Drowning there, however, wasn't optional. I inhaled lungs full of oxygen and went under, hoping to come out on a brighter side. Hoping to finally find the sunlight. Hoping to reach the shore. Hoping to discover the meaning behind the constant vision. Hoping to end its recurrence once and for all.

Being hopeful had never gotten me far. This evening, all proved to still be intact. Because, when I opened my eyes nearly thirty-nine minutes later, I was still in the same spot, as if my tired arms and exasperated lungs were liars.

"Midnight."

"Midnight," Aden repeated, confirming the time he was to return.

"Destination?"

"Roulette."

With a raised brow, he questioned, "Roulette?"

I wasn't to be questioned.

Without a response, I climbed the stairs leading to my front door. Met by Jennie, I was stripped of my jacket and shoes.

"Take the week."

"I'm sorry, sir. Come ag–"

"You heard me clearly, Jennie. Take the week."

"I, uh–"

"Have Royce put you somewhere nice, somewhere private. A week."

"Yes, sir."

Her five-foot frame scurried, ready to suit every need I had. Even one to be alone. It didn't matter. Jennie was here to serve and she took her role seriously.

Aaliyah. The name came to mind. Daughter of an associate. Procreating with her posed a conflict of interest. I quickly dismissed the idea.

Salem. Next on the list was a woman I'd encountered only twice, but had left a lasting impression on me.

The sound of her name rolling off my tongue made my dick harden, just as she had. Since I'd stuck my dick in a piece of pussy, I hadn't doubled back. Hers, it made me reconsider.

Within a month, I was stroking her walls, again. Back for seconds. However, her lack of independence worried me. She wasn't a thinker. She wasn't a doer. She wasn't a hustler. She was—nothing.

It was her beauty that stuck with me. It was her quiet that drew me to her. But, in reality, she wasn't a person of interest.

By the time the second name vanished, so had my threads. I was down to a pair of trunks that were part of an extensive collection. Before another name could arise, my face was underneath the water and I was releasing everything that consumed me.

It hadn't failed me. Ever.

Water.

It washed it all away. Helped me start anew. Embraced me in its cold, expansive arms.

THE **GREY** LIST

Black Prada shades veiled my eyes. Paired with a fitted cap, my identity was easily and preferably concealed. My slacks and Ferragamo Oxfords in the shade Nero had been replaced with dark denim, classic Prada trainers, a black and gray letterman with hints of crimson red in patches on the right breast and back, a black hoodie, and a set of gold teeth with encrusted diamonds filling the canines.

Private entry was an option, but surveying those I'd be among quenched a thirst my proactive nature was often prone to. A step ahead was the only solution because if I wasn't there it meant I was two steps behind. That was unacceptable.

Still bodies and lifeless eyes.

My vision had been altered.

Headshot. Cervical fracture. Chest. Face. Ear to ear. No.

I shook my head, dismissing the bloodbath I'd create, cutting from one ear to the other. Disturbing the fine threads on my body would piss me the fuck off.

Too messy.

The disorderly thoughts were in full effect. While they should've resulted in tightened pimple-covered skin, they made my heart pump louder and harder, and with vengeance would easily be served if necessary.

They made it clear that in the event, in an instant, I'd air the whole shit out with the extended clip on the Glock that made my pants sag slightly. The arsenal behind the bar and the one in the office I was headed to would put down anything it didn't. The clean-up crew. Their purpose was clear when I installed them.

"Are you sur–"

"Goodbye, Aden."

Questions. Fucking questions.

I climbed out of the backseat, daring my driver to reach for his door. The attention his presence would cause was attention I wasn't beckoning for.

"I'll be around back. Here when you need me!" he yelled over his shoulder before I slammed the door shut.

I strolled past the lengthy line, right up to the door. Groans and grumbles doubled as my presence was noted.

"Capacity my ass. This nigga just walked right up," a tenor that reminded me of one of the men I shared blood with bellowed with enough emphasis to stop me in my tracks.

"Quiet, man," Vic, one of the four bouncers, warned.

"Fuck you, dog. I thought you were at capacity. How this nigga get the green light?"

Too loud. Too entitled. Too broke. The loudest nigga wasn't usually the poorest. Mentally. Physically. Emotionally. Spiritually. Financially. I turned to find a tacky, tasteless clubgoer with a studded shirt and pants to match. *Too dirty.*

"This nigga paying you or you sucking his dick?" Boldly, he questioned.

My legs jolted in motion, propelling me forward at an unfamiliar pace. When I began to regain awareness, my hands were around Dingy's throat. His body rested against the pavement. Mine was only a few inches off.

The corners of my lips curved upward, toward my ears. A smile contradicted my actions, my thoughts, and the reason my tool was pressed against a stranger's teeth as he spat unrecognizable pleas.

"Hm?" I listened closely.

Tears streaked his face.

"Say what, my nigga?"

Only he and I could hear what was being expressed. It was nobody else's business. I pressed the gun deeper into his mouth, chipping his right tooth.

Shoot him.

Too many witnesses.

Lifeless eyes lulled me, but blood-stained skin shook me out of my trance.

"Next time anyone asks, tell them you've, in fact, met the devil and he doesn't fuck around," I whispered.

With the butt of my gun, I left a lasting impression right above his eye.

Something to remember me by, I reasoned as he yelped in agony.

"Send this man home, Vic, but only after he's apologized."

He's not welcomed with that tired-ass shirt that's lost its elasticity.

Aden's eyes were the first set I found as I shoved my tool in the back of my pants. He was no longer behind the wheel of the truck. He was out, posted next to it, waiting to pull me from the ledge I loved living on. With a shake of the head, he rounded the vehicle as I turned and continued inside the club.

Now, back to the task ahead before I was very rudely interrupted and accused of getting my dick sucked. I scoffed, removing the sanitizer from my jacket pocket and squeezing a portion into my hand. The blackness that rolled off his neck confirmed what I'd already known.

Too dirty.

Naturally, girthy asses and titties that stared right at you and welcomed me inside Roulette. The bass of the speakers drummed against my skin. The very familiar smell of printed bills tickled my nostrils.

Darkness sheeted the entire building. Soft, deflecting lights passed through certain areas with the sole purpose of spotlighting the women who were here to entertain.

My attention never diverted as I strolled the entire first level, ending at the door that was shielded by two men covered in black.

As I stepped forward, announcing my presence with the timepiece on my arm that had diamonds dancing to the beat of the drums in the background and the glistening chain in the shape of an Erlenmeyer flask, guards were lowered. Bodies pushed in opposite directions, giving enough space for me to continue forward.

"Chemist."

"Chemist."

One after the other, they greeted me. A dipped chin and tilted head sufficed. I crossed the threshold where the sounds from the main floor were suppressed and light was plentiful. Red paint-coated walls that led to two doors. Only one would lead me to my destination.

"How hard is it to follow rules?"

Hello was far too formal for the middle child. Possibly for the oldest, too. I imagined it was the reason our bond was tighter than the ones between me and the others. Or, maybe it was a false accusation she used as leverage over the others. My presence, however, supported claims she and I were closer. The jury was still out on the verdict, in my opinion.

"There are no rules, Roulette."

"According to you."

"Who else matters?" I probed, taking a seat in the chair in front of her desk.

She was pecking away at the keys of her computer, never taking a second to address me with her eyes.

"You're here. What's bothering you?"

"You don't have me figured out, baby."

"No one does, but I'm as close as anyone. So, tell me or get the fuck out of my office, Chem."

I got comfortable. Roulette was always in raw form. Aside from Rugger, and possibly Range, she was the rawest.

They'd adapted traits that suggested they were female replicas of my father. Improved versions of his one and only son.

Their only issues stemmed from circumstances beyond their control. Female organs, hormones, and hearts. Their downfalls in a business were built with men in mind.

It was a sexist, misogynistic, world we lived in. Our empire was more of the same. I didn't agree. But, because I didn't want them in the pits of hell with me, I stood by the commandments.

An heir.

That was why my contribution to the family was crucial. At no point in time was it permitted for there to only be a single living heir in an entity of The Triad of Ara. My father's sperm was potent but it produced one girl after another.

His soldiers were marching, but seemingly to the wrong tune. If his life ended before a son of mine entered the world, balance would not be possible.

My silence was the bane of her existence. She'd give everything in her bank account to know what I was thinking most times. The window she wished my eyes were to my soul, she'd pay to have built.

"Chemistry."

The halting of the keys led her eyes to mine. I massaged the hair that had begun to thicken on my face. Though I'd always kept it low and manicured, the length added definition to my face, framing it much better. I was fucking with it.

"Your father is dying."

"He's your father as well."

Her shoulders hunched forward. Though she didn't voice her insecurities and fears as they related to the topic of conversation, I sensed them. In her eyes, where I'd built the windows she dreamed of. And from her posture.

"How long, Chem?"

"A year at best."

Softened eyes etched away at the cage around my heart. This wasn't how or where I wanted to share this news, but I hardly had a choice. Roulette was the closest I had to a friend.

The others had proved to be enemies. And the one whose loyalty was not up for question was a member of a family in The Triad. Confiding in him was not an option.

"A year," she repeated, falling apart inside while keeping a straight face as she stared back at me.

"You don't have t–"

"Shut up." She choked, twisting her chair until her

pretty face was hidden and I could no longer see her broken heart through the bay window I sat at often.

But, I could still feel it. I, too, had one. And they were bleeding in harmony. Together. As a unit.

Sniffles of hers pushed a sigh from my lips. Baby was hurting. And unlike other times, I couldn't stop her pain. Though I hadn't expressed it, I shared the same pain. That hurt she felt, I felt that shit, too.

Two snaps of my fingers and her eyes were on me again. Dried, but coated with redness, they studied me.

"Ready?"

"Yes."

"I haven't made good on my promise. I haven't fallen through. And it's fucking with me."

"He wants you to give us a son."

"Needs me to."

"Chemistry, that's asking a lot of you in such a short amount of time."

"I wasted a lot more, baby."

"I know, but damn. How are you feeling?"

"It doesn't matter."

Her lack of response made my flesh crawl. The way she could pull things from me was impossible and made me uncomfortable. Simultaneously, it was comforting. Because, if no one else, I knew there was always Roulette.

I gambled my life every time I stepped into her office. Admittedly, I was addicted to the thrill. She preferred the challenge.

In so many ways, she was as twisted as our father, as

twisted as her brother. It was no secret. Our siblings knew it. So did her mother.

"Cornered," I released. "But it doesn't fucking matter."

"To me." She huffed. "Who else matters?"

"You're insufferable."

"Then why are you here? Time and time again."

"I was just leaving."

I stood. Immediately, she demanded I sit. Not with words, but with those penetrating eyes.

"You don't run shit, Roulette. Get that through thick ass skull."

Tiptoeing around her with words had never been necessary. She had tough skin, possibly tougher than all the others. But it was no match for Rugger. That motherfucker was in a league of her own.

"Can't knock a girl for trying."

Wordlessly, I strode, contrarily. As I moved closer to her door, eyes still trained on her, I waited for words I knew she was full of.

"Don't come back if you're just coming to start shit."

"Never accuse a man of getting his dick sucked by another man and you won't end up with a dental bill and bruised ego."

"Oh, please, Chem."

My shoulders lifted and fell almost immediately after.

"Why don't you blow off some steam in one of the VIP rooms? I can get one of the girl–"

"Not interested, baby."

"So serious. Loosen up. Tonight. Just once."

"I have to produce a son in the next twelve months or jeopardize the integrity of our family. You think I give a fuck about letting loose anywhere but in a woman who can give me that?"

Pushing out a heap of air was her only response. I turned and twisted the knob on her door, sure she was behind me. Heels clacked against the floor as we trekked down the hallway. Music greeted us when we reached the large room designed for entertainment.

My peripheral scan detected a diamond in the muddy plain, halting my movement and making Roulette slam into my heels. The thought of her expensive foundation smearing against my letterman forced my eyes closed.

"Fuck!" she spat.

I have two more, I reminded myself. The compulsive nature of mine left me with hardly a choice. Buying in sets of threes was a habit I'd developed after ruining too many good pieces to keep count.

I separated my lids. My line of vision became increasingly clearer as I zeroed in on stage.

Climbing the stairs as the music selection changed was a frame dipped in chocolate. Long legs, which seemed never-ending, led me to a waistline that barely existed, a chiseled back, a slender neck, and a ponytail that hung past the ass wouldn't allow me to ignore it if I tried.

Fucking flawless.

Black lace covered a bald pussy. The same sheer fabric covered dark nipples, but left little to the imagination. Her exposure angered me, drawing me closer to the ledge than I'd ever been. Without a second thought, I was prepared to jump and I didn't give a fuck where I landed or who I landed on.

That's her.

I recognized shit belonged to me without qualms. She was no different. From the top of her head to the bottom of the mile-high heels on her feet, she was mine. In this one and in the next lifetime.

Part of my personalia.

An unfamiliar yearning panged me. Though disgusted, I was receptive to the feeling.

My stomach flipped. My chest tightened. My blood boiled. My head spun. My temperature spiked. For the life of me, I couldn't determine whether I was more intrigued or infuriated.

"Chem–" Roulette warned, pushing me forward.

She read me like a book, though it was rather complicated other times.

"Who is she?"

My spine stiffened, straightening, and I planted my feet on the tiled floor. I made it very clear I wasn't moving, no matter how hard she pushed.

"She's promising, Chem, and it is her first night. She's going to bring us a good penny. They love her already. She aced the trial."

"This... this is her last night, baby."

I wished I was sorry, but I wasn't. Not even a little.

"She'll make me good money!" she reiterated.

"And me, pretty babies," I reminded her of what was more important.

She said nothing more. Regardless of what she had, one foot was already in front of the other and my body was headed toward the stage.

"Is she clean?" I tossed over my shoulder.

With a nod, Roulette answered, "Royce checked."

Royce always checked. Everyone was screened thoroughly. Anyone that we'd come into contact with regularly was vetted and approved after extensive digging. If Royce had given her the green light, then there was no reason I couldn't.

Everything around me blurred, including the sounds of the loudspeakers. She was the only clear object in my tunneled vision. Muffled sounds played in the background. Fixtures moved about, all around me as I avoided the steps and hopped on stage.

Smoothly, free from anxious thoughts or movements, I approached the lengthy vixen who rolled her body to a beat I didn't recognize. Not because I didn't know the song but because I couldn't hear that shit.

My presence alarmed her none. Seductively, she turned, placing her back against the pole as she waited for the inevitable. Waited for me to state my business or drop some bread.

No amount of money tossed in a night's time would amount to what I had waiting for her if she followed instructions well, sucked good dick, and could spit out healthy babies.

"You're obstructing everyone's view. There are men willing to pay."

"I'm willing to pay more."

Her bottom lip disappeared in her mouth. I imagined my dick next. Flared nostrils revealed the anxiety I'd considered myself free of.

"Giselle," she introduced herself using her stage name.

"Don't insult me."

"Eden."

"Pack your shit and meet me out front."

"I'm no damsel in distress."

"Do I look like a motherfucking knight in shining armor?" I asked, already feeling as though I'd used too many words and felt too many things in the few seconds I'd been standing in front of her.

I'm a fucking monster.

"Better," she challenged, making my dick press harder against my jeans.

"Don't touch shit on the floor on your way out. It's beneath you, now," I demanded, referring to the money scattered on the stage.

"I didn't get your name. My mother needs to know who to come looking for if anything happens to me."

"I didn't give one," I replied, turning back toward her. "And if anything ever happens to you, I'll find her before she finds me."

"Yes, sir."

If she was trying to get a rise out of me with her witty remarks, then she'd accomplished the mission she set out on.

"Five minutes."

"Or what?"

I made the short journey to her, once more, unsure whether I wanted her to hear me over the music or if it was because I hated feeling so far away. The magnetic force quickly grew between us making my blood boil.

Through gritted teeth, I admonished, "You ask too many fucking questions."

"They're the epitome of informed decisions."

"You don't have a decision to make. I never said you had a choice."

As she fixed her lips to speak, again, I used the steps to exit the stage. Through the crowd, I ambled until I reached the back of the establishment where I knew Aden would be waiting.

THE GREY LIST

Five minutes or forever, I couldn't decipher how long it had been before I witnessed a model-like physique dressed in black from head to toe, headed in my direction. The confidence she exuded was the sexiest of her attributes.

She reeked of excellence. A bitch, I was certain she was labeled in the world. A bad bitch, she was labeled in mine. *My bitch*, she had become in a matter of minutes. I just wondered if she had a clue.

Her new title wasn't demeaning in any fashion. It was an honorable one. One would elevate her beyond heights she'd ever imagined. The club couldn't take her places I had prepared for her. Or, give her things I had access to.

"Are you always this—pompous?" she asked, standing in front of me with folded arms and eyebrows that almost met each other right above her nose.

"Are you always this talkative?"

"I asked a question," she pressed.

"That's the problem, baby. You ask too many of them motherfuckers."

I opened the back door, tilting my head toward the seat. She ignored my silent instructions, taking a second to take me all in.

From head to toe, she scanned me with eyes that were large but cut like slits. The structure of her face was unique, reminding me of a feline. High cheeks led to her ears and eyes with winged backs that raced for her hairline.

"Find whatever the fuck you're looking for?"

"I'm not sure yet."

"Get in."

This time, she climbed inside without a rebuttal. I rounded the truck and slid into the seat beside her.

Already, I was sending a message to Abel, owner of Prime House, letting him know I was on my way and to keep the doors open after closing. Staff wouldn't mind the extra hours for the increased pay.

It wasn't until I shut the door did the fragrance of her skin registered with me. Riot. I remembered it vividly. Not because I wanted to, but because Rugger left me no choice.

It was the only fragrance she wore. I believed she was the only one keeping Huffington Fragrance House in business until now.

"Riot." I cleared my throat. "Good choice."

"Does your wife wear it, too?" Eden inquired, angling her body in my direction, waiting for me to fold.

Nodding, I latched on to the truth in her words.

"Figured," she sniggered. "Married men are the most single men on the planet."

With a shrug, I responded, "You're a lot prettier when your mouth is closed."

She found my observation humorous. My teeth ached from the grinding as her laughter reached parts of me reserved for a select few. Baffled, I chose silence. She was tearing down walls that were constructed for a fucking reason.

She barely had a right. Armed with a killer smile, fiery spirit, and a sharp tongue, she was rendering me defenseless even with my Glock off safety and the Tech under the seat.

"Does she know you're en route to some destination with some woman who was preparing to slide down a pole minutes ago?"

"Do you?"

As the response tap danced on her brain, I used the opportunity to hike the sound of the stereo with the controls in the back where we sat. Her silence was what I'd been longing for and I'd finally been rewarded.

When she spoke, she caused a ruckus. I couldn't

handle her words. Her loud thoughts. Her confidence. Her beauty. Her fire. Not all at once.

"The fire within your mother, it will be the characteristic that leads you to choose your mate. Your wife will be beautiful, but she will be hell. There will not be much that is gentle or sheepish about her. She'll be a force to be reckoned with and you'll love her beyond your understanding.

"Beyond anyone's understanding. She'll be the first and she'll be the only woman you'll ever love more than your sisters. More than your brothers. More than... even more than your mother. She'll be yours. And you'll know it the second you see her.

"Without a doubt, if death becomes the result of loving her, you'll leave Earth a happy man. Just like me. Just like him. Just like your stepfather. Just like Maurice."

My father's words haunted me. Tainted the moment. Made a mess of my thoughts. Rarely was he wrong. This instance was evidence he was, once again, accurate in his predictions.

Stop the car, Aden. Stop the fucking car, my conscience screamed, but no words escaped me.

Let her out. She needed to go. She wasn't welcomed. But nothing in me was ready for her departure. Even the thought locked my limbs and plagued my existence.

I busied myself with the keypad on my screen, giving Aden specific instructions, including the small project that needed to be completed by the time I made it home with Eden in tow.

Women weren't welcomed into my home or my heart, but there wasn't a doubt in my mind I'd be sliding into her warmth between the sheets I rested my head on nightly. Somehow, someway, the waterfront property and the penthouse suite felt beneath her. Beneath us.

Once instructions were finalized, I was ready to settle my thoughts and clear my head. I leaned against the seat, closing my eyes to catch my breath. The way my heart was hammering against my chest, it felt as if I'd run beside Olympians within the last hour.

Phalanges, those of the fingers to be specific, abruptly halted my peace tour. My eyes trailed a single arm, ending near my knee where Eden's hand sat. Because I'd been wired to resist any signs of affection, naturally, my body craved movement. But, I couldn't.

Stuck under her palm, I closed my eyes, again, blowing out the steam that had been building inside of me. Heat, transmitted from her body, elevated my temperature.

Eden, please.

She didn't understand the concept of personal space. She'd obliterated the little was between us. And I was too fucking intoxicated by her existence to chastise her.

Please, I begged of her.

To my dismay, the calm I was in search of to settle the brewing storm that raged within me arrived. The peace I couldn't find had found me. The disorganization of my thoughts was demolished. Concise thoughts replaced the others.

Fuck.

She bore no restrictions. As if she knew my body belonged to her. Just like I knew hers belonged to me.

How she was privy to such information was baffling. How I'd come to the conclusion so quickly and felt so strongly about it was even more baffling.

Slow down.

The beat of my heart was loud. Alarming. Intimidating.

Move.

Eden was fucking with my head. I needed her out of my space. And like she'd heard me, she moved. This time, closer. Our sides pressed against each other.

Opening my eyes, I prepared to send her to the other side of the seat where she belonged. But, she looked so fucking good next to me. She felt so fucking good against me.

Her empty wrist was disappointing. Diamonds against that skin would be too fucking stunning to not be our realities. I made it my first point of business.

I'd lost order in my world. My limbs went against everything they'd ever been programmed for. My arm laid across her leg, hand caressing her calf. Our position was repulsive. Simultaneously, it was soothing. Satisfying. Soul-stirring.

Her head lowered, slowly, until it met the fabric of my coat. And suddenly, makeup stains didn't worry me. Her comfort became the priority.

"No time for sleep."

My lips were moving before I was able to think about what was coming from them.

"How do you compete with peace?"

Her question sat with me, silencing me, again. We

shared sentiments. Whatever was transpiring couldn't be compared to anything else. It was unlike anything else. Competing was pointless.

To appease her desire, I, absentmindedly, traced the letters in my head on her calf. My intention was to bring her more comfort. More peace.

The fact that I was considering anyone's desires other than my own had me stumped. She'd become my responsibility so very quickly. Instantly, her needs were leveled with mine.

"She'll be yours. And you'll know it the second you see her."

It wasn't until the final letter had been traced and light snores tickled my eardrums that I realized what had been written.

Eden Childers.

A light tap on the leg, many minutes later, awakened the sleeping beauty. Prime House lights were lowered, but, undoubtedly, they were still open. Not publicly, but specifically to accommodate our needs and fill our hungry bellies to the brim.

I slid out of the truck, staring at my hand as if it was a foreign object. Its extension resulted in a strained neck and squinted eyes.

So naturally, I began to expand making room for

Eden in my head as if there wasn't enough going on in that motherfucker already.

She grabbed a hold, shifting her weight to make sure she didn't fall while exiting. When she was finally on her feet, I calculated her height. An estimate of six feet with heels would put her at approximately five-nine on bare feet.

Imagining her long legs wrapped around my neck wasn't enough. I needed to feel them motherfuckers and home was too far of a drive. I wouldn't make it.

Within a few steps, we were out of the cold and inside the dimly lit establishment. Our table was ready when we arrived. In the center of the private room was a thick cream-colored cloth covering a table made for four but set for two.

"Menus are on the table, waiting. The kitchen is open and at your disposal. Should there be anything you want that isn't available, please let us know. We'll make sure it becomes available."

A few steps ahead of me, the host motioned for the chair designated for Eden, pressing every button I was in possession of.

His decapitation flashed before my eyes.

"Don't," I advised, wanting him to make it home safely so his family wouldn't miss him.

"Yes, sir."

With a nod, he stepped aside. I slid the chair back so Eden could sit. When she settled, I slid it up with her help.

"Thank you," she said to me before turning toward the host. "And thank you, handsome."

Angling my head leftward, I fought the urge to unleash my thoughts. Her defiance wasn't accidental. She was fully aware, fully conscious. Yet, and still, she was fucking with me.

On the ledge, I noted. *Wrong fucking ledge, though, baby.*

"He wants to make it home, Eden. Don't end his life tonight because you're fascinated with the thrill."

It explained the occupation she'd chosen. *Stripper.* It explained her lack of hesitancy to leave with a fucking stranger. *On the first night.* It explained why sleep was possible in the arms of a man she didn't know the first thing about. *Risky girl.*

Nervously, she chuckled, looking toward the host. "I'm sorry about that."

"I'm not and neither are you, so take it back."

She turned to me, eyes tightening to slits.

Nodding, I encouraged her to follow instructions. Still, she remained silent.

Her hesitation was enough to fuel the fire within me.

"Now is not the time for defiance. A man's life is on the line."

Raised brows and upturned lips followed snickering. She was willing to call my bluff. I was willing to show her I didn't bluff. As my hand located the butt of my gun, words began flying from her mouth.

"I am not sorry," she admitted, a smile still visible on her lips. "Please, send our waitress in. Female, please."

The host scurried out.

Nobody's safe, darling. A new set of eyes wasn't the answer, her obedience was. Lowering until my lips were next to her ear, I paused to gather my thoughts.

I wanted to fuck her as much as I wanted to fuss at her. I wasn't sure who was winning the battle, but I focused on the bigger head while drowning out the pleas of the smaller one.

"I, too, admire life on the ledge, but please don't fuck with me, Eden. I jump often."

I rounded the table to find her tongue crossing her top row of teeth. The hunger in her eyes, in her posture, wasn't related to food.

She had developed a thirst only my semen could quench. And when the time came, I'd make sure she guzzled it. Hydration was key.

"I feel slighted. Cheated, in a sense."

I waited for more, knowing it was coming. I didn't need to respond for her to reveal whatever riddle she was speaking in.

"You know my name but I have no idea who it is that isn't a knight in shiny armor, has the power to calm the relentless storm within me to restore peace, and is willing to end a man's life because he thought to pull out a chair for me."

"You flirted."

"Barely."

"That's even too much."

"A jealous streak."

Shrugging, I shook my head and squared my shoulders.

"I'm insulted."

"That easily?"

She was a mind fuck. I had an inkling she knew it as well.

"You're a very inquisitive person."

"That's all beside the point. Name."

"My name isn't important. My position in your life is."

"Your position?"

"Eden, baby, do you ever just shut the fuck up?"

That smile, the one that could shatter earth in fifteen thousand pieces, reappeared.

"Am I upsetting you?"

"Not even a little."

"Then, why do you look so an–"

"Because I'm trying my hardest to be a gentleman and wait until I'm home before I feast on your flesh but continuing to run your mouth is making that pretty fucking impossible."

Her mouth hung open. After a few seconds, she recovered. "A man of great discipline."

"At least I thought so."

"I believe in you. You can do whatever you put your mind to."

Her words punched me in the chest, pushing my body backward. I leaned against the back of the chair, my eyes penetrating her skin and marking my territory with invisible ink.

I believe in you. Though strangers, there was truth to her words. And even if there wasn't, there was meaning. To me. That shit meant something to me.

"I'm Ursula. I'll be with you all tonight. Is there anything I can get started for you all besides water?"

Our waitress appeared from thin air. Too fixated on Eden, I didn't notice anyone else. No one else was relevant. No one else mattered at the moment. All I saw was her. All I felt... *was her*.

"I'll have a French 75. Neat."

She didn't fold. Her eyes were trained on me.

"Water."

I needed a clear head dealing with Eden. I'd already reached my limit. She was intoxicating enough.

College graduate. One of three children to a widowed mother. Thirty. Fashion enthusiast. Reader. I'd learned enough about her life to determine there was nothing interesting about it. Yet, she was intriguing. Unbelievably so.

She was six years younger but carried herself better than most women my age I'd stumbled upon. The most important details of her life included never being married and never having a child. Hadn't I genuinely wanted to know more about Eden, I would've stopped listening after discovering those two details.

But, here I was, nearly thirty minutes after medium-rare steaks and medium-well lamb had been set in front of us, still listening intently as she expressed herself with satisfaction carving her features. She loved hearing herself talk. Somehow, I was beginning to love listening.

"I feel like I've divulged for hours and you've given me very little."

"There's not a lot to me," I assured her. "I'm boring, baby."

"I find that hard to believe."

"Then, don't."

"Mysterious, but not boring."

With a shrug, I brushed off the observation. There was possibly truth to it, but I wasn't sure. I didn't care to investigate.

"Only child?"

"No."

"I guessed it. You feel like–like an elder. Like a protector. A provider. Father-like."

Her profiling was spot on, but I wouldn't give her any indication.

"Stable home. Two-parent household. Very structured. Father is very involved in your life, even in adulthood. He played a huge part in who you are today. You're probably a lot like him."

"Finish your drink."

It was her third one. I was ready to see just how influential it was on her body. The lust in her eyes was heavier than when we'd entered.

Her stares lingered. Her hands, they'd found my leg a few times. Her nipples hadn't softened in the last fifteen minutes. They must've been aching by now.

"Time to go, huh?" she asked, slowly.

Her resolve had softened. She was milder. She was gentler. She was... *better*.

I didn't think it was possible. I didn't think she could improve. I liked her the way she was.

But, the more mellow, calmer side of her soothed something in me I couldn't quite put a finger on. I felt her grab a hold of my heart and stroke it gently versus squeezing the life out of it as she had earlier. That was good, but this was even better.

Maybe he was wrong. My father's words looped in my head. Eden wasn't a pit of fire all by itself. She was calm waters, too, wrapping me in her expansiveness.

"Yes. It is."

"Where to?"

"Some place for you to do exactly what you were doing on stage tonight."

I didn't wait for a response. I was up and out of my seat in a split second. She wasted no time falling in line. Her fingers curled between mine, solidifying our connection. The fire rested between us set my body ablaze.

Not tonight or any other night did I want it to be extinguished. I wanted it to burn. Us to burn. Until we ashed, meshing so well we were unable to be distinguished. Sundered. Dissociated.

Back inside the truck, rounded nails gripped the elastic band of the blinders I handed to Eden, the woman who refused to acknowledge personal space. She held no interest in the rest of the seat that was open to her. Up against me is where she was comfortable.

"Mister," she called out, still unsure of my government.

I was still unsure whether I wanted her to have it. It didn't matter. It shouldn't have, anyway.

"It's not up for debate, Eden," I replied, lowering the seat we were on.

The partition had been customized for privacy and had already been pulled when we entered. Aden was no fool. He understood well what was happening in my world tonight.

I didn't need to explain that this time was different. I didn't need to explain that she was different. He knew. I knew.

"I do–"

"Pardon the discomfort you might feel. I promise to make it worthwhile."

I slid them from her hand and over her head. Distracting her was the only resolution for the precautions required. The journey to my residence wasn't one that was revealed under any circumstances, to anyone other than family.

Eden wasn't the exception, *yet*. It didn't matter how much I was feeling her or how my heart beat wildly for her. My location wasn't to be compromised.

"I can't see you." She gasped.

Pressing against her chest, I lowered her body on the third row. Her heels were the first to be removed. Black in color, they sported a red sole. Socks, sheer like the top and thong she'd worn on stage, covered her feet. I snatched them off immediately after.

Pants that fit like gloves gave resistance, but I prevailed. The coat she wore kept the seat from chilling her darkness. But, small, prickly bumps still pimpled her skin. Braless, her titties peeked from underneath the shirt I raised. Dark nipples made my dick ache.

Fuck.

"I don't need you to see me, Eden. I need you to feel me."

I palmed her right breast with my left hand and used my right to find her ankle. My tongue looped her toes before they went into my mouth.

"Mist—"

Chem. My name was at the tip of my tongue. That was what I wanted falling from her lips. But, I maintained my composure, watching as her stomach folded and her body grinded against the seat.

She was hot. She was bothered. Just as I wanted her.

The long legs I'd anticipated around my neck sat on my shoulders momentarily as I slid lower, not stopping until my knees were on the floor of the truck. Carpet brushed the fabric of my jeans as I was welcomed into Eden's world by the distinctive smell of her arousal.

Panties hadn't been part of her attire. She'd come to give her pussy up. Give it up to me. She knew she'd be sliding down my dick before she stepped off stage. There was nothing sexier than a woman with her mind made up.

I stroked her flesh with my tongue, instantly obsessing over the bittersweet blend. Her juice awakened something devilish within me. Something sacred. Something terrifying. Something special.

A current made the hair on my body stand. There was a shift within me. Of me. Through me. Externally.

Fuck.

Mentally. Physically. Emotionally. Spiritually.

What she was doing to me, I wasn't sure. But, I knew exactly what I was going to do to her.

First, I familiarized myself with her folds, licking from the tip of her pussy just beyond her hood to her slit. Migrating further, I explored her backside, finding pleasure in making her body quake.

Once.

Twice.

Three times, I repeated the same movements slowly. Gently. Patiently. Blindly getting acclimated with her garden as I determined the best way to activate her sprinkler system.

"My God!"

Don't mention another nigga in my presence, Choc. My demand was lost in translation. I was too invested in her pleasure to address the shit that grinded my gears.

Her clit was my next mission. Though I had intentions of prolonging her orgasm, I wanted her back on the ledge. Back in her comfort zone. Ready, but unable to jump because I wouldn't let her.

"*Puh!*" I wet her slit, though there was hardly a need.

"Ummmm."

I slid two fingers deep within her, turning them upward and curling them.

"Pleeeeeaasse."

Her ass bounced off the seat, searching for the warmth of my mouth. The pressure from my tongue.

Stripping her of her misery, I circled the external portion of her clit while massaging the internal portion. She lost the strength to hold herself up. Her body flopped down. Her head moved from one side to the other. Her eyes fluttered, closing more often than they opened.

"Misssssssster."

They'd been activated. That fucking sprinkler. Unfortunately, I wasn't ready to water her garden. I pulled back, halting the orgasm that was quickly approaching. Eden's chest rose and fell dramatically as she struggled to catch her breath.

"Please!" she begged, barely above a whisper, but forcefully.

She made it painfully clear her pussy had been mishandled. I made a mental note to dead every nigga who had wasted her fucking time before me. If life had allowed them time with her until my appearance, the least they could've done was fuck her well.

Manage her needs. See to it her desires were met. Treat her pussy good. Real fucking good. They'd missed the fucking mark and in under six minutes, I'd hit motherfucker.

Fucking waste. I grunted.

She'd been deprived enough. I wouldn't make her suffer any longer. I couldn't. Before the night was out, I'd make up for all the times she wanted to cum and couldn't.

Her pussy was my priority now. Her pussy was my responsibility now. When she wanted to cum, she would.

I dug into her, again. This time, massaging her insides with more pressure. I caressed her clit with my tongue, stroking it rapidly until her ass was off the seat and those legs were around my neck.

"Uh, fuck! Please. Please. Don't stop."

I won't.

"Fuck. Fuu—"

She fell into the seat at once. Her sprinkler went off, spraying my mouth, chest, and the back of the passenger seat.

A tilted head and nod displayed the pride I harbored. Not for me, but for Eden.

She'd been a good fucking girl. She'd be rewarded as such. A bunch of dick and the night of her life would be the ultimate prize.

She was beauty and she was beastly. I knew, without a doubt, when I slid inside of her all hell would break loose. A sucker for adventure, I was prepared for the rollercoaster waiting. Because that was exactly what the fuck Eden would be. A wild ride. I could feel it in my dark, tainted soul.

"Chemistry," I muttered, analyzing her half-naked body as she fought to regain her composure.

A piece of art.

Her masterpiece hanging over the mantle in the living room was easily envisioned and duly noted.

With low lids and unsteady breathing, she asked, "Hm?"

"We are arriving."

We'd reached our destination. The familiar scent of nothingness the water carried settled his heart. The comfort it provided was the reason I'd purchased property and had a home built on the edge of the city where water was plentiful and the views were immaculate. Seclusion was among the reasons I'd chosen the location as well.

Hidden in plain sight.

Carefully, I gathered her limbs in my hands with her shoes dangling from my middle and forefingers. The bag she'd brought along hung over my shoulder. It wasn't until we'd crossed the threshold, made it through the main wing, and entered the left wing of my home where a pole had been placed within the last twenty-five minutes that I lowered her.

A lone chair was a mere three feet away from it. An unopened bottle of Brandy sat beside it, along with a glass. Eden's feet touched the marble floors beneath us.

Slowly, she pushed forward. Seduction oozed from her frame. She was naturally gifted with a presence that was as alluring as it was addictive. I wasn't a user, but I'd be damned if I hadn't found a drug worth giving a try.

"Where am I?"

Eyes still covered, she turned in a circle as if she could see.

"Feels big... broad. Tell me," she said just above a whisper.

Chemistry. My name resurfaced.

Chemistry.

Chemistry.

Chemistry.

I wanted the syllables to fall from her lips. Roll off her tongue. Coat her skin. Smear her makeup. Fill her to capacity.

She was becoming the exception. Rapidly growing on me, in me, through me, *with me*. I'd known her less than three hours and was certain she'd have my last name.

There wasn't a woman in Clarke who hadn't gone to school with me, filled out my medical forms, issued my identification, or was part of my family who even knew I had a fucking last name.

Or a first one.

Names weren't important. Positions were. Benefits were. Funds were.

Home.

"My home."

She was the first to enter and would be the last. She didn't need those details. Not yet, at least. When time permitted, she'd know everything she needed to know. For now, all she needed was the surround sound and those fucking shoes she once wore.

This wasn't the stage she'd anticipated performing

on, but it was the only one she'd be allowed to wind her body and claim her victim. On this stage, funds were endless. Bills didn't run low. And ones were insulting. Twenties replaced them. And behind the chair I was in pursuit of, was a bag full of them motherfuckers.

"Can I?"

The fire continued to smolder. It was much more manageable than it was two hours ago. However, the small flame was evident. Given the right amount of oxygen, it would rage, again. I'd be waiting. My lesson hadn't been learned. For Eden, with Eden, I wanted to burn.

"Yes."

She slid the blindfold from her head, allowing it to fall on the floor next to her bare feet. She angled her body in my direction, a smirk lining her precious lips. Darkness traced them, making them appear bigger, *sexier*.

"Put that shit back on and meet me right over there."

My strides were pointless. I didn't go far. Couldn't. The allure of Eden wouldn't allow it.

"Mister," she muttered.

"Chocolate."

Smile lines creased the outer corners of her eyes. "Chocolate?"

"The dark kind. Rich in flavor. Royal. A step above milk chocolate. More memorable. Intriguing. Sexy, in so many ways. Good alone but better paired."

Circling her, I memorized every visible feature on her body. *My body*. Like a substance in my lab, I studied her.

Stalked her. And quickly determined just how I could improve her. Though she was fine without improvements, she deserved pieces of the world that hadn't been accessible in the past. She deserved flowers.

A fucking garden, I corrected.

A home. A wrist that froze time, literally. Diamonds on her skin. A dedicated team to service her every need— hair, makeup, manicure, pedicure, meals, what-the-fuck-ever. Cars. Whichever one her heart desired. A driver. A bank account the size of mine. Anything. Everything. Fuck, Eden. I could hardly contain myself as our gazes locked.

"Unforgiving. Smooth. Thick. Addictive."

A son.

"I'd agree."

You have no idea, baby. The things I have in store for you.

"You don't have to."

"I do."

"Good, then."

"I have a feeling I've bitten off much more than I can chew."

"I can confirm with utter confidence."

Her smile deepened, reaching her eyes and cheeks. Even her posture improved.

"Your addiction to the thrill will be the death of us, Eden."

"Won't it be a beautiful one?"

Within a second, my fingers had spread around her neck. I pulled her closer, watching as her neck slacked, rolling backward. Her flesh was beckoning for me. Giving in, my lips met the first layer of her skin.

My teeth waited to meet the second, possibly the third. My hunger for her was apparent. But I settled my desires by flattening my tongue and running it across her neck, ending near her ear.

"Ummmm."

"Get dressed."

"Release me and I will."

I can't. Physically, yes. Mentally, I refused.

Dark, devilish eyes peered up at me. She was in no hurry to leave my presence. I wasn't in a hurry to let her.

Those lips, they wouldn't let me. There hadn't been a pair my dick stood for in my lifetime. Not a pair I craved. Not a pair I adored. Not a pair...

"Ed–"

They pressed against mine, against my will. Her tongue entered my mouth, stealing my breath and feasting on her remnants. I could still taste it. Taste her.

Hungrily, she consumed me. It wasn't until she was full, at capacity, that she pulled away. Breathlessly, I sucked in a lung full of oxygen.

Everything inside of me had awakened and I had the right mind to bend her ass over and break her in half. However, I was a man of my word.

Niggas were willing to pay. I was willing to pay more.

I needed her to understand that shit, write it down, and take a mental picture if necessary. Whatever she needed to do to understand there wasn't a nigga in the world fucking with me. Not on the first night or the last. Not ever.

"Goodbye, Eden."

I nodded toward the door where she should've been long ago. With my right hand, I tried wiping evidence of her gratification from my lips, from my face. I only smeared that shit.

Pissed, I watched her walk away, fighting the urge to pull her tall ass to the ground by that long ass ponytail until she fell to her knees and filled her mouth with something other than my tongue. I promise I had something better. Something bigger. Something blacker.

Slowly, she ripped my flesh with each step. Intentionally exposing me. Intentionally stripping me. Intentionally luring me. Intentionally fucking with me.

Her ponytail swung from one side to the other, dramatic as she was. As our connection was. As our night had been.

The fucking devil wears red bottoms.

I shed the coat. The hoodie was next. Beneath it was a solid white shirt. My chain sat atop my chest. I discarded my belongings before taking a seat. When I opened the Brandy, I placed the bottle to my lips and sipped. She'd left me empty, thirsting for more.

The glass on the table sufficed for a while. I tipped it toward my face a few times before the slender figure appeared across the room. The threshold of the door housed her silhouette.

The automatic connection to my phone made the application of music simple. A few buttons and the speakers were activated. That smoldering fire within her was reactivated.

Full force. Unmanageable. Uncontainable. Unpredictable.

"Something's got a hold on me lately. No, I don't know myself anymore. Feels like the walls are all closing in and the devil's knocking at my door."

My thoughts. My feelings. My fears. My troubles. My faults. My sentiments. They were spilled over the beat that built intensely.

Money rained down on her. It didn't take but a second for me to determine I'd give her the entire bag. Lending my attention to anything other than her seemed to be against whatever rules she'd made up in her little head. Because, before I could reach for more, she'd kicked the bag away from me.

Goddamn. Eden spared me none. She was on me, fingers trailing my skin as she stared me dead in the eye, making my soul curl and my dick ooze. Hardened nipples doubled the saliva in my mouth. When she snatched the top off completely, it all dried.

The thong was next. As if she was in a hurry to break my bones, clutch my balls... key my heart–she stripped down to her skin. My skin. That fucking skin.

"Did I tell you I'm no good at being alone? Yeah. It's taking a toll on me. Trying my best to keep from tearing the skin off my bones."

Pussy lips greeted me as she bent over, grabbing both ankles. Her flexibility was commendable. I made a mental note to bend her, fold her in every goddamn direction.

Effortlessly, she disrupted me. Wholly. Nothing was intact. Not a single part of me. I became undone watching her.

She was magic. She was mystical. She was un-fucking-believable.

There's just no way, I protested. The distance was too much to ask of her. She gave me no air, staying close and giving me the best angles as she twisted and turned.

Eden bore no fear. Her confidence was part of her show. It was the only thing she wore at the moment. Shit looked good on her.

Delirium. Her naked body swaying to the beat catapulted me into unfamiliar territory. The room grew warmer. My skin crawled with bumps. Swallowing, I tried hydrating the dryness of my throat.

Scorching. Her fire was choking me, depriving me of oxygen. Dewy skin dampened my shirt. The room continued to shrink in size. The heat continued to rise.

"I lose control when you're not next to me. I'm falling apart right in front of you. Can't you see?"

Fuck. A foot rested beside me. Her hand tilted my head backward. The yearning within me intensified. I wanted every fucking part of her in my hands... in my mouth. I craved entry into every hole in her body.

I wanted... *needed* to gut her of everything that was troubling her. Everything that had ever troubled her. End anyone who had ever troubled her.

"Problematic. The problem is, I want your body like a fiend, like a bad habit."

Fucking impossible. She was perfection. Nothing, absolutely nothing, was above her.

In some lifetime, she'd been mine. I'd been hers, too. The way my body responded to her, submitted to her, let me know it had encountered her in another world. But, not even time had been enough for me to forget her.

"*I lose control.*"

Now. Unable to wait another second to have Eden, I lifted her in one swift motion. My legs didn't stop moving when I exited the room. Not as I rushed through the long hallway. Not as we entered the main wing. Not when I entered my bedroom.

It wasn't until I was in front of my bed and her body pounded against the sheets. They lifted as she fell onto them. My chest rose and sank with each breath I took and each one I released.

Entering Eden would be hell. I'd burn. And I'd burn. And I'd burn some more. But, I'd be damned if her pit wouldn't be a grand resting place.

My hand was around her neck in a flash. Her lips were against mine. In synchronization, we silently confessed our desperation. I'd never been desperate for a fucking thing until her.

I lowered my pants and pushed my boxers along with them. I hardly wanted to remove my shirt. It meant parting our lips. Even if briefly, it felt torturous.

And when my demon was finally unleashed, her heart rate sped. I could feel it against my chest as I felt her pussy against my achiness. Long, slim fingers curled around my dick.

"Baby." She breathed against my lips.

"I'm fucking throbbing, Eden." The low, disgruntled statement was followed by a single word that dazed me.

Baby. A term of endearment. A term I used for the women who meant most to me. A term I didn't easily expel but had at least once tonight. Maybe twice. It wasn't until the current moment that I'd come to the realization.

She gave me little time to gather myself. Spreading her legs, she built bay windows with her eyes, preparing them for the viewing of my soul. Up and down, she rubbed my dick against her wetness.

She was soaking. For me. For my dick. For my entry. For my time. For my attention.

"Fuck me," she begged, softly, eyes never leaving mine.

I struggled to tear away from her needy orbs, but the view of my dick sliding across her slipperiness made it worth the trouble. The pinkness was a perfect match for her chocolate skin. I watched as she guided me to her entryway where I sat, anxiously awaiting my ending.

"Put 'em in."

Her assistance wasn't required, but I wasn't ready for the coolness of our surroundings to replace her fingers as I slid in. Obliging, she broke her barriers, accepting me into her fold.

Everything around me stilled. Not even I could move. She'd taken me captive. Her pussy made silent promises to never let me go. I believed every fucking word.

Goddamn, Choc.

At once, she claimed me for eternity. Not even another lifetime would stop me from finding her again. Falling for her again. This one had proved our union was beyond all realms of life. It was inevitable. I'd be looking forward to the next.

"Miiiiisster."

Chemistry. My features rushed to the center of my face as her warmth embraced me. She left gratuity on my dick, coating it with generosity.

Her thanks made sliding in and out of her an effortless motion. To my dismay, lubrication was the least of my worries. It was almost useless because, like everything around me, I'd grown still. Paralyzed with pleasure. Any movement would cause an explosion.

"Fuck."

I closed my eyes, finding solace in a new place. Cool water came up to my chest as visions of the open sea enhanced my mobility. The fear of cumming prematurely subsided.

When I reopened my eyes, there she was. Though I'd never see the pearly gates, she was my little piece of heaven. Nothing had ever felt so freeing, so transcendental.

Eden. A supernatural being. She was ineffable. Mystical. Extramundane.

High cheekbones led to a fierce set of eyes that were wide and wondrous. Her skin was immaculate. Her limbs went on forever. There wasn't a part of her I'd discovered that I didn't like... that I didn't love. Not in an emotional capacity, but in general. Her physique was almost impossible not to fall headfirst for. And that shit made my flesh crawl with both desire and disgust.

Slow strokes made her toes curl and her eyes disappeared somewhere in her head. Her pussy pulled me back in every time I pulled back. It was a death trap.

"Fuuuuuuuck."

When I felt my nut rising, I fought against the current to eject myself. I tapped my dick on her clit. Her body jolted each time I landed on the swollen bulb.

"Plea–"

"Shut th–fuck up, Ede–"

My eyebrows creased on my forehead as I closed my eyes briefly and shook my head from one side to the other. I needed silence. Her voice would only lure me closer to the ledge.

Tap. Her wetness echoed in the darkness.

Tap.

Tap. Her mouth slacked.

"Ummmm."

Tap. She reeked of sultriness. It oozed from her center. It beamed in her eyes.

Tap.

"Uhhhhhhhh."

I plunged deep into her.

Shit.

I lost my way. Lost my head. Lost my cool. Inside of her, I swam as if my life depended on it. In many ways, it did. This union wasn't solely for my satisfaction. It was for hers, too. And for the family.

My strokes deepened. Her moans increased. Our bodies rejoined one another in the center. I held her up to me by the back of her neck as our lips met again. She had me so far out of my comfort zone, it was her lead I was following.

It was all unfamiliar to me. Her experience and the feeling down in my soul had become my guides. I held no jurisdiction in their court. I was merely a spectator.

"I'm cumm–Oh shit."

Her whispers against my lips threatened to end me as well. I defied the odds by pushing her body to the bed and using my thumb to bring her to her peak. My strokes halted, momentarily, while I made sure she splintered. Right down the fucking center.

She came. Beautifully. Loudly. Dramatically. Against me. It wasn't until her breathing steadied and her eyes reopened that I removed my rod and allowed her river to flow. She creamed as I watched, her pussy still contracting slowly. She was still in the midst of her liberation.

Good, Chocolate.

I pulled her to the edge of the bed and cleaned the mess she'd made. With my face buried in her pussy, I inserted my thumb in her ass.

"Waaaaaittt."

Her body slid off the edge of the bed. She humored me.

Not quite ready.

The places I was prepared to take her, her body

wasn't ready. I freed her, standing and peering down at the troubled being beneath me.

The damsel is indeed distressed.

"All fours, Chocolate."

I massaged my dick, watching as she climbed onto the bed and assumed the position I'd requested. A tilted head allowed me to see the little she hadn't exposed. Her pussy parted perfectly, giving me a lovely view of the creamery she was equipped with.

My knees met the sheets that were halfway off the bed. Eden was the perfect height. My dick met her opening without compromising the angle. I leaned down and spat a wad on her slit. She jerked forward. I pulled her back, immediately sliding into her.

A lifted hand pressed against my stomach.

Oh, baby. I groaned, internally. *Don't piss me off.*

Disagreeing with her logic, I pushed it away. Her back curled in response. She inched up but was intercepted before she was able to flee.

"Unn uhn," I corrected. "Fuck you going?"

I repositioned her, making sure she got every inch of dick I had to give. So she couldn't deny my access to her depths, I gathered both hands behind her back and held them in place with my right hand.

Our skin clapped. The sound of our union was glorious. It stole a breath during each lung cycle. Blood rushed through my body. Obscenities crowded my thoughts.

Her pussy was opulent, better than anything I'd ever manufactured in the lab. With each stroke, I got stuck in her secretion. It was the most beautiful mess I'd ever made.

And right at the height of it all, I stiffened. My release announced itself just as it began to spill from me. Feasting off her flesh, I sunk my teeth into her back as I emptied my semen into her womb. I was prayerful that my release resulted in my heir.

THE GREYLIST

Time hadn't stood still, though it seemed that way. Exhaustion haunted me until I gave in and fell asleep right next to the woman who'd milked me of my semen and made me break nearly every rule in my book. Beside me, she slept peacefully.

Wake her ass up. Call Aden.

The little soldier somewhere deep off in my head encouraged. I didn't have the strength. Frankly, I wasn't ready to part ways.

She can stay. As long as she needs to.

As long as I need her to.

Hoping that was enough to quiet the voices, I glared at Eden. Her naked body was tangled in my sheets. She looked as if she belonged there. As if she'd always been there.

Moonlight shone against her skin. Perfection supposedly didn't exist, but I had Eden as evidence of its presence.

Though she appeared angelic, she'd earned her spot in hell with me. The thought rolled off my brain as I slipped out of bed, careful not to disturb her. Bare, I ambled toward the sliding door and pushed it back far enough for me to exit.

Sunless waters stared back at me as the automatic shades retracted at the push of a button. I stepped out into the brittle cold, embracing the chill that followed. Another button lit the stoned fireplace stretched from one end of the balcony to the other. Simultaneously, heat flowed through the vents above me.

The temperature increased with each passing second, making the balcony a more suitable place to sit and mull over the morning I'd had. A more suitable place to think about the things I'd done. A more suitable place to entertain my obsessive, intrusive thoughts about her.

I rested my back against the cushioned chair that was as wide as it was long. A sip of something brown would have improved the moment, but I was still recovering from the drunken hours with Eden. Liquor had little to do with my intoxication. It was her. She was the culprit.

And just as the thought passed through my head, movement sparked behind me. I turned to find the fearless lioness in pursuit of my sanity. Quickly, I pushed the button on the remote in my hand to close the shades and conceal our location. Just as the two panels joined in the center, her leg met the balcony's threshold.

Expect the unexpected.

I'd learned, rather swiftly, that Eden followed her own set of rules. Much like me. Instead of taking one of the two seats available, her naked frame lowered onto mine. With a shake of the head, I rubbed the side of my face. She was disorderly as they came.

Always in my fucking space.

"Hi."

She had my undivided attention. Her nipples hardened against me. I could feel them as she laid her arms on my shoulders. Her closeness was bothersome, yet, I wanted her nowhere else. In front of me, on me, was right where she needed to be.

"Hello, Eden."

"Can't sleep?"

"Choosing not to."

Silence fought for relevance. Eden wouldn't stand for it. Within seconds, she was speaking again.

"Black or white."

"Black."

"Coffee or tea."

"Coffee."

"Basketball or football?"

"Golf."

"Air or sea."

"Sea."

"Sea?"

"I have arms and legs. I don't have wings."

"Fair enough."

"Breakfast or lunch?"

"Dinner."

"That's not how this works."

"It works how I say it works."

"A man that loves having his way," she concluded.

"It's the only way."

"Why me?"

Her curiosity wasn't becoming. I hated it. For now, at least.

"Too many questions, Eden."

"Then stop me. Tell me things and I'll stop asking."

"There's nothing to tell."

I gnawed the skin of my bottom lip. If she kept at it, I would spill. That's what the fuck I couldn't fathom. Rather was the only one. She was my therapist. I didn't need Eden poking around my brain, too.

"You're not exactly an open book."

"Books are hardly open. You have to open them yourself. Read them for your own understanding. In time, you will."

"In time, as in this will not be the last time I see you? Feel you?"

She was so smart, yet she was so fucking clueless.

A walking contradiction.

"If there was any indication that this was a one-time thing, then, I've failed miserably, tonight," I admitted, unafraid of putting my pride behind me.

Her smile caressed me.

"There's something about you– I'm not so sure what, but I'm almost infatuated. Feeling as though I need a little more."

"Ain't shit little about what I have to give you. Don't insult me."

I tipped her chin, bringing her face closer to mine.

Expectedly, she leaned in, sealing our lips. I grew rigid beneath her. The Eden effect was clear. She was out for my head. She was out for my heart. Right now, I'd give her dick. Hopefully, it curbed her appetite for more–so suddenly, so soon.

"Put 'em in."

She wasted very little time lifting and reaching underneath her to grab my manhood. I held her gaze as she found her opening. To avoid micro-tears caused by friction, she lubricated the head of my dick by pushing it in and then pulling it out of the first few centimeters of her opening. When she was ready, she lowered herself onto my thickness, soothing the achiness she'd caused.

She was in control. Had been since I'd noticed her on stage, it seemed. I wanted the wheel again. Needed it, again, like my next breath.

With Eden in my hands, I stood from the seat, pressed her body against the glass door, and spoke directly to her, wordlessly. She'd misunderstood her place. She'd mismanaged her power and mistaken her role for one that was equivalent to mine.

That wasn't the case. It would never be the case. To reclaim my spot, I dug into her, relentlessly.

"Fuck. Fuck. Fuck!"

Her nails clawed my back. The stinging made it evident she'd broken skin, possibly drawn blood. I didn't give a fuck.

Shit is downright ridiculous, I admitted to myself. *Damn.*

I pounded her pussy slowly, and right at the brink of

pleasure and pain. My intention wasn't to bring harm, and I was sure to make that clear. However, she needed to understand where she stood with me and my position in her life. A little pain wasn't the end of the fucking world, but her dominance would be the end of mine.

"I'm cumming. I'm cu–"

"Urgh." The growl had come from somewhere deep within me, somewhere that hadn't been explored.

Together we came undone. Her grip around me tightened. Mine loosened.

"Fuck." Against her lips, I spat. My dick throbbed as my sack drained.

Eventually, her body began to slide down the glass. Her arms never fell from around my neck. Her palms brought my face closer to hers. Heated breaths grappled for space between us. And once they both settled, our tongues began a scuffle of their own.

Ridiculous.

It didn't matter how much of her I had, I wanted more. I pulled away before I got too caught up in her rapture to be freed.

"You should rest."

Though she wanted to protest, she didn't. A nod followed the suggestion, but the fire in her spirit was visible in those rounds as she hesitated to move.

I dare you, Chocolate.

I waited for a rebuttal, a sly mark, or a slice from that sharp tongue. The wait was in vain. Instead of putting up a fight, she turned and headed inside.

I watched from afar as she grabbed the bottled water

beside the bed and finished it off. When she climbed under the covers without wiping my remnants from her skin or draining my semen from her soil, I was enamored.

Staggering... in every sense of the word.

I followed her inside with her dried fluids still coating my dick. I covered it with a pair of shorts from the third drawer of my dresser. A smile traced her lips.

Tittering, I communicated my thoughts without having to say a thing. She understood me. I understood her. Twin flames of sorts. Fire danced between us. We were inevitably drawn to one another.

I found myself still staring seconds later. I hadn't made as much progress as I'd believed.

"You're intolerable."

"Yet, here I am."

And here you'll be.

"Come back to bed."

"Soon enough. Get some rest."

With a sigh, she closed those pretty eyes of hers and left me alone to decompress. Back out on the balcony, I unlocked my cellular device and glared at the red letters on the screen.

The rate of my heartbeat changed. The air around me stilled. The weight of my body grew heavier.

4:07 a.m.

I tapped the screen, initiating the call. The hour of the day meant nothing. Four o'clock in the evening or four o'clock in the morning would render the same results without fail. A baritone etched in my brain struck the line.

"Malachi."

"I'm happy it wasn't an emergency. I called you five hours ago."

"Brother, had it been an emergency, I wouldn't be on your line. I'd be in your face. You find humor in insulting me, huh?"

"You should know me by now."

"And you should know there is very little I don't know about you and them other knuckleheads."

Losing a parent was never easy, but losing a mother took pieces of you you simply couldn't replace. The void my mother's death scarred me with made its presence known each time I saw or heard from one of the men I shared her with at one point in time.

To make matters worse, the day I lost her was the day I lost so much of them. Our distance nibbled on my sanity for years. Nothing prepared me for the despair their combined absences filled me with.

I was grieving her casualty and our closeness at once. Til this day, neither had run their course. I struggled, in every way imaginable, with the consequences of my mother's decision on a daily basis. Nothing in my world had been resolved surrounding the circumstances of her and Maurice's deaths. Everything just lingered. Hurt a little less, but hurt, nonetheless.

I loved my sisters to my core, but those boys had my heart first. They always would. Their ages, occupations, and relationship statuses never mattered and would never make me love them any less.

"You crossed my mind."

"I'm flattered," I exaggerated.

"Fuck you."

"Hey!" his wife protested in the background.

"Listen to your wife."

"I meant that." Malachi chuckled. "What's on your mind?"

"Same shit, Malachi. Same shit."

"The water. It's returned."

"Never left."

"It's your paranoia."

"Was it ever paranoia?" Sighing, I ran a hand down my face. "Or preparation."

"For what, Chem?"

"Shit, if I knew I wouldn't be worried, yeah?"

Before speaking again, he released a long breath. "You're fucking contagious."

"Am I or do you just aspire to be like your big brother."

"Fuck you, again."

"It's starting to feel like incest, Malachi. Anna is available. Why me?"

There was ruffling in the background before an angelic tone tickled my eardrums.

"Chemistry," my sister-in-love sang.

It was four in the fucking morning and far too early for the sweetness in her voice but that was to be expected. She was as bland as she was blissful. She was as calm as she was chipper. She was as poised as she was pert.

"Hello, Anna."

"I can feel your frown all these miles away. What's bothering you?"

Silence toyed the line. God had been gracious to Malachi, blessing him with a woman like Anna. She was everything our mother once was, it seemed.

Her gentleness didn't overshadow her grit. She was equal parts of them both, but it preceded the grime that Malachi buried within her. She'd been polished anew. Traces that she'd stumbled out of the same neighborhood as Malachi were erased.

Her hands were clean. Her heart was cleaner. My brother had designed a world for her that forbade her from lifting a finger or dirtying her manicured nails. She was put up. And well.

"Worry me."

I felt the ends of my lips curl upward as I dipped my head. How they did that so effortlessly would forever haunt me.

Fucking girls, man. I scratched the top of my head and sat forward in my seat, ready to worry her as she'd asked.

Roulette. Rather. Anna. I could never forget Anna. I wasn't sure if she was working for Malachi or simply gifted enough to pull things from me that were meant to remain hidden.

"Richie is dying." I clicked my tongue with a shake of the head, still not believing it to be true.

"Oh, Chemistry. I'm so sorry."

"Don't be. It's life, Anna. You live and then you die."

"Yes, bu–"

"There are hardly any buts. One day I'll go. One day you'll go."

Quickly, she responded, "Yes, I know my time is coming. We all do."

"So, no sympathy for a soldier, baby."

She quieted, recalling words we spoke often as boys. It was our way of declining sympathy from strangers and those close to us for the deaths of our mother and Maurice. That shit was useless to us. It wouldn't ease our pain or bring either of them back.

"There's something else."

"There is," I confessed.

"I'm listening."

"Why aren't you asleep?"

"Chemistry."

"I feel something is brewing."

"Something good?"

"I wouldn't have to worry you if it was something good, would I?"

"I guess not."

"When was the last time you took a break? Stepped back and really let yourself live outside of your daily routine? When was the last time you bent the rules a little?"

I peered through the glass door, finding Eden had fallen asleep.

Today.

"I don't know what that would help."

"It might. I'm not saying tomorrow or next week. But, soon, leave it all behind and free yourself for a little while. Come to Berkeley or go somewhere tropical, surrounded by wat–"

"Water," I finished with a nod.

"Yes. Water."

I listened carefully, but I didn't have a response. In fact, my attention had wavered and the topic of water left me craving.

"I must go now, Anna."

"Of course," she groaned. "Please take it into consideration at least."

"I will."

"We love you, Chemistry."

"In this lifetime and the others."

I ended the call and stared down at the black piece of matter. Anna's words circulated until I stood and stretched my body.

On my way inside, I disabled the heating system. I pushed through my bedroom, eyes fixed on Eden. My exit obstructed my view, changing it to meet the needs of my desires. I didn't stop moving until the chlorine from my pool raised my skin with fine bumps.

THE GREYLIST

One lap after the other erased evidence that time existed. It wasn't until my limbs grew too tired to continue and my skin threatened me with permanent wrinkling I climbed out of the water. Everything was better.

I rinsed under the shower just outside of the pool and dried my body before stepping into a fresh pair of briefs. I layered it with pants. The decrease in my body's temperature was inevitable. Socks clung to my feet as I stalked the hallway toward my bedroom.

The sun shined from the large windows throughout, bringing light to the richly-colored decor of my home. I reached the master suite in minutes. The massiveness of my residence was easily mastered by the length of my legs. Paired with the fact I knew the layout so well, my pants were on the floor and I was climbing in bed behind Eden rather swiftly.

She repositioned, allowing her body to melt against mine. Her warmth elevated my temperature. With her ass brushing my dick, she searched me for the unknown.

When her fingers curled around my wrist and brought my hand forward, her intentions were made clearer. I tucked my hand underneath her, pulling her even closer. I buried my face in the ponytail that hung down her back, hopeful sleep wasn't too far-fetched.

The idea of comfort with a stranger in my presence was absurd. It had always been. But, with Eden in my arms, there was a calm no storm could interrupt. Peace not even war could disrupt.

"Get some rest." She sighed, deepening our connection.

Choc, I'm trying. The final thought stuck with me as I began to drift.

THE **GREY** LIST

NOTE: *If you are part of the woman-hater's club, please refrain from moving forward. The Grey List is female-centered. The disdain, hate, or slander of women protecting their peace, sanity, careers, hearts, and feelings is not welcome here.*

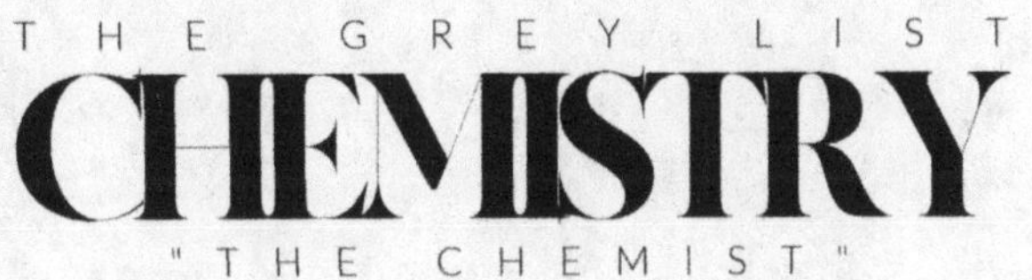

GREY HUFFINGTON

Between the covers of this book is **my** art piece —
beautifully paired words structured for **my** creative
satisfaction and later consumed by others for enjoyment.

It's **leisure for you**, it's **life for me**.
This is just a book to most. **It's art for me**.
My art. I've had *my* time. Have **yours**.

happy reading

GREY **HUFFINGTON**

ONE

Eden

Six nights ago...

Maybe he's an assassin. Or a Mobster. Or a drug dealer. Or a drug **lord**.

Definitely a drug lord.

Almost a full twenty-four hours later, I was still tangled in Mister's sheets.

I need a name.

I had two hours before my shift was to begin at Roulette. Missing it to lie with the unknown was tempting, but I had a job at stake.

My anxious thoughts didn't muddle the moment. I remained lost in the beauty of the complex creature that had carved a piece of me and stuffed himself inside.

But, do I? My inquisitive nature was hard to defy.

However, somehow, he felt worthy. Knowing nothing was much like knowing enough, for once.

Living in the moment was a tough task for me. This moment, somehow, required it. Obliging, I cleared my head and made space for my heart.

I threw caution to the wind, deciding I'd allow it to lead me. I hadn't engaged in anything as fulfilling as the night I'd had. Ever.

The fantasies I'd once kept buried inside were brought to life. That had to mean something about this moment, about this man.

I lifted a hand before lowering it on his deep brown, utterly obsessive skin. Every feature had been carefully, and strategically placed. God had broken every rule preparing him, making him extra special for someone special.

For me.

The strength of a man was almost always underestimated. But, the fingers coiled around my hand tightly, surely stopping the blood flow of my fingers, reminded me it was not to be misconstrued.

"Sorry," I winced, regretting not keeping my hands to myself.

His eyes popped open at once. Incoherent, he observed his surroundings, seemingly confused about everything and nothing, simultaneously.

"Eden?" He looked at me, loosening his grip.

I nodded, confirming my presence. Silence trailed as he sighed and released me. I watched as he came to, swiping a hand across his face.

So troubled.

He checked the clock next to the bed, finally realizing how long he'd slept since we'd eaten hours prior. Our fetish for one another led us back to bed where we'd started, but not before we revisited the room decorated with a lone pole.

I slid down it a few times before sliding down his. My walls were tender. My breasts were sore. The signs of a well-fucked woman were upon me. I hadn't experienced such pleasurable soreness since I'd first opened my legs at twenty years old.

"I should be leaving. I have work in a little over two hours."

He said nothing. His silence was agonizing. I wanted to know what he was thinking. I *needed* to know what he was thinking.

When he rolled out of bed, I was on his heels, quickly remembering I was nude. Chills stalked my body, instantly.

With his features contorting on his face, he pushed out a fresh stream of air as if I'd pushed the wrong button. The sheets came flying off the bed. The flat one coated my skin. Our eyes met as he tucked parts of it between my index fingers and thumbs.

He made it so hard to consider I brought him

anything but discomfort. The frowns. The stewing. The brooding.

It all left me wondering and feeling as though I was doing everything wrong. His lack of satisfaction made me thirst for his gratification, validation of some sort.

The flirty vixen he'd met the night before was a pile of mush this morning. She was vulnerable. She was submissive.

I searched deep within for the stellar version, summoning her before I made a fool of myself before and revealed the sheepish girl who still longed for things she was unsure of.

"Say something."

She was making it so hard for me. My exposure was pending.

"Quit."

Quit? His demand was incredibly stunning.

"Quit?"

My brows crinkled as I rushed behind him. Every step I took, it seemed as if he took five.

My God, where are you?

"You heard exactly what the fuck I said, Eden."

"I will do no such thing," I responded as a smirk tugged at my lips.

About time, girlfriend. I cheered, inside, feeling my power return.

Swiftly, Mister turned around, stopping in his tracks. I almost ran into him, but I halted in time to stop right in front of him. I could feel the heat radiating from him.

It made me slippery down below. Hadn't I been

recovering from the last twenty-something hours, I would've encouraged him to dive in. But, I had a job and he had... I wasn't sure what he had, but business felt plausible.

"Eden, don't test me, baby. I have no problem having your locker cleaned out and banning you from every club in Clarke."

"Clarke isn't the first or last to build strip clubs. Forcing my hand will only make me forget the night we had and the fact you exist, no matter how hard it might be," I divulged, feeling the hair on my neck stand. "Let's not become a tragedy so soon, Mister."

His eyes turned to slits. He contemplated what would come from his mouth next. And I waited, impatiently, needing him to say something.

He was well-calculated. Nothing came from him that he hadn't studied in his head a hundred times. He was always in his fucking head. And in mine.

"Forcing my hand will fill your conscience with guilt and have you paying your respects at a new funeral every fucking weekend. You won't have time to have your black dress dry-cleaned before you're putting it on again. And again. And again."

"For a man whose name I can't have, you are territorial."

"What's mine is mine, Eden. Understand that."

"I'm not quitting. Not yet. When I'm ready, y–"

"You've made yourself clear. So have I."

"I–"

"End of discussion."

He bore into me with dark eyes and a menacing glower. His merciless gaze pebbled my nipples and caused my breath to hike in my chest. I wasn't able to breathe again until he turned, leaving a pang in my chest that traveled up my throat, and sat.

He trudged toward the bathroom. Helplessly, I followed him. The man had struck me with unfathomably good dick and expected me to manage my own footing in his presence. I wasn't sure if half my brain was working, but I knew he was capable of thinking for us both tonight.

"Leave the sheet. Come shower so I can take you and that smart-ass mouth home. I'm seconds away from stuffing it."

Please.

The sheet fell to the floor as I escaped its expansiveness. Cold marble touched the tips of my toes. Mister stopped at the urinal and nodded for me to take the toilet not too far from it. Suddenly, the urge to relieve myself returned. I'd forgotten it when I opened my eyes and found him sleeping peacefully beside me.

I stared straight ahead, eyes trained on the empty shower as my release commenced. Mister's eyes hadn't left me, yet. He shot daggers in my direction, having never loosened the frown on his handsome face.

"Smile more," I demanded, craving his white teeth and dimpled cheeks. They'd hidden behind gold, diamond-encrusted plates the night before.

"When I have a reason, I will."

"Am I not a reason?"

Finally, my eyes met his.

"You're a thorn, Eden. Don't shit feel good about a thorn."

"I find that hard to believe, Mister."

"Believe it, baby."

"You've been contradicting yourself all night."

"I'm a glutton for affliction, it seems. Trouble doesn't follow me. I follow it."

"One minute, you're passion. Next, you're pain."

He took his eyes off me momentarily to be sure he'd shook himself dry. I wiped myself, smearing the results of ovulation from my center. Emergency contraceptive were on the list of things to consume within the next seventy-two hours.

"I don't like riddles. Be clear about whatever it is you're saying, Eden."

"You're a fascinating creature, but I despise your ability to make a fool of my feelings."

"Your feelings?" He kissed his teeth. "Should they matter yet?"

I scoffed, nodding. He was a fucking riddle. It was probably why he hated them so much.

I stood up and the toilet flushed automatically, startling me. My departure was imperative at this point. Seemingly, Mister had forgotten the night we'd had.

The day we'd had. The moments we'd shared. The spit we'd swapped. The kisses we hated to end. The bodily fluids we bathed in.

"I can shower at home. Is there a car waiting? Will you take me? How does this work? I can manag–"

I lost track of my thoughts as his chest neared me. My vision blurred as his scent engulfed me. My head spun upon realizing he wasn't stopping. And when he entangled our fingers, pushing them above my head and me against the wall behind us, I shuttered.

"Plea–"

"Eden, baby."

One minute, you're passion. Next, you're pain

"You're driving me mad," I admitted, aching all over.

His lips brushed against my ear, weakening me.

"They matter."

His never-ending quest to confuse me was always successful. *Right or wrong*, I wasn't sure if I was either.

Still, I longed for him. More of him. Regardless of what came from his mouth or how much he furrowed those thick brows, that any woman would kill for.

"You're intolerable."

He'd claimed I was, but I felt more of the same.

"I know."

Silence hovered before he spoke again.

"I don't know what the fuck I'm doing. But when I figure it out, I want you right here. *Still*."

He'd reached my core with his words. Leaving him so soon didn't feel possible anymore. I wanted to stay, but I knew I couldn't. It was time to part ways, as difficult as that might've seemed.

His lips rested against mine as he struggled, internally, with his next move. I made the decision for him. I wasn't as poised. As calculated. As critical. Not with him, at least. I sunk my teeth in his top lip, not pulling back until I heard him wince from pain.

When his mouth slacked in surprise, I stuck my tongue inside, desperate to taste the blood I'd drawn. His fingers loosened around mine. I felt them, seconds later, on the sides of my face, deepening our kiss. Deepening our connection. When he'd had enough, he pushed away.

Lowered lids and glossed eyes told of his inebriation because he wasn't willing. Drunkenly, we both stumbled into the shower where lingering touches and longing stares continued. We cleansed our bodies and exited the shower without exploring more of each other physically. Mentally, however, it was out of our control.

Blindfolded, he delivered me to my address without ever asking for it. I climbed out of the truck with him on my tail. Just before the entrance, he stopped.

I fought the urge to invite him up. He, too, was fighting something. Not even the dark shades, fitted cap, and hoodie could conceal his hunger.

"Eden," he called out, stopping me in my tracks.

"Yes."

He paused, confirming his next choice of words was suitable.

"I enjoyed every second of our encounter."

Stunned by his confession, I placed a hand on my chest where it hurt.

"When will I see you again?"

"When I'm ready."

"When you're ready? Miste–"

"I'm not selfish in my decision, Eden. I just have a lot

of shit going on up here. Give me time. I'm over-stimulated."

I'd been there. I understood exactly where he was.

"Then, a number. A name. Something. How will I contact you when I can't stand the time between us any longer?"

"When you need me, I'll know. And I'll come. Always."

Always. That must've been wondrous. Always having someone like him near.

"How?"

"I'm waiting, Eden. And I'm watching."

"Watc–"

"Goodnight."

In the blink of an eye, he was gone.

Presently...

"Earth to Johanson!" Jack yelled, snapping his fingers.

Out of your head, Egypt.

It was easier said than done. Seven nights ago, I met someone magical. Someone mystical. Six nights ago, he'd left me at the entrance of my building and I'd been swallowed into an abyss ever since.

Maddening, he was. And I was still trying to decipher my feelings. I wasn't sure if I was disappointed or completely dazed. His presence felt make-believe. Not as if it hadn't happened, but as if it was just unreal. Far too good to be true.

But, the thudding between my legs each time I thought of him assured me it was real. He was real. Regal, but real.

To make matters worse, I always thought of him. There was hardly a moment when he wasn't on my mind. Walking around with an irregular heartbeat in my chest and my cooch was torture.

"Have you heard a word we've said?" Macy asked.

A roll of the eyes wasn't enough to display my disdain for her. I needed her to hear me clearly. Unfortunately, I was unable to get my mouse across the screen to click the microphone button.

The mouse pad I'd pulled from my closet once given this assignment was bent out of shape and needed to be replaced. I'd told myself thirteen times I would grab a new one while I was out.

This time, I promise.

Frustrated, I picked the mouse up and slammed it on the desk, shoving the pad toward the edge. That didn't help much.

Finally.

I made it across the screen to tap the button.

"Macy, against my will, I have heard every word you've said. Sorry, Jack. Running over some details."

"Care to share?" Bradford chimed in, sipping the coffee from his mug.

Ugh. I sighed, wishing I could spend my mornings at the facility and not staring at my screen for morning meetings. Field assignments had their perks, but this wasn't one of them. I could smell the medium roast with creamer in his cup through the screen.

Two creamers. Four packs of sugar. I knew his preference because I fixed us both a cup each morning when I got in if I didn't stop by the coffee spot right at the corner of 2nd Street and Poplar. He was the only person I'd consider going the scenic route for. I loved my team, but they'd shown me time and time again they weren't worthy of my trust.

"Can you wait until this meeting concludes to finish your coffee? I'm jealous."

"You're put up in a beautiful loft you had a damn good budget to decorate, sitting in front of a desk in front of a window overlooking the beautiful city of Clarke. We're all jealous!" Bradford teased, taking a long sip. "Now, care to share?"

Shaking my thoughts clear of Mister, I tapped into the young woman on a mission to make her father proud. Though he'd left us years ago, I still felt him with me on each assignment. Like him, I'd taken a liking to problem-solving and landed a job in the same realm he'd held ranking for most of his career.

"I'm making strides. The owner still hasn't shown face, at least I haven't been able to put a face to the name."

"Name?" Macy questioned.

"Yes. I have a name now."

"We're listening," Jack told me, standing from his desk and moving toward the board we'd been scribbling on as a team for months. It should've been filled to the brim but we hardly knew anything. Many months of intel led us nowhere.

Someone had to get in the field. For three months, I took pole lessons twice a week to make sure that someone was me. There was no way I was giving the opportunity to Macy.

"The Madam."

"The Madam?" Bradford nearly choked on his coffee.

"Yes."

"So, we're dealing with a woman?"

"Supposedly. She, she, she. They're a very private bunch of women working, but when they mention The Madam, they're referring to a woman."

"Goddamnit. I wasn't expecting that." Jack gasped.

"There's a meeting happening soon. Apparently, they don't happen often but when they do, she selects a few women to attend for the entertainment of her guests. I need to be in that meeting, Jack."

"Does it look like you'll be in the lineup?"

"I will make sure I am. If I sit this one out, there's no telling when there will be another one."

"Good. Good. Yeah. We need you there."

"Any illegal activities you've witnessed so far?" Macy spoke.

"Nothing of importance. Nothing worth jeopardizing the investigation to pursue."

"Let's focus on the task at hand, Macy. The Grey List. anything else is irrelevant," Bradford added.

"Is there anything else?"

"No. Nothing I can think of."

"Alright. Check-in is next week. See you then, Johanson."

"I look forward to it more than anything."

I ended the video call, wondering if I was truly looking forward to the next meeting with my team more than I was my next meeting with Mister.

Not even a little, I admitted.

My legs stretched one in front of the other as I moved toward the large window. On the sixteenth floor of my building, I could see most of downtown Clarke. It was breathtaking, making me consider selling my home in Windridge to live the high-rise life.

Valet emptied your trash, parked your car, and handled your bags if you came in with any. Because it was only me, it still felt spacious as my home. I didn't have many complaints.

My arms locked underneath my breast as I leaned against the window. The city continued to move in his absence, but for me, life stood still. I couldn't seem to grasp the concept of moving forward. Everything stopped.

"Where are you?" I whispered.

There hadn't been a mystery I wasn't eager to solve since I was a child. It was the reason I'd landed the job I had and quickly rose to the top of the force. But this time, for the very first time in my life, the allure surrounded his mystique.

It was thrilling. Exciting, like the childhood memory of sticking your hand inside a box fan to slow down the blades or stop them from spinning completely. He was the blade.

I was the fool who was willing to try to slow him down or stop him long enough to notice me, *again*. Long enough to kiss me feverishly. Long enough to hold me through the night. Long enough to make my center cream like he once had.

"You could be anywhere out there."

But, you're near. I feel you.

His promise to always be there when I needed him hadn't escaped my mind. I was still trying to determine when he'd realized I was beyond the desire of him. My hunger for him had become apparent four days ago. I was famished standing next to the window.

My vibrating phone pulled me from the edge. I slid it from the pocket of my Levi's seeing my best friend calling. Without hesitation, I answered, hoping she could make sense of the situation I'd found myself in.

"Art."

"Hey, babe. What's up?"

"Nothing." I sighed. "Just finished another check-in with the team."

"Was it that bad?" she probed. "You sound disappointed."

"It went well."

"Good, then what's the matter?"

Our parents had been best friends since high school. They all left Clarke for college immediately after. It was a basement party for a mutual's return to the city after graduating that brought them all back together. My mother and Art's mom. My father and Art's father.

The two pairs of best friends reconnected over punch that was heavily infused with cheap liquor, handheld bites to eat, and Blues. Though the party ended, None of them were ready to go home, so they continued their shenanigans at my father's brand new, unfurnished studio apartment with a three-dollar box of pizza and a one-liter Coke in tow. My mother never left after that day. Art's mother and father became inseparable, too.

First, my brother joined the couple. I was next. They ended their child-bearing days with my sister. Art's parents had three children of their own as well. Two boys and Art. Like me, she was the middle child. We were born in the same year as well.

"Is it possible to miss someone you haven't truly met?" I dropped my head, staring at the new pair of black socks that covered my feet.

"Egypt." She paused, taking a deep breath. "You have."

"But, have I?"

"Yes."

"Then why don't I have a name or a number to contact him?" I chuckled.

Laugh to keep from crying. The saying registered with me at the moment.

"Tell me, Egypt, with honesty... would having his

name change anything about the time you spent together? Would it have made it better?"

"No."

"Then, don't worry. He's made it clear he's coming back. He just needs to clear his head."

"This is why you've been married as long as you have been. This is why your marriage is so damn successful."

"Why is that?" She laughed.

"Because you have the patience of a mother with five little ones."

"The thought of having five children isn't sitting well with me. Five is an odd number, so that's definitely not going to work for me."

"Then, four."

"Better."

"I have no patience for this man. I want him right now and having no way to tell him I– I'm just going on and on about me. I'm sure you didn't call to hear me go on about him, too. What's up, girlfriend?" I smacked my lips, trying my best to shake him from my thoughts. I failed. *Miserably*.

"Please don't agitate me," she warned as if it was possible.

I'd known Art her entire life. I could count on my fingers how many times she'd gotten bothered or had her panties in a bunch. And that was using one hand.

"Ugh."

"No way to tell him what?"

I was in no rush to spill, but with Art, I didn't have a choice.

"No way to tell him I miss him."

"Awwwww. My girl has the blues."

"Something awful, Art. As much as I want to, I can't deny it."

"I've been there. If no one else understands, I do."

She'd met her husband and spent a lovely night with him. Two days later, a business emergency pulled him away from her for three weeks. She was lovesick and positive she'd fallen for a man she'd only known forty-eight hours. Nothing in her world was right until he returned. When he did, he wasn't empty-handed.

"I know."

"So, listen to me when I tell you there is no need to worry. He will return. And when he does, you'll forget his absence existed because his presence will be so consuming. You'll forget everything except how good it feels to have him near."

"I need to forget today, then. Right now," I joked.

"Now is not the time," she replied.

"I guess it's not. Anyway, what are you up to?"

"Nothing. My usual. I just called to hear your voice. I might just miss you a little."

"A little? Should I hang up now or keep listening to you lie?"

"Okay, maybe it's more than a little. I was thinking we could do dinner sometime next week."

"The case, Art."

"God, how'd I neglect that thought? Right. The case. Maybe next month or next quarter or next year or ne–"

"Hush, lady. I will sneak away for you and you know

it. Just give me some time to carve a hole in my schedule big enough for us to catch up. This one is different from the others. I have to be careful. As simple as dinner might sound, it's not so simple this time around."

"Then, I'll wait."

"I'll find a way."

"I won't let you, babe. I will wait."

"Okay." I hated to disappoint her. "FaceTime date?"

"I'll take it," she sang.

"Good. Let's aim for a weekday. My weekends are spent on the case. A Tuesday, maybe?" I couldn't go into detail but I knew Art would understand regardless.

"Tuesday is fine," she agreed cheerfully.

"Okay. I'll send over the details later."

"I love you, Egypt. And I will be waiting for your message."

"Love you back, Art. Talk to you later."

The call ended and my emotionally charged stupor continued. Before I could pull myself from the window, light rain began to tap against it. It hadn't been in the forecast, but the clouds that hung low and sagged with water molecules were indications it might not hold off until tomorrow.

Gloom lingered, but there was something special about the way rain announced itself so subtly yet profound. It reminded me of *him*. So did the sign of the steakhouse on the corner next to the florist shop I visited often. The perfection of the lightly seasoned filet mignon from the night Mister and I dined made my mouth water.

"He wants to make it home, Eden. Don't end his life tonight because you're fascinated with the thrill."

His words taunted me. His confidence aroused me. I clung to everything that came from his oversized lips which were incredibly soft against my center. I remembered them most because the few times that turned upward, they revealed dimpled cheeks and regularly serviced white teeth.

Maybe Mister was wrong, or only partially accurate in his assumption. It was him I was fascinated with, too, not only the thrill. Maybe it was because, for as long as I could remember, following the rules got me further than disobeying them.

Following the rules had given me more awards than my shelf could hold. Following the rules was rewarding, in my career and personal life. I was the only one of three children who actually followed the rules, which was evident in the differences between my siblings and me.

Following the rules made my parents proud time and time again because if I didn't, their children would only be the source of sore memories. I had to follow the rules. I had to make them smile, for my siblings' sake. For our parents' sanity. I was the only hope.

But, rebellion, it felt so damn good. Too good, almost. I pushed out warm, pent-up frustrations as I continued gawking at the business across the way. My skin pimpled at the possibilities of my night if all went as planned.

It's not Prime House, but it will suffice, I reasoned, shoving a hand in my black jeans as I began to pace from one end of the loft to the other, searching my contacts for the newest addition.

Dyson. He'd insisted on entering his number in the event I was ready for the night of my life. He was oblivious, hardly understanding I'd already experienced it. To my despair, the man who'd provided it had been missing ever since.

Tonight, he'd be the replacement. A medium-well steak and attention from a new stranger I'd met during work hours would keep my mind occupied and off him long enough to breathe again I supposed. Or, somehow summon the beast. Either, I was willing to accept, but the ladder had moisture forming on the seat of my panties.

THE GREY LIST

Winters in Clarke were unpredictable. On this particular, late winter's night, temperatures were in the high seventies. The rain had dampened the streets, leaving such a muggy cast and prominent scent across the city.

I strolled into *Blanche Steakhouse* in a black satin number swayed with each move I made. Because the weather was perfect, I left the winter wear home and exchanged it for the strappy piece and platform sandals that matched its sex appeal.

With my chin upward, I searched for the bar, where Dyson claimed to have been waiting for the last six minutes. That's how long it took me to get from my complex to the doorstep of Blanche. Before I walked out of my door and wasted a look, I needed to make sure he'd be there.

I noticed the meaty fella almost immediately. His eyes were pinned against me, mentally stripping me of the few fabrics that graced my skin. I approached with an extended hand and a smile that felt unreal. Being in any man's presence other than the one who had left a lasting impression on me all those nights ago felt degrading. I swallowed the lump I'd caught in my throat.

"Eden," I introduced myself, deciding it was probably better than my stage name since our setting had changed.

"Real name." He chuckled. "We've made progress already."

"Possibly."

"Our table is ready. Decided to grab a drink before I took off and it was too hard for you to find me. It's a packed house tonight."

"I see."

Dyson tossed the rest of his drink back, allowing the alcohol to burn the back of his throat before slamming the glass on the bar top. I followed him, weary of my surroundings suddenly.

My eyes disconnected with the handsome man who'd been waiting for my arrival and began scanning parts of the restaurant that were visible to me. An unsettling feeling coiled my stomach, knotting it with a pang that was incredibly uncomfortable.

I could feel my brows hunch in disarray. I could feel my eyes roaming the openness with speed, carefully documenting each face. I could feel my heart rate increase. I could feel the atmosphere shift. I could feel everything around me slowly blur until finally we reached our table.

He's here.

I hadn't laid an eye on him, but his presence was that potent. I could *feel him* even though I couldn't *see him*. Hairs on the nape of my neck stood first. The rest followed, brushing against my dress as I sat down.

Dyson never pulled out his chair. He never joined me. Instead, he stood beside me, peering down at me as his fingers traced a circle on my shoulder. My attention was divided until I realized his hand was on me and he was saying something I should probably hear.

"I'm going to the restroom. I'll be right back, aight?"

I closed my eyes, trying to calm my raging heart. My head lifted and fell twice. "Okay."

When I was alone, I unsealed my eyelids, imagining he'd be right there. Right before me. Across the table, with curious, angered eyes, suggested he wasn't pleased with the choices I'd made.

Fuck. He wasn't. All that occupied the seat across from me was air. Mister was nowhere in sight.

I'm going mad, I admitted. *That man is not here and he's probably not even thinking about me right now.*

I shook my head clear of the haze and picked up the glass of water in front of me. With my other hand, I grabbed the menu to begin reviewing the night's selections.

Enjoy your night, Egypt.

I'd try my hardest. That was a promise I was making to myself so the success of my night didn't depend on a man who had possibly forgotten I existed by now.

I studied the menu, mapping my meal plan with precision. The first on my list was the lamb bites that were served with a house-made dressing as an appetizer. The seafood spinach dip was another appetizer I'd love to try. A salad was included with every entree. I'd settle for the caesar. Finally, a steak with loaded mash and broccolini would complete my meal.

Time stretched as I waited for Dyson's return. I altered between peeking at the time on my phone and behind me where he'd gone toward the restrooms. With each passing minute, his disappearance was becoming clearer.

This is why I don't care about entertaining men. I gnawed my bottom lip as I placed the call to his cell. It didn't stop ringing until the voicemail met me on the line. I tried once more and got the same results.

In total disbelief, I stood and pushed my chair back up to the table. Though I wanted to try his cell once more, I knew there wasn't a point. He'd been such a fleeting figure, that I wouldn't notice his absence. From the moment he'd greeted me at Roulette, I imagined he was all fluff. His disappearing act was all the evidence I needed to confirm my suspicions.

A fucking joke and a waste of effort. I strolled out of

Blanche Steakhouse with as much credence as I'd strolled in with. Only this time, it was coupled with annoyance and self-criticism that wasn't necessarily fair but reasonable.

Two feet out into the muggy air, my heart stopped completely. There he stood, hands folded in front of him, pressuring his shirt to expose more of his chest and the definition of his arms.

Dark, devilish eyes donned me. They hounded me for repayment, time lost, and the worry I'd caused. Before I could begin to acknowledge my debts and begin paying, his baritone stiffened me wholly.

"Get in the fucking car, Eden."

He lifted himself from the hood, stretching his body to meet his full length, and undoing me, simultaneously. Defiance was easier than compliance. I stood, unmoving, as he waited at the door of a matte black Mercedes with black rims made it look completely unreal in the dark of the night.

"Eden." He groaned, as if speaking to me at his current capacity was painful.

I hoped it hurt, just like his absence had made my heart tender and my head sore.

"Where is my date?"

"Get in the fucking car before I put you in the car."

"Where is my date?" I repeated myself, desperate to know where the man I'd come to meet had gone. It was obvious Mister had everything to do with his inability to return to our table.

"Now is not the time to test me. I will fail. I will fail

miserably," he grumbled angrily. "I have no limits, Eden. None. Don't fuck around or you will find out, swiftly and without remorse."

"Whe–"

In a flash, he was in my face, his breath making the strands of hair that were ring-curled and hanging swing backward.

"In the car. Right now." Slowly, yet forcefully, he demanded movement.

This time, unlike the others, I was swayed. My feet began moving before I could protest. In seconds, I was in the front seat with a seatbelt over my body and a furious driver. My back slammed against the seat as he burned the rubber of his tires, speeding down the street.

My God. I thudded at the center, realizing why he had a driver. He was a menace behind the wheel. It frightened and fascinated me at once.

TWO

Chemistry

Audacity.

It was the downfall of anyone who'd ever fallen victim to my wrath. The man slowly losing consciousness as his body shut down completely was the latest. Together, we made our way to the floor. Disgust plagued me.

Drop, I demanded.

When his body finally collapsed, on cue, I stood, grateful I didn't dirty my slacks on the restroom floor. His filthy nails and the sleep in the corner of his eyes were repulsive enough. It was difficult keeping my composure and I wouldn't last too much longer.

I removed the burner from my waistline and the

silencer from the pocket of my pants, preparing to put an end to the madness sooner than later. I hadn't planned for my night to go this way. A nice dinner, something brown in my cup, and Eden within arm's reach was the idea. But seeing her stroll across the street as if she was ready to claim her pageant crown had wrecked my fucking brain and almost made me wreck my fucking whip.

Witnessing her in another man's company was maddening. Witnessing another man lay hands on what belonged to me was incriminating. Seeing those fingers hadn't been cleaned thoroughly in hours, possibly days, was infuriating.

He'd sealed his fate when they grazed her skin, fueling the fire brewing inside of me already. To his detriment, I met him in the restroom with a closed for cleaning sign, a scorned heart, and my problem solver.

Pew!

The center of his forehead split, making room for the bullet I'd just put there. His body jerked, emphasizing the end of his life cycle. I was certain his bowels had movement. I wasn't going to stick around long to find out. He was in the right place to free them but at the wrong fucking time.

"Fucking animal."

A grunt escaped me as I straightened the wrinkles in my shirt. The warmth of my weapon rested against my back as I concealed it. With a scattered conscience, I unlocked my phone and snapped a picture of the diabolical human stretched out on the bacteria-prone floor. A text to Rugger reminded me it wasn't all for nothing.

Take him off your list. He's done.

Dyson Walker. He'd crossed our radar, not for his wrongdoings within the Triad, but because of his fetish for girls who hadn't quite reached puberty. He was at the bottom of the barrel, almost, hardly holding any ranking within the organization. We wouldn't miss him or his contributions.

Freeing the world of his predatorial ways and making sure young girls around the world were safe was higher on our priority list than the tens of thousands he brought in a month. Another nigga was always ready for his spot and was working hard to prove it every day. He no longer mattered to us the minute we discovered his disappointing desires.

The second text was erased before I could send it. I decided to call Royce instead. She answered on the second ring.

"Hey."

"Get Range. Clean up at Blanche."

"Have you made a mess?" She sighed.

"Don't ask questions you know the answer to, baby. Clear the camera feeds and erase any traces of our presence –including his date."

If she continues fucking with me this way, there might not be any traces of her to erase.

"Oh God. He was on a date?"

"He won't do that shit again." I scoffed, ending the call.

Taking a good look in the mirror, I smoothed my hands over my head. Because my beard was steadily growing, it felt unkempt. As a habit, I ran my palms along the shape of it, making sure there wasn't a hair out of place.

Not until I was satisfied with my appearance, did I exit. Thankfully, no one was waiting for the cleaning to end. It would be at least another twenty-five minutes.

The ambiance of Blanche was inviting. I floated through the steakhouse, easily finding the same bar that I watched Eden alert her date of her arrival. Blood filled my mouth, forcing me to let go of the flesh I'd bitten into. It wasn't until I tasted the copper-like liquid that I realized I was bearing down.

"What can I get for you?" The bartender bounced toward me while asking.

"Cognac. Neat. Double shot."

"Coming right up."

I wasted little time angling my body in Eden's direction. By the third time she'd tapped the screen on her phone to see what the time was and calculate the time her date had been gone, my drink was ready.

He's not coming, Choc.

I slid a fifty-dollar bill across the bar and stepped away with the glass in my hand. My DNA wasn't something I was willing to leave behind. I made my way through the restaurant, exiting with almost a full shot left.

Aden, I thought, taking a peek around the corner to see where the hell he'd gone. The sickening whip was mere feet from the entrance of the steakhouse and gave me something to focus on other than my missing driver and that fucking Eden.

Black on black. The BMW was a sight to see. It reminded me of the AMG GT I'd snatched off the ship four days ago.

Fuck. It was the vision of the matte ride that made me recall how I'd gotten to Blanche. It wasn't by way of Aden. I drove. My feet reacted before I could completely grasp the madness of the night. I didn't drive. Hadn't in over ten years.

With flared nostrils and teeth that were slowly grinding down with every back and forward movement of my mouth, I turned the corner. My car was waiting under the tree that held the rain's mist, loosely releasing droplets onto the black paint.

I finished my drink as I tapped the start button and unlocked the doors. The sleek midnight black whip was the only vehicle in the parking lot that chirped. Still aghast at my willingness to drive, I reached inside and sat the empty glass inside of the armrest.

The difference in this night and any other was becoming very clear. There was a common denominator in all the shit I'd been feeling, experiencing, and indulging in over the last week.

She hadn't left me, though she'd left me. Thoughts of her stayed with me. Stuck with me. They were relentless. So was she.

Fucking Eden.

"A head case."

I slammed my fist on the roof of the car.

"Fuck! Fuck. Fuck!"

Low, but very audibly, I released my transgressions under the large tree that partially shielded me from public view. My car managed to shield most of what it couldn't.

"She's not *that* special."

The lie rolled off my tongue easily but never settled with me.

"A lie." I followed up by shaking my head while attempting to silence the voices within me.

Eden was breathtaking. Not only her beauty was captivating but her personality, knife for a tongue, and eagerness to live life on the very edge almost every day of her existence. She kept me on my toes. Wondering. Guessing. Watching.

Like a fucking hawk, I watched her, sometimes through the window of her spot. As she admired the city from above, I admired her from below. On her way to work, I was sure she made it safely. And when she left, I didn't leave her until I was certain she was inside, safe, and sound asleep.

My addiction was rapidly blossoming. Whenever I managed a wink, she was the thought that woke me. When my eyes closed, she was the thought that lured me to sleep.

I was chastising myself for the body I'd added to my roster for her, but I knew without a doubt I'd lay a thousand more motherfuckers down if their audacity exceeded my limitations. They weren't at all unreasonable or difficult to follow. I found them rather generous, but the list was steadily growing as the days went by.

Look but don't touch.

Don't even look too motherfucking long.

Clear her path.

Say less.

Respect her the same dressed or undressed.

Do not entertain the thrill she seeks.

Never, *ever* enter her garden.

Eden made me boundless. By default. It was as if my destiny had been chosen for me the moment I set eyes on her. She was a means to my end.

"Maurice," I whispered, dipping into my ride and taking off from the parking lot at full speed.

He'd said a hundred times that my mother had been chosen specifically for him. There was nothing he could or wanted to do about it. Though I'd never understood logic, I was quickly learning this shit wasn't up to me. It was already written.

Seven days of defying the pre-written text I was supposed to follow had only done harm. No good had come from it, other than rescuing a slew of young girls who had no idea about the potential danger of Dyson.

I claimed the spot reserved for those who were utilizing valet. I didn't have a ticket and I didn't give a fuck. For the attendant's sake, who was looking at me with curious eyes, and hers, Eden had better make her way out of the door sooner than later.

On the hood of my whip, I prepared for the inevitable.

Still waiting for this nigga. My thoughts angered me.

Just as I debated going inside to pull her pretty ass out of the door by that damn ponytail, long legs in black satin rushed out.

She deserves silk.

At the sight of me, Eden's mouth widened and everything around us came to a screeching halt.

Be still.

My heart was wrecked. She was only a few feet away from me. Visions of bending her right over my car and allowing the entire downtown Clarke to see just how much magic we created when our bodies were entangled petitioned for fruition.

Stretch her out.

Fill her up.

Punish her.

Make her pay.

She'll regret this day.

I closed my eyes to silence the noise.

"Get in the fucking car, Eden."

Her beauty was almost convincing enough, but it didn't stop the rage her antics supplied. I pushed out of the car, unfolding my hands while matching her gaze. She was a fucking journey. A rollercoaster.

I was letting go of a piece of myself with each passing second, giving it to her and praying she did the right thing with it. Because she was a fucking head rush, I knew that was asking too much of her, but I couldn't deny her of what was rightfully hers.

She stood, unmoving, making me reconsider my

reservations and the delay of her punishment. Maybe spectators wouldn't be such a bad idea.

You've left a mess. Go.

I clicked my tongue, quickly putting that all aside.

"Eden." I groaned, growing tired of her defiance and even more exhausted with my inability to control the hammering of my heart.

"Where is my date?"

Audacity.

She had enough of that shit for us both. Her question was enough for me to strip her where she stood and stick my dick so far up her, she forgot any other nigga existed... *ever.*

"Get in the fucking car before I put you in the car."

"Where is my date?" she repeated herself as if I wasn't talking to her. As if I'd said nothing.

There wasn't anyone on earth I'd encountered who could say they'd successfully disobeyed me and the odds had turned out in their favor. Most couldn't because they were six feet under. The rest would have to write shit down because they couldn't speak to tell their truths.

"Now is not the time to test me. I will fail. I will fail miserably," I grumbled. "I have no limits, Eden. None. Don't fuck around or you will find out, swiftly and without remorse."

"Whe–"

Refusing to hear another word from her foul ass mouth or see her neck sway another time, I rushed to her side.

Maybe she didn't hear what the fuck I'd said.

Though I hated repeating myself, I'd made the exception. This, however, would be the last time. If Eden couldn't get in the car on her own, I'd happily put her in that motherfucker.

"In the car. Right now."

There was movement. I should've been rejoicing, but I was far from it. Out of my head and in a completely different world, I strapped her in and slammed the door.

Stupid.

Just fucking ignorant!

I slid into the driver's seat, mashing the gas and getting the hell out of dodge. Out of the corner of my eye, I saw her hands clutch the door handle and side of the seat as it began to cave around her. The seats were designed to contour to one's frame, suitable for all driving conditions, including mine.

It wasn't until we were on the expressway and the city noise was behind us that it quieted. All that was heard was passing cars and the purring of my engine. I gripped the wheel, forgetting how good it felt to be behind one.

A newfound appreciation was quickly acknowledged with a look in Eden's direction. No one had ever sat next to me in the passenger seat, not if we didn't share blood, and hardly then.

That position had been dedicated to her, created just for her. Without her influence, I wouldn't have copped the new whip. I was fine behind the tint of the truck I'd purchased for Aden to chauffeur in.

"Are you going to say anything?"

There was nothing to say. We both knew how we'd gotten here; there was no need to dwell. I'd been clear on the first date. She was chasing excitement that would end with niggas on her conscience every time. Reiterating myself with words was pointless.

Action. Eden needed to see shit caving for her to understand the severity of her actions. Until she figured her shit out, a body could drop every fucking day. I wouldn't lose a second of sleep because of it. The decision was hers. She could oblige or keep her black dress on standby.

"You could at least tell me where my date went!" She huffed, folding her arms in front of her.

To hell. I didn't let the words out, but I most certainly considered it.

"You was planning to give that nigga pussy that belongs to me, Eden?"

I struggled with words, finding it hard to convey my deepest, truest feelings. They felt useless. There was more important shit to digest.

"Miste—"

"Chem!" I stopped her before she could finish.

"Huh?"

"My name is Chem."

"Chem?" she whispered. "K-e-m?"

Because I didn't think she needed every detail, I simply nodded. That was not how my name was spelled, but I wouldn't correct her.

"Where is he?"

Throwing caution to the wind, I slammed on the

brakes, mid-expressway. Horns caved, sounding all around us. Screeching tires sent Eden spiraling. Her neck twisted from one side to the other. Her eyes grew three sizes larger. I watched as her chest raised and fell almost immediately after.

"What the f—"

"Don't eve—" Composing myself felt impossible, but I managed. "Don't ever ask me about another nigga, Eden. Don't so much as think of, remember, or dream about another nigga when you're with me."

The initial shock had worn off. The fact we were at a complete stop in the center lane of the busy highway still had her panties in a bunch, but the fear of it all had subsided.

She chuckled in disbelief. "You have some nerve, Chem. Barging into my life, treating me to a night that felt un-fucking-real, and then leaving me to fend for something at least half as decent because I wasn't left with a name, number, address, signal, or anything. And out of nowhere, you come waltzing back into my world, demanding all these things as if what I want doesn't matter."

"That's all that matters, Eden," I slipped. Those words weren't meant to see the dark of the night.

"Bullshit, Chem!" she barked. "Because I've wanted you for six whole days and you have not been reachable. You have been MIA."

I've been there the whole time.

Instead of revealing my hand, I revved the engine, putting the city further behind us. The pain in her confession had my chest hurting. Felt like fifty hollow tips had penetrated it at once. I struggled to breathe, struggled to think.

"Make better choices, Eden."

"What do you mean, Chem?" she asked, never tearing her eyes from the road to look at me.

She was furious. So was I, but I was ready to fuck that shit right out of her. Ready to remind her of the magic we'd made all those nights ago.

Too many nights ago, I admitted.

"His nails... they were dirty. Niggas of that caliber shouldn't have the privilege of seeing your face, hearing your voice, smelling your perfume, or witnessing your smile."

"What did you do, Chem?" she asked, finally taking a second to gaze in my direction.

"Sit back, Choc."

"You can at least tell–"

I applied pressure to the button beneath my thumb, hiking the volume on the stereo and muting Eden. She leaned forward and tapped the screen, turning the volume down instantly. Labored breathing displayed my annoyance.

"I was *actually* hungry."

Silently, I continued down the highway until she loosened her grip on her seat and finally understood her quietness was appreciated. As my exit approached, I cut across four lanes, sure not to miss it. Full speed ahead, we flew down the ramp, stopping at the red light at the intersection of the first main street. We weren't there for long.

With the light still red, I sped through, slowing the wheels of my whip when we'd finally reached the callbox at the fast-food joint.

Eden didn't deserve freshly cut and cooked steak. She deserved the quick, easy, processed food that was metaphoric of the character she'd chosen for the night.

"Welcome to Charlie's. What can I get for you, today?"

"Salisbury steak platter. Mashed potatoes and broccoli for sides."

"To drink?"

"That knock-off sprite."

I could feel Eden's eyes on me.

"Che–"

"You seem to be thrilled with generic versions tonight, why stop now?" I asked, reaching inside my pocket to retrieve a twenty-dollar bill.

She tutted, shaking her head as she rested it in her palm. She lay against the chilly window, staring back at me.

"Your change." The drive-thru employee beckoned for my attention.

"Keep it." I never tore my eyes from Eden. Nothing else was worthy of my attention at the moment. She was dazzling, even with the frown shaping her features.

"Can I have you pull up fro–"

"I'll wait right here," I assured the employee, finally taking a look in her direction.

"Alright. Give me a second."

A nod finalized our conversation and my eyes were

right back where they belonged. Even her fucking dress was generic.

"Don't ever put that dress back on, Choc. It's offensive."

"How so?"

"Silk is far more flattering."

"Since it's bothering you so much, maybe I should take it off now," she challenged.

"You should," I agreed.

With a huff, she rolled her eyes. I'd called her bluff. We fell into a curious silence. Our thoughts lingered, threatening to ruin the quiet we'd embarked on. Before either of us could, I was handed Eden's meal, fake-ass Sprite in tow.

Immediately after receiving the bag of food, she began devouring it. Watching her enjoy a meal she was supposed to despise and demand better left a bitter taste in my mouth. Nonetheless, I entered the expressway and began circling the city.

Sixteen minutes later and she was finishing up. With a napkin to her mouth and food digesting in her belly, she began taking into account our location.

"That was our exi–We're driving in circles, Chem."

"I'm aware. Unless you wanted to eat your food blindfolded, that was the only solution."

"Blindfolded?"

"Yes. Open the glove compartment and put them on."

"Seriousl–"

"Now, Eden."

She retrieved the blindfolds, but not without grabbing the box beneath them. I watched as her eyes glistened and a smile turned her lips upward. When she realized the blue Tiffany's box was hers to have, her neck rotated slightly, eyes landing on me.

"Mine?"

"It wouldn't be anyone else's, Choc."

She didn't understand the depth of my words now, but she would eventually. I softened around the edges, watching her dig through the box's content to find a heart-shaped pendant at the end of a thick, chained necklace known for its slogan, *Please Return to Tiff–*

"Oh wow."

Her long, slim fingers rubbed the gold, eventually picking up the receipt.

"Fifteen thous–"

"That's not for you to examine the price. It's for you to return in the event you don't like it."

"Che– that price can't be accurate. That's absurd."

"That's meager, Eden. Don't worry your pretty head about it."

Flabbergasted, she sunk into the seat, staring at the box. Though she was quiet, I knew her mind was in a million places.

"Penny for your thoughts." I cleared my throat, hating the gaping hole she was rapidly filling.

She turned toward me, mouth slacked as she waited for the correct words to find her. Unblinking, she gazed. It felt like I'd been waiting forever before she spoke.

"How are you heaven and hell, simultaneously?"

My intentions are good, Eden, I wanted to express. *I just have a fucked up way of showing it. I've never had to.*

"I'm fucked up, baby."

"What happened to you? What hurt you? What made you this way? Because underneath all the fire, I see the beauty."

My mother pushed me out into this world. Loved me like I was her entire world. Then left me in this motherfucker like I ain't need her. Like I ain't love her. Like she wasn't my entire world, too. My thoughts were revealed, but my mouth didn't have the capacity.

"Life, Choc."

"That's not enough, Chem. Tell m—"

"It's all I've got right now. Accept it."

"I—"

"Please."

The achiness resided in my words, making me sick to my stomach. I didn't want to, didn't need to say more. I wasn't ready to reveal my pain. I wasn't ready to expose my wounds. It made me vulnerable and that wasn't a trait I was ready to reveal either.

With a nod, she settled in the seat. Her eyes left me briefly before they were back on me. I waited, knowing she had more to say but unsure if I was prepared for whatever was to come from her lips.

"I'm no enemy. With time, you'll discover I'm an ally. One you can be open, honest, and your entire self around. Whether it is today or ten months from now when your walls come crashing down, I'm here to listen. Yes, you're a thrill but it's deeper than that. Much deeper.

You represent the darkness that surrounds my heart. That's why I'm drawn to you. We're inevitable, doesn't matter the capacity."

I tilted my head, slightly, attempting to reduce the discomfort. My throat was beginning to close. The car shrunk with each passing second. My heart ached. My head spun. My lungs tightened.

She hiked the volume on the stereo herself this time, drowning our thoughts. Thankful, I gripped the wheel and watched her place the blindfold over her eyes, accepting both of our fates without resistance. I made a promise to do the same. Just as that thought burdened me, another joined. I quickly lowered the volume, still focused on the road ahead.

"One more thing. Whatever nigga paying your bills right now, Eden, tell him to unpay them motherfuckers before his mother is forced to identify what's left of him."

Her jaws dropped. She wasn't able to say a mumbling word before the music was up again. I'd attempted to handle her balance for the remainder of the year, but there wasn't one. It had been paid up for some time. Instead of finishing the year's payments, I needed her balance to reflect a year's rent. Until then, there was a nigga's life on the line.

THREE

Eden

What am I doing?

I should be calling this in.

I should be taking him in.

I hunt men like him for a living.

I am bound, by law, to report behavior as such.

So, why is it my walls that I want him inside of instead of a cell?

He killed a man for Christ's sake.

Frustration budded, filling me with anxiousness. I wanted Chem far, very far inside of me to make me forget I had a duty to protect. I'd gone to school, worked my butt off, and graduated top of the academy. Yet, I was sitting in the passenger seat of a criminal who'd indirectly confessed to murdering a man an hour ago and threatening to end the life of another if the balance of my rent wasn't restored.

Egypt. Please. I groaned inwardly, trying to ignore the pulsating of my center. It was agonizing.

"This way," he demanded, his fingers wrapping around my arm as he guided me out of the car.

His touch set my body ablaze, cremating all the thoughts that sent me into a state of confusion. We made it up a set of stairs and into more warmth as I felt him hovering. Just as I moved to lift the blindfold, I was presented with another gift.

"Here."

Thorny stems picked my fingers.

"Ow!"

Finally, I was able to see. He'd taken the blindfold off. The dead roses in my hand hadn't been what I was expecting. Baffled, I stared at the beautiful mess, still soft to the touch but visibly dying.

"Chem?"

"I bought them earlier. Apparently, the trunk is no place for pretty things," he explained without remorse for the lifelessness in my hands.

Take the company's card off file, I reminded myself. Though it was deemed untraceable, it might not be the case with him.

"I'll do better next time, Eden."

He took me by the hand, leading me deeper into the house. I should've run in the other direction, but naturally, I wanted to go wherever he was taking me. It didn't matter how far. It didn't matter how unforgiving. I was in too deep, already. There was no turning back now.

We entered the master suite. I remembered it clearly. I'd gripped the sheets, hit the headboard, and been stretched out across the entire mattress.

I've missed you, I admitted, admiring its massiveness.

The small, dark brown blanket that was on top of it, folded neatly, startled me. My heart dropped as my brows furrowed. Swallowing, I asked the question I was fearful of the answer to.

"Uh, Chem, do you have a child?"

Slowly, he turned toward me, eyes delicate. "Are you expecting?"

Recalling the emergency contraceptive I'd swallowed shortly after spending time with him, I shook my head. "No."

Besides, it had only been a week since we'd been intimate. That wasn't enough time to detect a pregnancy if it was the case. For us, it wasn't.

"Then, no, Eden. I don't have a child."

He snatched the blanket from the bed and freed me of his hold. He disappeared into the closet and was back in the middle of the floor with me almost immediately. I was unable to react before my hands were free, my dress was on the floor, my panties were ripped, and my body was pressed against the sheets.

Chem's palms aligned with mine, above my head where he'd pulled my hands. As if I was the most precious thing on this earth, he glared down at me. His breath, I could feel it on my bare skin. I was a mess between the legs. He was driving me wild, slowly and deliberately.

"I missed you." I breathed out, sealing my lids to avoid the disappointment.

Needing to know he'd missed me too would kill the moment. Needing validation of my relevancy in his world would butcher my feelings.

He slid into me gracefully. The fabric of his pants rubbed against my bottom as he did so was evidence of his urgency. He longed to be inside of me. Once he was, he released a breath so relieving, that I felt the weight lifted from my world as well.

"I've missed you more," he confessed through a barely audible whisper in my ear.

There was resistance in his words. Regret. Reservations. Resignation.

He's undoing, I quickly noted. *He's unraveling right before me.*

His state wasn't taken for granted. Neither was it subject to judgment. It was welcomed. Embraced with my own truth.

Without urgency, he slid in and out of me. Though he was silent, he filled me with the validation I'd been seeking. Always sought. I was confirmed. I was validated. I was assured even when it didn't seem like it, I wasn't alone.

Just as he'd promised, he was there. And somehow, I felt as though I'd never be alone again. Not as long as he was part of my world.

THE GREYLIST

Morning had come. Morning had gone.

The afternoon had come. The afternoon had gone.

I stretched my limbs at exactly five-twelve in the evening. The sun was beginning to settle, casting an orange glow across the bedroom. The windows were too high to see out of, but they told stories my eyes couldn't, still satisfying my soul.

My feet touched the cold marbled floor as I rolled out of the massive bed. A yawn nearly ripped my face apart. It felt like I had been asleep for a month.

In his presence, I easily lost track of time. It didn't exist. Though it should've been troubling, it was comforting. On bare feet, I began combing the room for the man himself. The couch on the other side of it was my first stop.

Not here.

The shower was next. He wasn't there, either. I used the opportunity to relieve myself. As I sat on the toilet, I waited for him to burst through the door at any second. Waiting was in vain. By the time I'd washed my hands and dried them, he was still missing.

Without a cloth covering an inch of skin, I made my way into the hallway. I checked nearly every room before realizing he wasn't upstairs. I took the stairs to the first floor where movement seemed nonexistent. I pushed forward, regardless, determined to locate Chem. Not only was I missing the rhythm of his heartbeat, but I had one between my legs that only he could regulate.

"Sheesh!"

Startled, I placed my hand over my heart, completely forgetting I was nude.

"I'm so sorry. I'm so sorry. You must be Eden?" a woman dressed in a crispy uniform with her hair in a neat bun asked.

"Yes." Nodding, I tried catching my breath. Suddenly, I felt parched.

"I'm Jennie."

"Do yo-you know where Chem is?"

"Yes. I'll go get him. You just stay righ—"

"No. No. It's fine. I will. Please, where is he?"

Though she tried to keep her eyes on mine, she couldn't help their wandering nature.

"Swimming. The pool. Down the main hallway. Right. Follow the scent of water from there."

"Thank you."

Swiftly, I marched down the hallway, following the path as instructed until the scent of water led me the rest of the way. Drawn to it, just as I was drawn to him, I ended up at the door of the large, unusually lengthy pool area. Quietly, I crept inside, watching as Chem's dark skin swam toward the other side.

Amazed by his speed, I stopped at the edge of the pool, waiting for him to take a breath, lift his head, or stop. He did neither, instead, heading back toward the end where I was standing, still holding his breath. I watched him lap the pool, effortlessly, never coming up to refill his lungs. Not until the fourth lap. And when he finally reached for the concrete, there I was.

Water rushed from his skin in a hurry to get back to the surface. He glistened. His hair rested on his head and face, weighed by the heaviness of the liquid. He felt so far away. Too far away, in fact.

I slid into the pool, realizing its depth while praying I didn't make a fool of myself. Though I could swim, I wasn't as rehearsed as Chem and I wasn't, at all, equipped for depths like the one I was in.

My nipples hardened against his chest. Those perfect teeth slowly appeared behind slightly stretched lips. The excitement on his face was overshadowed by the capacity of his expression being met, but it registered, regardless.

"Hi."

I stared into those dark orbs, searching for the light I knew was buried in there somewhere. I was hoping it led me to his soul. It was crying for companionship.

I could hear it when he slept. Hear it when he spoke. Feel it when he looked at me as if I was his only hope. I didn't want to let him down, couldn't let him down.

"Good evening, Eden."

His voice was addictive. My obsession with him grew each time he shared his words.

Comfortably, we held each other's stare. Involuntarily, my body clung to him. My arms sat on his shoulders, hands gathering behind his head. And when I couldn't bear the allure any longer, I pushed forward, placing my lips on his.

"Ed– Don't do that shit, again," he fussed.

"Mmmmmmmm." I paid him no mind.

He clamped down on my bottom lip. I could feel the blood as it began to seep into my mouth.

Aroused by his violent sexual tendencies, I deepened our kiss. My legs wrapped around his waist. I could feel his arousal searching for my entrance.

And when it broke way, I gasped in despair. There was absolutely no reason on God's green earth for him to be so good. Feel so good. Fuck so good.

"Cheeeeeeeem." I moaned against his lips.

They lowered, sucking my right breast into his mouth. From below, he unclogged my thoughts, relieved my stressors, and wrote his name a hundred times. I tightened my grip around his neck, bringing our lips together again.

"Chem."

I was splintering. He touched parts of me only he had. That only he could. He was unfathomable. He was unreal.

"Give me a son, Eden."

His request sent me spiraling into another universe. Deep in his stratosphere, I searched for answers, signs this man wasn't for me. But, I found none. And though children were not on my radar, I'd give him one, gladly. Maybe not now, but eventually.

One day.

When his heart wasn't so cold. When his words weren't so hurtful. When his absence wasn't so depriving. When my career wasn't so demanding.

"I need a son, Eden." Almost as if he was begging, he repeated himself.

"Okaaaaaay." I purred against him as my orgasm subsided.

I was willing to agree to anything Chem said while he was inside of me. That's when my vulnerability peaked. I had no control over the things I said or did. I was putty.

Chem stiffened, signaling his end. His head lowered until it reached my chest. There, it hung with support. I wised up almost instantly, knowing he'd meant every word he'd said.

"Promise me you'll let me in and I'll give you whatever your heart desires."

I had demands of my own. I wanted to know more, see more, hear more... be more.

He never lifted his head as the words slammed into my chest, right where he rested.

"Whatever you want, Eden."

Minutes after Chem's response, I was still no less in a state of shock than I had been when it left his mouth. To hear him speak again, as he removed himself from my center, threw me for a loop.

"Do you know how to swim?"

"Ya– yes. Somewhat. Well, enough to save myself."

"Not enough to save me if you needed to?"

I'd find a way. Cut off someone else's arms if I needed to make sure mine didn't get too tired. My thoughts scared me.

"I'd find a way," I admitted, leaving the rest hidden.

"There's a way, Eden. It doesn't need to be found."

"I know."

"I'll teach you to swim better. It's important."

"To who? Because I have no reason t–"

"To me."

That settled it. That was all that mattered.

"Okay."

"Okay?" He sucked his teeth. "That simple."

"Yes."

He carried me, bridal-style, out of the pool.

"Is it dick that cures your defiance?"

"If answering yes will encourage you to give me more of it, then yes."

"Haven't you had enough, yet?"

"For now, yes. But, another week withou–"

"I apologize. I was unaware my absence had such a tremendous effect on you. I can't promise every day, but it will never be a week. Not if I can help it. Understand?"

Nodding, I allowed his words to linger instead of muddling the moment with mine. They were unnecessary. I wanted to use the energy I'd need to speak to believe him. My sanity depended on it.

Through his home, dripping wet, he carried me until we reached the shower. There was a shower in the pool area, but I assumed he wasn't interested. In his larger one, he removed his trunks and grabbed two bath cloths.

He's a caretaker. I noted another quality of his.

Chem wasn't the mess he claimed to be. He had ways, but we all did. There was something special at the very core of his existence, telling me he knew how to take care of a woman and provide her with a blissful life. Telling me he knew how to love. He knew how to trust.

As our time together continued, it was becoming very clear. I was anxious for more of him. More of that. Whatever it was.

"You must make your mother proud." I smiled, watching as he scrubbed the towel together to get the suds going. From the fruity aroma, I knew he wasn't preparing to cleanse his body. He was preparing to cleanse mine.

"Maybe one day I'll get to ask her. Around the fire pits of hell. I'm sure she'll be there when I make it."

I wish I'd found the same humor his smile exposed, but I didn't.

"Chem."

"Yes, Eden?"

"Is your mother al–"

"Turn around, baby. If we're going to talk, it won't be about my mother."

I gave him full access to my back. Gently, he scrubbed it with the towel.

"There are clothes waiting for you. You'll find them in the dressing room right next to mine. Dinner will be served at seven. Please don't be tardy, Choc."

"Dinner?"

"Yes. Aren't you hungry, yet?"

"Starving." I breathed. *For more about you. Your family. Your life. Your world. Your background. Your pain. You wear it right on your shoulders.*

"Good, then. That's settled. Seven."

"Seven."

THE GREY LIST

"This man."

Blushing, I ambled toward the black silk slip-dress on the bed. Black, strappy Gianvito Rossi slingbacks were on the floor in front of it. Another blue box was split in half, exposing the bangle inside. The receipt was missing, but a quick snap from my camera led me to the listing.

"Twenty-seven thousand dollars?" I whispered, hand over my mouth. "For a bangle? God, that's an entire car."

"Not the kind we drive, Choc."

I spun around to find Chem behind me. I hadn't heard him enter the room, but I should've smelled him. He was divine. Natural scent and added fragrance. Both were mesmerizing.

"Get out ya head and put that shit on."

He vanished, leaving my mouth wide open and the heartbeat between my legs irrational again.

I need to know more.

But why? I fought with myself, attempting not to let my inquisitiveness cheat me out of a good time.

Deciding against sulking or overthinking, I began preparing myself for the night. The dress, shoes, and jewelry weren't the only things waiting for me in the dressing room. So was a vanity, Dior makeup, a full brush set, and a note. The scribbles on the white paper were evidence Chem had written it.

Time is lost upon me when you're near. The sun has awakened me for thirty-six years straight. Since I laid eyes on you, it's been your face. Visions of you. The sight of you. The thought of you. I'm an imperfect man, so far from the person society tells women of your caliber to trust, to allow in your world, but fuck that. Fuck all of that. Fuck the world. Cause I'm fucking you, Eden. And since I've begun, nothing has made sense in my world. Everything is perplexing. I'm writing to let you know I won't always have the words. It's not often I do. But, I'll show you, every chance I get, that you're more than just a frame. More than just a face. More than just a thrill. You're something I look forward to, just like the rising of the sun.

I crashed the paper into my chest, crumbling it slightly.

He's troubled. Tears burned my bottom lash line.

He means well. I choked as the thought surfaced.

He's hurting.

Tears grew thicker. I swiped them away before they had the chance to fall. I placed the note on the table, knowing it had taken great courage to write, and sprinted out of the room.

I rushed down the hall, finding Chem standing in the master suite. My presence confused him. He didn't have time to deny me before my arms were around his body and my head was on his chest.

"Choc?"

Though he was confused, I felt him embrace me, hesitantly.

"For the things you don't talk about, I'm sorry. For the things troubling you, I'm sorry. For the things that keep you up at night, I'm sorry. For the things that have hurt you, Chem, I'm sorry."

He pulled away, unwilling to accept apologies that weren't mine to give. Soundlessly, with a rising and falling chest, he stared at me, baffled.

A tilted head led me to believe my words had hit their target. Satisfied, I left him in the middle of the floor, hoping I'd soothed at least a few of his aches.

I swiped a fresh set of tears from my cheeks, speeding toward the dressing room where I shut the door behind me and released a heart-shattering sigh. It left me breathless and unsure of what was happening between me and the man in the next room.

Breathe, Egypt, I coached.

He doesn't even know my name, I argued. *He deserves that much, at least.*

I inhaled.

I can— I can't blow my cover.

Though I was after an entirely different group of people, sharing confidential information with Chem was not an option. He was, undoubtedly, a criminal and I was an agent. I had no business here. Our worlds weren't supposed to mesh, under any circumstances.

I couldn't dwell on the future or let it ruin the plans Chem had for us. I put my thoughts on the back burner and sat down in front of the vanity mirror. My hair had seen better days. My body, however, hadn't. Chem was unbeatable.

I busied myself with the many purchases Chem had made. Either Jennie had good taste or he had another woman in his life who had expensive taste. I wasn't complaining. They'd done a phenomenal job.

Lightly, I applied a full face of makeup. The layers were so thin it was hard to see the enhancements once I'd finished.

"Perfect."

I checked the time on the clock on the wall. There were only twenty minutes left to spare. I used them to slip the dress on. Panties were not included, so I didn't bother searching for them in the bags lining the room. Without a doubt, I knew the contents inside of each one belonged to me.

When my once-over was complete, I had four minutes left. I exited the room, feeling like I was the only woman on God's green earth who had been assigned to Chem. Somehow, I felt as though he was specifically designed for me as well. We were tailored for one another.

I descended the steps, expecting to round the corner, enter the dining area, and find Chem. I didn't make it that far. Black legs that went on forever and greeted me just as I rounded the staircase. My body tingled, watching from afar as Mister took me in.

Stopping mid-way, because I was certain the sight of

him would cause me to lose my balance, I did the same. He was incredible. From his head to his toe.

His mother and father had made art. Fine, vintage art that was timeless and meant to be enjoyed and not captured to be locked in a frame on a lone wall.

"Eden."

"Chem."

"You are un-fucking-real, baby. Wondrous. Captivating."

"Have you been captivated, yet?"

"I have." He chuckled, nodding, simultaneously.

I'd never get over that smile. It wasn't often exposed, making it monumental. Time stopped every time I witnessed that glorious part of history.

"Good, then. I'm not alone."

"Not at all."

"You'r–I don't know that words are good enough to describe what you are, Chem."

"The feeling is mutual."

Silently, we shared appreciative gazes, and then, suddenly, he stepped aside. On a table I didn't recall being there earlier, he revealed a large box of roses. They were plentiful.

"These"—he cleared his throat—"They don't die, Choc."

I melted, instantly recalling the ones he'd killed accidentally.

"Chem!"

Finding my footing, I rushed toward him. Just as I

approached, I noticed something quite unusual. Quite out of character for him.

"Mister," I sang, cupping his cheeks.

"What?" He smiled, unable to hide it this time.

"Are yo—Are you blushing?"

"Hm?"

He brushed his hands over his waves, one after the other, stepping back so I wasn't so close. I stepped forward, not letting him off the hook.

"You are!"

His smile reached his eyes for a split second. The darkness lightened. The longing in them wasn't overlooked, either.

I'm right here, I thought, pressing a palm against the side of his face.

"Chem, it's okay. You understand that, right?"

A shake of the head confirmed his reservations.

"Someone broke your heart?" I asked, driven by the fear that was apparent.

He was traumatized. Life hadn't been the only thing to make him this way. *Someone* had helped.

"I told you I'd do better next time." He stepped aside, nodding toward the roses.

His words stole another piece of my heart. He was deflecting, but his sentiments were heard loud and clear.

"Who broke your heart, Chem?"

"My mother," he spat, the light in his eyes vanishing as the darkness returned. The Chem I was growing fond of quickly retreated, replacing himself with the colder, relentless version. "Dinner is ready, Eden."

His body stiffened underneath my touch. I hung onto his words as I followed him into the room where a table was set for one. As I sat in front of the plated steak and glass of water, I came to the conclusion I'd be the only one eating. However, I still needed to ask. Concern wouldn't let me keep quiet.

"Are you not hungry?"

"Food won't satisfy my craving. What I'm in the mood for is between your legs."

"Che–"

"I pulled you away from dinner last night and fed you food I wouldn't even feed a dog. I owe you a steak."

The brutally honest Chem was present. Instead of giving him a few words to chew on until dinner was finished, I decided to fill my belly. Hunger was ready to announce itself at any minute.

A few feet away, at the other end of the table, Chem sat with his eyes trained on me and a glass of brown liquid against his lips every few seconds. I squirmed under his scrutiny, wondering just how badly he was tearing me apart with those orbs.

My weight shifted every few seconds. My hands were unsteady. Cutting into the tender steak became a much more difficult task than it ever had been.

"Uh um." I cleared my throat, feeling the room grow smaller.

The temperature increased, simultaneously. I crossed my legs underneath the table. My posture slacked slowly, but I straightened my back the second I realized it was crooked.

Please. I begged him. My entire body was unsettled. I couldn't keep still.

"You're staring."

"I'm aware," he responded without remorse.

God, he's a fucking dream. There wasn't a part of him that was imperfect. He was fine. Unbelievably so. And his energy, whichever he was giving at the moment, made him so much finer.

"Chem."

"If my actions haven't made it clear, Eden, you don't get to choose another nigga. I've chosen you."

Lifted brows and piqued curiosity led me to drop my utensils.

"They don't belong there," he informed me, nodding toward the napkins on both sides of the plates.

I laid the knife and fork in their rightful places and focused on the man across the table.

"Have you?"

"I have."

"Do you know what that consists of, Chem? Choosing someone?"

"I don't. Not from experience, at least."

"I didn't think so."

"I'm learning day by day."

"You've never been in love."

I wasn't surprised. You had to be a special kind of woman to deal with a man like Chem. There weren't many of us in the world with the capacity to do so. Fortunately for us both, I did.

"No."

"I wasn't asking. I was voicing m–"

"That means nothing, Eden."

"For you. For me, it means several things."

"Your food will get cold. You should eat."

I picked up my utensils and continued chopping away at the flavorful steak.

"There are better ways to ask a woman to be yours."

"I wasn't asking."

I gulped water from the glass in front of me before clearing my throat. It was thickening to the point of discomfort.

"For what it's worth, I've chosen you, too."

Chem sipped the brown liquid in his cup. Soundlessly, he displayed his satisfaction with softened eyes and a nod.

FOUR

Chemistry

I lifted the cover to find Choc getting down to business. Her skills had awakened me from my sleep three mornings in a row. Even thinking about taking her back to her crib later had me vexed, but she was slowly relieving my anxiety.

"Good morning, handsome."

Eden plopped my dick out of her mouth to greet me. She held that motherfucker like a microphone and as soon as she'd spoken, it was back in her mouth. My toes curled, watching her get down the way she did. It was apparent she loved dick in her mouth and the thought of another nigga having the opportunity to put theirs in it swelled my nostrils.

I pulled her upward, by that fucking ponytail, bringing her lips to mine as I entered her from below. I hadn't expected creating an heir would be this rewarding. I hadn't expected to form a bond in the process. I hadn't expected to fall for the woman who'd brought him into the world. But, surely, with each passing second, I was deeper into the web she'd spun, not giving a damn about much else.

"Yeeeeeeeeees."

She was slippery between the legs. I hadn't dived into a wetter pool. Her shit was always soaking, ready for me to lap it until we both began to spit up.

"I told you. He's not paying us any mind," Royce complained, smacking her teeth.

"That's not becoming, baby. Don't do that," I advised, struggling to rejoin the moment. Eden made it hard to focus on anything but her and the money.

"He's been in his head for the last three weeks. Here, but never here," Royce continued, apparently frustrated with the lack of attention she and the others were getting.

My father's grunt led me to the smirk on his face. He cut into his smothered chicken with a shake of the head as if he knew something the rest of us didn't.

"Is everything okay?" Rather quickly spat, concern etched on her pretty face.

"Everything is alright." Roulette scoffed. "He's gotten a hold of something he can't quite let go of."

"Roulette," I warned.

"Meaning?" Rome questioned, meeting my eyes.

"Nothing, baby." I tried defusing it before the fire was actively destroying our dinner. "Eat your food. And yours, too, Roulette."

"He met someone," she spilled. "Why he's keeping her a secret is beyond me."

"Mind the business that pays you, Roulette."

"She is my business and she pays me well."

I'd quickly forgotten Eden's involvement with Roulette. I didn't have a rebuttal, so I remained quiet. My father's sniggers left me with a hung head. I focused on the food in front of me, ready to drown almost everyone out.

"So, you have met someone," Rugger inquired.

Her interest was rare. She cared very little about very little.

"Is wh–Wait, was she the date?" Royce began piecing the puzzle together.

"Royce, let it go," I suggested.

"She was the date!"

"You robbed me of the opportunity to end Dyson because he was on a date with a woman you're having sex with?"

"I'll keep crossing niggas off your list if they find themselves near my shi– Change the subject. We do not discuss business at this table."

"But, this isn't business. This is personal," Rugger countered. "In many ways."

"Who is she, Teddy?" Rome wondered with those big, pretty eyes planted on me.

"The woman I've chosen to give me an heir. That's it, Rome."

"But, it isn't," she protested.

Sometimes, her discernment was the curse and not the gift. Kissing my teeth, I laid my silverware down and shrugged.

"What is it, then?"

"You care," she revealed. "You care about her. It's been three weeks, which leads me to assume it's deeper than that, too. You're falling in– Chem."

She couldn't finish her statement. Bewilderment had her stumped. Her eyebrows crinkled. So did her top lip. Her nose widened as if she smelled something foul. The revelation she was having didn't sit well with her. Taking a look around the table, I noticed it didn't sit well with most of the women surrounding me.

"I'm proud of you," Roaman spoke up, wiping the sides of her mouth with the dinner napkin.

Just like the others, she reeked of wealth. However, Roaman was in a class of her own. Her gentleness was striking. She was a model woman. I couldn't remember a time she'd disappointed me or anyone else in our family. She was careful with her words, decisions, and actions. She was pure gold.

"Be more like Roaman," I told the others.

"Roaman doesn't even want to be like Roaman," Roulette taunted, making the others laugh.

"Roulette, you never know what you're talking

about. I doubt that's changed tonight." Roaman shrugged, not at all fazed.

"The idea of you seeing someone makes my heart smile," Rather shared. "Good for you, Chemistry."

Rather had been pushing for companionship for years. She thought it would be a part of progressive therapy and a way to help manage my emotions better.

"I'm invested. When ready, tell me more," my father added.

"Tell us more about her now," Rugger demanded.

I shook my head. "No."

"Please," Range begged.

"Next subject, baby."

"If you want to know more about her, just come to Roulette. Trust me, I don't have to say anything else. You'll know her the second you see her. She's breathtaking. And she'll be in the VIP room for our upcoming meeting. She's a gem."

"And she's a dancer?" Rome perked up, slightly.

"Nothing like the dancer you are, but one nonetheless," Roulette tittered.

"Not Chem done fell in love with a stripper," Royce teased.

"Don't speak that way, Royce. And if that was stated to offend me, it didn't."

"Not at all. It just added a bit of a plot twist that is rather exciting. I'm with Richie. I'm invested." She folded her arms and sat back in her seat.

"Please... find something else to invest in. Tonight, we're celebrating Rome."

"We are," Roulette agreed.

"And if you want your club to keep standing, baby, she better not see the paint of the VIP room. I will dismantle the entire club and build another one right where it stood –only when I feel like you've learned your lesson."

Her head flew backward. She found my claims to be humorous, but I'd meant every word.

"I don't have to convince you I'm not bluffing."

"You don't. I'd just like to see you do it."

She was not easily moved. Roulette was me. Sometimes, I forgot shit, but she was always quick to remind me.

"I have the address to your lab, *Chemistry*. Please don't mess with my money and I won't mess with yours."

A smile stretched my lips.

"Challenge accepted, baby."

T H E G R E Y L I S T

As I crept through the house, mind racing and still considering what Roulette had said, my phone began vibrating in my pocket. I assumed I'd left something behind and Aden was calling to let me know. However, the familiar number scrolled across the screen and told me otherwise.

"Benny. Talk to me."

"She left, Boss."

Over the last few days, I'd had my head in the game, fully immersing myself in its crevices to prepare for the meeting Roulette was having. Eden was no longer under my watchful eye, but someone from my team was sitting on her. I was learning the ball of fire, inside out, and I knew my absence would cause distress.

It wasn't intentional, this time. Business was priority. A few days and I'd be back in her space.

Eden was stubborn and becoming spoiled. A few days felt like an eternity for her. She'd beckon for me, any way she could. And when she did, I wanted to be notified. That was Benny's purpose.

"How long ago?"

"Twenty minutes."

"I should've gotten a call nineteen minutes and fifty-nine seconds ago. Why am I just hearing from you?"

"Because I didn't want to bother you about nothing. But, this is definitely something."

"When it comes to her, Benny, everything is something. When it comes to her, Benny, it's never nothing. Everything is something. Send me the location."

"Bet."

I headed for my bedroom, removing my clothes as I sauntered through the house. I changed my slacks and button-down, settling on a black hoodie, black sweats, and black sneakers. Without a doubt, there would be a funeral tonight. I wanted to be sure I was dressed for the occasion.

Only six minutes after Aden had dropped me off, I

was climbing into my Benz with my favorite problem solver reminding me it was lodged between my pants and waist. I muted the volume on the stereo, choosing total silence.

Head.

Neck.

Chest.

Blood of the faceless man spilled in the visions that repeated themselves, entertaining me as I erased the distance between Eden and me. It was difficult to decide just how I'd end my life tonight, but it was surely ending.

I peeked at the address once more, calculating the time remaining. It felt like eight hours though I only had eight minutes left before I made it to the bar. I'd never experienced a longer eight minutes in my life.

When I finally pulled up to the hole in the wall, shades and hat concealing my identity, I searched for the car that was registered to Eden. Within seconds, I located it, parking right beside it. I hopped out and headed toward the entrance. Thankfully, no one was covering the door.

The dark, smokey atmosphere should've obscured my vision, but I laid eyes on Eden almost immediately. I was drawn to her. It was inexorable. I could feel her, even when she wasn't around. For a few seconds, I watched her at the table for two, scanning the small building for any signs of danger.

For any signs of me.

I approached the unsuspecting victim, training my gun on his temple as I stood beside him. It was possible I was concealing my piece poorly, but my irrationality didn't allow me to give a fuck.

"Good evening, Eden."

Frozen in place, she looked up at me with wide eyes. I watched as she swallowed the lump in her throat. The smell of urine polluted the air. I tore away from Eden, momentarily, to address the man on the other end of my barrel.

"Revolting."

"I don't want any probl—"

"Trust me, there won't be any problems I can't solve."

"Ch–"

Sharp eyes cut Eden with precision, quieting her instantly. That was the reason my name was to remain a secret. That was the reason she hadn't deserved to know it.

"Get out of the chair and walk your pretty ass out of the door. If I have to tell you more than once, I promise this man's casket will be a closed one."

There wasn't resistance. Not even hesitation. She'd learned from experience I meant every word I said.

"Okay," she replied, hands in the air.

She dropped them shortly after, pushing herself back by the edge of the table. She was wearing another black dress, this one with long sleeves to battle the unpredictable March weather.

That ponytail swung from one side to the other as she pranced across the floor as if she didn't have a care in the world. It wasn't until she was out of the door that I lowered my gun.

Pew!

The silencer quieted the release of my bullet, but the pain of the injury made it useless. Like a wolf, Eden's date bellowed.

Next time it won't be the little head, I thought, making my way out of the door behind Eden.

When I arrived, she was standing next to my car in the parking lot. Liquid courage had her eyes glistening with lust.

I brushed past her, ready to get the fuck out of her face. Deciding between punishing her with my absence and fucking her right here in the open was too difficult of a task.

"Get in your car and go home, Eden."

"Chem." She purred like a kitten, gripping my forearm and pulling me toward her.

I didn't resist. Couldn't resist. She was unavoidable. She was my destination, no matter the circumstances. I was beginning to understand that. Understand us. Understand our dynamic.

My hand curled around her neck. Gently, I squeezed.

"I am not one for the games, Eden. Because I don't lose. Get that through your skull."

"I'm sorry," she apologized, lips close enough to kiss. I refused.

"Not sorry enough." I pushed off of the car, freeing her neck.

"Chem." She pulled me back, again. Grabbing my hand and placing it around her neck.

"Stop fucking with my head. I'm not right up there," I gritted, staring down and into her eyes.

"I'm sorry," she repeated while busying her hands with my sweats.

I did nothing to stop her from freeing my throbbing dick. She massaged it, never breaking contact. Our orbs were trained on one another as she brought cum from my shit.

The kind that was frequent as a young nigga because you knew you were about to smash something sick. Eden fits the description. Not only was I pressed to be inside my pussy, but she was sickening. Her body. Her face. *Her*.

"I'm sorry."

When her lips crashed into mine, I couldn't resist any longer. I hoisted her in the air and brought her down on my dick. Heaven was just as I'd remembered it.

Fuck.

Against my car, I stroked her long and I stroked her hard, sure I was making a mess of the black sweats clinging to my thighs. And just when I noticed her peak approaching, I dislodged myself and lowered her to her feet. Her disgruntled moan nearly made me reconsider, but I stood my ground.

"Get in your car and go home, Eden."

I unlocked the door of my whip as I approached the driver's side, pulling my pants up in the midst of the madness. When I slid in, I wasn't alone. Eden sat next to me, right where she belonged. But, not tonight.

"Go home."

She opened the glove compartment, hands trembling as she removed the blindfold. She placed it on her head and pulled it down over her eyes.

I watched in disbelief as she felt around for her seatbelt, securing it shortly after discovering it. When she rested her back against the seat, I reminded her she wasn't welcome.

"Go home, *Eden*."

"It's been four days." Her voice cracked. She was becoming the version of Eden that softened me. The version that could have anything from me. Ask anything of me.

"I don't give a fuck if it was ten. I was coming back. I'll always come back. I am a businessman. I have business to tend to. Once it's done, I'll always come back. What part of that shit don't you understand?"

"I'm sorry."

I snatched the blindfold off her face and tossed it in the backseat.

"I can't babysit you. I won't babysit you. Do whatever the fuck you want, Choc. Just make sure you're able to live with the consequences, because I will have no problem doing so. I didn't see you for four days. This time, let's make it ten."

"Don't do th–"

"You don't get to decide. You've made your bed. Lie in that motherfucker. Goodbye, Eden."

The burner that I'd purchased for communication would be at her doorstep by morning. I just needed my baby to hold out a few hours longer and I'd be at her fingertips. But, in Eden fashion, her impatience had written a check her ass couldn't cash.

She unbuckled the seatbelt and climbed out, reluctantly. I could still smell her arousal long after she was in her car with the engine running. I could also smell the traces of blood lingering.

Disappointment tugged at my heartstrings. She'd had her period. I quickly calculated her next ovulation window. Two weeks from now, I'd have the opportunity to plant my seed.

Three weeks of her madness and I was ready for a lifetime of adventure. She kept my adrenaline pumping. Kept me wondering. Kept me on my toes. Kept reminding me women of her caliber were hard to come by and I'd be foolish to let her slip away. I didn't plan on it.

The city lights became fewer and farther apart as I got closer to home. Just as I backed into the garage, I contemplated making another trip downtown. Eden had gotten under my skin, but now I wanted her against it.

Stand your ground, I finalized before shutting my door behind me.

I headed straight for the shower where I discarded her scent and washed away the evidence of the day I'd had. By the time I pulled back the sheets, I was ready to call it a night. I had an early morning and having a late night would be an unwise decision.

Stretching my hand across the bed, I gripped my sole source of comfort other than a body that was miles away, feeling the discomfort her lack of composure caused. The brown blanket was all that was left to commemorate the bond I shared with my mother.

I slept with it nearby. For a sense of peace. For a sense of stability. For a sense of normalcy. For *her*. Because, since she'd been gone, nothing was the same anymore.

FIVE

Eden

The ceiling fan whirled above me as I lay flat on the bed with my nose toward the sky. Misery had crept into my bones and made itself home. Not even my mother or Art could rescue me from the funk I was in. They'd both tried. There was only one solution.

Him.

It was day nine of punishment and I was praying I still had a piece of my sanity by the time midnight rolled around. I had four hours before my fate was revealed and I was counting down the minutes. Because I had work in a few, I knew lying around sulking wasn't possible, but I'd lay as long as I could while technology failed us all.

The flowers that never died were on my kitchen

counter. Gifts, several he'd funded, had filled the living room. Deliveries showed up at my door daily. Each time there was a knock, I was hoping to find him behind it.

A new cellphone, one that had only one number stored and a photo of me wrapped in his sheets for a wallpaper, made the perfect, useless accessory for my nightstand. I'd called Chem nearly ten times in less than ten days, still, I hadn't heard his voice or seen his face.

Parts of me had regretted the second I accepted Tre's invitation to the bar a few blocks away. We'd crossed paths in the lobby a few times. His smile was radiating. His conversation was interesting. My center was aching. His invitation couldn't have come at a better time.

This wasn't a ploy to summon Chem, but when the opportunity presented itself, I didn't let it slip away. Because, without a doubt, I knew he'd come. I knew he'd appear. And I wasn't wrong. The results weren't in my favor, but they were results, nonetheless.

"Johanson! Can you hear me?" Bradford yelled into the com, nearly deafening me.

"God." I gasped. "Yes. Loud and clear. Can we turn it down?"

I sat up in bed, ready to snatch the tiny bulb from my ear. It wasn't visible to the naked eye and I was hoping it didn't get lost in my ear canal. The device was small in stature but packed a punch. It felt like my partner was right beside me, screaming his head off.

"Turn it down, Rodgers," Jack told our tech guy.

"Sorry, Johanson," Rodgers apologized.

The volume was much better.

"It's fine."

"Get to your desk, Johanson. Let's brief before you get out of the door. We need to make sure we've covered everything."

"Yes. Of course."

Though I'd much rather ball up underneath my covers, I rolled out of bed and made my way to the computer. Dread sank in as I looked down at the mouse pad I'd yet to switch out.

"Have you checked your mail?" Bradford asked on cue.

A quick scan over my living room reminded me mail had been delivered to my door all week. The service the building offered was a godsend.

"Yes."

"Good, I sent you something. It's in a black box. The sender name should be scrambled."

Discretion was detrimental. We weren't dealing with the average criminals. We were trying to infiltrate a criminal empire that was air-tight, sophisticated, and had eluded our radar for years. Hadn't a string of events begun to connect and a lone witness gotten caught with his hand in the cookie jar, we wouldn't know they existed.

I searched through the boxes, locating one of the two black ones. The letters on the shipping label had me squinting, trying to figure out what they said. To understand that, I had to unscramble them. I grabbed a pen on my way to my desk and began scribbling on the desk pad.

The – I managed to get the first word.

Grey – the second came and the third was a no-brainer.

List.

"Really clever, Bradford." I chuckled, opening the box.

To my surprise, I removed a much-needed piece of foam that fit right in the corner where my mouse rested day and night. The tan mouse pad had the same words, scrambled about, written across the bottom.

"Thanks, that would be great. Tired of hearing you bang that mouse on whatever surface near."

"Can we get down to business here?" Macy sighed into the phone.

"This is business," I responded. "I'm logging on, Jack."

"Good. Good. Bradford, give us a quick overview."

Three faces appeared in three different squares on the screen. I was the fourth. The volume was muted because we were still testing the dependability of the com since there wouldn't be a unit near to cover the audio. The new technology supposedly needed no assistance and could transmit a signal for miles and miles, resulting in clear, concise audio.

"We're all familiar with the case numbers in front of us. Beside each is the occupation because names aren't information we're privy to, yet. We're hoping to break ground tonight inside of this meeting.

"Up until now, we've discovered very, very little. We're working with breadcrumbs here, people. That's why this meeting is so important. We've profiled each and every member of this elite, very intelligent group of people. Johanson, this is new information to you, but here's what the profiler has finalized."

I straightened my posture, excited to hear the new leads in the case. It wasn't often we had any, so this development was much-needed encouragement and a step in the right direction.

"The Chemist –our number one subject. The initial target. The big guy. With him in our custody, the rest of this empire will crumble. Nothing moves unless he moves it. We're certain of it. According to his profile, he is arrogant. Calculated. He lacks remorse and empathy. He is someone who has impeccable schooling.

"A scholar. He's possibly the head of a major pharmaceutical company, fucking drug administration board member, or something. The bottom line is, that he's into drugs. The science of it all. He's a fucking genius," Brad explained, completely enamored.

"Can we move forward?" Macy asked, seeing his eyes blossom as he discussed a man we were all fascinated with.

"He's a ghost. According to his profile, he's hidden in plain sight. He's someone we'd walk past and never suspect committed a crime his entire life. Keep an eye out for him!"

"Noted."

"Next is possibly his right-hand man. The person who does all the dirty work. He doesn't mind getting his hands dirty. The Hunter. He is as deadly as he sounds. More than likely very quiet. Says less. Acts more. He's readily available whenever his boss needs him. No one is off-limits. Not even us, so please be careful.

"Find the quietest in the room and it will likely be him. He's connected to this killing, we're certain." Bradford pointed at the crime scene of a murder we'd yet to solve, mainly because the suspect was on the list with seven others we were trying to get our hands on.

"Bradford, I need to be out of here in ten minutes or less."

"Right. Right. Speeding this up. The therapist. No therapist at all. Actually, a fucking nightmare. You never want to see him. His tactics are far worse than we've seen in the military, foreign countries– anywhere.

"By any means, he will extract information from you. You'll find he is most likely a very caring being. Possibly an actual therapist in his daily life. He's inquisitive. It's in his nature. One to ask questions. Expound on theories. Work your brain before you even know he's working your brain. This man is a fucking weapon."

He shook his head. "Please, steer clear of this one. We do not need him picking any part of your brain. If so, we're all toast."

"Got it."

"The Handler. Profile says he's resourceful, very. Can handle anything you put in front of him. Very good at cleaning messes, along with the next one on the list. The Cleaner. Likely in the legal realm. A paralegal. Lawyer. Something. He cleans the legal messes.

"If we could find someone under their wing who has had legal trouble, I know we can find him. We're just not sure if it's one person or an entire fucking team of cleaners. The workload must be massive."

"I doubt it. They are wise. Very. I doubt they get into much trouble," I reminded him.

"Didn't think of that. You're right."

"The Madam, we've learned is a woman. Her sophistication will likely be the red flag. She's a woman of class, one that's not easily impressed. According to her profile, she's a take-charge woman. She has demands and expects them to be met.

"She gets her way. She's outgoing. Charming. Likeable, but deadly if crossed. The women she employs are loyal because she is good to them. Generous. And has the potential to change their lives at the snap of a finger."

"I concur." I nodded. They were blindly loyal. I'd never seen anything like it. It wasn't a cult, but it felt like it at times. The way they cherished their leader and protected her at all costs.

"We fall flat there." Bradford pointed to the last of the list.

"We're aware there are at least two others involved, possibly four. But, we have nothing. Absolutely nothing on either of them."

The —

The —

The final names on the list were blank, but we were holding space for them because we knew they existed. With time, we'd have them pinned on the board alongside their occupation, too.

"After tonight, we might have answers. Don't worry, team."

"We have faith in you, Johanson. We'll stay out of your ear so you can pay attention. We're here to listen." Jack concluded.

"I need to get out of here. Debrief tomorrow?"

"Yes. See you tomorrow," Bradford confirmed before logging off.

I did the same. Attire was provided, so I stepped out of the door dressed in a black co-ord set that would be perfect in the gym. I made a mental note to revisit it before I made use of the state-of-the-art equipment downstairs on the amenities floor.

THE GREY LIST

It was Ego Ella May who led me straight to Roulette where I parked in the designated area for the women who made the place the success it was. I'd spent three weeks within the upscale exotic establishment and it lived up to every bit of the hysteria of the city. It wasn't the average strip club. Nothing about it was average.

The architect. The women. The tailored audience. The ambiance. The furnishings. The structure. The talent. The rules. The staff. Absolutely nothing was average. It was a fantasy. From the second you crossed the threshold, you could feel the shift and it was a significant one. It felt like you walked right into a dream. For most, they did.

The women were all exotic, ranging in many shades of black. From the darkest to the lightest, you'd find everyone was unique. Unrealistically intriguing features made you wonder if you were in a real place. High cheekbones, thick eyebrows, massive lips, long noses, round bottoms, perfect toes, breasts of all kinds, and bodies that were sickening as a collective roamed the facility daily.

I hope.

I hope.

I hope.

I want this love to last forever and ever.

Do you?

Do you?

With my eyes closed, I listened to Ego Ella May confront her feelings for her lover. In twenty minutes, I'd be completely transformed into a more confident, more radiating version of myself. But, for now, I allowed the effects of Chem's absence to dwell in my spirit.

Just as the song ended and another began, my phone rang. Because the song never stopped running, I realized it wasn't my main line. The phone that was ringing was the one I stared at for hours on end, hoping for a returned call.

My eyes popped open and I immediately started digging through my bag in search of the vibrating device. Its tone led me straight to it. I slid my finger across the screen, frantic and praying I caught it before it stopped ringing.

With the coolness pressed against my ear, I released a stream of air. Involuntarily, my eyes closed, again. I waited, soundlessly, to regain my composure before speaking. There was no question about who was on the other end. I could feel Chem dominate my existence without even a word being spoken. And when he finally spoke, my emotions toppled over.

"Hello, Eden."

"I've missed you," I rushed out, breathlessly.

He consumed me.

"You're not alone."

Hearing his voice on the other end for the first time soothed every ache I had. Things began to make sense, again. The gloom that was cast over me lifted. The sun began to shine, again, though it was pitch black outside.

"I'd like to see you," I admitted, drawing circles on my thigh, nervously waiting for him to respond. Silence followed my declaration. And when he was ready, he responded.

"I've hated myself every day for the last nine days."

"I'm sorry."

"So am I."

"Ch–" I paused.

"Yes, Choc."

"I want to see y–"

"You don't have to tell me twice, Eden. You never had to tell me twice. I heard you the first time. I felt you even before then."

A smile tugged at my lips as I nodded. The sound of knuckles on the window startled me. I looked up to find

Rachel, one of the sweetest girls I'd ever encountered knocking. I rolled the window down a bit to hear whatever she was saying.

"We have less than twenty minutes to pull ourselves together. Come on in, babes."

"Yes. Of course. I'm on my way inside."

"Okay. See you in there."

When I resealed the window, silence coated the line. "Hello?"

Defeat slumped my shoulders and curved my spine. He'd ended the call. The yearning plagued me for nine days straight and four days before that returned.

Fuck. I contemplated dialing him back but decided against it. I had a long night ahead of me. My team was counting on me. Sitting in the parking lot in my feelings would not help us solve the case we'd been working tirelessly to end.

"Hello. It's me–" Bradford teased.

"Cut it out, Bradford. Stay out of her personal shit," Jack demanded.

"Please!" I added.

With my nose piercing the air, I strutted through the parking lot, reaching the door in only a few seconds. When I approached the dressing room, I was rushed into makeup and wardrobe. An artist lightly polished my face for fifteen minutes. The final five, I was given a two-piece and a full-body suit I was to choose between. Because I loved the way the bodysuit hugged me, I settled with it.

"I love it. I'm not as half decent," Rachel complimented as we both made our way into the dressing room.

The room was brimming with good energy, sex, and determination. The depths the girls were willing to go to please customers that didn't etch away at their character, value, or principles were almost as admirable as it was concerning. They were born caretakers, even if it wasn't the medical or childcare field they specialized in. The people they took good care of were men, very wealthy men who simply wanted part of the fantasy created effortlessly at Roulette.

"You look beautiful, Rach."

She was dreamy in the two-piece with earrings that dangled on her shoulders and rhinestones glued in the small inner corner of her eyes. More were in a scattered pattern from her temple to her cheeks. Loads of blush made her appear bashful, slightly younger, and perky.

"Thanks, Giselle."

Pet names. Names that didn't make much sense. Unique names. They weren't allowed in Roulette. We were given a simple alias if we couldn't supply one of our own. The goal was to be memorable, even by name.

Rachel. Giselle. Brandy. Ash. Lola. Irish. Jamie. Valerie. Simple names that wouldn't easily slip the elderly clients' minds and didn't sound like something out of a wildlife magazine. It made the task enjoyable and not as difficult as I'd imagined. In some life, Giselle fits the persona. Fit the description of the woman I was when I entered through the back door. Fit my own personal fantasy.

I prepared to exit the dressing room. We'd been instructed to meet in the Red Room where we'd be given details about the expectations, rules, and specifics for our guests. Tardiness wasn't accepted, so I began to make my way down the hallway before the others.

"Jack," I whispered. "You guys there?"

"Yes. We're here, Johanson."

"Good."

I made my way down the never-ending hallway. My heels slapped against the tiled floor. I could feel as I shed my skin, transforming into Giselle with every step I made. And just before I turned the corner to enter the Red Room, my body was snatched in the opposite direction, behind a long black curtain, and down a separate hallway. One I didn't know existed.

And then, finally, after making it only a few feet down the extensive hall, I was pushed against the wall. Long hands roamed my body. Familiar lips pressed into mine. Labored breathing stole oxygen right from my lungs.

My eyes lowered with lust, with desire, until they closed completely, submitting to my fate. It was a beautiful one, just like the man responsible.

Our tongues danced as his hands caressed every inch of me within reach. I melted in his embrace. My fingers curled around his shirt, hanging on as if he'd disappear.

He felt surreal. So did the moment. I wanted a do-over. And over. And over. And over. I could have him six-hundred-thousand times and it still wouldn't be enough. I could overdose on him and die happily.

Sultriness streaked his words, lessening mine. He

whispered in my right ear, reminding me I had a device in my left.

"I don't want to end anyone's life tonight, Choc. But, if you go in there, you'll leave me without a choice. I'm hungry and my dick is hard. Come with me. No fussing. No fighting."

He stepped back, taking me in and fucking me with his gaze. My center pulsated. My body burned. And as he completed his statement with words that matched my desperation, I died a hundred times. To know he felt it too stripped me of life and then reimbursed me almost immediately.

"I miss you bad."

I can't fuss.

I can't fight.

Not tonight, Chem.

Whatever you want. Whatever you need.

In the skin of his I loved so much is where I wanted to be. And although my team needed me, I knew he needed me more. The thirst in his voice said so. The longing in his touch said so. The look in his eyes said so.

"I have to work," I whispered back. "Please don't make me choose."

"The choice has already been made."

He knew it and so did I. *He* was undeniable. *I* was undeniable. The choice had made itself, almost.

"Ch–"

"Eden."

With his brows raised, he pressed two fingers against my center. I shuddered, knowing I didn't stand a chance against him. He'd discovered my seething garden. I needed a hose down. I needed watering. I needed hydration. And he had the tools to replenish me.

"Please," I mouthed, aware people were listening on the other end and could hear everything I was saying.

A shake of his head finalized the decision he'd made and magnified the choice I'd made. He pulled me in the opposite direction from the one I was headed in and into a private suite. Waiting for me was a beautiful cream two-piece. The top was a collared shirt that had gold buttons down the middle. The pants matched in color and style.

"Get dressed, Choc."

Chem laid a chilly piece of jewelry in my hand before stepping off and sitting in the red chair against the wall. I uncurled my fingers to find a Van Cleef bracelet in my palm. It was beautiful and paired well with the clothes waiting for me.

In seconds, I was out of the bodysuit and in the two-piece. It fits me perfectly. How he'd guessed my size so perfectly, twice, was a mystery, but so was he. I couldn't wrap my head around the fact I was putting my career and the case on the line to accompany him at dinner, but the distance between us made it impossible to deny myself the opportunity.

Because his eyes hadn't left me, I hadn't been able to remove the communication device from my ear or disable it. When the chance came, I'd do so. The last thing I wanted was Chem in the line of fire. I never knew what to expect from him, but I didn't want my team to get wind of his existence or the lengths he was willing to go to protect whatever we were trying to build.

The trouble I had getting the bracelet on my wrist lifted him from his seat. He fastened it almost instantly and then grabbed me by the hand. He led me out of the door and into the parking lot where his car was waiting.

Something deep down inside of me made it clear that I'd walked out of Roulette for the very last time. How I'd convey that message to my team, I didn't know. But, I doubted Chem would allow the building to stand if I ever re-entered.

The speakers drowned out the com, managing to keep me content during the ride to our destination. The lights danced across Chem's skin, making it glow every other second. I couldn't tear my eyes away from him.

Every time he was in my presence, he was like a dream. Looked like a dream. Felt like a dream. Smelled like a dream. Walked like a dream. Talked like a fucking dream.

The distance between us made my heart ache. Slowly, I slid my hand across the armrest, invading his personal space. When close enough, I took his hand into mine, linking our fingers. His collapsed around mine before pulling them toward his lips where he kissed them tenderly. Each and every one of them, without haste.

Pinky.
Ring.
Middle.
Index.
And thumb.

Every time his lips touched my skin, I watched parts of his shed. He was revealing the man I knew was inside of him somewhere, one that had been afraid to show himself prior. His comfortability had grown in his absence. I was grateful.

He never let me go during the eighteen-minute ride. It wasn't until we were in front of *Charred* that we separated. He exited the car with a valet attendant waiting outside for him.

"Good evening, sir," happily, the guy greeted, eager to make conversation with a man who had very little to say.

Chem nodded.

"And let me get the mis–"

"Don't open her door. Not unless you can live without fingers."

Chem only said a few words. They didn't concern his car. They were a warning for the precious cargo inside.

"I, in fact, have no intentions of doing that, so I will let you have at it."

"Wise man," he concluded, making his way around the car.

He opened the door and assisted me onto the curb. When I was close enough, he pressed his lips against my ear.

"You're almost too fucking good to be true."

My cheeks peaked as my body prickled with tiny bumps that made areas of my skin painful. I pushed forward with Chem leading the way. He was dressed in a brown, long-sleeved shirt with pants that matched. His hair was freshly cut, adding another layer to his sex appeal. Under the word fine in the dictionary sat a picture of him. I was convinced.

Long legs paraded toward the entrance. I cursed every woman who'd ever seen what was between them. He was definitely a man over six feet. His dick, it was measuring at nearly four feet, itself. I was almost certain.

He was carrying a miniature version of himself between his thighs. A third leg. A pole. A water hose. A bat. And when he swung, he always hit his target.

So wrapped up in his charm, I hadn't noticed we'd reached our seat or we'd entered through a private wing and not the actual front door. I'd missed my chance to sneak off to the restroom and ditch the com in my ear. Our waitress was waiting on us, watching with a smile that reached her eyes as we took our seats.

Please, love. This one is mine.

He was rubbing off of me. The ping of jealousy stung like a bee. But, the way our waitress was eyeing the man who belonged to me left me with a bitter taste in my mouth.

Chem made his way around the table for four and had a seat after making sure I was settled. The knots had begun to form in my stomach, coiling it in twelve different directions. I could feel the gas as it bubbled and rolled around the areas that weren't constricted and curled.

It was imperative I visited the ladies' room much sooner rather than later. By now, my team was aware I was no longer in Roulette. Where I truly was, I never wanted them to find out.

"Welcome to Charred."

Fuck.

"I'm Taylor. I'll be serving you tonight. It's such a pleasure having you and it is such a pleasure seeing a familiar face."

With raised brows, I jogged my memory. I didn't recall the face in front of me. But, the chances of my name being revealed sent me into a panic. It wasn't long before I realized her eyes were still trained on Chem. I was invisible to her.

Giddily, she bounced, ready to be acknowledged. Ready to be affirmed. Chem said nothing. He simply expanded his limbs and grew more comfortable in his chair. My nervous, sweaty hands pressed against my pants, relieved I wasn't under the watchful eye. Having my cover blown would've ended my night and possibly my life.

Though I was freed of concern, I grew increasingly suspicious of the woman before us with a smile bright enough to light any room. The twinkle in her eyes let me know she'd had or craved more of Chem. Jealousy pushed my nostrils out further on my face. My heart drummed against my chest.

"A familiar face?" I chuckled, getting Chem's attention.

"Yes. Yes. Since–oh my God. Forever. Chemistry Childers."

Hearing his full name was quite surprising. I hadn't

taken him for a Chemistry, but as I repeated it in my head, it began to feel like the perfect fit. It was sophisticated, much like him.

"Oh," I sniggered, catching his eyes, hoping he was reading mine. "The whole name?"

"Umm. Hmm. We go waaaaay back. I hate Rome and I drifted apart the way we did. I still miss her and keep telling myself I'll get down to the theater to see her perform. How is Roulette? I tried getting into her club a few months back. Apparently, I don't make enough to get on the guest list." She laughed.

"Oh, God. I miss each and every one of those girls. They were like sisters to me. Everyone is on the right path, thriving and just continuing to be the girls I've always admired. I bumped into Roaman. She told me she finished school and finally became a surgeon. From my understanding, Rather has her own practice. I'm going to have to go sit on her couch one day. Every time I leave this place, I need therapy, but don't we all?"

She looked over at me for a response. A sly smile stretched my lips. The agitation on Chem's face matched the discomfort on mine. While it would make my job so much easier if she continued talking, I couldn't help but want her to shut the fuck up—*and fast*.

I dug in my canal, moving the com around, hoping to scramble the device and make communication difficult. There was so much going on in my ear, my head, and my heart. I was torn a twenty-six ways, it seemed.

"And Range. I saw her on the cover of the local magazine. First female to make partner at her firm. She was always so fierce. I knew she'd be great. Hell, I knew they all would. The way your family was structured just– I never had that. That's why I spent so much of my time with Rome. Tell my girl I miss her and I will get down to the theater to see her. I promise."

"Cognac, neat," was Chem's only response.

Silence was mine. The influx of information I'd received in such little time was so overwhelming, that I was unsure of what it was I should do next. Vomit threatened to spill from my core. It was made abundantly clear the man I'd spent the last two years searching for was right in front of me, had been inside of me, and I'd fallen head first for him.

"Cuvée," he finalized.

"Same ole Chem. Nothing more to say," she teased, entering his drink on the small handheld device she'd been holding.

"You've said enough. When you return, either shut the fuck up or direct another server to our table, Taylor Finlen."

Her eyes grew three times their size. I wasn't sure if it was the revealing of her full name that he'd obviously remembered or his request that had her scurrying from the table without my drink order. I didn't mind. The water that was waiting would suffice. I peeled the paper from the straw and submerged it. Before it could hit the bottom, I was halfway through the glass.

"I need to use the ladies' room," I announced, catching my breath once I'd finished three-fourths of the water.

I didn't wait for a response. I was up out of my seat in a flash, heading down the hallway and through the restaurant. Because I'd never been inside the prestigious establishment, I had no idea where I was headed, but I was determined I'd find my way.

I didn't need assistance. I needed fresh air. Because I didn't want to make a run for it, the restroom would suffice—*for now.*

Oh God.

This is all bad.

Hot flashes made me feel like I was drowning in a pool of sweat. The walls of the restaurant were getting tighter, and closer. My throat burned though I'd just had almost a full glass of water. My thoughts were jumbled. The knots in my stomach locked, squeezing it for dear life. Panic had set in and it was taking me for a ride.

This can't be happening.

What are the fucking odds?

I grew ill. It was all beginning to make sense. How I hadn't pieced the puzzle together before now was baffling. I was blinded by his charm. His sophistication. His, everything.

"The Chemist —our number one subject. The initial target. The big guy. With him in our custody, the rest of this empire will crumble. Nothing moves unless he moves it. We're certain of it. According to his profile, he is arrogant. Calculated. He lacks remorse and empathy. He is someone who has impeccable schooling.

"A scholar. He's possibly the head of a major pharma-ceutical company, fucking drug administration board

member, or something. The bottom line is, he's into drugs. The science of it all. He's a fucking genius."

Bradford's words revisited me as I located the sign with the skirt on it.

Chem– The Chemist. CHEM. Chemistry. My thoughts raced.

I shoved the door to the restroom open and found the nearest stall. Hovering over the toilet, I pressed a hand against my chest to stop my heart from plummeting out. At any second, I knew I could find it on the floor.

"Johanson!" Jack screamed.

"Hey. Joh–"

It wasn't until then that I began to hear the voices in my ear. The voices in my head had been so loud. The galloping of my heart had been so loud. My breathing had been so loud. I was deafened.

"Y–"

Before I could speak, the door of the restroom flew open. I hadn't set my eyes on him, but I could feel Chem. He was so fucking demanding. Spellbinding. Entrancing.

My God.

I snatched the small device from my ear by the tips of my fingers. It fell into the toilet, exactly where I'd intended for it to go. I flushed it, watching it swirl before wiping the sweat from my top lip and straightening my posture. When I turned around, I was face to face with the man himself.

SIX

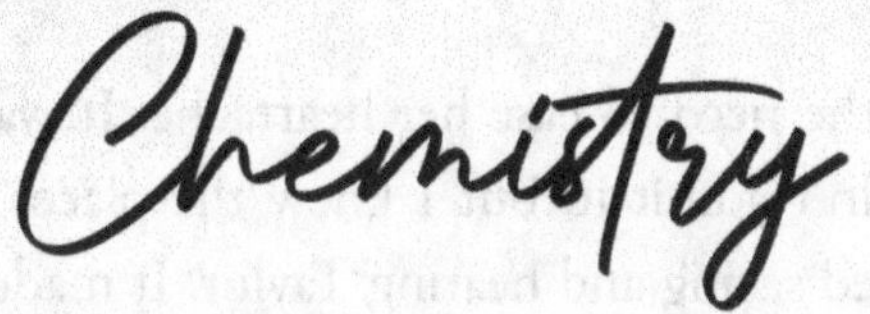

She was struggling. The lack of oxygen that had her short of breath reminded me of the way I felt when I saw another man in her presence. That darkness that shaded my orbs had formed a cast over hers. I reached behind me, removing my tool.

She flinched, causing irreparable damage to my heart. I'd never hurt Eden. The fact she considered it had my head ringing.

Address it later.

"I'll make sure to clean the mess you make," I assured her, holding the Glock out for her to grab.

"Chem–"

"I know what that feels like, Eden. That jealousy.

That anger. It'll swallow you if you let it. If I refuse to let there be a nigga on this earth who can make me feel that way about you, then I'm not the exception and no one is exempt."

She gasped, mouth slacked and eyes wide with shock.

"They won't ever know you were here."

"Are you telling me to k–"

"I'm telling you to do whatever it is your heart is telling you to do. I'll clean the mess if it comes to it."

"I am not that person. I–I am not that woman," she claimed, taken aback by my admission.

"Then, so be it." I shrugged, adjusting my Glock on my waist.

I felt the need to ease her heartache. It was possible she wouldn't admit it, but I knew the places her mind had traveled seeing and hearing Taylor. It made me want to stuff her big ass mouth with something that would shut her up for good.

I cradled her face between my palms and inhaled deeply. I exhaled shortly after. I employed her, wanting her to follow the same steps Rather had forced me to time and time again. When she began inhaling and exhaling, I could see the weights being lifted from her shoulders.

"She couldn't handle me, Eden. Not even if I gave her an instruction manual and read that motherfucker to her like a bedtime story. It's only you. It'll only ever be you."

My words composed her. With a nod, she put my worries to rest.

They could never be you.

Her silence was disheartening. I needed to hear her to know all was well. The look on her face made it hard to believe.

"A penny for your thoughts."

"I don't want to be here." She sighed. "I'm sorry."

It felt as though those words ran so much deeper than the surface. Instead of responding, I took her by the hand and led her out of the door in which we'd come. The valet was close, but my car was closer and I was certain the key was inside. It was one of the reasons I loved *Charred*.

Their clientele wasn't the average Joe. At any second, hell could break loose, and waiting for the valet to hand you keys and pull your car around shaved off precious seconds that could mean life or death.

Within seconds of stepping out into the brisk air, Eden was in the passenger seat and I was whipping off the parking lot, burning rubber to put distance between us. My appetite had intensified, but it wasn't for food. It was Eden I craved, mentally, physically, and surprisingly, emotionally.

I wouldn't stop digging into her until tears streamed down her face and she felt me deep, deep in that soul of hers I wanted for myself. Selfish, I was, but only when it came to her. She'd become the prize I didn't think I needed in my possession. But, now that she was here, I'd do anything and everything to keep her.

My phone vibrated. I hesitated to answer the call, but

it was rather hard ignoring the baby boy. He was persistent. He'd only retry until he got an answer.

"Yes," I greeted him.

"Yes?"

Because I refused to feed into his apparent ignorance, I remained silent.

"What's up? What are you doing?" Milo asked, making small talk. It led me to believe the call was pointless, but I couldn't end it. It wasn't often he or the others wanted anything much, but their calls let me know my presence was missed. If nothing else in life felt good, that did.

"I'll be there soon," I informed him.

It was news to me, too, but when their hearts grew heavy with my absence, it was my duty to lighten their load.

"Say no more. One love."

He ended the call without a response.

Spoiled fuckers.

He wasn't the only one. Makai was the leader of the duo. It didn't matter that they were grown-ass men. Even distance couldn't deny our bond. It hadn't been very long since Mercer had been behind bars, but every day I contemplated setting his ass free. He didn't want to live his life on the run, which was the only reason I hadn't.

My eyes wandered, landing on the woman who made everything and nothing make sense, simultaneously. Her hands were tucked between her legs. The furnace was keeping her fingers warm. It wouldn't be long before I replaced them with my head and then my dick.

The night sky was as breathtaking as she was. Clarke was such a beautiful city, but at night, she was something straight out of a magazine.

Catherine.

Catherine.

Just like Catherine.

I blinked away the images of her casket. It was only a few inches away from Maurice's. They were buried side by side.

A fucking love story tragic enough to make you despise the idea, the feeling. I hated it. My mother had made me.

Though I tried thinking less of her, she stuck with me. Day by day, thoughts of her plagued me. Catherine was as stunning as Eden.

As sure. As thought-provoking. As breathtaking. As fierce. As striking. There were similarities I wished I hadn't noticed but were there.

And just like my father had explained to me time and time again, she was addictive. She owned me the second I laid eyes on her. I hadn't shaken her ass yet.

When the city lights disappeared and we began traveling north, I removed the new eye mask from the armrest and handed it to Eden. She accepted it without hesitation, pulling it over her eyes and reclining her seat, slightly. Her level of comfort stretched my lips across my face. I felt my head as it nodded, approving her state of contentment.

"Are you staring at me?" she broke her silence to ask.

"I am," I admitted with a tilt of my head.

She said nothing more, but I was reminded of the restroom incident.

Where was her comfort? Her contentment? Her satisfaction?

"Eden."

"Yes?"

"I need you to understand something," I explained, readjusting myself in the driver's seat.

"Okay."

"I'd never hurt you."

I was short but I was honest.

"I– I– I know."

Her uncertainty was baffling.

"Don't make yourself out to be a liar, Eden. You don't know that. I can hear it in your voice you're unsure. But, my word is one you can trust."

"I know, Chem."

That's what I was in search of. That vote of confidence she had when she responded then. She knew I'd stand on my word. She didn't know she was safest with me, more than with any motherfucker on the planet.

It's all good.

I'd make her a believer before it was all said and done.

"Don't ever be afraid of what I'd do to you. Be afraid of what I wouldn't do for you."

Burn the city.

Fight a bull.

Shoot anything moving.

Open up.

Entertain the possibilities of love.

Consider the rest of my life with you.
Admit what's mine has become yours.
Fall.
And fall swiftly.
Kill.
Conquer.
Destroy.
Die... preciously.
Anything.

I'd do whatever for those lips to form a smile in the end.

Instead of dwelling with words, I decided to rely on my actions. Choc would understand that it wasn't me against her. It was us against everything and everyone if it ever came to it.

We rode quietly for some time. Eden's hand roamed, in search of mine. I curled my fingers around hers and brought the back of her hand to my cheek where it rested.

"Can you play something soft?" Her voice was riddled with sadness.

It hacked away at my resolve. Discomfort lingered.

"What's wrong?" I needed to know.

"Nothing," she lied.

"If you're dishonest, I can't fix it."

Pushing out warm air, she exhaled. "Not everything can be fixed, baby."

That last word, I clung to it. It clung to me. A new height had summoned us. We weren't all bad, it seemed.

We were on our way. To where, I wasn't sure, but it had to be somewhere good.

"Then, you don't know me, Choc."

She turned in my direction as if she could see through the eye mask on her face. Her mouth opened, ready to spill, but then it closed shortly after. Whatever was going on in that head of hers, she wanted to divulge but simply wasn't ready.

I granted her request. Gentle, voiceless music flowed through the speakers. I watched as she melted into the seat, softening against my hand.

We reached my home by the time the eighth song ended. I helped Choc out of the car and into the house where she shed her blindfold. Distressed eyes stared back at me, forcing a smile.

What's the matter, baby?

Her beauty was present, but it was overshadowed by the despair that radiated from her. It was silent but obnoxious. Invisible but holding more space than it deserved. Until we both felt better, I'd plant my head between her legs. Maybe that would strip away her stress.

"I'll be in the kitchen," she announced, catching me off guard.

"For what?"

"You were very clear when you said you were hungry, Chem. It's my fault we didn't have dinner. I'm taking my rightful place in the kitchen so I can feed you."

Stunned by her declaration, I scratched the hair of my chin. Words swirled in my head. I chose the correct ones carefully and stepped closer to Eden. I tipped her chin upward, wanting to make sure she understood every word I spoke.

"Your rightful place is wherever the fuck your heart desires. I'm not a man who believes a woman has certain duties and certain areas of the home where she belongs. I've got staff for that shit. I'd rather peel my eyes from my skull than watch you slave over a stove if that's not where your heart is.

"I'm not around this motherfucker building engines and making home repairs. You won't ever see me get my hands dirty. Not in that sense. It's loathsome. We delegate, Choc, so we can spend our time and energy on progression.

"That's all that ever matters. *Progression*! Leave the inconveniences to the others. They're compensated well and love their jobs. I can think of a few ways you can feed me right now without stepping foot in that kitchen unless that's what you truly want to do." I paused. "Is it?"

She shook her head from one side to the other.

"Well, then. That's settled."

I leaned down, tapping my shoulder. She placed her hands on both and lifted her right leg. I slid a shoe off one foot and followed up with the other. She shrunk a few inches but was still a considerable height.

By the hand, I guided her up the stairs and toward the master suite. When we arrived, I wasn't in the mood for small talk. Eden was too fucking remarkable in that two-piece. My dick was growing rapidly, tenting my pants and causing discomfort.

As I unbuttoned my shirt, taking her all in, my requests began. I needed her stripped down to nothing much sooner than later.

"Take them clothes off, Choc. And stretch out. I want to see that pussy."

There was an immediate shift in the atmosphere. Her eyes grew lazy. Delayed blinks and lingering stares were evidence I wasn't a fool. She was covered in lust. Her entire demeanor had changed. Sex oozed from her body.

She shed one piece of clothing at a time. I didn't miss a second of her disrobing. Her dark nipples pierced the air. Her arousal coated the room, fondling the hairs of my nose. She smelled divine.

Ovulation was on the horizon. My heir would soon be more than an unfertilized egg in her womb. Sperm could survive for days. With my luck, it would. Just in case it didn't, I'd refill her in two days, when I was sure her body was ready for reproduction.

Eden rendered me speechless as she climbed on the bed on all fours, turned around, and spread her legs. She grabbed her ankles, stretching them as far as they would go. Her pussy glistened with moisture, the bright pinkness of her insides exposing itself slightly.

Definitely burn down the fucking city, I concluded, lowering to my knees in front of her. *Kill some shit. Empty my fucking accounts.*

My tongue lapped her pussy, ready to help her reach the finish line.

"Cheeeeeeeem."

Her pearl had hardened and was peeping from

underneath her hood so I didn't have to search for it. Eden's fingers gripped the sheets beneath her. Though I wanted to stay awhile, from the convulsions of her body, I knew she wouldn't last long. She had been deprived. Her orgasm wouldn't wait. Couldn't wait.

I apologize, I wanted to tell her, but the thought of her flesh slipping from my mouth wouldn't allow me to.

"Oh fuuuu– Yesssss!" she squealed, barely above a whisper.

My fingers pushed through her barriers and were immediately drenched in her creaminess. The lubrication allowed me to slide my hand up and down my dick as my fingers wrapped around it. As I massaged her pussy with my tongue, I massaged my dick.

Up and down. I kept a steady pace and applied pressure, knowing it was the key to a successful, intense orgasm. Eden began gyrating her hips beneath me, matching my rhythm. Her body was moving involuntarily, preparing to reach new heights.

"Yessss. Please don– don't stop."

I won't.

Her walls came crashing down. She released the built tension onto my tongue.

"I'm cumming. Ummmmmm," she moaned, completely stilling before sudden jerks prevailed.

"Oh fuck. Oh fuck."

Her legs tightened around me. Even at her peak, I knew she could climb higher. I sucked her clit until she was reaching for the stars. Her body went limp as her core stiffened. And then, the floodgates of her personal heaven opened and poured out a blessing so plentiful that I thought I'd drown.

"Chem. Cheeeeem. Fuuuuu–"

My dick had stretched to the point of pain. It was hard as a fucking brick. I was up on my feet as Choc fought to come down. She wouldn't. That mission was pointless. I wanted her mounted where she belonged until I was finished with her fine ass.

I buried myself inside her. Those plush, inviting walls quilted around me. My eyes went to the back of my head. My toes curled, and my spine followed. The tips of my fingers dug into her skin as I wrapped a hand around her neck and squeezed. Lips pressed against Eden's ear, I began to mumble the secrets of my heart.

Secrets that weren't meant to be shared.

Not yet.

They put my life and my vulnerability on the line.

They softened me.

They weakened me.

They haunted me –day and night.

"I'm falling."

Shit, I'd fallen. *Past tense*.

THE GREYLIST

The ponytail she wore was on the other side of the room. Her natural hair was wild and untamed, obscuring my vision and covering parts of her face I needed to see. I thumbed the thick strands, pushing them out of the way to reveal her beauty.

Though fucked and flushed, I was still in awe of her. The disoriented, bewildered image was as fascinating as the well-groomed, polished Eden.

She can do no fucking wrong. My wires were crossing. The lines were blurring.

Weary lines creased her forehead. She stared back at me, absentmindedly, obviously in a place far away.

"What's wrong, Choc?"

A single blink brought her back to me. She scooted closer, pursing her lips to kiss mine. Then, she slid backward, reconnecting with eyes that made me wonder if this was what heaven felt like. I'd never know, because I'd never get there. But, this must've been the closest thing to it.

"Why are you always looking at me that way?"

"Because." I sighed, regretful of the words forming before they left my mouth.

"Because–" she stressed.

"You remind me of someone I used to know."

Her eyebrows gathered near the center of her forehead as she inhaled deeply. Mixed feelings engulfed her, showing on every inch of her face.

"Did you love her?"

With a nod, I admitted, "I did."

"You still do," she posed, pain ripping through her pretty features.

Closing my eyes, I brushed aside the intrusive

thoughts, fighting to stay in the moment. Confidently, I reopened them.

"She broke my heart."

Her eyes softened. So did her resolve. Long, slim fingers stroked the side of my face as she looked down on me with pity. I wouldn't stand for it.

"No sympathy for a soldier, Eden."

"Is she still breathing?" she mustered as her body grew rigid.

With a titter, I shook my head. "Am I rubbing off on you, baby?"

"Is she?"

"No. She isn't."

"Fair enough."

"She was my mother, Eden."

A gasp filled her lungs with oxygen and swelled her eyes twice their normal size.

"I'm so sorry. I– I thought you mea– like an ex or–"

"It's okay."

"It's not. I'm sorry. I had no ide– Oh my God. I'm sorry."

"Stop apologizing. It was her decision. There's no need to be sorry."

"Her decision? I don't understand."

"And I don't care to explain. I have other things in mind."

"Che–"

"Come on, Choc."

I was up and on my feet before she could protest. She was in my arms and we were headed down the hall before she could digest all that had been revealed. Down the stairs, through the common areas, and into the pool area, I carried her as she continued to apologize.

"Please," I groaned, lowering our naked bodies into the water.

"I have been wondering what happened to you. What made you this way? What sealed your heart? What hardened your edges? And it's all beginning to make sense. I wouldn't wish that amount of pain on anyone."

She spoke from experience. I wasn't sure who she'd lost but it was apparent parts of her were missing, too.

"I'm this way because I'm this way, Eden. Don't try to figure me out. I'm no puzzle you can put together. There will always be missing pieces. You'll drive yourself mad trying to finish."

"I don't want to finish. Ever. That means the experience has come to an end and I don't want that, Chem. Can your mystique last forever or is that asking too much?"

Her words were grounding. I planted my feet where they were, not taking another step. The crystal-colored water reflected on her dark skin.

Paradise.

Eden was hammering at my walls. The way she broke them down with such ease was baffling and demanded a study on the ability alone. I tilted my chin in her direction, wondering if she knew what she meant for me, *to me.* She couldn't have, because I'd never be able to put that shit into words.

"Nothing you desire will ever be too much."

"Well, then." She chuckled, exposing those fluffy cheeks. "That's settled."

"Definitely fucking rubbing off on you."

Laughter knotted my stomach and twisted my heart. With a shake of the head, I pulled Eden closer as I pushed toward the deeper end.

"Let's see just how much."

"Baby, this is too far out," she whined.

"Sink or swim. Those are your only options. Whining isn't."

"I can't swim very we–"

"You will before the day ends."

I silenced her, wanting nothing more than to enjoy the two things that made me feel my best. Made all the voices disappear. Made me forget the demons I fought on a daily basis. Made everything okay.

Her arms rested on my shoulders as her hands gathered behind my head, pulling me closer to her. Legs wrapped around my waist. I used every ounce of resistance I could muster to keep from sliding into her. If I did, she'd never learn the lesson I sat out to teach.

SEVEN

Eden

As Chem's grip around my neck tightened and our kiss deepened, the reality of our situation toyed with the moment. His tongue was down my throat, making my center throb and head spin. One hand was pressing against my trachea and the other was cupping my ass so firmly I thought he'd leave an imprint.

My God, Chem. I ached all over.

He'd primed and punished my flesh for the unknown all weekend long. As if he knew things I hadn't revealed and was preparing me for the inevitable. It all felt so good, so final. So unfair.

I was severely intoxicated, struggling to keep my eyes open and my mouth closed because he'd soaked me with the sweetest, most pleasurable energy I'd ever experienced. Lust coated my skin. My features. Made both my head and heart heavy, because I knew eventually I'd be forced to break the heart that I wanted so badly.

"Be a good girl, Choc," he warned with a finger.

"Promise."

I didn't recognize my voice as I responded. I swallowed the pain of it all, but he hadn't missed the crackling. He never missed anything. His attention to detail was appalling.

"Don't do that to me, baby," he begged.

Chem didn't beg. I'd learned this rather quickly. To hear his pleas was unsettling. My eyes welled, but I managed to smile in spite of.

"I ju– I just miss you already." I lowered my head, swiping my face before he could see the tears fall from my eyes.

Because no matter how amazing he was, how much I'd enjoyed the last thirty-six hours with him, how hard I'd fallen, or how much I loathed his absence, I had a job to do. I had a case to solve. And he'd broken it without me knowing it, expecting it, or *wanting* it.

"Business calls."

"What is it you do, Chem?"

Please say you're into real estate. Own a restaurant. Own laundry mats. Into the oil trading business. Make clothes from scratch. Something. Anything but–

"I'm a Chemist, Eden."

My chest caved. There was no denying it. The man I'd lost sleep over and had been studying the little we had on was standing in front of me, holding my heart in his hand.

"Wha–"

He wrapped his arms around me. I melted into his chest. He was safe. Felt safe. Safer than any space I'd ever been in. Safer than any person I'd ever encountered. Safer than any love I'd ever known because though we weren't there yet, I knew people like Chem didn't love often.

And when they did, they gave it everything and anything they had. That's what I wanted. That's exactly what I needed. Exactly what I deserved.

"Don't worry yourself with my boring ass, very fucking uninteresting occupation. None of that matters. Just wipe those tears and let me go so I can get back to you."

"Yeah?"

I looked up at him with curious eyes.

"Yes."

He kissed me deep and then let me go, again. This time, I stepped off, knowing it was time to rip the bandages off and face my reality.

"I'll see you later, Choc."

Goodbye, Chem. The finality of the moment gutted me.

Words felt too much like torture, so I saved them, headed toward the entry of my lofts, and started for the elevator. My world was crashing around me. I was completely shattered while simultaneously disappointed.

The second he'd revealed his hand and participated in criminal activity with my knowledge, he was supposed to be reported to the agency. Things would've never gotten this far.

But they have.

I pushed the button for the elevator, sick to my core at what I was leaving on the table. Chem wasn't perfect, but he was the very first person in the world I truly believed was mine. Mine to have. Mine to hold. Mine to love. Mine to live with until my dying day.

I finally exhaled as I stepped onto the elevator, allowing the bottled-up emotions to come tumbling down. I covered my mouth with a hand to prevent the whimpers from spilling into the lobby.

My heart broke one thousand and twelve times for one hundred and twelve reasons. And just before the door of the elevator closed, the number one reason stood in front of me with a stretched arm and anguished eyes.

"You trying to make a nigga say fuck it–"

"Chem–"

"Whatever is happening right now, I don't like it, Choc."

Me either.

"Why the tears?"

I gnawed the inside of my lip, drawing blood as I chose my words carefully.

"I asked a question," he reminded me.

Shifting my weight from one side to the other, I prepared to share things with him that were meant to remain private.

I'm an agent, Chem, hired to bring down your entire empire. Last night, at dinner, more was revealed about the case than we've been able to find in years. The women I've learned are your sisters, they're all wanted. You're wanted. You're the most sophisticated case we have right now. Almost everyone has been pushed aside for your capture.

I'm not at Roulette because I want to show my ass every weekend. I'm there because my career depends on it. We've been hunting you for so fucking long, baby. Obsessing over you. I understand why. You're as clever as we anticipated. You're smart. You're charming. You're calculated. You're everything we knew you'd be. Everything The Grey List is.

My God. This is all so fucked up. And... and... my name isn't Eden, for crying out loud. It's Egypt. Please call me Egypt.

"Eden."

"I thi– I think I'm falling in love," I admitted, choosing my battle wisely.

His posture slacked, something that wasn't witnessed often. The elevator began to buzz, letting us know the doors had grown tired of being parted. Neither of us bothered to adjust our stance.

"Is that what I'm feeling?" He breathed out, running a hand through his facial hair as he looked around, finally relieved to have an understanding of what was happening.

I nodded. "Yes."

He rushed into the elevator, pressing his palms against my cheeks. "Then what's with the sadness?"

Seconds passed as we stared back at each other. The doors finally sealed.

"Answer me."

"You feel so– incapable."

The confession coiled my stomach. Vomit threatened to spill. I waited for him to tell me I was wrong. I waited for him to demand I take my words back, but he didn't. Instead, he nodded, keeping my face between his hands.

"I am, Eden. I am incapable. Probably undeserving, too, but–" he explained, pressing his forehead against mine before continuing. "Dammit, I'm not impossible. This is not impossible. We're not impossible. I have a fucking heart. And that motherfucker beats every time I think of you, see you, hear you, feel you..."

He pulled back, eyes on me, again. "If I never get anything else in my life right, I'll get this right. I'm loyal to a fault, Eden. Let that be the mustard seed. Our mustard seed."

When our lips rejoined, the elevator began climbing. I pulled away, unsure of where it was taking us. I pressed the button that would lead us to my place swiftly, knowing if I missed the opportunity there wouldn't be any telling when we'd make it to my floor.

Anxiety swelled in my throat as we waited for the unknown to reveal itself. Chem never took his eyes off me. I could feel him a few feet away, in the corner of the elevator with his hat pulled down over his face. He was breaking protocol for me. This was completely out of his norm. I was completely out of his norm.

The second he decided to step outside of his comfort zone, it was into the arms of a woman who was employed to apprehend him and everyone he was associated with. I grew dizzy thinking about the pain it would inflict on us both.

Luckily, the doors opened exactly where I needed them to, and with perfect timing. Chem stepped off right behind me. He wasn't very close, but he wasn't very far as we strolled down the hallway.

When I made it to my door, I hesitated, waiting for him to catch up. To my surprise, almost immediately after stopping, his hands slid down the front of the black leggings he'd supplied. His index, middle, and ring fingers caressed my pussy, making my head fall backward onto his shoulder.

"Cheeeem."

"I'll be back, Choc. And I won't be long. This shit better stay put until I return. You hear me?"

"Ummm hmmm," I groaned, grinding against him to increase the friction.

Abruptly, he pulled out, and before I was able to get myself together, he vanished. From one side to the other, I turned, trying to figure out where he'd gone. The pinging of the elevator shifted my line of vision. Just as the doors closed, I noticed the black jacket of his suit. The hat he wore covered half the back of his head.

Incognito. A ghost. I'd known him all along. Studied him. Searched for him. And there he was, taking off with pieces of me I'd never get back.

I stormed inside of my place with the heaviest heart one could bear. I didn't make it past the threshold. The door slammed behind me and my back slammed against it.

My body sunk deeper and deeper until my bottom was on the floor and my heart was beside it. Pulling my legs up to my chest, I laid my head against my knees. And for the first time in almost three years, I wept.

Not because of the task at hand but because the precious soul was at stake. One who'd seen awful things. Though I didn't know exactly what, he was proof. His demeanor. His reservations. His tone. His boundaries. His barriers. His walls were slowly coming down, exposing uncharted territory that was so damn warm and welcoming. The monster he could be was nothing in comparison to the man I knew he was deep, deep down inside.

Pull yourself together, Egypt.

I remained. Tearful cheeks soiled the fabric against my body. The leggings caught the discarded saltiness that fell from my eyes. Wishing I could blink and it all made sense, I joined my lids and rocked from one side to the other.

THE GREY LIST

Two hours later the floor was still my resting place. The sound of the blaring cell pulled me out of the dump I'd crawled into. I found it hard to catch my footing as I stood and fought to balance myself.

Aimlessly, I ambled through the flat, immediately forgetting where I was headed and why. I flopped onto my bed, allowing the silence to overcome me. It was welcomed. My thoughts had eaten me alive already. Unfortunately, it was contaminated with the annoying sounds of the cell I remembered coming into the room for.

Shit. I shuffled around the bed, reaching over and pulling the desk drawer out. I retrieved the cell and pressed it against my face after answering. Resentment thickened the air around me.

Swollen eyes tightened as I spoke, greeting the caller on the other end. For the first time since he'd been introduced as my partner, I had no interest in talking to him.

"Yes?"

I tucked my chin and lowered my head, sighing as I patted the soreness around my eyes.

"Yes?" Bradford scoffed. "We've been worried sick about you, ready to round up the troops."

"You know the rules, Bradford."

Forty-eight. If I was obviously compromised and didn't make contact within forty-eight hours, the team was to come searching for me. Even if they had, I doubted they'd find me. Chem was much too smart for us. He'd evaded us for years. I was the only thing that could change that and knowing I had made me crumble inside.

"And they were the only reason we didn't comb the city looking for you."

"We've combed the city for years and found nothing. I doubt you would've found me."

"Jack has been calling you all fucking day, man. Even

Macy was worried. God, Johanson. Do you know what the hell you've done for us? I have been trying to wrap my head around this shit for nearly two days. Crack it wide open!"

"I know."

Sighing, I laid back on the bed, staring up at the ceiling. I couldn't get comfortable, so I found myself sitting up, again, staring out of the window.

"We're all getting online at three. He wants you there."

"I'll be there. I missed the meeting at Roulette and there's no telling when there will be another one. I had–"

"Roulette? Roulette?" Bradford chuckled in disbelief. "We're not worried about Roulette, Johanson. We have the big man himself. Jack is pulling you out of that club, effective immediately. He wants you to give Mr. Childers your undivided attention."

Chemistry Childers. I'll never forget that name.

"How much did you hear?" I wondered aloud.

"Enough. Enough to do some digging and discover every single name on The Grey List happens to be a Childers. They're all fucking siblings. We were so fucking off. Way left field, partner. This family is fuc– just brilliant. And they're all women. Every one of them except The Chemist. You couldn't have paid me to believe this shit if I hadn't heard it for myself. Women? This powerful? This clever?"

"You say that like men aren't the dumbest creatures on earth."

"I'm not saying that, but what I am saying is, is that

who you'd expect to be running a criminal empire of this caliber and under the radar, nonetheless."

"Well, it seems to me as though it's the reason why the empire is so successful. Women."

"Maybe you're right."

"Maybe."

"You sound like you're ready to hit the sack, so I won't keep you. See you at three. We have so much ground to cover. It's all starting to make sense. The pieces are falling in place. The puzzle is almost complete."

The puzzle will never be completed. I'd marked Chem's words.

"See you at three. I look forward to seeing what you all have put together. I'm happy I could contribute to the success of this case. It only took forever." I yawned, feeling the restlessness catching up with me.

"Later."

"Later."

My energy has depleted. I waited until Bradford hung up because I simply didn't have the strength. When the call ended, I tossed the phone where it had been resting and scooted closer to the head of the bed. Pillows gave me something soft to land on.

Still lying down, I began to strip my body of the clothing I wore. A big shirt he'd pulled over my head before helping me get my leggings up as if I was disabled. I appreciated the gesture and the kiss that followed our success.

I closed my eyes, prayerful the tears that began to sting my orbs retreated. When it was safe to open them, I did. Simultaneously, the phone I'd just put away began beeping.

Frustrated with the progression of the case, suddenly, I retrieved it again. A text with an address and the three o'clock timestamp. The phone rang as I concluded its reading. I answered immediately, sitting upright in bed.

"Yes?"

"Jack wants you to meet us there."

"Bradford, we all know I can't just meet you there. He has eyes on me. I know it. And he's no fool. He'll know something is up."

"He won't know anything other than you're going to tell a friend named Chrissy all about dinner and the time you spent with a man you just met. Women do it all the time, Johanson."

Nodding, I agreed, silently. "Tell Jack I'll see him at three."

"Will do."

"Don't call back. I'm cutting this thing off. I don't know what happens next, but I refuse to let an outdated Android blow my cover."

"I'm with you on that. Tuck it away nicely."

"Later, Bradford."

This time, I ended the call, curling up in bed and flipping the cover over me. I closed my eyes, wondering if sleep would find me. With so much going on in my head, I wasn't counting on it.

Boom.

Boom.

Boom.

A knock at the door alarmed me. I was up and on my feet within seconds, pulling the leggings back on while rushing toward the door. I hopped on one foot as I pushed the other through the last hole.

"Who is it?"

"Delivery for Eden Reid."

Delivery? I thought, peeping outside. Michael from concierge stood on the other side of my door. The familiar face prompted me to open it.

"For you," he said, handing over a bag and a phone with a fully lit screen.

"Thank you, Michael. Who do I thank–"

"I have the slightest idea but someone is waiting on the line, adamant I keep it open until the phone is in your possession."

"Thank you so much."

"My pleasure."

I stepped inside with the phone and black bag. Chanel was written in a simple, yet captivating font. It held the least of my interest. The cell, however, had nearly every ounce. I pressed it against my ear, finding my way to the window in the living room where I peered down toward the street in search of my suitor. I wasn't psychic, but I didn't need to be to know who was on the other end.

Silence coated the line for seconds, dragging on for what felt like minutes. And then, when he was absolutely ready, he spoke.

"Get off the phone, Eden, and get some rest. Pick it up again and it's going to lead me to believe whoever on that line doesn't cherish their life."

"You're insufferable."

"Addictive. Interesting. Even a bit concerning, but insufferable? Not anymore, Choc."

"I was talking to a friend."

"With balls and a dick. Don't insult me."

Chuckling, I said, "Maybe once upon a time, but she's transitioned."

"Let me find out otherwise and she's going to transition again. To her final resting place."

The dull silence on the line made it clear he'd hung up. With worried eyes, I searched the busy street for signs of Chem. There were none.

Where are you? I wanted to know. I *needed* to know. The phone vibrated in my hand. I answered instantly, not waiting for it to ring a second or third time.

"Don't worry yourself. If I wanted you to find me, I'd be at your door and not on your phone."

"Where are you?"

"Wherever I'm at," he teased. "You need rest. You've hardly slept a wink."

"I miss you," honestly, I breathed out.

So much it hurts. And it would keep hurting because no matter how far we'd come, we'd taken a hundred steps back at dinner the other night.

"I miss you more, Eden. I miss you more," he rattled off, sucking the skin of his teeth. Afraid he'd hang up, again, I rushed more words from my mouth though they came out calmly, slowly.

"I can't sleep."

"I'm aware. Inside your bag, you'll find a very special tea. Have a cup and you'll sleep for hours. Only a cup."

Or half. Three o'clock is not very far away.

"Tea?"

"Get some rest, Choc."

The line died without any more words exchanged.

Goodbye. With a groan, I made my way into the kitchen where I'd set the bag on the counter. Just as Chem had mentioned, there was a small tin of loose tea. I masked my excitement for the newest gift, prioritizing my health instead.

Without sleep, I'd be delirious. I needed the rest before I stepped foot outside of my door in anticipation of meeting my team. Their lives depended on my sharpness and so did mine.

I stared at the brand-new phone I'd placed on the counter beside the sink. It was then I realized the last phone he'd given me was no longer in my possession. He'd obviously gotten hold of it. Where it was now, I had no clue. Frankly, I didn't care, either.

Save yourself while you can, I begged him, internally. *Run.*

The smell of fresh tea made my tastebuds tingle and my mouth moist. I heated water in the kettle on the stove and waited for it to begin steaming while I grabbed my favorite clear mug and a tea strainer. With both situated, I moved along my new list of things to do.

The black bag made a ruckus but eventually settled once I'd lifted the large black box from it. I loosened the bow around it, allowing it to fall onto the counter as I removed the top of the box. Paper and a dust bag covered a black, quilted bag with interlocking Cs on the flap.

I brushed my hand across the leather. The quality was impeccable. So was the man who'd purchased it. I removed the medium-sized bag and held it against my body. It was the perfect size.

The squealing kettle jarred me from whatever daydream I was in, prompting me to complete the task I'd started. I filled the tea strainer almost halfway and did the same for the cup. Honey was piled at the bottom of the glass before giving me a chance to stir it into the mixture. The purple mixture made it clear lavender was a key ingredient.

What am I going to do with you, Chem? I placed the warm glass to my lips and sipped slowly.

EIGHT

Eden

"Hey." Macy greeted me as her arms encased my body.

Peeved by her closeness, I warned her it was too much at once. "Please, let go of me."

Macy had joined us five years ago. Since she had been trying to prove a point that didn't need to be proved. She wanted priority on our caseload and to be put into the field. Although she was ready because Jack knew this and kept her behind the desk, her jealous streak began. It hadn't ended yet.

"You're not alone, Johanson. Play the part. We're sitting ducks until this meeting is over."

Deciding the team's safety was more important than my disdain, I curled my lips and accepted Macy's embrace. We couldn't confirm I was being tailed but we weren't going to deny it, either.

We all knew who we were working with and their surveillance was heavy. Chem's especially. If it wasn't his eyes that were on me, there were eyes on me, nonetheless.

One after the other, we entered the unfamiliar home, still moving our mouths and smiling as if we were catching up. I tossed my head back in laughter just as I stepped inside. Macy closed and locked the door behind us.

She led me through the home, into the basement, and through a set of doors that opened in a long hallway. After a lengthy walk, we climbed stairs and ended up in a completely different basement of a completely different home. One that was two homes away from the one I'd entered.

"Seriously?" I sniggered, finding Jack and Bradford waiting.

My partner handed me a fresh cup of coffee and began. "Welcome to the makeshift bunker, Johanson. We have about fifteen minutes before our subject realizes no one is in the home you entered and gets suspicious due to the lack of movement inside."

"Then, let's get started," I responded, sipping from the cup.

Mmm. It felt so good to have a thick, ceramic mug in my hand with freshly brewed coffee inside while chatting with the team.

"Johanson."

"Jack," I greeted the man who'd started it all, put

together the team to close a case that would've forced anyone else at the firm to give up due to lack of evidence, leads, and breaks. But, patience had gotten us here, to a place I was both proud and apprehensive about.

"Alright. Here's what we have," Bradford began, swirling my sanity like a sandstorm in the desert.

The amount of red marks, clippings, strings connecting dots, images, names, occupations, and other information that filled the corkboard made me nauseous. My stomach turned with each sentence that left his mouth.

"Roulette – the madam. Not sure how we missed that one. It was right there, in our face. Rather, licensed therapists with a thriving practice. Roaman, we don't have much on this one, but we pulled her records. Clean. Board-certified surgeon. We're not sure how she is connected, but we're sure she's connected."

I massaged my temple as thoughts collided with my feelings. I wanted to, but I couldn't keep silent. I was battling myself as the words began to spill.

"She isn't a factor in the operation. I can bet my money on it. She's simply a helping hand when someone is injured and they don't want anyone at the hospitals asking questions."

"Bingo!" Jack yelled.

"See, four heads are better than three," Bradford added, writing beside Roaman's picture.

She was stunning. Every woman on the board was stunning.

"Any input on this one?"

Images of the sweetest girl, dressed in footless ballet tights, a leotard, and ballet flats captivated me. The innocence in her eyes told a story the wisdom in them wasn't willing to.

Without a doubt, I knew she was something special, someone special to Chem. Though the others were as well, this one was different. She had his heart. A big chunk of it.

"She's the youngest of the eight."

That explained a lot. And because I knew her brother's protection was something she could depend on, the job was easily delegated. I, too, found the need to protect her and the innocence I once prayed for. But, life had different plans for me.

"She isn't involved. She's useless," I lied, feeling as though it was the furthest from the truth.

Some way, somehow, she was connected, but instead of trying to determine her role, I wanted her to disappear. She didn't belong beside the others who had very clear, very crucial positions in the criminal empire they'd created.

"Jack and I thought the same thing. She's nineteen. I doubt she's gotten her feet wet," Macy explained.

"They could also be sheltering her, keeping her away from the life they've created outside o–"

"Right. She probably has no idea what they do outside of their day jobs. Let's not disregard the fact they all have incredibly impressive schooling. Top of their class.

"Each one of them. And we're talking college. A

doctorate in five to seven years, it's unheard of! They're doubling up on college credits, taking on twice the load of a normal student.

"That's not easy, no matter how you try to spin it. But her, top of her high school class, and then goes on to Hillard? To twirl in circles?" Macy made points that we all took into consideration.

"Their dance program is the best around. Education is a factor."

"But, these people have real—well, very complex majors that Hillard's education just doesn't compare to. Doctor Chemistry Childers. Doctor Roaman Childers. Doctor Rather Childers. Range Chi—" Macy explained.

"You're right," Jack admitted. "You're right. They're pacifying her. Probably don't even want her in college, majoring in anything useless because they'll surely use it if they can."

"Agreed," I replied, sipping from my cup.

"I can see that. So, no ballerina?" Bradford asked, removing her image and tossing it in the bin where I assumed they'd removed everything on the board.

"No ballerina," we all said in unison.

I breathed a sigh of relief, pacing the floor while keeping an eye on the board and the man presenting to us all.

"Range Childers is the lawyer, who happens to be on some pretty high-profile cases. She hides behind the firm's name, but she's all over the cases of some of Clarke's most notorious criminals. I can't help but wonder if the entire firm works for them."

"They own it," I concluded.

"Hm?" Bradford and everyone else in the room was baffled.

I was repulsed by my knowledge and the ability to share it. I craved silence. I preferred silence. But, this had been our case for years and this had been my career even longer. I couldn't help myself, although I felt the need to help Chem.

Caught between a rock and a hard place, I resorted to what I knew best. Who I knew best. Egypt Johanson, the agent. I'd just met Eden. She had little influence at the moment.

"Open your eyes, people. They own the firm. Check the tax documents. Investors. Client list. Compare it all and I can guarantee you'll find them at the end of the rainbow somehow, some way," I gritted, disgusted with myself.

Fuck. Just listen. Don't say anything else. Just listen.

"Rugger Childers. Has to be my favorite. A ghost she is, indeed. She has a degree in forensics. She mastered it as well. *Double, actually*. Science and psychology. She's a fucking weapon," Bradford whispered, looking over the files in his hand.

She was as fierce as she'd been described.

"She's a total fucking nerd. So is The Chemist. These two are very similar. Given her occupation, her studies have aided in her ability to remain unseen, and unscathed.

"Untouched. She knows how to manipulate a crime

scene or leave one without even a trace of evidence. We know she's The Huntress.

"Who or what she's been hunting, we don't know. We haven't linked her to anything or anyone. The case we thought she was involved in, they picked up a guy for last week.

"We thought he was our guy, The Hunter, but that couldn't have been furthest from the truth. We're back at square one with her. She'll be the toughest to nail. The girl practically doesn't exist."

"We'll get her, just like we'll get the others," Jack assured him.

"What is the plan?"

"You start digging. Now that we know we're in the right place, start digging."

"It won't be easy."

"We're aware," Jack confirmed. "But we believe in you. Whatever you have to do, Johanson. It's time we nailed these fuckers. Been a pain in my ass for way too long."

"Check-ins won't be as easy, Jack. This is personal for him. I'm not business and up until now, neither was he."

It would be best if you took me off the case, completely. He doesn't deserve what I will bring to his door. No matter how much havoc he's caused Clarke, he has only brought me joy. Elation. Peace. And so many orgasms I lost count.

The thought never pressed through. It remained just that–a thought.

"Whatever it takes, Johanson. It's gotten personal for him, which is exactly what we want. He needs to trust you. The minute he lets his guard down, then you start digging. In the meantime, is there anything you can tell us about his residence? His lifestyle? Any habits? Anything that will stick?"

He ended a man's life because his dirty nails grazed my skin. My neighbor has irreparable damage to his male parts because he asked me on a date. Bradford is on thin ice. The call I had with him put Chem in his feelings. If we're not careful, he'll find each and every one of you and end your lives.

"No." I shook my head. "Just like we thought, he's a criminal of another caliber. He's smart. Calculated. Very careful. We've only had dinner here and there."

"His home?" Macy asked.

"I have nothing," I lied with a shrug.

I don't have much, at least. I'm always blindfolded.

"You think we could get a tracke–"

"I'm not risking my life, Jack." From side to side, I shook my head. "No wires. No trackers. No phones. Nothing that will alarm him. He is unlike anything I've ever encountered.

"There is hardly anything that'll get past him. He's always watching. Seemingly waiting. Paranoid in a sense. Like he feels something on the horizon. I can't explain it.

"But, it feels like he's always preparing for something. He's restless for the most part. Always thinking. Planning. Working. Even when he says he isn't, I can tell by the way he completely zones out.

"Sometimes it feels like he isn't even in the room. But, his presence is so magnifying I can't help but acknowledge it." Not until I'd finished did I realize I'd trailed off.

The smile on Bradford's face was as wide as his head. He nodded. "That's definitely our guy. You are on the money describing him, his demeanor… his profile. Fuck, you're a Godsend, Johanson."

"I need to get going," I reminded them, taking a peek at the time.

I'd been over for twenty-three minutes. That was far too long.

"Yeah. Yeah. You're right," Jack stuttered. "You should get going. Hang out with Macy for about another hour and then head home. Make it believable and not like you actually hate each other."

"Hate is such a strong word." I headed for the door, ready to split in thirty minutes. I wouldn't give Macy more than that.

"It's almost accurate, though," Bradford added.

"Whatever. Nice seeing both of you. I look forward to putting this behind us so I can get back in the office."

"Same, same." Jack nodded.

"Later, Bradford."

"Later, Johanson."

This time I led the way. We re-entered the modest home, heading straight for the kitchen where I found the liquor cabinet. I needed a drink, possibly three. With everything unfolding the way it was, I was struggling to keep my head and heart out of the dumps.

The nagging pang in my stomach made it clear I was

going against everything I'd sworn when I took that oath, but I hardly had a choice.

I'm on no one's side, I reasoned. *I want everyone to win in the end.* That was impossible, so I knew I had decisions to make. Decisions that could cost lives. Decisions that could cost my career.

I wasn't dating a low-life criminal. Chem was cold-fucking-blooded. He'd proved it on the very first date and continued thereafter.

I tossed back the first shot and immediately followed with a second one. Macy joined, having a shot of her own. When my glass smacked the counter for the second time, I breathed out the warm air and laid my palm against my chest as the stinging subsided.

"Argggh."

"I don't know how you do it," she snickered.

"Do what?"

"This. For once, I'm happy I'm not in your position. I would fold."

I have, about twenty times. In every position. He's that fucking good.

"Well, good thing you're not in my position."

"That man is fine."

My nostrils widened with disgust. Hearing a woman refer to Chem as anything other than a decent human had me in my feelings. Suddenly, Macy's life didn't matter as much as it had before those words left her mouth.

Definitely rubbing off on me, I cringed.

"He is."

And he's mine.

"Have you two— you know?"

"I don't. Have we what?"

"Sex."

She smiled, waiting for a response. I contemplated leaving her in the dark, but, realistically, she was the only one I could openly discuss the case with.

She didn't want to know if I was fucking Chem. She wanted to know if he was fucking me well. Her eyes widened as she waited in anticipation.

"Yes, his dick is as good as you imagined it must be. It's even better."

"Dammit. I knew it," she gasped. "I can tell by the way he stands. The pictures do him little justice."

I won't do you any either if you don't find something else, someone else to swoon over.

"Not even a little."

His possessiveness was growing on me. I, too, wanted to be the only person who admired him the way only lovers and friends with benefits should.

"To the couch?" Macy asked, finally changing the subject.

"I imagine so. You have about twenty minutes before I'm out of here."

"Jack said an hour."

"Unless you want The Chemist at your doorstep, taking note of every feature on your face and sketching it in his memory bank, then I suggest you listen to me. Jack doesn't know him, Macy. I do."

Nodding, she headed toward the couch. I followed

her, but not before fixing a drink. Vodka and pink lemonade from the fridge was the perfect match. They were not preferences but would suffice. The timer began ticking the second I touched the plush sofa.

Within thirty minutes, I was nearing my complex with a heartbeat between my legs and ovulation on my brain. It was a crucial time of the month for me. And before Chem, I didn't have anyone to caress my aches.

Now that he was a factor, I knew there wouldn't be another cycle I spent massaging my clit or watching others indulge in sexual acts I dreamt of in my sleep and while wide awake.

The valet slid into my driver's seat as I slid out. Dressed in black from head to toe, I strolled into the lobby and then into the elevator. Seconds later, I was headed down the hall, ready to crawl into bed with another glass of tea.

The rainfall was set for seven and I could hardly wait to watch it from my bedroom window. Because it was floor-to-ceiling, the effects were dramatic, just as the beating of my heart when a familiar face stilled in my sight.

"Chemi–" I halted, stopping myself from saying his full first name.

With his chin angled, he stared at me. Silently, he studied me. I wasn't sure if I should run in the opposite direction or shove him into my apartment, against my door, and strip him of his clothing.

"Come inside," he suggested, holding on to the handle of my door.

He turned the knob along with my stomach. The fact he'd been inside of my temporary home without me there to monitor him made me weary.

"A burglar as well? My, my... so many hats."

"I haven't stolen anything in my life, Eden. Don't insult me."

He held up the key I hadn't given him. I shook my head, following him inside.

"So, you saw the mess I left, huh?"

"I haven't been inside. I was waiting on you."

"Because you knew I was on my way home?"

"I did."

"Of course, you did."

"It's better if I know where you are at all times, Eden. Things aren't black and white with me."

"Why not?"

"Another subject for another day. Right now, I just want to rest."

There it was. The answer to the nagging feeling in the pit of my stomach. Chem's presence had never felt so bleak and mild. It was bold and obnoxious. It was quiet but loud. It was consuming. But, now, it felt meek. Mellow. *Mild*.

Without allowing him to take another step, I whipped his body in my direction, forcing him to stop in front of me. His resolve was baffling.

"Chem," I started, looking into those dark, wondrous eyes.

"What's up, Choc?"

Anxious limbs wouldn't keep still. Chem was hardly in a rush to do anything, to go anywhere. But, for once, he was in a hurry.

"What's the matter?"

"No–"

"Chem."

"Feels like I'm coming down with something," he admitted finally, clearing his throat in the process.

It was then that his warmth resonated with me. He was feverish.

"Why aren't you home? Getting rest. You need it. Your body i–"

"Home is wherever the fuck you are, Choc. Not a place. Not a location. Not a structure. I'm right where I need to be. Just show me to the bed and let a nigga get some sleep."

"I find it hard to believe you don't know where my bed is."

Or the entire layout of my loft. I'm sure you've studied the blueprint.

"Smart woman." He chuckled softly.

The diminishing of his personality scared me. I hated to see him feel anything but joy, happiness, and content-ment. Neither of those felt obtainable for him at the moment.

I watched as he shed his clothes, making it into my bedroom in only his briefs. His hands held his head once he landed on the comforter.

Poor baby.

I depleted the distance between us, kneeling in front of him to lift his head. It didn't belong there. It wasn't meant to hang.

"Baby, have you eaten?"

A shake of the head was all he could muster.

"Anything in particular you're in the mood for?"

Another shake of the head followed a deep, throated sigh. His long frame scooted up on the bed. He laid his head on the pillows of doom. He wouldn't stand a chance on those.

Sleep would lure him quickly and pleasantly. That's exactly what he needed. I stood, preparing to leave him alone to get some rest. I didn't make it out of the room before he called out to me.

"Choc," he said just above a whisper.

"Yes."

"Come lay with me."

His vulnerability unearthed me. It was quiet. It was calm. It was gentle. It was generous. It was confirmation I wasn't the only one feeling all these things.

Chem had come to my home instead of facing the music alone. That meant something to me. To us. *For us*.

There is no us. I tried reminding myself, but quickly cast those thoughts aside. There was. And in some other lifetime, there would be, again.

I peeled off my clothes, laid them on the chair of my desk, and then climbed into bed. His open arms accepted me, flaws and all.

Against his chest, I laid my head, making it up in my

mind that as soon as he was asleep, I'd start to make him a healthy broth to kick-start his healing process.

Whatever was happening with his body, I despised. The quicker it subsided, the quicker I could have him back. The overwhelming, inconsiderate, and incredibly charming Chem. It had only been a few minutes, but he was deeply missed.

Our breathing was in sync. So was the beat of our hearts. They drummed, slowly, completely at ease in each other's presence.

"Hey."

"Yeah?"

"A penny for your thoughts," I replied, scooting so close the contours of our body began to mesh.

"Where have you been?"

"At a friend's."

"Not today, Choc. I know where you've been."

"Then when?"

"This whole time. If I knew you'd feel like this, I would've found you a long fucking time ago."

"How do I feel?" I probed, taking advantage of his willingness to divulge.

"Like nothing I've ever felt before." He shook his head from side to side.

"And how does that feel?"

"Like love," he released with a sigh, pulling me into him.

Slowly, he kissed my forehead. Chills ran the lining of my spine. Words faded in the back of my head. And soundlessly, I digested the new information I'd been given. It changed everything.

I feared for our future. Mainly because it didn't exist. To even consider one with Chem was pure delusion.

I was on the other side of the law. My kind and his didn't mix. The day he discovered my truth would likely be the day it all ended—the relationship, the comfort, the care, and possibly my life.

I wasn't ready. I wouldn't ever be ready, either. While I had the chance, I'd enjoy what we were building and mourn what we'd lose at a much later date.

His breathing altered a little more with each passing second. Eventually, I realized I was the only one still awake. After his confession, Chem was able to rest. A hasty departure wasn't my intention, so I stayed a little while longer, listening to his heartbeat and embracing the connection.

Time stood still in his arms. Gravity pulled me deeper into his embrace. If I could, I'd lay right here forever. But, life wasn't so simple and neither were we. I gathered my bearings and ripped the Band-Aid he'd placed over my heart just minutes ago. It was difficult but I managed to tear away from him.

A few feet away, light snores erupted. A smile made my cheeks rise and my eyes tighten. Chem wasn't a dream. He was the dream.

From head to toe, he'd been carved so perfectly. His heart was gold. His money was never-ending. His dick was long and he knew how to use it. There wasn't much more a woman could ask for. There wasn't much more I could ask for.

"I feel you staring." He grunted, rolling over as a cough shook him to the core.

"I am waiting for you to make your point."

He didn't respond. He kept his eyes closed and his head planted on the pillow beneath him. "What is it?"

His annoyance wasn't authentic. Not even a little. Had it been, I couldn't say I cared much. Back on my knees, crouched on the side of the bed, I pulled his hand into mine and laid my cheek against it. My eyes never left the sleeping giant.

"It does," softly, I claimed.

"Hm?"

"Feel like love."

NINE

Chemistry

The sun hadn't quite kissed the sky when I opened my eyes, but it was near the horizon. Eden's still, warm frame reminded me I wasn't in my bed. I'd made it to hers and crashed, slightly disturbed by my level of comfort.

Heat transferred from her body to mine. One leg was draped over my lower half. An arm curled around my stomach. Her head hadn't moved from my chest since she'd discarded the dishes she'd used to serve the soup that was possibly responsible for my health this morning. I was much better than yesterday.

Sickness was knocking at my door and I damn near answered. Instead of driving the distance, Aden brought me downtown where I wanted nothing more than to be in Choc's presence. She was all the medicine I needed, but I wasn't opposed to the idea of soup when she woke me from my slumber in the late hours of the night.

If only shit was this way always. The purple and orange hues of the rising sun, Eden in my arms, and the silence of the morning was peace I'd never encountered.

It made me wonder if it was even real. Because it should've been impossible for something so simple to be so impactful. So satisfying. So gratifying. So amplifying.

Just like the sun, Eden brought light to my dark sky. She illuminated my world, establishing her position and becoming a critical part of my day. Without her, I was operating in darkness. That's how it had been since I laid eyes on her.

"You're stewing." She groaned, turning over.

With her ass pressed against me, she found comfort again.

"I'm thinking."

"Hmm. About what?" Choc yawned, sleep still apparent in her voice.

I maneuvered my hard dick out of the hole of my briefs and began massaging it while turning over.

"How good this feels."

The soft fabric slid up her thigh with ease.

"This?"

"Waking up with you in my arms. Forgetting the rest of the world exists, even if only for a little. Yes, Eden. This."

Because she had one leg hiked and the other straight, I had access to her portal. Up and down, I rubbed my dick against her pussy until it was coated with a thin layer of her lubrication.

"That's all?" She moaned as I entered her, carefully separating her walls.

They accommodate me well. No resistance. I slid into home base with ease.

"And this, too."

"And this," she agreed, twisting her neck until her lips met mine.

Involuntarily, my lids gathered, blackening everything. Though I couldn't see a fucking thing, I could feel every fucking thing.

Eden's canal as I stroked her long and slowly. Eden's body as it begged for more of what I had to give. Eden's heartbeat was thunderous yet steady just like mine. Eden's desperation. Her surrender. Her power. Her divine feminine energy. Her light. Her love.

"Cheeeeeem."

Her scent permeated the air. The sound of our skin meeting, over and over, became the soundtrack to our soulful session.

"Fuck," I whispered in her ear, pulling her closer with my arm underneath her chin and a hand at the back of her neck.

Her pussy was silk.

"Fuck, Eden."

As the words left my mouth, my back hit the sheets. She flipped us over, claiming me for the hundredth time as if she didn't have enough of me already. I hardly recognized the man I was becoming because of her and I wasn't sure if I was supposed to run for the hills or continue running toward her.

She spelled out *trouble* for me. But, I'd never been one to evade its uncertainty. I embraced it. I embraced her and whatever came with her.

She established her dominance while still remaining unfathomably feminine. Gentle. Reserved. Sexy as fuck.

Her fingers caressed her tresses as her head fell backward and she continued to come down on me, sliding down my dick so beautifully.

Like something from the hands of a skillful artist, she became art I wanted on my wall. Down every hall in my home. On my body. In my head. The sun's rise as her backdrop was monumental.

"Ahhhhhhhh." Labored breathing muffled her moans, yet they remained the greatest sound ever heard.

I gripped her waist, ready to send her flying off the edge. From beneath, I drilled into her, searching for the diamonds she had hidden in her pussy. With my ax, I hacked away at everything eating at her, everything worrying her, everything hindering her, and every doubt she had about us.

Before she came into my life, I was incapable. Things had changed. I was changing. And in the end, Eden would have the privilege of saying she'd experienced a love not even the books compared to.

Her climax was my goal. I needed her to glisten. Just as she had so many times before. As her body grew rigid, I knew it wouldn't be long. My baby was near and I was right behind her.

"Yessss. Yessssss. Oh—"

"This dick about to cum, baby."

"Oh fuck!"

Eden hunched forward, curving her spine as spasms from her center made her quiver. Contractions served their purpose, extracting my semen and filling her with my minions.

"Shit."

Our movement halted. Both of us struggled to regulate our breathing. Once she had hers under control, Eden spun around on my dick and leaned forward. Her tongue traveled the length of my mouth, tapping the roof and then swirling around as if it were unfamiliar territory.

"Choc." I chuckled, knowing exactly where this was headed.

"Shhh." She gyrated her hips, slowly, awakening my softened tool.

She was truly amazing. From head to toe, I was still in awe of her.

"Whose is it, Chemistry?"

Staring up at her, I was rendered speechless. My rigidness allowed her to move freely. With her hands on my chest, she placed her feet flat on the bed and bent her knees until she was squatting. Eden never broke eye contact as she unmanned me with her slippery pussy and rare beauty.

"Whose is it, Chemistry?"

My government rolling from her tongue had me ready to bust in her shit, again. I cupped the sides of her face, bringing her down a notch and gaining full control of her destination, the time frame, and the intensity.

"Say my name again."

"Whose is it?"

She deprived me.

"Ede–"

"Whose is it?" She moaned.

"Say it."

I pushed forward, lifting from her bed and pinning her to it. I pressed a hand against her head and lifted her ass with the other, making sure she couldn't run from the blows to her back.

Her defiance would cost her, but it was punishment she thirsted for. It was obvious by the way she scooted her legs upward, shortening her body to deepen her arch.

I fucking love this woman, I confessed with a shake of the head. *She'll be the fucking death of me*.

I was balls deep in her shit, stroking with the intensity that matched my feelings.

"Ummmm," she whimpered but never moved. Never attempted to alleviate the pain. Like a fucking champ, she ate every blow I threw at her.

"Say it, Eden."

"Whose is it?"

"Yours." I grunted, giving in first without an ounce of shame.

"Fuuuuuck. I'm cumming."

"Shit, baby. Cum on this motherfucker."

"Chemistrrrrrrrrry."

THE GREYLIST

Mesmerized with her skin, I watched the water trickle down her chest and drip from her nipples. She was squeaky clean. I'd administered her cleansing myself, so I was sure of it.

Perky, dark areolas stared back at me as she massaged the facial cream into my skin. According to her, if I was sleeping over, then I had to abide by her rules, starting with the eighty-six-step skincare routine.

"That's enough, Choc."

"Quiet. I'm almost finished."

She'd said that shit three times, yet we were still standing in the shower. She claimed it would keep my pores open so the product could penetrate and do its job. I didn't give a fuck whether it did or not, my skin was immaculate without it.

"Is this the last step?"

"Two more," she hissed as if I was bothering her. As if her hands weren't in my face and I hadn't been ready to call it quits minutes ago.

"Baby!"

"Okay, one, then."

Afraid she'd start the entire process over, I refrained from shaking my head. A heavy sigh sufficed as she picked at the nothingness on my face.

In my opinion, she was only still in my personal space

because she wasn't quite ready to part ways. Her fear of my departure after we dressed was in vain. I wasn't going anywhere, yet, and neither was she.

"You're not returning to Roulette."

"Okay."

That simple. She didn't fight me on the decision. That was new, but it was perfect timing. That smart-ass mouth had toned down tremendously.

I wasn't sure if it was the dick I was giving her or the facade wearing off. Eden was all smoke and mirrors. Baby was gentle at her core. She craved attention, affection, time, and energy just like any other woman with a person she cared deeply for.

"Where are you going when you leave and when will I see you again?"

So fucking predictable. Eden was easy. Quality time was her language of love. Though I didn't have much of it, I pushed shit aside to make more.

"Wherever I'm headed, you're going with me."

"Really? Where?"

"It doesn't matter, Choc. Don't start with the questions. Just know that when you're with me, you're safest."

"I know," she admitted, stepping back and taking me in. "Done."

"Yeah?" My eyebrows raised. Relieved, I didn't bother shutting off the water before I stepped out of the shower and onto the plush rug. I'd been held captive way too long.

"Don't act like you didn't want to be in here with

me!" Eden yelled over her shoulder as she turned the knob to disable the water. "You love the silence. The calm. The–"

"Which is why we're headed out, so we can have uninterrupted time together. More calm. More quiet. More comfort. You don't have to hold me hostage in a fucking shower for that. All you have to do is ask."

I tossed a towel in her direction and grabbed the second one for me.

"Technically, I didn't hold you hostage. I—"

"Just shut up, Choc, and come on. We have shit to do."

"Like pack. How many day—"

"Don't insult me. You don't need anything when you're with me. Are you hard of hearing or some shit, baby?"

I took her by the hand leading her into the bedroom where we both began to get dressed. The same slow tunes she'd cut on before we headed to the shower were playing in the background, setting the tone for our day. It was gloomy and gray, the perfect weather for the mood we both seemed to be in.

My cell chimed on the nightstand where I'd left it. A peek at the screen and I noticed Aden's name. He'd sent a text, likely assuring me he was downstairs and waiting whenever Eden and I were ready.

I quickly realized I wasn't the only one interested in my screen. Eden's neck stretched as she studied it as well.

"My driver," I explained.

"Hm?"

"If it's another woman you're worried about, then stop worrying right now."

"What are you talking about?" She tried walking off, downplaying her inquisitiveness.

I pulled her long ass right back, wedging my chin between her neck and shoulder. Before sinking my teeth into her skin, I reminded her of the obvious.

"I'm all yours. For now. Forever. This lifetime and the next. Now that you're in my system, I can't shake you. And frankly, there's no room for anyone else. My heart is full, Choc."

Her confidence spiked as I freed her. It was in her walk. And the words that left her mouth next.

"It'll be trouble if you ever tried to shake me," she claimed, switching toward the closet.

You're trouble, Choc. Don't matter whether I was trying to shake your fine ass or not.

She tossed me a brand-new pair of her socks. Without complaint, I slid them on my feet.

"You were right."

"Me?" she questioned. "That's nothing new, Chemistry. You have to be a little more specific."

"What's with you calling me by my full firs—"

"Taylor called you by your full name and you had nothing to say about it. Please don't piss me off again. I'm growing tired of thinking about how smitten she was with you."

"You wouldn't be exhausted if you'd handled your business." Shrugging, I continued, "And nothing is wrong with you calling me Chemistry. I prefer it. I like the way it sounds coming from your mouth."

"Good, because you look so much more like Chemistry."

"It's the same thing as Chem, Choc." I laughed, folding my hands in front of me while watching her finish up.

Stopping momentarily, she peered in my direction. "What was I right about?"

"I'm an older sibling."

"I could tell from the moment I met you."

"How?"

"Your demeanor. It probably sounds weird, but the older children are always natural caretakers. Despite your grumpiness, I saw the true Chemistry. That's who I trusted with my life that night."

"What about now?"

"It doesn't matter what Chemistry I'm getting, I know they all mean me well now. I trust you, wholly. More than I've ever trusted anyone in my life."

"Seven girls."

"Hm?"

"Seven girls. My father had seven girls, all younger than me."

"So, you have seven sisters? Seven whole siblings?"

"Seven sisters. Eleven siblings. I was raised by my father. I have four brothers who were raised by their grandfather. Our mother committed suicide and murdered my stepfather before she did it. That's where we're headed."

"To meet your sisters?"

"No. To visit my brothers. It's not often I'm allotted time to see them, but there are times I force myself to drop everything for them. It's important to me they understand their positions in my life have never and will never change."

Eden stilled, taking in all the information I was dishing. After a few seconds, she was active, again.

"You know, Chemistry, you have so many layers to you. I wonder if I'll ever finish peeling them back."

"You won't."

"I couldn't agree more."

She ruffled the sheets, patting them down for any items. I grabbed the other ends, straightening them on the bed as she did the same. Once it was made, we both moved to the floor where underwear and random items had tumbled.

"Where are they?"

"Berkeley."

With a nod, she replied, "Berkeley is nice."

"It's where I was born."

"I'll admit I'm both surprised and honored to be on the receiving end of these new developments. You're so guarded. So hard to penetrate."

"I have my reasons."

"I understand."

"This is my family, Choc. I don't fuck around when it comes to them. None of them. When you step out of that door out there, everything you know, see, hear, or learn about them must be locked into a vault somewhere in the back of your brain—never to be opened, mentioned... nothing.

"This is not up for negotiation. I'm not silent because I simply want to be. I'm silent because I have to be. I have people to protect. Continuing this thing with me means you're vowing to do the same."

She paused, peering at me with sincerity in those big eyes of hers.

"As much as I can, I'll protect the things and people you love. Cross my heart, hope to die."

A hand crossed her chest.

No matter how invincible you think you are, you're human, son. And there's only so much you can do.

Her words reminded me of my father's.

"Fair enough. Are you ready?"

Tittering, she shook her head. "I'm a woman, baby. You have seven sisters, have you learned anything from them?"

"In other words, you'll be awhile?"

"Not exactly, but at least another fifteen minutes. Would you like orange juice or something else from the fridge while you wait?"

"A bottle of water. I'll get it. Just finish up in here."

A kiss landed on my cheek as I stalked across the room toward the door. My stomach flipped four times.

This fucking girl, man. My face flushed with heat. The feeling was inexplicable.

"Soooo, he blushes," she announced in celebration.

I didn't respond. Her fridge was the first stop. After grabbing a bottle of water, I headed up the set of stairs that led to the loft area above the kitchen. I'd gone over the floor plan several times before ever stepping foot in her place, but seeing was believing.

The very simple, minimalist decor in the space made it look more expansive than it was. White sheets lined the guest bed. A mirror covered nearly the entire wall opposite the bed. I imagined our naked bodies tangled in the sheets and reflected in the mirror.

I took a seat in the chair near the corner that was surrounded by faux greenery. The warmth of Eden's home made it clear no amount of rooms, expensive pieces of furniture, oversized televisions, staff members, or square feet could make a house a home. It was the people within the space. I'd spent years in my residence, and there hadn't been a time I felt grounded the way I had when I stepped inside Eden's space. The feeling hadn't subsided.

I lost track of time, lost myself in my thoughts as I rested my mind and body on the upper level. Rather had noticed the progress of my mental capacity and the positive effects Eden was having on me. Though she hadn't realized my progression was due to companionship until Roulette revealed that detail, she noticed the change. That sat well with me.

You'll fail. You're not equipped to love anyone. Not even yourself.

Quiet.

Grunting, I sipped from the bottle.

It won't work. You're the devil himself. She's an angel.

Quiet. I shook my head, focusing on the good parts of the unruly thoughts.

She is.

But, she's a woman. You can't tr–

"Quiet."

"Hm?" Eden startled me. I hadn't heard her come up.

Deflection was my only ally. Jewels I'd purchased clung to her skin. She looked as amazing as I'd imagined she would dripped in ice. She was slowly transforming from an extraordinary woman to one who reeked of wealth and entitlement. The haughty kind. The kind I desired.

I didn't mind a woman with expensive taste. I had the budget. The only niggas who didn't were those who couldn't satisfy the bill. I preferred my women established, entitled, expensive, and egotistical. Nose in the air and hand out every chance she got. Because, anything she wanted from me, she could have.

Additionally, it led me to believe most niggas didn't have the financial range to fuck with her or fuck on her. Though Eden was the first to check every box, I'd determined my type through the years as I floated through the sea of women beckoning for my attention and getting my dick as a result. It was almost all I ever had to offer until now.

"Is black your favorite color?"

She nodded, confirming what I'd known all along.

"Do you like the Chanel bag?"

"I love it."

"Figured you could use a black bag for the countless black pieces you have."

"Thoughtful," she responded, smiling with her entire body.

"Are you ready, Choc?"

"Yes."

I took her by the hand when I stood. She trailed close behind as I descended the stairs. She wore slim black pants and a black, snug shirt that exposed her navel. Not even the models in Paris were fucking with Eden. I was still in yesterday's clothes, but there were clothes waiting where we were headed.

On the elevator, I pulled Eden into me while planting myself in the corner so I could watch everything around us and so the view of the camera was obscured.

"Mister." She kissed my lips.

"Tell me your dreams, Choc."

Tossing her head back, she chuckled. When her eyes returned to me, the smile on her face softened. She understood quickly that comedy wasn't my intention.

"My dreams?"

"What do you want more than anything else in life?"

For a few seconds, she pondered.

"Ease."

"Ease? Explain, please."

"Ease. Life has its way of making me feel as though there isn't a better version possible. Or that I should be grateful for the one I have and not want a better one. So..." She paused, swallowing slowly. "A life of ease, that's the dream. That's my dream. I don't have this big, fancy idea of what life should or could be.

"No big dreams for me, Chemistry. Just... I just crave a more simple, less daunting life. One where I hardly lift a finger or don't feel guilty for lying in bed all day if my heart desires. Quietness. Calm. Slowness. I love that. I hate rushing through my skincare routine. Rushing through meals. Rushing to answer the phone. Rushing home. Everything is always moving so fast. In my dream, everything slows down. Even me."

"Sounds obtainable."

"I think it is. I don't think it'll happen in this lifetime, but maybe the next."

"Have you not learned anything about me, yet, Choc?" I asked, pushing the spiraled strand from her face.

She was rocking a ponytail, but it wasn't cascading down her back. It was her natural hair in a ball of some kind with two strands hanging in front.

"I have learned quite a bit."

"Then you should know that I wouldn't ask if I couldn't deliver."

The elevator doors had stood open for some time. They were preparing to close when I nodded toward the exit.

"We can stay right here for as long as you want or we can get moving."

Eden barely made it through them. They reopened fully, allowing me to pass through as well. We strolled across the lobby and out of the door where Aden was waiting. He widened the door of the truck and greeted Eden, simultaneously.

To avoid additional cameras, I slid in behind her instead of walking around to the other side. As soon as we settled, she continued the conversation we'd cut short.

"It's not your job to—"

"Eden, don't make me gag and bound you for talking senseless."

She didn't have a quick, witty remark, so she kept quiet.

"You didn't ask for the world, baby, though I was more than willing to give it to you. Your request was simple. You want peace and quiet. That's exactly what you'll have. I won't wait to give it to you, either. Consider it done. From this moment forward, nothing you desire will be out of reach for you. Tell me. Just tell me and I'll handle it."

"Who must I thank for creating you? They did a fine job."

"You'll meet him soon enough. I just have one question, Choc."

"What is it?"

"Does that include motherhood? The life you dream of?"

With a heavy sigh, she nodded. "Yes."

"Then it's settled."

Within the hour, we reached the small, private airport where the family's plane was gassed and waiting for our departure. I was the first out of the truck. Eden was next, stunning everyone within view with her never-ending legs and confidence. She trekked the runway beside me, looping our fingers and staying close enough for our arms to remain at our sides without stretching forward or backward.

"Mr. Childers."

"Wendy."

Staff waited on the tarmac for our arrival. As we boarded the plane, they filed inside behind us. Eden didn't loosen her grip on my hand until I showed her to her seat. Even then, she pulled me down with her, refusing to lose sight of me. I leaned over, lips to her ear, and teased.

"Did you use super glue?"

I lifted our hands, reminding her she was still holding onto me. She released me, finally.

"Sorry."

"Stop apologizing, baby. Is there anything you need before I head to the back?"

"To the back?"

"To rid myself of these clothes."

"I– I'm fine."

I leaned forward again, this time kissing her cheek before I reached her ear.

"Liar."

I grabbed her by the hand, forcing her out of the seat and toward the sleeping quarters where there were clothes and shoes waiting. I closed the door behind us and ushered her to the bed.

Easily reading Eden was becoming my favorite task. She wore her feelings on her sleeves now. Hiding them from me wasn't a chore she cared for. Her laziness was my secret weapon.

"Stop pouting, Choc."

Her lips parted and curved upward into a smile. "You think you know me so well."

"I could always know you better."

I discarded the clothes I had on, exchanging them for something more suitable. A pair of black denim, a Louis Vuitton top, and shoes that matched felt much better, and less restricting.

"The feeling is mutual."

"Thirty-six. Berkeley bred. Eldest of twelve. Mother committed suicide. Father– father won't be around too much longer," I shared, feeling an ache in my chest, but continuing anyway.

"A chemist. Earned my doctorate in five years. Swimmer. Could've been an Olympian but that wasn't where my heart was. Childless, *for now*. What else is there to know?"

"Since you put it that way, I guess there isn't much more you can tell me. Everything else is learned."

"Agreed. But I know hardly anything about you."

"Chemistry, I find that hard to believe."

"Fuck what I've discovered. Tell me what you want me to know."

"The middle child. I have a brother and sister, both took wrong turns in life and ended up on the wrong paths. Master's degree in social work. Discovered later that it wasn't the career path I wanted to continue down. Quit and stayed home for a while and then boredom consumed me. After leading a black-and-white life, I wanted a bit of color. That led me to Roulette."

"And then, me."

"And then you," she uttered with her lips puckered. Her eyes wandered until she broke into a full smile.

"Fuck you smiling so hard for, Choc?"

"You tell me, first, then I'll tell you."

I dipped my head, shaking it from one side to the other. My smile was so fucking big, the sides of my lips were beginning to crack. Whatever voodoo she'd put on my ass was strong and wasn't letting up.

"Come on. We have to get back up front or the plane will never take off."

She started behind me, baffled by my declaration.

"Why not?"

"Because..." I paused as we crossed into the cockpit. "No one will be up here to get it off the ground."

"Chemis– Chemistry. Yo– you're– Wait."

Eden was lost for words, stuttering like a kid with a speech impediment.

"Sit there and grab a headset."

She sat down where she'd been instructed and grabbed the headset.

"You chose water."

I was instantly taken back to the conversation we'd had some time ago.

"Because I have arms and legs, not wings. But, I never said I couldn't fly."

"You're full of surprises, Mister."

That smile returned, stopping my heart momentarily.

"Would you have it any other way?"

She shook her head from side to side.

"Good. Now, settle down and put on the headset. Tour the beauty of the state of Huffington, shall we?"

"Yes. Please."

I began the pre-flight checklist as she adjusted.

"Checklist complete," I confirmed, speaking into the headset. Daniel was on the receiving end, waiting for my signal.

"Childers 3082, cleared for takeoff," Daniel responded.

"Staff, prepare for takeoff," I warned everyone onboard. "Choc, keep your eyes open. You don't want to miss the views as we ascend."

The plane started down the runway, and slowly, the nose tipped toward the sky. Our speed increased and so did our altitude as the wheels lifted from the ground.

"Wheels up."

We continued to climb until we neared the clouds. Once we'd reached the designated height, I was able to relinquish control.

"How are you, Eden?"

I turned around, watching her cheeks peak and her thumb rise.

"I'm well."

"If you look to the right, you'll see the Holy Woman statue. Straight ahead is the Cambridge Connect, the longest, highest bridge in Clarke. It leads to three cities in Huffington. One bridge, three cities. She's a beauty."

"She is."

"Cambridge Clearwater River is just beneath her. As hard as it is to believe, the water is drinkable. Scoop a cup and you can see right through it."

"You feel so far away," she said into her headset, staring daggers in the side of my face.

"I'm not, Choc. I'm right here."

I extended my arm and placed my hand on her knee. She rested her hand on top of mine.

"Right here."

Her body relaxed against my palm. Whatever was troubling her pressed forward, giving her a chance to enjoy the moment, enjoy me. That's all I wanted for us both. With time, she grew more comfortable and began pointing out familiar structures herself. We've delved into the history of our city and others we passed through on our route.

Every wonder of Huffington that was in our path, I was sure to give Eden an aerial view of. We arrived in Berkeley unscathed and in one piece. Fresh off the plane, we piled into the Bentayga and headed for my residence in The Highlands.

THE GREYLIST

The clock struck eight before I could get a grip on time. Nevertheless, tardiness wasn't excusable, so I was dressed and waiting when Eden descended the stairs in a pair of pants that widened tremendously at the bottom. Her shirt was silk, cut deep down the middle, and tucked in her pants. The risk of boob exposure added a bit of excitement to our night.

I'd have a time watching and waiting for the moment it announced itself and declared the end of our night. Because at the moment, I wouldn't be able to stop my dick from tearing through my briefs in an attempt to pleasure Eden.

Red soles added character to her attire. She was the prettiest. Her hair was pushed behind her ears, hanging down her back with swirls and swooshes lining her face. Not a hair was out of place. The new earrings I'd gifted her upon arrival were perfect, and so was the clutch that was part of a large wardrobe that was prepared in her absence. It would remain at the house in The Highlands for our impromptu visits.

"Sorry, I took so long. My hair," she explained, standing in front of me.

"No need to explain, Choc. It was worth the wait."

"You like it?"

"I do."

Bashfully, she dipped her head. I lifted her chin. "Let's ride."

Hand in hand, we exited. Shortly after, we were cruising through the streets of Berkeley, having ditched the driver.

My city. It didn't matter how long I resided in Clarke, Berkeley would be home forever. The nostalgia was disheartening. The memories made my time in the city more complicated than it needed to be. But, I was determined to diminish their effects this time around. Eden was with me. Things would be different.

My phone lit up the cupholder. Choc's eyes were on it before I could see who it was calling. It was becoming abundantly clear she'd experienced things she hadn't talked about, yet. Someone had led her to believe men were cheaters, all of them. She was responding to trauma. It wasn't her fault, but I wanted the head of the nigga whose fault it was.

"Who fucked with your heart?"

She whipped her neck in my direction. "Hm?"

"Hm. You heard me, Choc. A name."

"Chemistry, you can't go shooting everyone I've crossed paths with."

"You really don't fucking know me." I scoffed. "A name."

I picked up the phone, seeing it was Pops. I didn't want to keep him waiting, but she wasn't off the hook, either. If she didn't give me a name, I'd start digging myself.

"Pops, good evening."

"Heard you're in town and haven't been by to see your old man. You're not too big for me to lay you across my knee."

"I got big guns now."

"Then I hope you know how to use them." He chuckled.

"I do. But I haven't been here long. A few hours. I'm meeting those knuckleheads for dinner. Before I leave, I'll be over."

"Alright, just making sure you haven't forgotten about me."

"Impossible."

"Well, I'll see you, then."

"See ya."

I ended the call, ready to continue the conversation. Eden wasn't interested. She hiked the music playing on the radio station, caring nothing about the genre or tune. To my dismay, it was some bullshit. Thankfully, we weren't very far from *Saint*, the restaurant of choice.

TEN

Eden

Dark faces surrounded me, all standing as I took my seat along with a woman who was in possession of the type of soft skin other women dreamed of. I didn't have to touch it. The texture was visible from every side of the table.

Anna. Chemistry had introduced us seconds prior. She was as gorgeous as her name and just as elegant. The strappy top she wore with a skirt to match was the perfect combination. It said a hell of a lot without saying very much. Her slim frame seemed glued to her husband's hip. Their happiness was apparent.

From the tip of her head to the soles of her feet, she loved him deeply and that was quite obvious. The adoration was on full display. Longing stares, touches, and words. She clung to everything he said though it wasn't much. Milo and Makai, they'd said more than Chemistry and Malachi combined.

They'll never hear it from me, I promised myself while settling in my chair and watching the men around me do the same.

Though every bit of information was crucial to the investigation I was part of, this was a piece they'd never have. I'd meant every word I said to Chem. To the best of my ability, I'd protect what he loved.

I waited for the waitress to appear and collect our orders, thirsty for something with a slight kick to get me over the hump I was struggling with. Beautiful black men, all resembling the one I was growing closer to each day, had all lost the most important person in their worlds at a point in time.

To see them well and thriving was a blessing in itself. Yet, my heart still broke for them. My father passed away years ago, while I was a fully grown woman, yet his death knocked the life out of me. For an entire year and a half, I struggled to get off the couch and rejoin life. Aside from work, I was failing at everything else in my life when he left us.

Since Chemistry entered my world, I felt like something within me had been restored. To discover he was the man behind the case who would make or break my career as an agent was like thorns to the heart. Of course, I wanted to advance in my career, but I was beginning to believe I wanted what he was offering me even more.

Don't think like that. I tried, but it was useless.

"So, Eden, correct?" Anna began as drinks approached us before being set on the table.

We hadn't ordered anything. I hadn't, at least.

"Thank you." Baffled, I smiled at the loving staff.

My eyes wandered, but didn't have far to travel before they landed on their mark.

"Everything was prearranged," Chem explained.

With a nod, I turned and faced Anna. "Yes. Eden."

"Such a beautiful name. Are you enjoying Berkeley so far?" She sipped from her glass with the sugared rim. I did the same, loving the silkiness of her voice. I wanted her to continue.

"It's only been a few hours, but yes. So far so good. Any time I get to relax in a city other than my own, I'm all for it. That's also when the exhaustion shows its true colors."

"That's true. What is it you do?"

I hesitated, unable to share my true occupation. I had to settle for something less satisfying, less truthful. But, just as the words formed, Chem cleared his throat.

"Nothing."

Anna's chin tipped toward him. Her brows pulled inward and her mouth slacked as she waited for him to explain. "Nothing?"

"Or whatever she wants. She's still undecided but if it's left up to me, *nothing*."

Malachi placed his glass on the table, agreeing with his brother. "You remind me more and more just how much we think the same."

"Wouldn't have it any other way." Chem shrugged.

"And you?" I asked Anna.

"Nothing." Malachi sniggered, picking his drink up again.

She smiled, taking another sip from hers and nodding. She couldn't deny the allegations and I didn't want her to, either. If this was what ease looked like for a woman, then I was ready to submit–to the lifestyle, to the person who could provide it, and to my aspirations of acquiring it.

"For the most part, but I help my husband manage his business otherwise."

A life of leisure. She was the poster girl and I'd noticed it from the moment of her entry. She was waiting on hand and foot. The men made her the center of their attention when she was around and everyone stopped to listen when she spoke. She was treated like a literal Goddess and to have the same treatment was blowing my mind.

They're different, I surmised. *These men are different.*

The lone fact that they were his brothers catapulted me into a new space. I saw things from all angles and knew from experience that involving yourself with a person meant involving yourself with their family as well. Most people positioned themselves as acts in the circus that had multiple shows a year, all featuring family members with a hundred tricks up their sleeves.

Second-hand embarrassment was shameful until it knocked on their doorstep. And then, instead of laughing at the family shenanigans, you were part of them. Voluntarily or involuntarily. From deadbeat grandparents to uncles who needed to be underneath the jail for their crimes against the youth of the family, I'd seen and heard it all, and even investigated some.

Nothing about this family stood out to me. Nothing screamed for me to run for the hills. Nothing tried to convince me I didn't belong at their family reunions, dripped in diamonds just like the ones Anna was covered in, with my head high and my belly swollen.

My family had drifted apart slowly as my sister and brother got deeper on their paths to nowhere. When my father died, that was the end of us. My mother, grandmother, aunts, and one of my uncles were the only family I was clinging to. The idea of joining one three times as big, wealthy, and sophisticated excited me.

"Any children?"

"Not yet, but someday soon, I imagine."

I wasn't sure why my eyes scoped out Malachi. The smile on his face as she said those words made it clear to me that he couldn't wait until the day.

"You?"

They landed on Chemistry next. He waited, unmoving until I responded.

"Not yet, but someday soon, I imagine."

Dramatically, Anna nodded, lifting her palm for me to match. Her fingers curled around mine as she slowly shook my hand back and forward. Chemistry stared daggers into my heart, but his satisfaction was notable.

More servers joined us as Milo and Makai returned to the table. They'd stepped away as everyone got situated in their seats. Appetizers of all kinds were placed in the center for us to freely indulge. The salmon bites were first on my list of treasures.

"You niggas ain't spiked my shit, have you? Because I'd go home with you willingly," Makai began, sipping from his cup.

"If we did, it's far too late now. You've killed it."

"Just keep it PG and have something rolled. I don't mind being kidnapped."

"Shut up, Makai," Milo suggested. "Stop acting like a fucking fool in front of company."

"If she's at this table with this nigga, she ain't company, Milo. She's family." He pointed out.

"Fact," Chem agreed.

"What's your name again?" Makai asked.

"Don't bother," Milo warned me.

"E–"

"Eclipse. Right. Right."

The table grew silent, everyone staring in Makai's direction. It was apparent he was the life of the party, the one to bring joy and laughter to the incredibly serious and highly sensitive nature of his family. And I enjoyed that.

"Yeah. Eclipse." I laughed. "Mountain. My name is Eclipse."

"Ahhhh. A sense of humor. I like her, ugly ass nigga," he claimed, speaking to Chem.

"Niggas been dropping 'bout liking her. I don't think that's the one to like, Makai." Chemistry shook his head as he fired off with a warning.

Oh God. Please, I begged inside.

"It's Mountain," he teased. "Standing tall– wide a–"

"My safety is not on, Makai. Don't fuck with me."

"She said it. I didn't."

"Fuck you."

"See, I knew I shouldn't have had that drink. I'm feeling a little woozy and you hollering out suspect ass shit like that. Milo, please don't let him take me home. You hear that bass in his voice? I'm going to have a long night if he doe–"

"Makai, please." Anna sighed. "Eden, forget everything he just said. Makai is the... *special one* of the bunch."

At once, he quieted. The utmost respect being for the woman at a table full of men had my cheeks aiming for my eyes.

"Now that he's quiet, we should all toast to Chemistry and his very interesting venture," she announced, holding her drink up into the sky.

"That's not going to cut it, baby. We need a few bottles. Shit like this doesn't happen often," Malachi stated, immediately searching for a server to put in the request.

"You're right." Anna lowered her glass.

"Has it always been that bad?" I whispered to Anna, wondering why it was so hard for everyone to believe Chemistry was seeing someone and things were serious enough to be introduced to part of the family.

"Worse," Anna shared. "And I mean that with love. Chemistry swore he'd never fall for a woman, let alone trust one with his heart again."

"Again?"

"Catherine."

Nodding, I digested everything she'd said. Gazing at Chem, I gushed at the pure contentment on his face. He was in his comfort zone. He was happy here.

With pursed lips, I blew an air kiss. His teeth peeked through his bashful smile. In a swift motion, he grabbed the kiss I'd blown, mid-air, and placed it on his chest, right over his heart.

Bottles in buckets of ice sat beside each man at the table. At once, the corks were removed and the champagne glasses were filled from one end of the table to the other. Silently, the servers waited for our glasses to lift.

"To Chemistry and Eden," Anna chanted.

"To Chemistry and Eden," everyone else joined.

"To us," I mouthed, facing the man himself.

"To us," he repeated.

Empty glasses barely hit the table before they were filled again. Chatter began and didn't end until dessert was cleared and we began dispersing from the table. I didn't have a single complaint. The appetizers, entree, and dessert were all pleasant.

I found it hard to leave the people I'd shared the last two hours with when it was time to depart. I clung to Chemistry's arm, trying to stop my head from spinning as we made our way out of the door. My head leaned onto his shoulder when we finally made it to the valet station where the truck we were in was being pulled around, along with the cars of the others in our party.

I watched Malachi and Anna speed off into the darkness.

I want that type of love. Visions of Chem and I ten years from now felt irrational, but they still played in my head as the tail lights got further and further away from us.

Milo and Makai were next. They'd rode together. Rubber burned as they exited the lot. Chem and I were last to go. He held the door open, waiting for me to climb in. As he locked the seatbelt around my body, his lips caressed mine. Passion erupted as emotions encouraged the vulnerability between us both.

"Hi." I breathed heavily when he finally released me.

"Hi."

Unable to contain myself, I wrapped my arms around him, peering into those dark rounds, searching for his depths. Searching for his core.

"I enjoy spending my days with you."

"You have the rest of them to spend with me, Choc."

"Yeah?"

With a nod, he responded.

"I admire the love between Anna and Malachi. It's so pure. So effortless."

"They've been together since they were kids. If you've never seen soulmates, there you have it." He tipped his head in the direction they'd gone in. "In this lifetime and the next."

"Do you ever dream of a love like that? Like theirs?"

"I never dreamed of love a day in my life, Eden."

Disappointment scrunched my nose and brows.

"Until you," he continued, finally bandaging my pain. "And it's nothing like what my brother has because that's theirs. What I want with you, for us, is something unlike anything else. Monumental. A little dysfunctional, possibly. Very fucking intense. Unshakable. Unbreakable.

"Something that can't be penetrated. Something solid. Something real and unconditional. Something that remains the same through the good, bad, ugly, and unfathomable. Something misunderstood by most, but makes perfect fucking sense to us. Is that something you dream of, Eden?"

"Yes."

It was like he'd stolen the vision right out of my head. One word in particular stuck out to me.

Unconditional.

In a perfect world, he'd mean that in every way, and what was on the verge would only be an obstacle we both used to build our bond. But, that was a perfect world and we didn't live in one. Once everything erupted, I'd be happy to still have breath in my body. Even that would be a blessing because having Chem wouldn't be in the prayers of things God granted me.

"You're staring," I teased.

"Can you blame me?"

I shook my head. "I'm guilty, too, thinking about the things I want you to do to me tonight."

"I'm thinking about the number of zeros that'll be absent from my account after tomorrow."

"Tomorrow?"

"We're shopping, Choc. So, after I fuck you good, I need you to sleep good because we have a long day ahead of us."

Learning how freely he moved in Berkeley was rewarding. He was quieter, less visible in Clarke. If you weren't searching extremely hard for him, then you wouldn't find him. He was invisible.

"Yes, sir."

After another peck on the lips, he made his way around to the driver's side. 6lack played as we cruised through Berkeley. The city was beautiful with a skyline worth drooling over. Chemistry took the scenic route, in hardly a rush to get back to the immaculate home we'd be in during our stay.

This is it.

The sunroof was pulled back, blowing my hair in the wind. I reached out, catching it in the palm of my hand. Equanimity calmed my being. Freedom toyed with my happiness. If only life for me was as simple as this late-night, slightly inebriated night with Chem, all would be well.

For now, I'd pretend. Because it felt better than anything I'd ever felt before. Both hands out of the sunroof led me to my knees. I climbed onto the armrest, sticking my upper body into the open air. April was such a beautiful time of the year. The temperature was perfect.

Everything was still as it prepared for the transition from winter to spring. Signs of life were noticed. Color began visiting the colorless parts of nature that the cold had ruined. All was well. There was restoration after such a brutal season.

This is everything.

Chem's hand snaked up my leg, halting on my ass. He held me steady, making sure the alcohol I'd consumed didn't interfere with the moment.

He's everything.

I wanted to drown in his affection. Fall freely for his love. Surround myself with his happiness. Lay in his contentment. And contribute to his never-ending gratification.

My God this feels good.

The wind chilled my cheeks as Chemistry warmed my heart. I fought to stay in the moment, forgetting everything that could destroy it or destroy us for just a minute. My eyes closed, slowly, and my head tilted backward.

God, please, let us be okay when the dust settles. I can't bear the thought of him hating me, not when I want his love more than anything I've ever wanted in my life. Please.

Suddenly, the distance between us was overwhelming. In a swift motion, I lowered myself into the truck and into his arms.

"Baby," he called out, remaining poised.

The lack of control of the wheel mattered none as I planted my head between his neck and shoulder. I wrapped my hands around him, pressing our bodies against each other. If any way possible, his skin was my destination. I wanted inside.

"Eden, what's the wrong, baby?"

"Nothing," I admitted. "Everything is right."

Almost. Almost everything.

Silently, we continued our journey. I never returned to my seat. He'd become my resting place.

Upon our arrival, we filed out of the car. My feet never touched the ground. He carried me, with my legs wrapped around his waist and my arms around his neck, to the front of the truck. The door of the house was just too far away for us both.

My eyes were heavy with lust, my center throbbing to the point of discomfort. His dick was threatening to bust through his slacks. We wouldn't make it. It was now that our unity was required.

When my back collided with the warmth of the hood, I winced, slightly, but recovered as the heat began melting my juices. They soiled the thong between my ass cheeks.

"Cheeeeeeem," I moaned, feeling the wind hit my nipple. It was in his mouth a millisecond later.

Quickly, he undressed me, never parting ways with my breasts. From one to the other, he switched back and forth, making me delirious with desperation. Conflict developed with each second passed. I wasn't sure if I wanted Chem buried in my mouth or my walls. I was still deciding when I felt his warm meat against my leg. But, as it tapped against my clit, it became very clear where he wanted to be.

"I want it in my mouthhhh." I winced as he entered me.

"I'll put it wherever you want me to, Choc. Just let me inside for now."

My body parted for him, making way for his girth. Weeks and weeks and weeks and weeks with him and he hadn't disappointed me yet. Mentally, physically, emotionally, sexually.

"I've got plans for us," he groaned, taking my ear between his lips. "So many fucking plans."

The sincerity in his voice tap danced on my heart. I knew he meant every word. It was the fact I also knew we'd never get to live them out that made it hurt.

ELEVEN

Eden

Detangling our limbs on the second day of our trip was more complicated than we'd imagined. We tried again on day three. Success had evaded us both. It wasn't until the fourth day that we managed to pull ourselves together and make it beyond the threshold of the bedroom with the intent to leave the house once and for all.

The aroma that filled the home and the lack of warmth next to me helped me down the stairs and into the kitchen. I leaned against the entryway, staring at the man who'd held me captive the last few days. His slim frame swayed from one side to the other as Jay Z played in the background. Word for word, he spat as the rapper talked about imaginary players in the game.

The same mouth he used to sample the meat he was cooking had devoured me six times since we'd made it to the beautiful home I learned was his. Two floors, a left and right-wing, seven bedrooms, ten bathrooms, a sauna, an indoor pool, a six-car garage, a pond, two balconies, a theater, an entertainment room, two kitchens, a fully furnished basement that served as a third floor, and so many other things about the home had made me fall in love. The walk-in fridge and pantry he'd had stocked before our arrival were among my favorite parts.

"You going to just stand there watching me, or are you going to join me?" Chem asked, never looking up from the skillet.

"I'm still deciding."

"I've waited long enough for you to wake, Choc. Don't make me wait any longer."

I cleared the distance, nearly sprinting to his side. He pulled me in and leaned down to plant a wet kiss on my lips. He released me too quickly. I stuck around, standing behind him as my hands roamed his stomach and chest. I laid my head on his back, inhaling his scent, exhaling, and then inhaling again.

"Good morning."

"Good morning, Choc. How'd you sleep?"

"Well, until I noticed I was alone."

"I heard your stomach growling in your sleep, so I knew you'd be hungry when you woke up. I have to feed you."

"Shut up, seriously?"

"I'm not in the kitchen just to be here right now. Yes, seriously."

My cheeks flushed as I buried my face in his shirt. "Argh. What are we having?"

My words were muffled but still easy to make out.

"Chicken quesadillas. Something to hold us over while we shop. We're having dinner tonight."

Dinner was Chemistry's favorite time of the day.

"You love dinner so much."

"It is my favorite meal of the day, yes."

"Why?"

"Because, by dinner, my day is done. I can sit down without as nearly as much on my mind or plate as there was when I sat down for breakfast or lunch. It's my time. I cherish those moments."

"As you should. Slowly, it's becoming my favorite part of the day, too."

"We're not as different as you think."

"Yet, we are."

"I won't deny that. How is this?"

He forked a piece of chicken and turned around with the fork aimed at my lips. I opened, accepting the serving.

"Ummmmm. Yes. That's perfect."

Juicy. Tender. Seasoned to perfection. I didn't need bread and cheese with it. The chicken was perfect all on its own.

Chem turned off the burner and slid the skillet to the other side of the eight-burner stove. It was massive and I'd tried to make it down more than once to use it, but I was unsuccessful. However, the dinner we'd collectively cooked last night was worth the wait. The stove itself was a beast. If you weren't careful or had anything up slightly higher than it should be, you'd regret it. Chem had jeopardized our potatoes twice, but they survived.

"Can I help?"

"No, thank you, Eden. All I need is for you to have a seat at the table and wait for me to serve you. Water or lemonade?"

"Lemonade?"

"Made it this morning," he informed me.

"Will you ever stop doing that?" I asked, planting my head in his shirt again.

"What's that, baby?"

"All the right things."

"I'll try my hardest not to. I've gotten it wrong a hundred times before, Choc. This time is different and I just want to get it right. Over and over again."

"Thank you."

"Don't thank me. You deserve it."

"You deserve it."

I'd learned a few things about Chem and nothing bothered me more than his lack of entitlement as his life pertained to love and companionship. He found it difficult to accept as if he wasn't worthy of either. He was wrong. All wrong. And with the little time we had, I'd show him.

"Not talking about me."

"I am. And I want you to know you, too, deserve it. Okay?"

He paused, turning his body around to get a glimpse

of me. In his arms was exactly where I wanted to spend the rest of my days. I stared up at those dark eyes.

"Okay?"

"Whatever you say, Choc."

"Yes, Choc," I corrected him.

"Yes, Choc."

I stood on the tips of my toes and pecked his forehead, right cheek, left cheek, and then finally his lips. After lowering, I did as I'd been instructed and had a seat at the massive table that had the ability to sit at least twelve.

Chemistry joined me five minutes later with piping-hot quesadillas and a glass of water. His chiming phone reminded me to check mine for notifications. It was time for me to check in with my mother. Suffering through my absence while I was working cases was the bane of her existence. She despised each passing day we didn't make contact.

However, completely disconnecting from my world was necessary to see things through and tap into my aliases. But, somehow, Chemistry made it difficult not to think of her, want to call her and hear her voice. Everything about this case was different from the others.

"A penny for your thoughts."

I didn't realize how long I'd been spaced out until he pulled me from my head where I'd tucked pieces of my reality. My quesadilla was halfway gone and the bottle of water was a few sips away from emptiness.

"Returning my mother's call. I'll do that when we make it back to th–"

"Do it now."

"No, she won't mind. I—"

"Do it now, Eden. That wasn't a suggestion."

It was a demand.

"I–I don't have my phone. It's upst—"

Before I could finish the sentence, he'd left me alone. In a flash, he was gone. With a shake of my head, I finished my meal and waited for the inevitable. Calls were prohibited in his presence. Chem made sure my phone was powered off or on airplane mode whenever he was around. He never answered or made calls either. However, being in Berkeley changed everything.

Only a minute had passed and he was back, in front of me, and seated with my phone on the table in front of me.

"If I could call my mother, I would. That's a privilege I won't let you or anyone else around me take for granted."

The pain was evident in his voice, in his eyes, and in his posture.

"Your father never remarried?"

"He did, to an amazing woman I love but she'll never be or never replace the woman that birthed me. That's a different type of love, Eden. Much different. I can't explain it, but as much as I love my stepmother, I love my mother a hundred times more.

"The love was engrained in me. It was automatic. I didn't have to learn to love her. The love was part of me. Part of my identity. It was big and bold and overwhelmingly expansive. No one could ever—" He sucked his teeth, and then continued. "I can't explain it, but you have a mother so you know exactly what I'm referring to."

"I do." Nodding, I confirmed.

"So, call her."

I unlocked my phone and instead of calling Pamela, the woman who was on standby and had been assigned by the agency as my alias' mother, I found myself dialing the number I knew so very well. If I didn't introduce them, I wouldn't be able to live with myself. If I fed Chem any more bullshit, than I'd been trained to, I wouldn't forgive myself.

He'd quickly become one of the most important people in my tiny world. She was the other one. It was imperative she had the chance to hear his voice and see his face. Exposing my identity was the least of my concerns. My mother never referred to me by my government name, especially while on assignment.

It didn't matter whether I was alone or in the company of someone else. That was her way of never slipping. It was also why she bit the bullet and allowed so much time to pass in between points of contact during cases.

After dialing her, I quickly erased the number and opened the FaceTime app where I tapped her name from the short list of calls I'd made, missed, or received. Art was right underneath. I made a mental note to call her before our time in Berkeley ended as well.

My heart galloped in my chest as I waited for her to answer. When the phone stopped ringing and her freckled face appeared behind a new set of glasses, it smiled. I smiled. And at a glance, I caught a glimpse of Chemistry's smile.

What? I mouthed.

"Nothing," he said, shaking his head.

"Evening, baby!" Excitedly, my mother greeted me.

Staring at her was like staring in a mirror. She was flawless and I'd inherited her beauty. If she was any indication of how I'd age, I was looking forward to it.

"Hi, Mom. I was calling to say hello."

"Well, thank you. I've been wondering when you'd ring my phone. I'm so happy to hear from you."

"Me, too. I have someone I'd like you to meet. I know this isn't ideal, but he's right here and I figure there's no point in waiting, right?"

"Right. Who is it, baby?"

"His name is Chemistry and he's the man responsible for the painful muscles in my face. I haven't stopped smiling since the day we met."

I watched as Chemistry folded under the pressure. He wasn't accustomed to praises. He was a mess hearing anyone gloat about his presence in their world and the massive difference he made. I could see that just by examining his discomfort. Yet and still, there were subtle signs of appreciation hidden in his sly smile.

"Easy, Eden," he pled, shaking his head.

"It's the truth, Chemistry. Accept it."

"You sound like my sister," he whispered.

"Take it from me, Chemistry. This call itself means it is very much the truth."

"Here."

I extended the phone. Hesitantly, he accepted it. I watched his face light up as my mother came into full view. He looked over at me, tilting his head with curious eyes.

"Splitting image."

"Yes," I agreed, chuckling.

"Hello," Chem greeted my mother, filling my heart to capacity.

"Hi."

"Nice to meet you as well, Mrs–"

Johanson, I wanted him to say, but knew that wouldn't happen.

"Reid," he finished.

Playing into the narrative, my mother said, "Nice to meet you as well, Mr.?"

"Childers."

"Good to know my daughter's last name," she joked.

Chemistry looked up at me under those busy brows. It was my turn to crumble under the stress.

"You're staring."

Blushing, I hid my smile behind my arm as I laid my head on the table.

"Eden Childers."

"Chemistry, please."

"Head up, Choc."

"Is that your home?"

My mother was obsessed with home improvement television. I kept her sanity most days. When I walked into Chem's second home, I knew she'd love it. I didn't blame her.

"It is."

"Oh, that is beautiful. I can't see it all, but the little bit I can see is gorgeous."

"We can change that," he told her.

"Change wha–"

"You can see it in person if you'd like. I can have a car there to get you in twenty minutes."

"No! Of course not. Maybe one day soon. For now, I want my daughter to enjoy her time with you. She deserves it."

"I keep telling her that."

"Don't worry, she hardly listens to me, either. Her father was the only person who could get through to her, I believe."

"Well, I'm trying to change that as we speak," Chemistry bragged.

We both knew the truth. He could get to me, through me, under me, on top of me, and inside of me. Wherever. Whatever. However. Whenever. Forever. Nothing mattered but his word nowadays.

"Good. Good. You're on the right track. I know that much, at least."

"We're about to get our day started. I'll talk to you later, Mom!" I yelled across the table as I stood, prepared to get dressed and outside.

"Alright. I love you, baby."

"I love you, too."

"Chemistry, nice meeting you and I look forward to meeting you."

"The feeling is mutual."

"Be safe, you two. Talk to you later."

"Later," Chemistry responded.

He extended my phone in my direction. As I tried retrieving it, he pulled me down onto his lap. My bare ass sat atop the fabric of his shorts. I was in one of his shirts, which didn't quite cover my bottom half.

"Fuck you going, Choc?"

His nose tickled my neck as he inhaled, consuming my scent.

"To put on some clothes so we can get our day started."

"Without me?"

"I'm afraid if you come, I'll never get dressed and we'll never make it out of the door."

"You have every right."

His rigidness lined my ass cheek.

"See."

My appetite for Chemistry felt insatiable. It didn't matter how much of him I had, I still wanted more. Today was more of the same. I untangled our limbs and stood up from the table, turning around so that I could free his dick.

"Promise we won't stay inside all day."

"I promise, baby."

"Five minutes."

"All I need is four."

I lowered until my knees touched the cold tiled floor.

Chemistry had grown a third leg in a matter of seconds. Saliva pooled in my mouth at the sight of the dark, slightly discolored at the tip, missile.

"You gon' stare at it or put that motherfucker in your mouth?"

The strain of his features revealed his desperation. Making him wait wasn't part of my plan. But, I'd be damned if I didn't openly admire the prettiest piece of meat I'd ever had the pleasure of tasting. I put him out of his misery, opening wide and shoving him into my mouth until he reached the back of my throat.

"Shit."

His fingers curled around the loose bun I'd thrown up before coming downstairs. He pushed past physical boundaries, challenging me to swallow more of him. My gag reflex was activated instantly. Simultaneously, tears stung my eyes. Saliva trickled from my mouth when he pulled his dick from my mouth. Immediately after, he shoved it in, again, repeating the same movement.

"Fuck, Choc."

He released me, allowing me to slide up and down his shaft with teary eyes and enough saliva to drown an ant hill. A blubbering mess, I circled his head and transformed into a human suction cup, ready to bring his semen to the tip of his dick only to leave it there. I wanted it so deep within me, I'd need a month's worth of emergency contraceptive pills to extract it.

The bulge started from his nut sack rose with every stroke of my neck. Blindly, I searched for his hand. Upon locating it, I guided it toward the back of my head, urging him to exert his authority.

His ass lifted from the chair as he began to fuck my mouth, slowly but forcefully. The grip on my hair tightened the second our eyes locked. His nostrils widened and brows furrowed. Even scrunched, his face was still so beautiful. He was still so precious.

"Goddamn, Choc."

The bulge neared the tip. My time on my knees had ended. I had a job to do and I'd done it well. In a swift motion, I removed him from my mouth. Saliva trailed from my face to the head of his dick. My erratic breathing, running nose, and teary eyes were all condoning my belief that I'd carried out the task well. Slowly, I stood, climbed onto the chair, and grabbed Chem's throbbing manhood.

Staring into his now hooded eyes, I positioned him right at my opening. His lids joined each other, halting my motion.

"Look at me," I demanded.

He was barely able to open his eyes, thoroughly intoxicated by our entanglement.

"Chemistryyyy—"

He pulled me down onto him, entering me with vengeance. I planted both feet beside him, balancing myself on the chair. My hands rested on his shoulders. My eyes never left his.

Up and down, I stroked his dick just how he loved it. Slow. Methodical. Magical. A hand wrapped around my neck, bringing me down to his lips. He kissed mine, exploring my mouth as if it was foreign territory. And then, suddenly, he pulled back. Our eyes met, again.

"I'm about to cum all in this pussy, Choc. Keep fucking me just like that."

Obliging, I continued rubbing against my clit internally, using his dick to caress my insides.

"Fuuuuuuuuck."

I began to rupture. Tingling started at my toes and traveled up both legs, ending at my center where I exploded.

"This dick cummi—Fuck."

He jerked, tightening his grip around my neck while racing to my lips. Deeply, intensely, he kissed me. Passion erupted between us as we both reached our peaks.

THE GREY LIST

As promised, we didn't stay inside. After showering and getting dressed, we were out of the door. In The Highlands of Berkeley, we strolled the long strip of luxury brands that were surrounded by fine dining, a small golf course, and cars one could only dream of owning someday.

My government salary didn't afford me the luxury I was witnessing and indulging in. It was bittersweet to even consider. Criminal money stretched for miles and miles, seeming to never end. We'd confiscated millions at a time during operations. Most of them had so much money they wouldn't be able to spend it in one lifetime. Some time it was so old it crumbled.

I wondered if it was greed or a trauma bond with money that was a result of childhood poverty. For some, they hadn't seen a struggle and didn't know what one looked like, so greed was their only explanation. Others, like Chemistry, I couldn't quite put my finger on their purpose for acquiring more than they could keep track of.

"Welcome, Eden. I'm Diane, and I'll be shopping for you today."

We stepped into Prada and were greeted almost instantly. I wasn't sure how the personal shopper knew who she was speaking to, but I'd bet my last dollar Chem had orchestrated the entire thing. A glass of champagne was shoved in my direction. I accepted it, placing it to my lips after returning the gesture.

"Hey, Diane."

"Good evening, Diane."

"Always good to see you, Mr. Childers. Anything we're looking for in particular this evening?"

"Not exactly. Whatever she wants. If she stares a second too long, put it on my tab."

"Sure thing. Right this way, Eden."

With the Bottega Veneta bag swaying in one hand and a Chanel bag in the other, I pushed forward. Chemistry was loaded down with bags as well. He'd made a few purchases in Louis Vuitton and wouldn't leave until I decided on something. When I hesitated to choose between the monogrammed and plain bag, he made Elizabeth, our shopper, add both to his bill. We'd also stopped by Christian Louboutin and grabbed shoes that matched in style.

"I'm going to get a dressing room started for you."

"Thank you."

I melted into the plush couch, realizing how much my muscles ached. Aside from having my body contorted in every position possible over the last few days, we'd been walking for what felt like thirteen hours. The sneakers and two-piece athleisure fit Chemistry had waiting on me when I exited the shower was a God-send. I should've known then this shopping experience would be unlike anything else.

"What's the matter?"

"My body aches."

I sipped from the champagne while admiring the man who was almost too good to be true.

"I'll get that taken care of."

"Taken care of?" I chuckled. "Is there anything you can't take care of?"

"Not when it comes to you, so let's not worry about that."

He was resourceful and didn't mind using those resources. I appreciated that. He didn't wait to be asked. At the mere mention of discomfort or desire, Chemistry sprang into action.

Caretaker. A good one.

"Whatever you say, Mister."

Shyly, I sipped and scanned the bags that were

encased and on shelves that glowed. A black, very simple piece caught my eye just as Diane returned.

"Galleria. Isn't she beautiful?" Diane pointed to the bag I had my sight set on.

"Yes," I claimed.

"We have her studded or simple black leather. She's versatile. An everyday bag, work bag, classic bag, or special occasion bag."

"Do you like it?" I turned and asked Chem.

"I do. You?"

"Yes."

"She'll take both," he finalized.

"Bab—"

"She'll take both," he reiterated.

"Great. Now, would you like a look at more bags or shall we move on to the shoes and clothes?"

I hesitated, knowing I hadn't gotten to spend time with the lovely bags on display.

"A little longer, Diane." Chem was observant. His attention to detail allowed me to remain silent as he expressed my hesitancy with words that failed me.

"Okay. Anything in particular you're interested in?"

"The triangle bag and the small bucket."

"Let us see the backpack as well."

Diane gathered the bags. One by one, I placed them up against my body. My reflection in the mirror made it difficult to choose. I finally accepted the fact I didn't have to as I slid the backpack off my shoulder.

"I want them all."

Chemistry's eyes lit up, though his face was void of emotion.

"Alright. Adding these to your order."

"Thank you."

"To the shoes or are we stopping here?"

"I imagine I need at least one pair of shoes to coordinate."

"Or five," Chem added.

"I don't need five." Tittering, I finished the champagne.

As it hit the small table next to the couch, another one was placed in my hand. The strategy was to get customers loose enough to spend willingly. However, that wasn't necessary. Chem would spend regardless. He didn't need a drink in his hand or influence of any kind.

"Whatever you say, Choc."

His attention never wavered. Not once had he picked up his phone. His eyes were planted in my direction, no matter where I turned or what I was doing. I had his undivided attention and the way my skin prickled under his watchful eye let me know I was fascinated by his willingness to stop his world from spinning on its axle to visit mine.

Prada was a success. It was abundantly clear it was a store I'd fallen head over heels for. The plethora of black pieces sold me almost immediately. Tanks, blouses, tees, dresses, pants, and skirts... I'd snagged a little of everything. By the time we exited, I was ready to call it a night. The sun would be setting soon and there were more bags than fingers on our hands combined.

"I'm going to put these in the truck. Stay put, Choc."

"I can he–"

"Thomas is on the way out with the rest of the bags. He'll help. Just don't let nobody snatch your pretty ass."

"What would my man do if they managed to pull it off?"

"Start the bloodiest war of our time. It would be noted in Black history for decades to come. The War of Eden. No one will be safe until your return. No one."

He pecked my cheek and took off in the direction of the truck, leaving me flushed with a giddy smirk lining my lips. I believed every word that came from his mouth. When he returned to grab more bags, I couldn't help myself. I pulled him closer.

"The Battle of Eden sounds better."

"Whatever the fuck you want to call it." He scoffed with a shrug.

Thomas pushed through the doors of Prada with hands full of bags. He followed Chemistry to the car where they began organizing the purchases. A hand on my shoulder startled me. Simultaneously, I was hit with a whiff of a familiar fragrance.

"Tired yet?" Anna asked as she rounded me, finally putting me at ease.

With a hand on my chest, I sighed. "You scared me."

"My apologies."

"What a coincidence? Chem is just over there, trying to stuff what he can inside."

"No coincidence, babe. Malachi came to steal your

man for a quick second and I came to free you from their unanimous shopping addiction. It'll go on for hours more if we don't intervene."

"Thank you!" Breathlessly, I pulled her into a hug. "Shit, I didn't know I'd ever need saving from a shopping spree, but God."

"I won't be around to save you every time, but consider it done if you're here in Berkeley."

"Again, thank you."

"Don't sweat it. Have you eaten? There's a really nice spot just a few feet north of here. The drinks are amazing, too."

Chem approached us with a scowl on his handsome face.

"Where is that nigga and what does he want?" he questioned Anna just as we heard a horn honking.

A stunning, green G-Wagon stole the breath from my lungs.

"Get in, loser. We're going drinking."

"I'm busy!" Chem hollered toward the truck.

"You done tricked off enough for the day!" Malachi yelled back. "There's always another day."

Chem turned to me. The hesitation was appalling. He was waiting for permission. Chemistry wasn't one to wait for anything and ask for nearly nothing. Quickly, I nodded, encouraging him to take his brother up on the offer.

"I won't be long," he promised, kissing my forehead and then my lips.

"I'm not worried. See you later?"

"Without a doubt."

"I'll be sure to get her home safely. Just make sure my husband makes it back to me in one piece, okay?"

"That goes without saying. I'd sacrifice myself before I let anything happen to him."

"Those knuckleheads are meeting you all. Prepare yourself."

Milo and Makai. Without hearing their names, I knew that's who she was referring to.

"It's not Milo. It's that fucking Makai. Our mother dropped him on his head a few times. There's nothing that can convince me otherwise."

"Me either."

Chem leaned in and landed a kiss on Anna's forehead before taking off toward the truck. Horns honked behind Malachi. Impatient drivers wanted him out of the way so they could get to their destinations sooner rather than later. To their dismay, they'd honked at the wrong truck, on the wrong day, with the wrong passenger present.

Chem's visible waistline knotted my stomach. I watched the barrel of his gun as maneuver until it was airborne, pointing toward the unruly drivers behind Malachi.

"Blow that motherfucker again," he dared.

The driver of the first vehicle quickly took note. The second didn't until the barrel was tapping his window. Chem never made it to the third vehicle. It reversed and headed in the other direction.

"Baby!" I bellowed, hoping to snap him out of whatever trance he was in.

"I'll see you back at the house, Choc," he responded, blowing an air kiss as if he didn't just scare the shit out of three unsuspecting victims.

I turned toward Anna, expecting an explanation. She didn't have one. Her shoulder lifted and fell just as she grabbed my hand and pulled me toward the restaurant she'd mentioned. Still in a state of shock, I followed.

The sun began setting as we approached the intricate dwelling with roped solar-powered lights and small pods decorating the patio. Rich, yet bold colors covered every inch of the space we entered. The chairs and tables were thrifted at some point in time. None of them matched, but they were all perfect additions to the vintage-inspired space.

"Reservations?"

"For two. Anna Domino."

"Yes. Yes. Your table is ready." The hostess tapped the iPad a few times and then led us toward the door, which gave us access to the patio that I'd fallen in love with from afar. Standing among the beautiful chaos made me fall a little deeper into the unique space.

"Pod six. Alex will be with you shortly."

"Thank you," Anna responded, taking a seat on the right side of the egg-shaped fixture.

I sat on the opposite side, taking note of the confidence Anna exuded. It was quiet, but it was so fucking loud. She reeked of wealth, good fortune, and knowledge.

Her face disappeared behind one of the menus that had been sat on our table. I took the opportunity to study the other one. When I waitress asked, I cared to know what I'd be starting with.

"He's in love with you." Anna's voice carried through the rounded pod where we were seated, halting the beating of my heart. Immediately after, it restarted. Harder. Louder.

"Chemistry?" The question was never meant to leave my head, but somehow, it had surfaced.

"Well, surely, I'm not referring to Malachi."

With a smile, I nodded. "Right."

"He won't ever admit it, but he and Makai have a lot in common. The death of their mother ended their interest in companionship. They avoid commitment. Not because they want to but because their hearts aren't ready. It feels good, really good, to know Chemistry's heart has progressed and his brokenness hasn't rendered him helpless. He's a gem, Eden. Though he might seem cold at times, his heart is pure."

"I know," I confessed.

"Don't break it," she warned. The softness of her voice had subsided and was replaced with a stern, firmer combination that made the hairs on the back of my neck stand.

I don't want to.

"Hi, I'm Alex. I'll be waiting for you this evening. What can I get started for you ladies?"

Our waitress appeared with a smile that could light

any room. Dressed in a black and white ruffled dress, she blended well with the vintage decor.

"I'll have a French 75."

"I'll have a dirty martini."

"Alright. Will you ladies be having appetizers?"

"Yes, but we're still undecided. When the drinks are delivered, we will have decided on something."

"Great. I'll be right back with those drinks."

Alex hurriedly scurried from the table as if she was in a rush to be somewhere else.

Anna's words were still ringing in my ear when we were left alone again. As she continued scanning the menu, I tried piecing my heart back together. The thought of breaking Chem's shattered me every time.

TWELVE

Chemistry

I strolled into Rather's office and had a seat on the couch that held the secrets of many. Aside from her unorthodox method of extracting information from those assigned to her through our family's empire, she was a damn good therapist. The best, in my opinion. She was talented and could perform well in both arenas, just like the rest of us.

Rather wasn't always on duty. In fact, her cases were few and far apart. There weren't many people in possession of the information we needed and couldn't retrieve ourselves. With Rugger, it was more of the same. When she wasn't ending the lives of those deserving, she was tucked away in the lab, discovering the mistakes of murderous criminals so she didn't make them in the future.

Our operation was seamless. Everyone had a role. Roulette was the first point of contact. She kept a watchful eye on her customers. When a prospect entered her establishment, spending an obscene amount of money, she made note of it and followed their paper trail until they revisited.

It's Roulette. Gamble on your life. It'll never be the same.

They always doubled back. Roulette wasn't a place you visited and forgot. The experience was one of a kind and built to leave a lasting impression on everyone who entered the doors.

Once she was ready, she invited them to a private meeting where they were given the chance to observe Rome at the theater as she wowed everyone in the audience in a leotard and ballet flats. Her gift of discernment was utilized to the fullest extent and the most critical part of our process.

To get to me, you had to get through her. That shit wasn't easy. The baby face and gentle persona had fooled plenty. Yet Rome was far from the naive girl they suspected she was. To make matters worse, her unwavering love for me made her quest to protect me a bit more intense.

If you weren't worthy of my presence, she could sense it from a mile away. Not many made it past the viewing. A select few made it backstage to meet her and shake her hand, a sign you'd moved on to the next stage. If cleared by Rome, I was the next face one would see.

After our introduction, operations were filtered through Royce. She handled client affairs, serving as the liaison for both parties. Client affairs weren't the only thing she had her hands in. She wore many hats. Whatever one needed, she could acquire.

Messes that needed cleaning were where Range entered the fold. Whether it was a case that wasn't looking too good or a body that never needed to be found, she was the person to call.

Roaman worked less and worried more. As the oldest girl, she couldn't help but stress about the flow of things each and every day. Yet, she remained quiet and useful when she could be. Not everyone could make it to the hospital and not everyone could go to the hospital in the event of an emergency. She was on call most nights. Her days were spent in the operating room, saving the lives of patients on her roster.

Step One: Roulette –scouts potential clientele

Step Two: Rome –determines whether a potential client is good for business, crucial to the longevity of operations

Step Three: Chemistry –distributes formula for unique strands that elevates client's operation, 10xs the growth of their business and clientele

Step Four: Royce –liaison and point of contact beyond

the distribution of formula, keep everything and everybody in line

Step Five: Range —responsible for handling clients in legal battles and cleaning messes that have been made while they're on the roster

Step Six: Rather —extracts valuable information from those who pose threats or those aware of threats to the operation

Step Seven: Roaman —nurses those who've been in Rather's chambers back to health as well as operates as an on-call surgeon for those who can't visit the local hospital without suspicions being raised

Step Eight: Rugger —death. The last face you'll ever see. A visit from her marks the end of life.

My mind wandered until I heard the sweetness of Rather's voice, pulling me back in.

"Hello, Mr. Childers."

She looked up from the glasses that were sliding down her face. She pushed them up with the pen she'd been writing with, giving me her full attention.

"Not today, baby."

"Please, Rather. Or, Doctor Childers will suffice. I'm not your baby this evening, Mr. Childers. I'm your therapist."

"Rather, not today."

"Is there something we should discuss? Something bothering you? You seem vexed."

"Nothing is bothering me."

"I find that hard to believe. You seem to have a chip on your shoulder. Who pissed in your Cheerios?"

My head fell backward, leaning on the couch and sliding down slightly.

"Catherine," I revealed.

"There. Now we can get started."

She was aware of what was bothering me. It was the same topic almost every session. Though we discussed it fifty different ways, the topic remained the same.

"How was your trip to Berkeley last month? Is that what triggered this"–she paused–"episode?"

"Seeing the people who share my pain always triggers me."

"Yet, you still choose to see them every chance you get. Whenever they call or make contact, you drop everything and run in their direction."

"I'll always do that, baby. My heart won't let me disregard them."

"I know and that's the point I'm making. You have to give yourself credit. Even though it shatters you, it doesn't stop you from showing up for them. Time and time again."

"Yeah."

"So, I find it hard to believe that is what's actually bothering you. Be honest with me, honest with yourself."

I bolted to my feet, only to pace the floor slowly, trying to articulate what I was feeling.

"I have time, so don't rush it. I'm here to listen when you're ready to talk. And if it's silence you need, I can provide that as well."

I shook my head. "That's not it. Just finding it diffi-cult to put this shit in words."

Rather placed her notebook on the table and removed her glasses. She lifted one knee over the other and interlocked her fingers. Doctor Childers no longer existed. The professionalism remained but everything else had changed.

"Chem, it's me you're talking to. The words don't require perfection."

Halting, I nodded with a shrug. "Though my actions have contradicted this statement time and time again, I don't hate women. I don't hate the idea of partnership. Companionship isn't on the list of things I despise. In fact, it's the complete opposite. I'm very self-aware, baby. And I knew if there was ever a time I let my guard down and tapped into the side of me that thirsted for those things, I'd fall head first."

"I never thought you hated women. You're surrounded by them and you love us dearly. I, too, knew when the time came, it would be monumental."

"I've fallen, baby. Fuck not trusting her, I don't trust my-fucking-self. The things that go through my head. The things I think about. The things I obsess over. And dare I say, there's never been any-fucking-thing I've ever been afraid of in my life, baby, but I am scared of that woman and what she represents for me. I am whole in every area of my life but that's where I fall short. I don't think I'm equipped to love her at the capacity she deserves and that shit drives me mad."

"Che–"

"The way my mother ripped my heart out of my fucking chest that day, balled my shit up and tossed it in the trash, was brutal. She took something from me I can never get back. So, when it comes to love, it renders me speechless. I'm lost. Confused. Uncertain. Fucking fearful. Those aren't words I ever want in the same sentence as Chemistry. Because Chemistry is fearless. Certain of every-fucking-thing. Careful. Bold. Knowledgeable. I don't know shit about any of this, Rather. And I'm none of the things she makes me."

"Who makes you?"

"Eden."

"Her name is Eden," Rather said with a smile.

"Yes."

"And she's altered your comfort."

"In every way."

"Good or bad?"

"Both, I assume."

"Is it actually bad or is she forcing you to confront everything you've avoided since that tragedy?"

I paused, digesting the words spoken.

"She's forcing me to confront everything I've avoided."

"So, a good thing, correct?"

"Painful. Frustrating. Handicapping."

"Grief doesn't have a timeframe, nor does it look as pretty as the other emotions. Sometimes it hides in corners. Sometimes it is front and center. Sometimes it's dormant. Sometimes it lingers. It shows up in different places, appears differently in all its stages, and even makes us believe it has gone on its way sometimes.

"When it's all said and done, it stays with us. It sticks with us. It becomes part of our identity. It helps us make decisions. It keeps us from making repeated mistakes. It navigates our lives for the rest of our lives. And that's what's happening, Chemistry.

"Your grief has helped you navigate every aspect of your life but nothing has truly made you confront your feelings. You avoid things, places, and circumstances that will uproot that grief and make you feel it right there where it hurts most."

She pointed at my chest.

"You can only run for so long before it hunts you down and walks you like a fucking dog. It's not always pretty, the aftermath. But, yours can be as beautiful as you make it. Sacrificing your sanity to be whole again and to come out on the other side with a wife and hopefully children that love you unconditionally someday seems worth it to me.

"Trust me, she's not asking for the perfect love. Just a good love. One she can bet everything on because that's exactly what the heart is. It's everything. When it stops beating, you're dead. Don't end her life because you're afraid to live yours."

Shit. Rather preached, ending her sermon with a smile.

"I believe in you, Chemistry. So does Eden."

"Yeah?"

"It's been almost three months, Teddy. Of course, she does."

I plopped down on the couch, feeling the weight I'd felt on my end lifted from my shoulder. It had me anchored since we'd left Berkeley a few weeks ago. I hadn't seen much of Eden because my schedule was in recovery mode from taking a full week off to spend time with her.

I'd ditched my bed to sleep in hers at least two times a week. But, when the morning came, I dragged myself out of her pussy and out of her bed to meet Aden downstair so I could get my day started. It took a lot of willpower, but I managed.

"Now, when will we meet her?"

"Soon, baby. Really soon."

"And your head? How is it up there?"

"I feel better when she's around. I'm not easily distracted by the voices or the irrational thoughts because my attention is almost always on her."

"Nothing's wrong with that. I implore you to spend even more time with her. Carve out space every day."

"That's the goal, eventually. Right now, it's not obtainable. I lose focus with her in my mix."

"Well, that's my homework for you. It doesn't have to be immediately, but within the next three months, I want Eden to be a part of every day. Physically. Not over the phone or through text messages. Skin to skin. Mouth to mouth. Di–"

"I think this session is over."

"Wait, I didn't even get to the best part."

"I get the fucking point, Rather."

"So serious."

"That's not an insult."

"Anything else on your mind?"

Pops. "Nah, nothing I care to talk about right now."

"Then maybe next time."

She stood on her feet and prepared to walk out of the door in front of me. After every session, we indulged in a wind-down. It was time Rather and I spent alone, free of thoughts and conversation relating to topics we'd discussed in her office. With seven sisters and an entire empire to head, time was limited.

Whenever I could, I slid in a few minutes or even a couple of hours with one of them. Dividing my time and attention between seven girls was a struggle I faced graciously and proudly. Luckily, one of them didn't give a damn about spending time alone or my attention. She lived in a bubble and it was hard for any of us to penetrate it at times.

Rugger was a different breed. Nothing about her was average. Not even her height. She was six feet of chaos. When one saw her coming, it was in their best interest to run in the opposite direction. But even then, she'd hunt you down and complete the assignment. There was no escaping her wrath.

She stopped at the door's threshold, plaguing me with confusion. The regretful smile on her face said what her lips had yet to.

"Not today?"

She shook her head. "Not today, Teddy. I have to prepare for the night's assignment."

I nodded, understanding what she was up against. Altering her capacity and mindset completely for a few hours, sometimes a few minutes, robbed her of precious time.

"Perry?"

"Yes."

"You won't be long, baby. They won't last but a few minutes."

"It seems that way," she agreed. "Nevertheless, preparation and decompression."

"Understood."

"See you later?"

"Of course."

"I love you, Chemistry."

"In this lifetime and the others."

"How will you find me?" She chuckled, accepting the kiss I placed on her forehead.

"Don't worry. I will."

I exited her office and headed straight for the truck, which was right outside the main door of her practice.

"I'll be waiting," Rather called out to me.

"You better." The last two words were tossed over my shoulder before the sunlight threatened to blind me.

Inside the truck, with both palms flat on my slacks, I reconsidered my plans for the evening. On one hand, a brief visit to the warehouse to assist Rugger and Rather weighed in. On the other hand, kidnapping Eden for the night seemed to hold the most weight. The decision was one I wasn't ready to make, so I didn't. Instead, I began checking things off my itinerary earlier than planned.

"To my father's," I instructed Aden.

"Alright."

Out the window of the Escalade, I watched as the city passed me by. Its beauty was undeniable. The peace was unobtainable anywhere else.

"Hmph."

I kissed the skin of my teeth with a shake of my head. The presence of four Perry motherfuckers had threatened the peace and the beauty of the city. I'd known it since the first mention of them crossing state lines. Boldly and stupidly, after three months in town, they'd set up shop in territory that was claimed.

The Triad of Ara covered every inch of the city, in every direction, in every dimension. No grounds were unclaimed. They'd learned it the hard way. And unfortunately, it would be the last lesson they learned.

Rugger wouldn't leave a single trace of their existence and would walk away from the warehouse as if nothing had ever happened. Because, to her, nothing would have. She'd return to her lab and obsess over something seemingly insignificant to others but was a key component for her next mission.

Thirty-two minutes and we were through the gates of my father's home. Upon arrival, I exited the vehicle and climbed the steps where the staff greeted me. Beyond the entryway was Rhea, waiting to usher me down the hallway and into whatever room my father was in.

"Good evening, son."

"Good evening."

I pulled her into my arms and released her shortly after. She made a fool of time. Made me wonder if it was even a true concept or if it was truly passing us by. She hadn't aged more than a few years since I'd met her. She was still flawless.

"Don't you look fancy. Headed anywhere special?"

"Not exactly. Just left Rather."

"Is that why you're still wearing a mug?"

"Am I?"

"You are."

Suddenly, I could feel the contortion of my face. I relaxed the muscles, hoping I resolved the crinkles and creases that revealed where I was mentally.

"That's better."

Because their home was massive, there was a chance he could be in one of fifteen spaces. To narrow my search and save me the headache, Rhea showed me to the great room where he was.

"Wasn't expecting you so soon."

"Rather canceled."

"She'll have her hands full tonight."

"That's why I'm here."

"Well, then, have a seat. Are you hungry? I can hav—"

"I'm fine. I'll have something when I leave."

My father lifted his glass and pointed in my direction. Veronica rushed to his side to retrieve it. The brown liquid inside was low. I observed closely as she refilled it and poured some into a glass for me. Trust was a word I rarely used and hardly believed. It didn't matter Veronica had been staffed eight years ago and showed unwavering love toward the family.

At any moment, that could all change. When it did, I didn't want to be blindsided. That went for her and anyone else around us. She handed us both our glasses and stood off to the side, waiting for more instructions.

"What's on your mind, Richie?" I sipped, letting the liquid burn my throat as it trickled down.

"I was going to ask you the same. There's been a notable shift, son. I don't know if I should be worried, yet, but I'll let you decide by what you reveal today."

"A shift?"

"Yes. A disconnect of some kind. One that hasn't hindered business in any capacity, but I'm more than a mentor and chairman of The Triad. I'm your father. That's who you're speaking with right now."

"With a straight face, you're demanding I tell you my personal business?" I chuckled.

He shrugged. "I guess you could put it that way."

"Business is good as usual, so there's no other way to put it. This is personal. You could've called me on the phone to ask who I'm fucking, Pops."

"That wouldn't have been very polite and I'm aware of who she is. My question is what and how much does she mean to you?"

I paused, taking a second to expand my mental and

emotional capacity. Eden forced me to see beyond myself and my limitations. She pushed me to be better, do better, and think better.

"Everything," I admitted, relieved. That simple word alleviated so much for me simultaneously. I released the breath I didn't realize I'd been holding. Soothed by the idea of Eden, a smile lifted my cheeks and guided my head backward and forward, repeatedly.

Satisfied? A voice asked.

Very. I responded.

Quietly, my father took a sip of his drink. He gazed in my direction with worry lines creasing his face. He took another sip and then a third one, finishing it off. Veronica scurried over, but he dismissed her with a hand in the air. She fell back, blending with the fixtures of the home so effortlessly.

"Then what I have to tell you doesn't matter, do it?"

"It doesn't," I admitted. "I'm all in."

"Well, I assume this is who you've chosen to carry on our legacy."

"Yes. She is."

"Good. Good. Will there be a wedding soon?"

"Will you live to see it?" I asked with empty lungs.

I couldn't pull in a single particle of air until he responded. The possibility of him never seeing me walk down the aisle was crippling. Months ago, the chances of me wedding were extremely slim to none. Now that I knew without a doubt I'd be walking Eden down an aisle after reciting vows, his absence was unacceptable. Richie and I had so much history. He was everything I could've dreamt of in a father.

And when our loneliness grew to be too much to bear, he sought companionship, doubling the love he had for me. Rhea was the quiet to his storm. Though she was a woman of few words, her presence spoke for itself. She gave us seven girls that would go to the end of the earth for us and vice versa.

"Should I lie to appease you? Pacify your feelings? Or should I ruin your day with the truth?"

"They need to know." I referred to my sisters.

"Yeah, yeah." He sighed, sitting back and lifting his glass.

Drinking away his sorrows wouldn't make the situation any better, but it would bandage the ache for a bit.

"When will you tell them?"

"Next month."

"Next month is no good, Richie," sternly, I denied.

"Why not?"

"There are four birthdays within the next sixty days. Don't be the thief of joy. Let them enjoy themselves."

If he was going to break their hearts, at least he was to be considerate.

"In two months, I won't have to tell them. They'll see it for themselves. I can hardly keep a meal down. My appetite doesn't exist. I'll be as thin as that damn stick over there in two months."

A hard cough rumbled his body.

"If we have to feed you through a fucking tube, then so be it. But, you will not break those girls' hearts on my watch. Not anytime soon, at least. So, get your shit together, Richie. The defeat in your tone, it's unfamiliar and very fuc—very offensive. The man who taught me defeat was never an option–" I scoffed, straightening the wrinkles in the jacket of my suit.

"You don't get to give up on yourself, Pops. I will shove food down your throat myself. Please do not let it come to that. Forget everything those doctors are feeding you. The Man upstairs is the only doctor we listen to aside from the one Rhea gave birth to. You hear me?"

Roles had swiftly reversed. After years of hearing my father preach to me and demand, that I approach every obstacle with grace and excellence, I was giving him the same speech. He never showed remorse. I wouldn't either.

With a titter, he shook his head. "You're your father's fucking son."

"That's a compliment."

"As it should be. So, tell me about Eden."

I lifted my glass for Veronica to refill. When the brown liquid swirled the middle of the glass, again, I relaxed in my seat and the words began to flow.

"I met her during her debut at Roulette."

"There are beautiful women in Roulette, son. What made this one so special?"

"She's no chameleon. She doesn't blend with her surroundings. An inexplicable gravitational pull led me straight to her. I couldn't stop my feet. They birthed a mind of their own and didn't stop until I was face to face with the brazen beauty. I thought my heart would break free of my chest at any second. Though I remained composed, it took almost everything out of me. She had my adrenaline pumping. Thoughts running rampant. Trigger finger itching. I knew from the second she opened her mouth niggas would have to die behind her."

"They have, so I've heard."

"Stop listening so hard, old man." I chuckled, pulling at my growing beard. "I don't regret any of it."

"Why would you?"

I lifted and dropped my shoulders. "Three months of bliss. Three whole months. I haven't grown tired of her yet. In fact, I crave her presence more now than I did three months ago. As our connection ages, my hunger for her grows. At this point, it feels insatiable. Like, I'll never have enough, no matter how much she gives me."

Laughing, I caught my head in my left palm. "Arrr. I can't believe I'm even saying this type of shit, Pops."

"I can."

I whipped my head in his direction at the declaration. "Why?"

"Because I always knew it was possible. You just needed to bump into the right one. There's one woman for every man who will stop him dead in his selfish tracks and make him forget he even exists because all he will know is her. Eden has sunk her teeth into your skin and her venom is running through your veins. You'll never recover."

"I don't want to."

"Haaa!" He fell back in laughter, clapping his hands and stomping his feet on the floor. "That's my boy."

"She drives me mad."

"Let her."

"She wants all of my attention."

"Give it to her."

"She eats away at every bit of sanity I have, but simultaneously keeps me stable. She's good to me, Pops."

"Protect her."

With a shake of my head, I continued. "Feels like I'm losing all self-control. I don't know this person I am when she's around or even when I'm thinking of her."

I looked up at him with weary eyes. "Now that she's here, I don't want to live without her."

"Then, marry her."

Rhea and my father wed twenty-eight days after they met. *Time waits for no man.* It's one of the many mottos he lived by. Within the first five months of their nuptials, her belly began to grow with Roaman maturing inside her womb.

Every year after, and twice in one year, in particular, she produced a child. My father wanted another son. Rhea wanted a house full of children. They were a match made in heaven. Though my father never got the second son he dreamed of, he was prideful of his tribe. None of us had been led astray.

Everyone was involved in the family's business while still thriving in their respectful careers. My talents didn't end in the custom lab I'd built and spent time creating for our clientele. Pharmaceuticals were my passion. And drugs I'd perfected over the years were managing diseases and alleviating the pain of millions.

"I will. I just need to know my old man will live to see it."

"Promise." He sucked his teeth, shaking his head. "Promises they're meant to be broken."

"Not ours."

"Nothing I'll say will make this any better or hurt any less."

"Assuring me you haven't and will not give up, that'll make all the difference."

"I won't give up, son."

We allowed the silence to dwell. I sipped from my drink and he did the same. Nothing more needed to be said.

THE GREY LIST

Eden rushed toward the truck with Aden and an umbrella hovering over her head. My nostrils flared at even the thought of the rain touching her in places that were restricted and reserved for me. I swung the door open as I ended the call I'd been on.

Nothing mattered anymore. *Nothing*, now that she was in sight. Eden slid in, not stopping until her hands were on the back of my head, pulling me into her.

Electricity flowed freely through my body as her tongue twirled around my mouth. She tasted like a strawberry cream soda. The Lost Cherry perfume she wore was divine. It mixed perfectly with her natural scent. Our lips twisted and turned until we both pulled away, breathlessly with smiles that nearly split the corners of our lips.

"I've missed you," I confessed.

"I've waited by the phone for your call. Felt like it would never come."

"My call will always come, Choc. Always."

She settled beside me, refusing to acknowledge personal space and I wasn't in a hurry for her to do so, either. I enjoyed the feeling of her skin against mine. She rested her head on my shoulder and sighed heavily.

"Have you eaten?"

She was in her favorite color. Prada sneakers and a nylon Prada bag quickly reminded me I had a cart full of items I needed to complete the checkout process for. Eden represented me so well. Joining the entourage would be a breeze. Just like my sisters, she was born to be pampered, spoiled, and to have her way.

"Yes."

"How long has it been?"

"Two hours, possibly more."

"Then dinner will wait. I can push our appointment up."

"Our appointment?" She stretched her body, sitting up straight and pressing her back against the seat behind us.

"I didn't stutter, Eden."

"You didn- Where are we headed?"

"Just sit back and look pretty. Don't worry yourself too much. You'll see soon enough."

Instead of pushing her luck, she scooted to the other side of the seat and lowered her back until her head was in my lap and those big, round eyes were staring up at me. I saw my future in them, *in her*.

"Hi," she snorted, sniggering at whatever she found funny.

"Hello, Eden."

I brushed a finger up against her cheek. She leaned into my hand kissing it tenderly. I missed her dearly. That smile of hers. That mouth of hers —for the things it said and the things it did to me. That laugh of hers. The sound of her light snores revealed her level of contentment. The softness of her skin. The beat of her heart. Her silence. Her pussy. Her selflessness. Her.

She pursed her lips, closed her eyes, and waited for me to grant her soundless wish. I complied, leaning down and pecking them. By the time my back hit the seat, again, her eyes were open and I felt myself falling deeper than I'd been seconds ago. Minutes ago. Hours ago.

"Whaaaaat?" She blushed.

"You're beautiful, Eden."

With her hands, she covered her face. I pulled them away one after the other.

"Don't hide."

I've done enough of that for us both.

"You make me feel so fuzzy inside. My God, I feel like a kid with a crush."

"I'm no kid and this ain't no crush, Choc."

"I'm well aware," she admitted. "You've made that abundantly clear."

"There is something else I want to make abundantly clear."

I brought her hands to my lips and kissed her fingers, one by one, stopping at her ring finger where I'd one day place a ring. She waited with bated breath for me to continue. My stomach flipped fifty times. My mouth dried as I fought to release the words on my heart.

"I've been trying to convince myself I'm in too far over my head but every time I set eyes on you, I feel like I'm not even halfway there. So much darkness, so much nothingness surrounded me before you stepped and lit this motherfucker up.

"Your light exposed wounds I've been needing to heal for two decades. Your light exposed parts of me I had tucked away, hidden, and hoped they were never discovered. Your light brought me clarity. And a bunch of fucking feelings I fight to control every day. I lose every time, Choc.

"Because this feeling isn't meant to be controlled. It's all-consuming. It's wide. It's large. It's deep. It's better than anything I've ever felt. For once, I don't get to dictate. My submission is required and until three months ago, I had intentions of leaving this earth without submitting. But here we are and now that I'm here, I'll never return to that emptiness I experienced, that abyss I was once in.

"You've helped me more than you'll ever understand. And I thank you for that. They say perfection doesn't exist, but I have the proof in my hands right now. I love you, Choc. yesterday. Tomorrow. Next week. Next month. Next year. Next lifetime. Unconditionally. Wholly. Completely. Without reservation. Without shame. Without fear. Without regret. I love you. And I've known it for some time now.

"Possibly the moment I laid eyes on you, but I convinced myself it was impossible and again, I was in too far over my head. But, fuck my head and fuck time and fuck all the restrictions society puts on us. There's no timeframe. No amount of days. No amount of nights. No amount of dates can change my mind about how I truly felt that night.

"It's clear now because my feelings haven't changed. They've only intensified. My love has grown. Expanded. Blossomed. It's almost too fucking big for this heart of mine. But, that's alright because it's growing too, to accommodate you... to accommodate us."

I shook my head. "Fuck."

I couldn't wrap my head around the things coming from my mouth, but I didn't need to. I was no longer speaking from my head where logic existed. I was speaking from my heart where love existed.

"And I know I'm saying a lot but in short, I love you. I love you. I love you."

Tears fell from her eyes, rolled down her cheeks, and soiled my pants. Her chest caved and stilled as I continued.

I kissed her forehead. "I love you."

I kissed her right cheek. "I love you."

I kissed her left cheek. "I love you."

I kissed her lips. "I love you."

She released a breath. "Chemistry."

"In this lifetime and the next, Choc."

"I need to te– tell you som–" She choked, tears as plentiful as her emotions.

"We've arrived," Aden announced, pulling us both above ground level where the tsunami of tears threatened our wellbeing.

"What is it?" I asked, still invested in our conversation.

Hesitantly, she shook her head from one side to the other.

"What's the matter?"

She lifted, fixing her clothes as she wiped her eyes. "I've known it all along, too. I tumbled and have been falling for a mighty long time. I love you. I feel it in my heart from the moment I open my eyes until I close them. And when I fall asleep, you're there too. You're not alone. Don't ever think you are. I feel it too. I feel it all."

Her words soothed me. I wasted little time exiting the truck that had grown clammy in the midst of my divulging. Eden followed. Before taking off, I pressed her body against the back door and smoothed down her ponytail. Her eyes had swelled slightly and still had signs of moisture. I cleaned it with the handkerchief in my pocket.

"Choc," I began. "There is something you have neglected to mention."

"Is there?"

"The name of the ex that broke your heart."

"Chemistry."

"His name."

"No, because he has a wife and family now. I will not allow you to take him away from them."

"He doesn't get to live peacefully while you continue to live with a broken heart."

"My heart okay, Chem."

"Oh, I don't doubt it. I'm going to make sure of that. But, you still live with the results of his actions."

"No."

"Yes, Eden."

"Then, promise you won't lay a hand on him."

"I promise."

"I feel like you're lying."

"I haven't lied to you yet. I'm not starting today."

"Adonis. Adonis Von."

My thumb slid down my tongue. I cleaned the tear stains from her face with the saliva assisting.

"Good. Good. Thank you, Choc."

"Don't lay a hand on him, Chemistry. Don't even say a word to him. Don't break your promise to me."

"I'd never, Choc."

"Did you really just use spit to clean my face?" She chuckled.

"You let me."

It wasn't until she began to resemble the Eden I knew and not an emotionally scarred, shockingly gorgeous model who'd been turned down for her dream gig that we pushed through the private entrance of the family jeweler. She took the hand I was extending for her to grab. Her empty hand reminded me of why we were here.

I was ready to weigh Eden's finger down with a block of ice, but there was one problem. I didn't know her size. That was the point of our visit. Once that was settled, I could get the ball rolling. Before my father took his last breath, Eden would take my last name.

THIRTEEN

Eden

The stress of the case was weighing on me. Familiarity wasn't debatable at this point of the investigation. I missed my mother. I missed my best friend. I missed the freedom of going and doing as I pleased. And I missed the time I spent with Chemistry before I discovered his identity.

"It will all be over soon, Johanson. We just need more specifics. Where does he live? Does he have any secret locations we should know? Tailing him has led us nowhere. I am afraid I'll lose one of my agents if he catches wind that we're following him so we fall back. You're our only hope."

"I understand Jack. But I keep making it clear that he is not like the others. He doesn't make mistakes. I stumbled upon him by chance. Hadn't he approached me, we'd never know who he was. He's given me nothing," I lied, gnawing at my bottom lip as I did so.

Chem hadn't given me much, but there were a few things I was obligated to report. I hadn't. The house in Berkeley. His family's jeweler. His driver, Aden. His staff. The amount of time it took us to get from his place to mine. The amount of turns we made. The exact turns we made. Yet, I had nothing.

"That sucker has his shit air-tight."

"He's unlike anything I've ever seen before. I'm beginning to feel like we'll never dismantle their operation. We don't have enough on him."

"What we have, we'll make stick."

"The word of a dealer that simply wants a way out of his own troubles?"

"Well since you put it away, I guess we don't have much on him."

"Give me some time. Maybe he'll slip."

"Let's hope he does. Otherwise, we'll bring him in on what we have, shake everyone around him down, and piece some shit together from there. Once he's captured, I'm sure someone will come forward with some information."

"Possibly so. Have you finalized the profile for my best friend?"

"Yeah. Yeah. We're finishing up. It should be ready in a few days or so."

"Make sure it goes back to childhood. Just in case, Jack. I don't want to bring any harm to her or her husband. But, this case is taking much longer than I anticipated. If I'm going to continue, then I at least need someone I love on speed dial for those days I need some fresh air and normal conversation. If it's not one of you all I'm talking to, it's him or my damn walls."

"Understood. Just hang in there. We'll take care of it and make sure everything checks out, down to the school yearbook pictures."

"Good. Talk to you later."

"Talk to you later, Johanson. And good work out there."

"Tell me that when this is all over." I sighed.

"I'll tell you again then."

He ended the call, freeing me from bondage. The cafe's restroom wasn't exactly where I wanted to be on the private call, but it was the only solution for Jack's impromptu call. I swirled the iced matcha I'd ordered, hating the fact I'd brought it in the bathroom with me. However, the stirrer that stopped it from spilling out of the small opening at the top that offered some sort of relief.

I emerged, reentering the crowded cafe and heading straight for the door. My loft was two blocks away. The wind swept my ponytail over my shoulder. I adjusted the YSL sunglasses I'd picked up in Berkeley with Chemistry's encouragement. He was such a fucking influence.

Even my altered strut was inspired by him, his lifestyle, and the parts of it he offered me. My head was a little higher. My nose pushed into the air a little more. My shoulders were a bit more squared. My spine was straighter. My words were fewer. As if everyone around me could sense who it was I was bending over and busting it wide open for, I entered spaces differently, now.

I belong to Chemistry. I imagined there was a sign pinned on me somewhere that let everyone know. The way groups parted to give me unrestricted access on the sidewalks, held doors open long before I approached them, greeted me so pleasantly, and accommodated my needs with me hardly having a chance to ask, I assumed the thought wasn't too farfetched.

Make him proud, Egypt.

It didn't matter how many miles away he was, his presence was always felt. Though he wasn't around physically, he had eyes on me. That much I knew. When the report was made, I wanted to be sure it included how much of him was beginning to shine through me.

Downtown Clarke was a melting pot. Its beauty was undeniable and my promise to explore it more hadn't been broken yet. Each day I wasn't climbing from under Chem's covers or lying beside him underneath mine, I made my way through the lobby and into the sea of opportunities downtown presented. Today, I decided to try iced matcha for the first time. Tomorrow, if my schedule permitted, I'd try the ramen spot just three doors down from the cafe.

I arrived at my building with matcha lining my lip. It

had a pleasant, very potent taste to it while remaining mellow. Smoothly, it ran down my throat, soothing its warmth. The walk to and from the cafe in the Clarke sun had my temperature slightly elevated.

"That's good." I moaned, tasting the honey I'd added to my order.

Oblivious to my surroundings, I strolled through the lobby, into the elevator, down my hallway, and to my door. I entered while finishing off my drink and scribbled in a trip to the cafe onto my mental schedule. They'd definitely be seeing me soon.

"Oh shit."

My path to the kitchen was obstructed. The sound of sturdy boxes and my ice nearly hitting the floor forced me to pay attention to where I was going. The new additions to my place hadn't been there when I'd left. A smile creased the corners of my lips as the culprit came to mind.

This man.

Brown boxes lined the floor, apparently brought up to my place by concierge. I hadn't ordered anything online as of lately, but Chem had. I imagined he'd burned a hole through his credit card. On the shipping label of the brown boxes were names of every store we'd visited in Berkeley and a few we hadn't gotten a chance to.

Does he know when to quit? Where will I fit all of this?

On cue, another phone he'd provided me began to vibrate. Carrying so many of them around was becoming a headache. I kept the phone I'd been issued home for the most part, tucked away until it was time to check in or I received a notification through email to answer a call that would be placed at a designated time.

"Do you ever quit?" I whispered into the phone, setting the cup of ice on the counter and heading to the bedroom closet where I stored the agency's phone.

"Spoiling you? No. Why would I?"

"Maybe because I'm running out of room at my place."

"That's why we have a big ass house with big ass closets, Eden. If they're not enough, then I'll build you one that is."

"Chemistry, no more."

"I just thought I'd tell you sorry in advance."

"Sorry? For what?"

"You haven't been in your bedroom, huh?" He tittered.

Before responding, I exited the closet, back peddling into my room where things began to become clearer.

"Did you– I know you didn't– Wait. Where is my bed?"

"I get the best sleep in it, Choc."

"Does that mean you just come jack it from my place?"

"What other choice did I have?"

"I don't know, maybe find one like it," I suggested, holding my chest as I laughed.

"Why when yours was right there."

"Chem, this is insane."

"Have you learned anything about me yet?"

"I have, which is why this shouldn't surprise me."

"It shouldn't. Besides, I'm a reasonable man, Eden. If you want to sleep in your bed, then fine. I understand. But, whenever the feeling arises, there's only one place you'll find it. Me and the bed are a package deal. To sleep on it, you have to be sleeping with me."

"Isn't that some crap?"

"It's fair. Don't lie. Just think about it."

"In the meantime, what will I sleep on?"

"There's a bed in the loft area."

"I don't want to sleep up there. I like being near the window."

"Then you know what you have to do," he teased.

"Sleep with you."

"You say that like it's bad news. I'm going to need you to sound a bit more enthused."

"Chemistry, do you know what days without you are like?"

"You've mentioned it."

"So, you should know I am losing my mind right now. Nights with you are good for my body, my heart, my head, and my soul. Nights with you bring me peace, comfort, joy, and *ease*."

Ease? Effortlessly, Chemistry had managed to culti-vate the life I aspired to have. He'd done so without breaking a sweat. It had been so seamless, I hadn't real-ized until this very moment.

"Ease," I repeated just above a whisper. "How do you do that?"

"Do what, exactly, Choc?"

"Be so damn good to me while simultaneously keeping me distracted so I don't know what's happening. And then moments like this bring clarity and I realize what you were up to the entire time. How'd I miss that?"

"Because your life with me is supposed to be so easy you don't see it. You just feel it a little more and more each day. Eventually, it becomes so normal nothing feels out of the ordinary. By the time you're having a moment like the one you're having right now, all the chips have fallen into place, and because you weren't worried about where they'd land... you actually had the chance to enjoy their journey. Enjoy your journey."

I rested my back against the window, looking down at the shoes I had on. I was every bit of him, from my head to my toe. He'd bought every piece of clothing I'd worn over the last few weeks, down to my underwear.

"I love you, Chemistry."

"Then show me. Be ready at seven. If I have to come upstairs and get you, we won't make it down. I'm going to fuck you right where you're standing, right where your bed used to be."

Swiftly, I turned, trying to find him in the sparse crowd of people walking in downtown Clarke. I had no luck.

"Where are you?"

The silence on the line let me know he was no longer with me. He'd ended the call. I placed the phone on my chest. A chuckle escaped me. There was no denying what I felt for Chem. He had quickly become the center of my world. It wasn't the case or my career that kept me up at night. It was him.

"Then show me," I mocked him. "Be ready at seven."

I pranced around the room, filled to the brim and unsure of what I'd pull from my closet to wear tonight or what look I was going for. Then it dawned on me. There were boxes in my kitchen. More than likely, Chemistry had already chosen what I'd be wearing.

T H E **G R E Y** L I S T

6:54 p.m.

I bolted out of the door, nearly crashing into Michael. He stopped just inches short of me. Long-stemmed red roses filled his hand.

"I-I assume those are mine."

"Yes, yes indeed they are, Ms. Reid."

"Thank you, Michael." I reached for the gorgeous arrangement, but he stepped back.

"I've been instructed to get these in some water. Move along, now. I hear you have a very special date with a very special gentleman tonight. Tardiness will not be accepted."

"Thank you so much. There's a vase under the third cabinet under the sink!" I yelled over my shoulder.

"Enjoy your night."

I will. Chem would make sure of it.

With my head high and my heels higher, I strutted out of the lobby and right into the arms of the man waiting in black from head to toe. He'd learned fairly quickly that it was always the first choice and fell in line. Now, whenever we were together, we coordinated. It was intentional on his end, I supposed, but looked effortless.

A set of gold teeth gleamed under the light when his lips pulled back and a smile exposed his dimpled cheeks. My heart stopped. Time stood still. Everything around us evaporated. There was just him. There was just me. There was only us.

His hands gripped the butt of my jeans, cupping both cheeks. I stared up at him, completely and utterly obsessed with every inch of him.

The slit that ran down the center of my shirt exposed my skin. Chem's hand rested against my stomach as his lips convinced me of their lonesomeness. I shed them of their misery, parting them with my tongue so I could explore the familiar warmth.

"Ummmm."

Liquor. Peppermint. Pineapple.

Very unique, very distinctive flavors confirmed what I'd discovered the second he was in full view. Chemistry's blood alcohol level was elevated.

"Good evening, Choc."

His smile was contagious. So was his energy.

"Good evening, Chemistry," I replied, biting into the peppermint that didn't belong to me.

"After you."

He ushered me into the truck and then joined me.

Unable to keep his hands to himself, he wrapped one around my neck and shoved it backward. Involuntarily, my mouth slacked, giving him unrestricted access. Deeply and unapologetically, he kissed me.

My body grew warmer. My skin thickened with fine, tiny bumps. My breathing grew unstable.

Fuck.

My center throbbed. My chest caved. My heart ached.

Please.

As if he had telepathic powers, he released me. Breathlessly, I panted, trying to gather myself.

"Thief."

The peppermint was no longer in my possession. Not even a crumb from the three pieces it had split into under the pressure of my teeth.

Gnawing on my bottom lip, I scooted to the end of the row we were on. Distance was required if exiting the truck was in the plans at some point in the evening.

"That won't save you, Choc."

Chuckling, I pleaded with the man a few inches away. "Just let me pretend."

"If you must."

Chemistry crossed a leg over the over after grabbing a glass from the compartment in front of us. He swirled the liquor in his glass before sipping. He, then, extended his arm in my direction. Graciously, I accepted the drink. Pineapple was the first to strip my tastebuds of the toothpaste I'd used minutes ago. The cognac was next. I squeezed my eyes together in hopes of relieving the intensity of the burn. Luck wasn't on my side. I handed the concoction over without having another sip. One was more than enough.

"Argh. That is awful." I breathed out. "The splash of pineapple juice is fighting for its life in there."

Finding my complaint humorous, Chem stared at me with a silly smile on his handsome face.

"Women–" He paused.

"Are the greatest gift from God."

"Are dramatic," he challenged.

"Oh, I thought you were ready to admit that other thing."

"That's true as well. I can't deny it. I'm surrounded by them and I wouldn't trade it for anything."

Chemistry's logic was interesting. He valued women, their contributions to the world, and everything they stood for. However, he didn't care to cultivate relationships with women who didn't have the same last name as him or one of his brothers. Not until me, at least.

We quieted down. When my system was regulated, I inched closer to Chem. The distance easily got the best of me. As I snuggled against him, a silk fabric was lowered over my head, not stopping until my eyes were covered.

"Home?" I questioned.

"No."

Instead of tossing questions out and hoping something stuck, I quieted down and settled in. The volume of the music increased, drowning my thoughts. Lauryn Hill's voice boomed throughout the truck.

Ready or not.

Here I come.
You can't hide.
I'm gonna find you.

The words were fitting. In the back of my head, I knew whether Chem was ready or not, my team was coming to find him. And now that he was in our line of sight, there wouldn't be any hiding. He was too precious to our investigation. We knew exactly what he did and how he did it. What we didn't have was evidence connecting him to his crimes.

He was not a drug dealer. He was not a smuggler. Neither was he a handler. Those occupations made our jobs easy. They laid the trap for themselves and were quickly captured with the evidence in bulk. Chem's role was a bit more intricate. *Advanced. Revolutionary. Innovative.*

We wouldn't capture him with shipping containers full of kilos or stash houses full of baggies. He forced us to do our fucking job and doing it well would be the only way we'd break the case. However, he made it impossible because I couldn't separate my feelings from my fate. Truthfully, in no world could we exist. In the end, we'd end. There was no way around it. Hanging onto him was only prolonging the case.

The moment I disassociated and focused solely on the task at hand I'd crack it wide open. But, I wasn't ready to burst the bubble we were in. I wasn't ready to destroy all the progress we'd made. I wasn't ready to undo all the things he'd done to me, for me. I wasn't ready to break his heart or mine.

The wheels stopped spinning shortly before the wind whipped around the open door and into the truck. Chem's warmth evaporated. He'd left me alone, but only momentarily. His hand was around mine, guiding me out of the backseat within seconds.

Careful not to tip over and fall head first, I took one step at a time. The echoing of my shoes urged the belief that we were in a large, open space. The chill narrowed the location down to three or more possibilities. However, I was almost certain of one place in particular. When my eyes were uncovered, my assumption became my reality.

A warehouse.

"Mmmmm. Mmm!"

Muffled sounds beckoned for my attention. Straight ahead, only a few feet away, I laid eyes on a bound and gagged figure. I stepped forward, trying to comprehend what was happening and why the person seated looked so familiar. Squinted eyes and a closer look confirmed my suspicions.

"Ch–"

"Aht. Aht," Chemistry warned with a finger in the air.

"Wh– why is he– You promised you wouldn't lay a hand on him."

My body flushed with heat. Hyperventilating, I began to run through the scenarios, the conversations, and all the information Chemistry had possibly gotten from the man in the chair.

"And I haven't. If I'd laid a hand on him, Choc, he'd

have a hole in his fucking head. Does this man have a hole in his fucking head?" He asked, pointing at Adonis.

"Mm! Mmmmm!"

Chem tilted his chin, closing his eyes in an effort to maintain his composure.

"He's a noisy nigga, so yes, I'd love to put my hands on this bitch, but I'm a man of my word. I haven't spoken to him and neither have I touched him."

"Why is he here? I thought we were having din–"

It was then the aroma touched my nose.

"We are."

"With him?"

"Of course not with him. I have other plans for him."

Flustered, I began to feel my skin crawl. Whatever was happening had my stomach in knots. Adonis was a huge risk. I wanted to kick my own ass for ever mentioning him. I was so caught up in the moment, interlocking my world with Eden's world that I gave a name that wasn't supposed to be given. There was a complete work-up for Eden. Ex-boyfriends included. *Fuck.*

"I don't understand what's going on," I disclosed.

"Not a nigga alive will successfully break your heart and sleep peacefully at night as if that shit never happened. I think it's time he got to experience what you dealt with... what you're still dealing with."

"I'm not."

"Keep telling yourself that, baby, but when you're ready to talk about it, you can sit on my sister's couch."

"Okay, maybe there is still some underlying pain there, but it's not that big of a deal."

"Every time you screen my calls, it becomes a big deal. The fact that you're panicked if my time and attention aren't devoted to you makes it a big deal. The way that you hold me at night as if I'm going to slip away and into somebody else's pussy while you're asleep makes it a big deal.

"How you tried to sabotage our shit before it even got started makes it a big deal. Instead of trying to piss me off by dipping and dabbing, I figured getting down to the source would help you begin to heal whatever this fuck nigga did. At least that's what my therapist suggests."

I hadn't found a lie in his statement. I wished I had a rebuttal, but I didn't. Though I'd completely blocked those memories, that hurt Adonis had caused, I hadn't forgotten it. Daily, it was manifesting in my relationship with Chem.

Since Adonis, I hadn't committed myself to another relationship out of fear history would repeat itself. Chemistry didn't give me the opportunity to run from him. He was too addictive. Every change I got, I was running toward him with my mouth agape and my pussy drooling.

"So, we're going to have a nice, quiet dinner in the room right over there. It's soundproof. And together, we're going to watch this niggas heart crumble."

"Mmmmm. Mmmm. Mmm."

Adonis sounded off as Chem's driver handed him a

device that he pointed at the wall. The bright lights lowered and a large screen appeared on the blank wall. A recording began to play. Baffled, I stood beside Chem waiting for instructions.

"A few weeks ago, Eden shared your name with me. Simultaneously, she shared that you were happily married with a wife and children. I put my boy Benny to work almost immediately. I was a bit taken aback when he reported back just three days later with your wife's cell number, your home address, her office address, and an invitation to dinner on the one free night she has each week while you spend time with the kids alone."

"Mmmm. Mmm."

The guy I'd seen near my building on multiple occasions came into view. Shannon, who I'd learned was the woman Adonis had married years ago, stood in front of the camera moments later.

She's an old friend.

Don't worry about her.

I'm not fucking her Egypt.

Me and her are just friends.

I wasn't with Shannon.

The lies came rushing back but were silenced when Chem's voice rang out. Everything began to make more sense as he continued.

"That was two weeks ago. She's been trying to give up that pussy ever since. Unfortunately, you weren't staying with the children this week because you were set to catch an impromptu flight this afternoon for business and not return for three days. Because she couldn't get to

Benny, she told Benny to come over at eight when the children were sound asleep."

Shannon wasted little time undressing. Completely naked, she climbed onto the bed and beckoned for Benny to join her.

"After picking her brain and learning her kinks, he discovered she'd always fantasized about having sex in the bed she shared with her husband while being recorded. In the event she discovered his work trips were not really work trips, and were in fact time spent with another woman, then after she won the custody battle, their home, and half of everything he made for the rest of his life, she'd send him that fucking tape."

Chemistry laughed with a shake of his head. Adonis had grown silent, his eyes big as saucers as he peered at the large screen where his wife was stuffing her jaws with Benny's dick. He wore no protection. Tears touched Adonis' cheeks and the sobbing began.

"Luckily for you, I'm on your side, Adonis. You don't have to wait to see what your wife is up to when you're away on business. Because I'm showing you."

She quickly made a mess of the act. Saliva trailed down her chin and began to drip onto the bed as she bobbed, allowing Benny to stroke her mouth, simultaneously.

"I don't know, man. It doesn't look like her first time putting another niggas balls in her mouth. She's way too comfortable but I could be wrong. But, uh, I have no interest, so I'll leave you alone. I have a meal waiting for me."

By the hand, Chemistry led me in the opposite direction. Relief washed over me. Learning Adonis wasn't allowed to speak and hadn't been spoken to resolve the tension in my chest, but it didn't clear me completely.

"Chemistry," I called out to him as we entered the private room that was lit with candles and smelled divine.

"Yes, my love?" Tenderly, he bit into the strawberry he picked from the small fruit bar against the wall.

"Sometimes I don't understand you. There's no reason for Adonis to be down there."

"I never asked you to understand me, Eden. I've made it clear that it's an impossible task."

"Explain this to me." I groaned.

"Eye for an eye."

"Is that your explanation?"

"He should've chosen wiser." He shrugged, picking up another strawberry, nearly making me lose my train of thought.

I wanted him to handle me that way. Gently. Carefully. Lovingly. Right off the table and into his mouth. That's what I needed to forget everything happening downstairs.

He continued to make himself clear. Over and over. He'd wage war if it meant my happiness. He'd shed blood if it meant his. Still, as a woman of the law, I found it hard to wrap my head around it. Around him.

"Had he and we wouldn't be together. It would be me who he'd married."

"Had he and his life would've tragically ended if that meant having you to myself. Have you not gotten it through your skull, Eden? We're inevitable. We were going to happen regardless. Now, fix your face before I think you're in your feelings about that nigga and I end up breaking my promise. Let that man make it back home to his children, at least, because his wife is as good as gone."

His hands were around my waist before I could protest. His lips pecked my forehead and then my cheek before I could push him away. I didn't have the strength for either. He weakened me. Handicapped me. Stripped me of all my powers.

"You're insufferable." I sighed into his mouth.

"Suckable?" he mumbled. "I couldn't hear you. Is that what you said?"

"I–"

His pants hit the floor instantly. The sound of his belt crashing into the concrete sent me spiraling.

"Then suck this motherfucker, Choc."

I was on my knees in a split second. He'd never have to ask me to consume him twice.

I devoured him. He gripped my ponytail to gain leverage and slow me down. I fought against him but lost in the end. But, so did he. He pulled me up by the hair and kissed me with a vengeance as our food was delivered to our table.

We started with appetizers. Chem ended that course with me. We ate our entrees. Chem washed his down with more of me. Instead of dessert, I took Chem into my mouth, again. And by the time our plates were cleared off the table, my body had landed. On the cream linen, he fucked me as if the world was coming to an end.

By the time I pulled myself together and made it down the stairs. There wasn't a sign of Adonis. Aden stood next to the truck waiting for our arrival. We climbed in and found comfort fast. He stroked my arm with two fingers, putting me at ease. Within minutes, I was asleep.

FOURTEEN

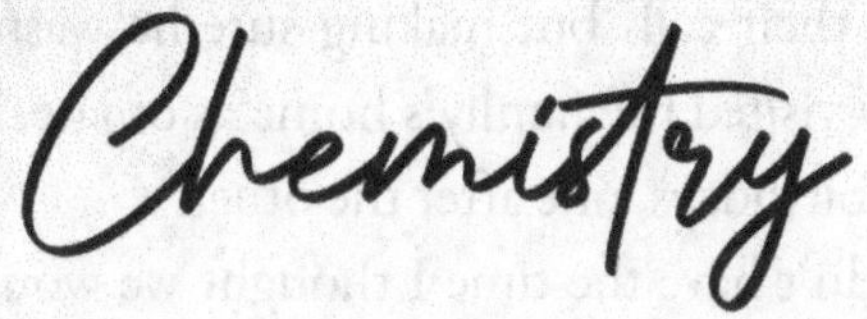

Backward.
  Forward.
  Backward.
  Forward.
  I lapped the pool with the intention of releasing the stress that built each time I saw my father's face. He was dying. I could smell death in his home. I saw it on his face. I heard it in his voice. He'd done what he'd promised he wouldn't.

He's given up.

It angered me. Knowing he was the glue holding my sanity together and that I was losing him made me sick to my stomach. Losing him was never in the plan. At least not so soon. He was supposed to grow old and die of natural causes. Having cancer end his time on earth made me feel robbed.

Wasn't my mother e-fucking-nough? I questioned God as I fought the water, pounding my fist into its depths as I came up for air.

It had been two days since I'd last seen him and I hadn't slept a wink. Getting through Roaman's dinner celebration would be impossible without questions arising. Those women were a lot of things, but ignorant wasn't one of them.

My father had managed to elude them for weeks now, answering their calls but making sure he wasn't around when they visited the family's home as of late. But, there were four birthdays, one after the other.

We didn't have the time I thought we would to keep his condition under wraps. Everything was changing for him and fast. He'd have to face them and his reality. He wouldn't be with us much longer.

"FUCK!"

I climbed out of the water and grabbed a towel from the warmer. It didn't matter how much I tried over the last forty-eight hours, I couldn't find peace. Not even thoughts of Eden soothed the aches my father's sickness caused.

"Fuck!" A bit more defeated, a bit more defenseless, I whispered into the towel I used to pat my face.

Under the steady flow of warm water, I shed the emotions that weakened me and broadcasted my vulnerability. There were seven girls I'd need to remain level-headed for. When they crumbled, falling alongside them wasn't an option for me. My time to lead the family had come.

No sympathy for a soldier.

I ended the shower and ambled out of the pool quarter without a single thread clinging to my skin. I'd given my housekeeper the week off because I was in no mood for human interaction, not unless their name began with an E and ended with an N.

There was a pang in my chest at the thought of her. Though I hadn't found peace in the last forty-eight hours, she was the closest thing to it. That's why I kept her near. Her presence just made sense in my world.

Up the stairs and in the master suite is where I found her. Sprawled across the bed I'd taken from her place, she slept without a care in the world. The ease I promised her had Eden living softly. Gently. Carefree. Just the way women were created to live.

I slid into a pair of briefs, hating the idea of waking her but I knew we'd be late if I didn't. I wouldn't hear the end of it from my father and I wouldn't stop chastising myself, either. Even being on time in our family home was considered late.

In a fresh pair of briefs, I sat next to Eden on the bed. Her skin was glowing. She took her precious time oiling her body from head to toe every day. It was one of those things I could sit and watch her carry on with forever. It was slow, careful, and deliberate. Every movement. Every detail.

I pushed her hair out of her face. She'd spent the

night with me and hadn't gotten out of bed to do anything but bathe, eat, and use the toilet. I depleted her of her energy every chance I got, trying to relieve the stress that was riding on me. Between her pussy and the pool, which didn't feel very different, I thought I'd feel better now. But, I was wrong. Nothing could soothe the pain of losing a parent. In my case, your only biological parent.

"Baby," I whispered.

She didn't budge, but I was certain she'd heard me.

"We have to get dressed and out of the house by five."

"Hm?"

She maneuvered in bed, ruffling the sheets. Against her dark skin, the contrast to the white sheets was remarkable. We'd make beautiful children.

"Wake up, Choc."

She reached over and pulled me into bed with her. I didn't resist, because the urge was already present. I was struggling to keep my composure, but it was hardly useless. Eden would always win.

Whatever she wants. Whatever she needs.

"Just lay with me. Please. For ten minutes," she groaned, making my heart skip a beat.

"Five."

I wrapped her in my arms, allowing her to get five more minutes of rest. She deserved it. She'd been working me over, extracting nut from my sack for over twenty-four hours. I knew she'd need more time to recover. Time wasn't on our side, though. We had a dinner to attend.

"Fine." She yawned. "Seven."

I compromised, setting the timer on my phone for seven minutes. Because I knew I wouldn't sleep through it, I closed my eyes for a few minutes as well. As Eden's breathing changed, mine did as well. Together, we snoozed, wrapped in each other's warmth.

"Baby." Choc's voice stirred me awake.

"I'm up."

"You're literally asleep." She chuckled, sleep still evident in her voice.

For the first time in days, I found a bit of peace and it was stolen minutes later by an annoying alarm and the woman who visited my dreams more often than not.

"I'm up. We should get dressed."

"We should."

I was thankful I wasn't blinded by the main light in the suite. The low lights that were scattered about the room and automatically shined in the darkness were perfect. It was a small detail Rhea was adamant about during the build, but I'd thought was pointless at the time. I'd spend the rest of my life thanking her for the suggestion. They grew brighter as motion was detected and dimmed again when motion was no longer detectable.

"I should've figured out what I was wearing before I laid down."

Eden couldn't keep her mouth closed. She yawned again, stretching her arms in the air. Her bare body was hardly covered in sheets. Her nipples hardened as the

AC unit kicked on, sheeting the entire room with cool air.

She shivered. With both her hands, she rubbed her arms and slid out of bed. I stood, gathering my bearings as well. Eden made her way toward the closet where her wardrobe was growing. I stopped her in her tracks.

"Your things are in the guest room, Choc, on the bed waiting."

She twirled on her heels, a smile stripping the restfulness from her eyes.

"You can't help yourself, can you?"

"You don't give me much of a fucking choice, baby."

"What if I told you I don't want to be alone as I get dressed? I haven't left out of the room and you already feel too far away. You made me sleep alone last night and this evening. If I get dressed alone, I'm going to start thinking you're tired of me." She blew smoke up my ass, pouting all while doing it.

"You don't believe that shit. It doesn't even sound good coming out of your mouth."

I approached her, wrapping my arm around her neck. I pulled her into my chest and grabbed a hand full of her ass.

"Stay put. I'll go get your shit and bring it in here."

"Thank you."

"A fucking shame, Choc."

"What?"

"Rotten!"

"Would you have me any other way?"

"I'd put your pretty ass back where you came from," I confessed.

Spoiling was my ministry. Years of catering to my sisters had given me lots of practice. I exited in pursuit of her things. I returned moments later finding out she'd migrated to the bathroom where she was brushing her teeth. I joined, grabbing my brush and placing it underneath the dispenser.

My heart galloped, hard and viciously as I stared at our reflection. The person I saw in the mirror this evening was not the person I saw months ago, in the same mirror. Mentally, I'd grown. Emotionally, I'd matured. Physically, I'd changed.

No longer was I that empty shell of a man. The person beside me filled that void. Made me whole. Made me hopeful. Made me happy.

"A penny for your thoughts," Eden turned toward me and requested.

She'd finished cleaning her teeth and was preparing to gargle. My semen was hiding in parts of her mouth that the toothbrush couldn't reach.

I spat in the sink before using the running water to rinse my mouth.

"Thank you."

"Me?"

Her eyebrows raised, forming squiggly lines on her forehead.

"Yes, you, Choc."

"For what, baby?"

She was clueless. She hardly understood the magnitude of her influence.

"For everything and nothing. For your presence. Your patience. Your light. Your love. Your energy. Your fearlessness. And for fucking with a nigga like me."

"And thank you."

She peered at me through the mirror with a smile. We were alike in a lot of ways, one being the way we felt the need to reciprocate the praise given because we didn't want the spotlight shining too bright or the flaws would begin to show. The day she came to terms with her flawlessness in my eyes, she'd grow comfortable with my ovations.

"Nah– thank you." I countered. She continued, eyes never leaving mine.

"For your attentiveness. Your attention to detail. Your delicacy. Your gentleness. Your curiosity. Your willingness to explore. Your ability to love even when the capacity was limited. Your vulnerability even though it's hard. Your wisdom. Your— *Everything*. If I had the chance to do this all again, I wouldn't change a thing, Chemistry.

"Not about you, about me, or about us. You bring me so much joy. So much happiness. So much adventure. I'm not sure what my life was without you, but it must've been hell. Because in some strange way, it feels like you're my slice of heaven."

"Niggas like me don't make it there, baby," I reminded her.

"But, you must know what it's like because you've created it for me in the midst of all the flames."

I didn't try to elude her or the feelings the moment birthed. Rather had forbid it. Those days were over. I was ready to step fully into my role as Eden's partner and that started with the difficult conversations, ones that were unbearably uncomfortable and packed with emotions.

"Admittedly, I don't know what the fuck I'm doing, saying, or even feeling right now. What I do know is nothing has ever felt this way, or made me feel this way. I doubt I'll ever feel this shit for anyone else, again. My father is dying of cancer and before he takes his last breath, I promised I'd produce an heir.

"That hasn't come to fruition and even if it does, our child wouldn't enter this world before he leaves it. Time isn't on my side, Eden. Before he goes, I want to make you my wife. I'm not asking for it to be tomorrow, next week, or even next month. But, before he–"

"Is that why we went to the jewelers last–"

I nodded.

"I'm so sorry to hear– I– I lost my father to cancer. It wasn't until you appeared that I forgot how good life can be when grief isn't swallowing you whole. I'm so sorry, Chemistry."

"Don't be. It's life, Eden. You live and you die. Those are the only two sure things life gives us. Everything in between is no guarantee."

"What about chemo?"

"He's old, Eden. Chemo would kill him before it could

begin to heal him. This isn't his first battle. He promised if it ever returned, he'd accept his fate. Those toxins nearly destroyed him. I didn't see him for sixteen months. I remember it vividly because it was the worst year and four months of my life. It was before my mothe—yeah." I paused.

"Baby–"

"I've been given one person, but it feels like it's at the cost of another. It's fuck up. This life guts you and then digs your grave."

"Is that what's been bothering you? Your last visit with your father?"

"The last few, but the one two days ago hasn't left me yet. It won't allow me to rest. Every time I close my eyes, there he is in a casket."

"I wish there was something I could do– something I could say–"

"You being here right now, Choc, that's all I need from you. Baby, it's all I'll ever need from you. Just stay by my side. I've got the rest. Always."

She stood on the tips of her toes and wrapped her arms around me.

"I love you."

"I love you, too."

Every time those words left my mouth, a weight was lifted. Eden was my peace. Even in the midst of this storm, she managed to offer some amount of solace.

"In this lifetime and the others," she responded, looking up at me with a smile.

"You gone find me there?"

"I promise."

"I'm holding you to that, Choc, 'cause a nigga gone be waiting."

<h1 style="text-align:center">THE GREYLIST</h1>

A fleet of luxury cars lined the driveway of our family home. In addition to my siblings, there were a host of guests that included associates of the birthday girl and some family from Rhea's tree. Mother Sheryl, the matriarch of the Franklins. Father Westly. Heather. Lindsey. Jermain. Jacob. Kendra. Kassie. And a handful of fully vetted associates who cared to celebrate Roaman's special day.

Eden clung to my right side as we took the steps. We had only made it up two of them when the loud, thunderous bass in the distance summoned us both. Out of her newest addition to the collection, Roulette bolted before the engine had come to a complete stop. With a shake of the head, I observed as she checked her reflection in the side mirror and swept a thick piece of hair behind her ear.

She strutted past all the cars and met me on the second step, hardly giving me room to release the frustrated air that had begun building the second I heard her loud ass speakers. Realizing what she'd chosen to add to her fleet increased the pressure.

"Hello, Roulette."

"Well, hello, Chemistry."

"Giselle." She nodded toward Eden.

"Eden," I corrected her.

"Same difference," she replied, sucking her teeth.

"Hi," Eden greeted her. "And yes, it's Eden."

Tilting her head with a nod, she exposed the gum she'd been rolling around her tongue. "Okay. I knew I hired you for a reason. I love the little campfire you always have going. Please note I'm an entire field of fire. Wild. Untamable. Easily agitated. Hard to maintain. Even harder to smolder."

I chuckled, finding her speech comical. "Good thing she's fucking a fireman, baby."

Eden's neck whipped in my direction at the realization it was Roulette I was calling baby and not her.

"She's a lot of mouth, Choc."

"And action. Don't forget that part, Chem."

"Oh, I won't," I assured her. "But that's nothing she has to worry about."

"Umm. Hmmm. You two are cute together. You–"

She held her index fingers close to one another. "Fit so well. And you're dressed alike. This is so sweet."

"Please, Roulette."

Eden was all teeth, smiling from ear to ear as her cheeks blushed a dark purple.

"Black is my favorite color. Well, and red," she blabbered, rolling her eyes.

She tapped the key fob, securing her whip.

"You locking that motherfucker like somebody wants it. Better not let Pops see that disgrace in his front yard. He might get that shit towed."

"What's wrong with it? It's an i8!"

"It's a BMW. And the B stands for bullshit."

"Like the B in Ben–"

"Mercedez Benz."

"Whatever."

"Magnificent. Memorable. Ma–"

"I get it," she sassed, lifting the top of the box in my hand without my permission.

"Baby, what are you doing?"

"This better be pre-owned." Roulette scoffed.

By the flaring of her nose and the way she looked up at me with eyes slimmed to slits, I knew she was unhappy.

"That's insulting."

"This is insulting."

"The 30 Jaune Ambre– Croc– All I got was a vintage Kelly."

"They're both Hermès, Roulette. Both Birkins."

"And the B in mine stands for bullshit."

"It was vintage, not worn."

"Do I look like a vintage bitch?"

"You don't look like a bitch at all, baby."

"You understand what I'm saying."

"I don't. Clarify."

She sighed. "Tonight isn't about me. Tonight is about Ro. But, you owe me, Teddy. This bag is at least $15,000 more than the one you–"

"Exactly, so why are you pouting? Just tell me you want something better and I'll get you something better."

"She wants something better." Eden laughed. "Surely she wants something better."

"Thank you. And you should get her one to for all the chaos you've caused out here tonight."

"I haven't caused shit. That's all you." I chuckled as I watched her put the lid on the box.

"Whatever." She walked off, on her way inside to cause more hell.

"What did you get her, since you're complaining about my gift?"

"Nothing. That's from us all."

"No, the fuck it's not," I countered, unable to contain my laughter. Roulette was so fucking full of herself that you couldn't help but love her.

"I am the gift. Having me as a sister is a privilege. Not everyone can say they have a Roulette. I'm rare and very fucking expensive."

"I won't deny that last bit."

"You can't deny any of it."

"Take your ass back outside if you didn't get baby anything for her birthday. If no one else deserves a gift, she does. She's put up with the foolishness of six women who came after her, all stepping on her nerves for a different reason and in a different way. Not to mention, besides Rome, she's the only one with real sense."

"I'm happy you didn't include yourself because you're the most senseless of us all."

I couldn't deny that, either. The doors opened when we approached, welcoming us into our territory, a place where we could disrobe and become the people our parents had raised instead of the people they'd made.

"I got her a gift, Chemistry."

"Then where is it?"

"It's not anything tangible. It's a vacation. Seven days, to a very special island off the coast of Ja–"

"You're full of shit," I tittered, knowing exactly where this was going.

She was referring to one of the three islands I owned. On two, I'd managed to begin an entirely different civilization from the one we knew and grew up in. The other was private and a place for family to vacation when they needed to get away. All three were equally gorgeous.

"Take my plane. Stay at my home. What part of the trip do you begin contributing?"

"Shopping. I think that's where I come in. Any shopping she wants to do while we're there, I promise I'll handle."

"She hates shopping."

"Even better."

"You're full of shit, Roulette," I called out to her as she tiptoed toward the large dining hall.

"I got her a new Rolex. The one she's been wearing is busted!" she yelled over her shoulder.

It was in her nature to bring us hell, but she meant no harm. Growing up in a home where jokes were few and far apart, Roulette had them lined up and ready to spit whenever the opportunity presented itself. In the field, she was nothing like the woman we'd just encountered on the steps.

She was a weapon. She was nontolerant. She ran her business with an iron fist. If she ever cracked a smile, someone had better be worried.

"That's Roulette. I'm sure you've met her before."

Stunned into silence, Eden shook her head. "I haven't. I mean uh– not exactly. I was going to me– meet her the last night I worked, but then you came and–"

"Well, then, that's Roulette."

The doors of the dining hall opened. Family and a few unfamiliar faces filled almost every chair around the table. Roulette had even taken her seat. I placed Roaman's gift behind her, against the wall where the others were. She slid her chair back and stretched her arms wide, accepting my love.

"You must be Eden?" she asked, still holding onto me.

"Yes."

"Thank you for coming, I'm Roaman."

"Happy Birthday."

She cut me loose, ignoring Eden's extended arm. She pulled her in for a hug instead.

"Nice to finally meet you."

"It is," Eden expressed, stepping away and immediately searching for me with her hand.

I put her mind and heart at ease, lacing my fingers through hers. We made our way to the head of the table where Richie and Rhea were.

"Eden, this is my father," I introduced my old man. "Rowan. You can call him Richie."

"Richie?" She whispered.

"His middle name is Richard."

"Nice to meet you, Richie."

My father stood, getting a firm grip on Eden's free hand before shaking it.

"The pleasure is mine."

He was a man of few words, especially when it came to strangers, so I wasn't surprised when he sat down and allowed us to continue.

"Rhea, Eden. Eden, Rhea, my mother."

Stepmother was her title, but she was much more than it entailed. Catherine had birthed me, but Rhea had molded me. She was a lifetime of stability in a mother figure, something I'd experienced in my mother until it was all snatched away.

When her mental health started to decline, so did my happiness. So did the happiness of everyone around her. That's what I was afraid of most while fighting my own mental health battle.

I'd never experienced a crisis, but I knew I was capable. I understood that my mind wasn't as flawless as it seemed and there were parts of me I couldn't control if I wanted to. My impulsiveness was a sign of my illness. My thirst for blood was another one. It wasn't my soul that was satisfied after; it was something deeper, something inexplicable that was fulfilled.

There were many dimensions to me, so many, I was still trying to discover the paths to them all. That's why I needed Eden to stop trying to piece together my puzzle. Some pieces didn't fit and they never would.

"Hello, Eden. I'm so happy to finally put a face to the name."

You've had a face to the name, I thought. I was no fool. My father had shown her Eden's picture, probably back as far as her grade school photos. She lied with a straight face, nearly forcing me to laugh.

Richie's damn wife.

"Rather, Royce, Range... Eden."

I made it around the table, leaning in to hug Rome.

"Baby, this is Eden. Eden, this is my youngest sister, Rome. She's the baby of the family. She's my eyes, my ears, and my heart. She's also a ballerina. She has a big show coming in a few months. We'll be there."

"I can hardly wait. Nice to meet you, Rome."

"Likewise."

I'd waited as long as I possibly could to poke the resting beast. Rugger sat next to chairs designated for Eden and me. I contemplated leaving well enough alone, but Eden nudged me as we prepared to sit, urging me to make the introduction.

"Rugger," I called out.

She didn't move an inch. Her eyes remained on the glass in her hand twirling it while possibly thinking of a hundred ways she could unalive Eden with it and sleep well tonight knowing she had.

"This is Eden. Eden, Rugger."

"Nice to me–"

"Another round, please, Veronica?" politely, she asked.

The disrespect was intolerable. Instead of getting

comfortable in my seat, I stalked hers, not stopping until I was in front of her with it pulled out from underneath the table.

"I don't like making scenes, Rugger. We have guests, baby. But, if you want to take it there, make sure you're ready to take it all the way there. I've never disrespected you, not even once. I expect the same from you.

"By disrespecting Eden, you are disrespecting everything I stand for. You will fix your fucking face and you will smile and you will greet her just like the others. If you have a problem with that, we can take this shit outside. Have I made myself clear?" I whispered in her ear.

As I gave her space to digest everything I'd said, I smoothed the wrinkles of my jacket with a smile. "Clear?"

Chuckling, she nodded. "Very."

Rugger was every bit of me. Every bit of Richie. Rhea was nowhere to be found. We'd marked the poor girl.

"Well, then," I concluded our conversation without having to say another word.

I leaned in and kissed her forehead. Slowly, I turned her back around and pushed her forward until her chair was almost under the table. However, it was facing Eden, who was too startled to speak.

"Good evening, Eden."

"U-uh... Hello."

"Now, wasn't that easy?" I asked, close enough to her face so only she and I could hear.

"I can think of something much more satisfying and easi—"

"Rugger."

"Hello, Chemistry." She sighed, falling in line though she'd much rather be defiant.

"That's better."

I patted my palm against the side of her face, gently. Rugger was a fucking headache, but she had my heart. When I looked at her pretty face, I saw so much of me. If there was any chance a woman could head the family business, it was her. I believed it wholeheartedly. But, unfortunately, they weren't given the opportunity.

"Eden, everyone. Everyone, Eden."

I'd made my rounds and introduced Eden to the people she'd encountered most. The people who meant the most to me. At a later time, I'd be sure Mother and Father Franklin had a chance to chat with her. For now, they were too busy trying to stay awake. Their bedtime was at seven, exactly when dinner started.

Everyone around us had fallen back into conversation by the time Rugger and Eden had been properly introduced. I wasn't sure if the other conversations had ever stopped. Maybe it was time that stood still when a woman I love shunned another I loved. Or, maybe it was everything around me. I wasn't too sure, but something had stopped. Maybe it was my heart.

Salads were the first on the table. The menu had been planned months ahead of time. Roaman had chosen her favorites but gave wiggle room for those who might've preferred things that weren't on her shortlist. She was the most accommodating of them all. Had it been anyone else, they wouldn't have given a damn what anyone else preferred. I couldn't say I would've either.

Eden chose a Caesar salad. I went with the house selection. Though mine looked and smelled divine, I picked off her plate until I'd had a decent helping.

"Now... yours."

She pulled my plate in her direction and began forking my greens. Suddenly, I was interested in the salad I'd chosen again.

"It's good."

"It is," she agreed. "What kind of dressing is this?"

"Rhea makes the dressings from scratch. I'm afraid I'll botch the name and disappoint her if I try to pronounce it."

"I'll have to get this recipe."

It was creamy and rich, thick in texture with hints of garlic and citrus.

"I'll make sure it gets to you. She's been creating a cookbook for the girls since they were babies. She has over five hundred recipes, now."

"Seriously?" Eden's eyes blossomed like flowers.

"Rhea!" I belted, grabbing hold of her attention.

"Yes, son?"

"I was telling Eden about your recipes. You're up to five hundred or so now, correct?"

"Oh, Chemistry, you're behind. I'm well into six hundred. The last time we chatted about the book was over a year ago. It's grown tremendously since then."

"Does dad know? Or has he been around for the

results, because it doesn't look like he's had anything to eat all month," Royce pointed out. "Are you on a diet we don't know about, old man? Preparing to look good on a beach? I need that amount of discipline."

Clicking his tongue, my father sucked his tongue. "Not voluntarily."

Worry lines creased my face. Tonight was Roaman's night. Her heart wouldn't be able to stand the bomb our father would drop on it.

"I've de–" I was cut off almost instantly.

"I'm moving forward with the Berkeley plan. Roulette is expanding. Two sister-establishments. Securing locations is the next step. I have two in mind, both currently owned and operated by others."

Roulette looked over at me with that adorable smirk of hers that I loved so much. With a wink, she let me know what she'd done was lightweight and handling the stress of a situation only she and I were aware of was nothing.

Thank you. I mouthed.

"They'll be yours by tomorrow if you'd like."

If Roulette wanted to expand, then Roulette would expand. Whoever was in her way would have to move or be moved.

"I'm in no hurry. Busy is slow. They'll be ready to sell everything by the time I am ready."

"Good. Whatever you need, baby."

"The way you refer to them as baby," Eden whispered. "That's adorable."

"Doesn't matter how old they get. They'll still be babies in my eyes. Mine, more specifically."

"I promise to let you know."

"She'll bleed your pockets dry," Range warned.

"I doubt that's obtainable, Range." I sucked my teeth and sat back in the chair I was in.

"Does this mean you're leaving us?" Royce forked her greens as she posed the question. The pained look on her face let me know she wasn't too happy with Roulette's news.

"No. But, I will be back and forth–a lot."

"Oh." Royce sighed, releasing a visibly deep breath.

"Would you have missed me?"

"Y–"

"I would've," Rome admitted.

"Me, too," Range chimed in.

"Of course, I would've." Roaman nodded.

"Me, too," Rather claimed.

They all waited for Rugger to speak. They'd be waiting forever and we all knew it. Laughter erupted around the table.

"Rugger," my father called out to her. "Be nice."

Appetizers appeared as his warning surfaced. They were sitting in between each set of chairs for easy access. The helpings were large and diverse so sharing was encouraged. The deviled eggs and sweet chili salmon bites were the first to be transferred to my plate and the first to be demolished.

"Try this, baby," Eden convinced me, holding a fork to my face.

I accepted the piece of grilled shrimp and bell pepper tossed in a savory marinade she'd pulled from the skewer.

"Good, right?"

Because my mouth was still full, I nodded. It was clear I'd leave with a few pounds and an upset stomach in tow. There was at least one more birthday dinner before the month ended, so history would only repeat itself.

Chatter was minimized as everyone began to explore their palette, some expanding it while others stuck to the foods they were most comfortable with. Eden had a bit of everything on the appetizer dish. I looked around the table and discovered my sisters had all done the same. Just as I'd imagined, she fit right in.

To my surprise, she had pulled Rugger from her dungeon. The two were involved in chatter, Rugger explaining the importance of the work she does as a forensic specialist. Eden didn't blink once. Her interest was piqued.

Rugger then began to explain the occupations and hobbies of the rest of the bunch. She skated right over mine as if it wasn't as useful as the others. Rome twirled in a circle for a living and if she lived off that salary alone, she'd be out on the street.

Her monthly allowance kept her afloat. Yet, Rugger spent the most time convincing Eden of how special Rome's talents were and how much more intrigued she was with her in comparison to everyone who needed an education to seek their dreams.

"So, Eden." Range's curiousness saved Choc from Rugger's rare spill.

"Yes. Range, isn't it?"

"See, you're learning fast."

"Trying to keep up here," Eden disclosed.

"Range. Roulette. Rather. Rugger. Rome. Royce. Roaman." She pointed at everyone, giving her a final crash course.

Beside Range, Rome summoned me with a visibly pained expression. When our eyes met, a very hesitant, ingenuine smile barely came to fruition on her beautiful face. My stomach knotted. My heart fell into the soles of my shoes. I'd seen that look before. I knew exactly what it meant. The nature of it, however, I was unsure of.

"What's the matter, baby?" I mumbled, aware she could read my lips.

She shook her head from side to side, leaving me baffled. I tilted my head in the opposite direction, suggesting she meet me in the foyer.

"I'll be back in a minute or two." Leaning over, I explained to Eden, "Don't let them convince you of anything. None of them except that one over there. She's the good one." My finger was aimed in Roaman's direction.

"Okay."

"Excuse me."

I excused myself from the table and headed toward the entryway where Rome would be meeting me. It wasn't long before her heels were clapping against the floor. She was ravishing in the black tulle. Her hair flowed down her back and shoulders, covering almost everything her haltered dress didn't. With open arms, I pulled her into me and kissed her forehead delicately.

"It feels like it's been weeks since I've seen you." She breathed, emotionally charged and disturbed.

The imbalance was both frustrating and disheartening. Rome's gift cursed her sometimes. Tonight felt like one of those nights.

"What's the matter, baby?"

Pausing, she stepped away and began pacing a small area she drew invisible bordered around.

"Rome."

"I don't know how to say this without– I just–"

I snapped my fingers desperate to flip the switch in her head.

One.

Twice.

Immediately, the words came tumbling out.

"It's Eden," she exclaimed. "Something doesn't feel right with her."

Taken aback by the declaration, I halted. Everything around us disappeared as I digested what was being presented to me. Rome had never steered us stray. She had my best interest at heart.

However, she'd never witnessed a platonic or romantic relationship between me and another woman. Upon hearing I was seeing someone, she fought with her own feelings, her own selfishness as it pertained to me. I raked through the hair on my face as I gazed at Rome.

"I just need to ask you one question, Rome."

"Anything, Teddy."

"Is she no good for me or is it your heart that's hurting at the thought you'll lose pieces of me that have been yours since the day you were born? Is it discernment or is it heartache, baby?"

There was a thin line between the two. I just needed to be sure.

"I– I can't be sure. This feels like nothing I've ever experienced before."

"Because it is something you've never experienced before. This is new for us all. I am not dismissing what you've said to me. I'm locking it in here." I pointed to my head.

"But, until you can decipher... until you can separate your feelings from this matter... give me a definite answer, nothing changes, okay? But, when, and if you say the word, Rome, I'll handle it accordingly."

"Okay."

The worry lines that creased her forehead were repulsive.

"Listen, don't worry about me, okay?"

"You say that like it's so easy. It's not."

"Just don't, baby. I'm alright. I can handle my shit."

"I've never worried about you because I know that already. But, things change."

"And so do people. Please keep that in mind when you're finalizing your decision. Alright?"

"Okay."

"You look beautiful, Rome. Has anyone told you that tonight?"

"You."

"Good, then. That's enough right there."

I took her by the hand and led her down the hallway. Just before we entered the dining hall where everyone was waiting, Rome stopped.

"What is it?"

"I do like her," she told me.

"But, not for me?" I chuckled.

"The verdict is still out."

"You want your big brother to yourself and I get it. But, how will he give you nephews and nieces if you don't want him to find someone to give them to him?"

"Yeah. Yeah, Teddy." She chortled.

"When you're ready, let me know, okay?"

"I will."

A final kiss on the forehead and we were headed back inside. Seeing Eden had changed seats and was occupying Rome's chair to get closer to the action and a healthier distance for ease of conversation, made parts of me smile. But the pang in my chest was potent, forcing me to disregard everything else for a moment. It wasn't until she was by my side, her palm was against mine, and she was unveiling those three words I often yearned for that I settled.

"I love you," she confessed, resting her head on my shoulder.

FIFTEEN

Eden

Seeing Art's face after so many months gave me all the feels. I didn't want to let her go.

"Argh. I wish I could hold on to you all day."

"Then we'd never have a chance to chat or have anything to drink," she teased, taking her seat.

The simple denim pants and shirt she wore were as adorable as she was. Art was a minimalist. In her world, less was more. I'd adapted a number of her ways and they made life so much simpler.

"I need something very strong, so I guess it makes sense to let you go, after all."

"Hiiiiiii," she exaggerated, grabbing my hands from across the table.

"Right. It feels like forever has passed us by."

"I love your hair. Is this how you've been wearing it for your new gig?"

"Yes, but I'm thinking about adding it to the rotation when it's all over."

My heart crumbled at the thought.

Oh Chemistry.

Art dipped a chip into the salsa as her head bounced. She agreed with the decision.

"Yes. I think you should."

"Yeah."

Sadness blanketed me. I'd grown anxious over the last twenty-four hours. I spent a full two days with Chem and family, falling head over heels for each and every one of them for different reasons. The girls were the epitome of elegance. Their brains weren't full of air like most women born into wealth. They were knowledgeable.

In the short period we'd mixed and mingled, they had taught me so much. Chem had put most of them on a plane and sent them on vacation for Roaman and Royce's birthdays. They'd filter in until everyone arrived. I'd been convinced to join them and would when Chem wrapped up his schedule on Friday evening and could accommodate me.

"Start talking, babe. I don't like the dread I hear in your voice."

"I messed up, Art. Royally."

I palmed my face, groaning as Chem's handsome face appeared behind my lids.

"Hi, ladies. I'll be your server this afternoon. Can I get you started with some appetizers or something to drink?"

Though I couldn't see our waitress, I heard her. The bubbly energy she exuded was such a privilege I wished had been bestowed upon me this morning when I crawled out of bed. Unfortunately, there was too much on my mind, too much on my heart.

"Give me something strong."

"Give her something strong, preferably fruity. As for me, I'll have a strawberry martini."

"Alright. I'm going to put those in and come back in a few to take your orders."

"Sounds good."

The vibration in my hand prompted me to view the screen on the phone I waited near on the days Chem and I were apart. It was glued to my skin. When the opportunity to talk to him presented itself, I didn't want to miss it.

He was calling. His presence surrounded me almost immediately. The guilt made my eyes burn from the tears waiting to fall.

"Hello?"

"Head up, Choc. What's the matter?"

"Are you near?"

My elevated temperature made me hot all over. As requested, I lifted my head and pierced the arm with the peak of my nose.

"If you need me to, I can be."

"I am having lunch with a friend I miss dearly. That won't be necessary."

"You still haven't told me what's wrong."

"Bad news."

"I'll com–"

"No. You don't have to. I need this."

"Would you like me to come after?"

"No. I'd like it if you continued preparing for vacation. I'm okay, Chemistry."

"She's pretty, by the way."

I looked over at Art, who was freeing the hand of the waitress who'd brought over our drinks and those who belonged to the table near us.

"She says thanks."

"No, she didn't, baby."

"She will once I tell her."

"Alright. The meal is covered. Have a ball, Choc. I have to go."

"Thank you, Mister."

"I love you."

"I love you more."

He ended the call as I began to squeal into my hands and stomp my feet underneath the table.

"Okay, apparently, there's a lot I've missed."

With remorse sketched across my features, I nodded. "Oh my God, Art. Yes."

This is what I'd been missing, what I'd been needing. The first taste of community I'd had in the last few months happened to be the night of dinner and the following day when I joined the girls for a shopping trip.

We were all in need of vacation pieces and Chem was paying. Nothing was off limits. They'd made it clear I was entitled to any and everything my heart desired.

"Then start talking."

"One second."

I took a massive gulp of the purple concoction. It was better than I'd expected. The alcohol was potent, but not overpowering.

"This is good."

"Egypt."

"Okay. Okay. And it's Eden," I whispered.

"Sorry." Remorsefully, she apologized.

"I fell in love–" I sighed, taking another sip.

"Okay, what's the issue?"

"With the target."

I peeped around the restaurant which was covered in greenery and bold colors. Art had chosen the location. I would return surely.

Her already large eyes grew bigger. "Eg–Eden!"

"I knoooow. And it's bad. It's big. It's bold. It's breathtaking. He's– he's breathtaking. I'm letting my team down, Art. I'm letting myself down. I'm le–"

"Woah. Woah. Let's stop there. What do you mean, you're letting yourself down? I'm a lover, Eden. I know what that feels like and why it feels that way. Maybe you have let your team down, but yourself, you haven't and it's exactly why I won't agree you've messed up, babe.

"You've decided to live. And as you should. It's just a job, Eden. It's not your entire life. Whenever you're gone, they'll have someone to replace you before the dirt hardens over your casket. Don't let them choose how you live. Shed your unhealthy commitment to the clock, to your career. Let down your hair. Free yourself, friend."

Her logic had me reevaluating every doubt I had about Chem and me.

"I didn't know he was the target when we met."

"So? Even if you did. You have control of a lot of things, babe, but the thing in your chest... you don't."

"I was already gone by the time I discovered it. And nothing changed. Nothing. I think I was even more intrigued."

"I would've been."

"Ugh. It's just frustrating because the reality of us being together is... it just doesn't exist after everything comes to the forefront."

"Then you have two options. Choose yourself or choose your career."

"What are– I don't understand what you're saying."

"You understand exactly what I'm saying, babe. Put in your notice or bring him in. It's simple, Eden."

Her directness was startling. Art was the more reserved of our duet. However, her discourse on love as it pertained to life always unleashed something within her that was buried.

"It's not."

"Yes, it is, because we both know the obvious solution. There's no amount of promotions to convince me to ignore my heart if I am confident the man I've fallen in love with is for me."

"I know."

"Does he check every box?"

I nodded. "Even boxes I didn't have before him. He's added so many to the list of expectations. He exceeds them all. Advance in every way."

"How many boxes does your career check?"

She squinted, waiting for me to give her the answer.

"One," I murmured.

"One." She chortled. "So, please spare us both the unnecessary conversation and tell me about this man of yours. He sounds like a dream."

"Art, you have no idea. He is the dream."

She took a final sip of her drink as the server appeared.

"We're going to need more of these. We'll be here a while."

Flushed with excitement, I quickly finished my drink and began ordering appetizers.

THE GREY LIST

I'd taken Art's advice.

Sleep on it, Egypt. When you wake up, your heart will tell you what is best for you... if it lets you rest.

My eyes darted across the living room where the digital clock displayed the time of the morning.

5:28 a.m.

I'd worn down the first layer of polish on the floor. A full hour ago, my pacing began and hadn't stopped. A hundred scenarios played through my head at once. The phone I'd been issued was in my hand with Jack's number on the screen. I planned to press send the second I correctly configured my words.

I wasn't ready to give up everything I'd worked so hard to obtain in my field. Simultaneously, I wasn't ready to give up Chem. Asking to be removed from the operation was the only solution.

I'll never have them together.

Tossing caution to the wind, I plopped down on the couch and pressed send. Jack's phone rang twice before he picked up. It was five-thirty in the morning, almost. The commotion in his background was least expected. We weren't in the office until around seven each morning. Baffled, I began to stutter. I was expecting to catch him while he was home and able to hold a conversation. With the chatter and movement happening, I knew that wasn't possible.

"Morning, Johanson. Got something for me?"

"Actually, Jack, I was calling for something else."

"Talk to me. What's going on?"

Pausing, I filled my lungs with oxygen before exhaling.

"Johanson. You there?"

"Yes. Just needed a second."

"Is everything okay?"

"It's the case, Jack. Things have gone far beyond my control. Prior to knowing who he was, Chemistry and I had begun forming a personal bond. I'd already gotten too close to the subject to be very effective in this case.

My reason for calling this morning is to ask to be absolved from the–"

"Johanson." He sighed. "We're agents, my friend. We're not fools. We've known for some time now your feelings were affecting your judgment and ability to help us close this case. I would've pulled you out two months ago, but we were afraid you'd blow the whistle before we got to him. We needed more time to build a case on our own with the little we did have."

"Jac–"

"We got his phone number and were able to obtain a warrant to search his records and data. We narrowed his home and lab down to one of the three locations he frequented most. One was your place. The other two we discovered were his lab and his home, which we are preparing to raid as we speak. The lab looks promising. We got him, Johanson."

My mouth descended so low it nearly swept the floor.

"What do you mean, you're preparing to ra–"

As the revelation hit me, I sprouted from the couch in search of the phone Chem and I used to communicate. My heart hammered against my chest, so close to leaping out, I held it inside with my palm. The loft began to spin. Every inch of me felt the pain of my future. I grew anxious waiting for a response from Jack.

"Jack! What do you mean raid?"

"I'm sorry, Johanson. You were compromised. It happens. The raid is happening."

I ended the call without my heart in my hand. My feet were moving faster than my brain. By the time I made it to the room, I'd forgotten what I had come for. But, the pain, it was clear. It knocked me to my knees. The air from my chest evaporated.

Underneath the bed, the rectangular device lay on top of the sheet that had fallen off the bed when my anxiety crept in this morning. My memory was jarred, instantly. I grabbed the phone, cradled it in my palm, and unlocked it. Chem's number was the only one on the contact list. I tapped the screen to initiate the call.

"Pick up!"

Pick up.

Pick up.

Pick up.

"Please, baby. Pick up."

Tears cascade down my cheeks. The wind was expunged from my lungs with each ring.

"Chemistry. Please!"

I redialed his number.

"Wake up, baby. Please."

Chem was a man who hardly slept, so it was hard to believe he was still asleep. However, it was the only possibility that kept my sanity intact.

Pick up.

Please.

Chem.

When the voicemail came on again, I sprang into action. Panic-stricken, I pulled on a pair of sweats as quickly as possible and paired them with shades to conceal the tears still running from my eyes. The T-shirt

I'd worn to bed was freshly washed. There was no need to change it.

With only one shoe on my foot, I bolted out the door. Continuously, I called Chem, hoping he'd answer. He'd never ignore the barrage of calls I'd placed, so the chance that I was too late was heavy on my mind. Persistence pushed me further faster, it didn't matter if the chances were slim, I didn't let it stop me from eagerly shuffling my way through the hallway and trying my hardest to make it to him before my team did.

Baby.

Pick up.

"Please, baby. Pick up for me."

I had already made it to the expressway before I realized I didn't have a clue where I was going. Each time I'd been to Chem's home, my vision was obstructed, his head was between my legs, or mine was between his. However, there were very distinctive characteristics I remembered with each trip.

The voicemail came on again. Finally, I concluded I wouldn't be getting an answer. It was time to focus on the task ahead.

Fuck.

I swerved into the line beside the one I was in. A loud horn startled me as I tried merging into the next one.

"Oh shit."

I waited until it passed to make the switch. From there, I accessed the second and then last lane. The obnoxious sound that erupted upon entry into the emergency lane made every inch of my flesh crawl.

"Think, Egypt. Think. Think."

Closing my eyes, I jogged my memory.

Expressway.

Northbound.

Twenty-four.

No.

No.

Twenty-two, maybe.

Yes.

Twenty-two.

No, maybe twenty-five minutes.

Oh God. I can't fucking remember.

Twenty–

I'll never make it

"Come on, Egypt. Come on."

Elevation.

Trees. Lots of trees.

My ears.

My ears pop.

The mountains.

Mount Clarke!

He lives on Mount Clarke.

"Fuck, that area is massive."

Fuck.

Fuck.

Fuck.

"I need help," I cried out. "I need... I have to... My God, Chem. Pick up the fucking phone, baby. Please."

With trembling hands, I dialed the number that had sent a text confirming my date and time of arrival on the island. On the very first ring, Rugger's voice appeared on the line.

"Eden."

Quietly, I wiped the tears on my face, attempting to gather my bearings. It was pointless. They just continued to fall. My heart had finally escaped my chest and was bleeding out on the floor, right under my feet.

"Where is my brother, Eden? Is Chemistry well? Is he breathing?"

I couldn't speak. There was a large, immobile lump in my throat. It wasn't letting anything through. I struggled to catch my breath. The oxygen levels in the car were fleeting. Everything around me blurred. I couldn't see through the tears that fell over and over again.

"Eden!"

"I'm so... I'm sorry. I didn't kn-know."

"Answer me, bitch!" Rugger's cold, icy tone sent chills up my spine. Though she remained calm, the shuffling assured me she was up and headed out.

"Please don't come."

"Where the fuck is my brother? You'd better start talking."

Her voice cracked. The pain that rested in the crevices turned my stomach. I'd only known her for a few days, but I understood a few things about her. Everything we'd gathered and created her profile with was accurate.

Cold.

Calculated.

Apathetic.

Ghostly.

Emotionless.

Collected.

Detached.

Distant.

The tears I couldn't see rolling down her face were felt. Wholeheartedly. Every emotion she felt, I did a hundred times over. The guilt wasn't going to let me forget how I'd betrayed Chemistry, neither was the sound of Rugger's heartbreaking on the other line.

"I need his address, Rugger. Pl— I- Please."

"Tell me where Teddy is at this moment."

"Ho- Home. He's home. Please. I need his address."

"Eden, if–"

"My name is Egypt Johanson. I am an agent who has been studying your family's empire for the last two years. The Chemist. The Madam. The Huntress. The Cleaner. The Handler. The Therapist. And we just learned of The Ballerina and The Surgeon. My job was to infiltrate through Roulette.

"The first night of my employment, Chemistry pulled me off stage and the rest was history. I'd been hunting him for years and still have no idea what he looked like, where he was, or how he operated his business. We assumed everyone was a man. It wasn't until I'd fallen for him that I learned his true identity.

"It all happened so- I didn't- I have spent the last five and a half months trying to do my job but the love I have for Chem made that hard. My team is aware I am in far too deep and took it upon themselves to close the case with the little information I have provided.

"It wasn't much. It was never much. But, this is what we do. All we needed was a little. This morning they're headed to his home to raid–"

She cut me off, mid-sentence.

"When I find you, I'm going to slit you from one ear to the other. I will not show you any remorse, and I will leave you in front steps of your precinct so the pigs won't have to come looking for you. You'll serve as a warning that the game has started and it won't end until everyone involved in my brother's demise is in hell, waiting for me to join them just so I can kill them again. 8237 Mt. Catherine."

His mother. I ached all over. With every detail, the pain intensified a little more.

The call ended and though my life had been threatened, I was relieved to have the address where Chem rested. Traffic was still light when I merged into the first lane. I accelerated the gas, attempting to cut the drive down by several minutes.

Come on.

Come on.

Time seemed to creep in as I put my home further and further behind me. The air pressure punished my ears as my car elevated. What felt like a lifetime was only twenty-four minutes. I typed the address into the GPS system and was happy to learn I was only seven minutes from his home. I could get there in five.

I disobeyed the traffic signs and laws set by the city

for residential streets. Every few seconds, I used the shirt on my body to clean my eyes. The waterfall of tears made it impossible to see.

Houses became more sparse the closer I got to the address until I finally pulled onto the secluded street where Chem's home and approximately fifty government-issued cars were parked.

"Fuuuuuuuuck!"

Defeated, I pulled close to the curb and snatched the shades from my face. Sobbing, I released the tears I'd been holding onto since the night I discovered who I was completely obsessed with –mentally, physically, emotionally, and soulfully.

The phone I'd tossed in the passenger seat began ringing. I didn't recognize the number calling. Regardless, I answered the call, hoping Chem wasn't inside and had found a way to contact me.

"Hello."

"It's Rome."

They'd all hate me. My time with Chem had ended. His sisters were his entire world. And after this day, neither of them had any reason not to despise the very ground I walk on.

"I'm sorry."

"I know. I felt it the night I met you."

Her response halted the tears. I wasn't expecting it.

"This isn't a friendly call, Eden. This is a warning. If you value your life, find a far, far away place and pray to God every day my family doesn't find you. They will not spare you."

"I–"

Another call ended before I could say another word. I look up, catching a glimpse of the long, slim figure I'd laid with a hundred times more. It belonged to the man I loved, unconditionally and without reservation. It belonged to the man I'd betrayed. The man I had crossed.

In an instant, I was out of the car, rushing toward Bradford and Jack, who were both escorting him to their car. The shades were back on my face, masking the emotional turmoil I found myself in.

In Chem-fashion, he strolled slowly, refusing to increase his speed under the silent demands of the agents. The defeat I'd imagined I'd witness on his face was nowhere to be found. In an immaculately tailored suit, his usual attire, he was dressed. Baffled, I tried making sense of his attire at six o'clock in the morning.

His chalky skin made it clear he'd lapped the swimming pool this morning. His face was the last to be moisturized and it was usually after he was fully dressed. Eagerly, I cut through the sea of cars.

"Johanson," Bradford called out once he'd noticed me.

Jack and Chemistry turned simultaneously. "Johanson."

"Can I... I need a minute with him, Jack."

"Can't do that, Johanson," Jack stated firmly.

"Jack. Please. A few seconds. I–"

"Johans–"

"Jack!" Singer yelled, waving him back into the house. "You might want to see this."

"Get him in the car and don't take your eyes off him."

"Got it, Boss," Bradford assured Jack.

He took off in the opposite direction as Chem lowered his head and sat in the backseat. The sight was terrifying. Though he'd committed countless crimes, he didn't belong there. He was better than that... better than this all.

"Brad–"

"Don't beg, Johanson. I always hated when you did that."

"A few seconds."

"Thirty," he agreed, nodding toward Chem. "Just crouch down. I don't want Macy or Jack seeing you."

"Thank you so much."

I rounded him, coming into close contact with Chemistry. I'd expected the pain residing in his eyes. I'd expected the look of disappointment. What I hadn't expected was the smile on his face. The same way he'd looked at me since the day he'd demanded I meet him outside in five minutes was the same way he was looking at me now. Only this time, there was so much regret, emotion, and love in those eyes.

"Hello, Egypt."

"I'm sorry," I claimed, lowering my body so Bradford wouldn't get the fire that would come from his disobedience.

"You are," he disclosed.

There was so much hidden in those words. Of

course, I was, but hearing him say it made it so much worse.

"I didn't mean for any of this to happen."

I felt around in my hair, in search of the thin, black bobby pin. It wasn't long before I located it. I was responsible for his capture. I felt equally inclined to assist in his escape.

It didn't matter how much I was putting on the line, my heart was hurting and it wouldn't beat properly again until Chemistry was free. At the moment, he was my priority. Not the force. Not my friend. And not my boss.

"I'm sorry. I can fix th–"

"The damage is done, Choc. Save yourself."

"Chemistry." I cried, moving closer because I needed access to the cuffs.

My chest ached as I watched him scoot further away.

"Do your job."

"This is my– this is my job."

My words were useless. Chemistry had ended communication with his last statement. My thirty seconds were over, and Bradford was headed toward us. I shoved the bobby pin back in my hair and placed my hands on my knees in front of me.

"Chemistry."

I was met with silence.

"Alright, Johanson."

He wouldn't even look at me.

"I'm sorry."

Silence.

"Chem– Please. Say something. Anything."

"Fuck you," he said, calm and collected. "Disrespectfully, my love."

Bradford ushered me away from the car. The door slammed with a thud and a gust of wind that took my heart away with it.

"You should get home and pack, Johanson."

"Pack?" Low whimpers accompanied more tears. The pain of losing my father was nothing in comparison to what I was feeling. Everything hurt.

"Jack is setting you up in protective custody. This is– this is big. You're not safe, Johanson. Their money is long and their reach is deep. Hell, you shouldn't even be here right now. For your safety, we didn't tell you."

"Bradford, I can't go into protective custody. That's no life for me. I–"

"Will die if you don't."

"I'll die if I do."

"You have a better chance at life, though, Johanson. We didn't just come to his home. Simultaneously, we busted every address listed for his siblings. No one– I mean, no one has been found except The Chemist."

They're not here. I doubt you'll ever find any of them.

"Everyone else has disappeared without a fucking trace. It's almost as if he was expecting us."

"I didn't," I told him.

"I'm aware. You didn't know, either. But, when we entered, he was sitting at the table. Fully suited. Un-fucking-bothered. I've never seen anything like that before and I've been on this fucking job for twenty years, Johanson. Our presence didn't disturb him, not one bit. I almost turned my ass around when I saw him.

"Something about this man says he means business, man. *Shit.* He's been cooperative, dictating our moves without saying a fucking word. This shit is– I don't know. Just take the fucking protection."

He was right. The agency was the only chance for survival.

"I will."

Egypt

The loft felt nothing like it had when I'd left hours prior. Though filled with the most extravagant, expensive pieces, it was desolate. An abyss I wanted to fall into and never crawl out of. A dark, black ball of nothingness.

Even the anxiousness and worry I experienced when walking through those doors over the last few months was better than this. Because he was still here. Still around. Still lurking.

I was tasked with gathering my things and preparing my entry into protective custody. I hated the idea of it all, but there wasn't much I could do at this point. Things had gone haywire quicker than I'd imagined and nothing on my end had been set up to stop the inevitable. There was only one entity I sought protection of and it wasn't the one I was employed with.

My back pressed against the door, slamming it shut. I removed the black shades and slowly lowered my body to the floor. I pulled my knees up toward my chest and rested my head on them. Darkness surrounded me as I closed my eyes and released a tearful sigh.

The day I'd been dreading had come and the things I felt were far worse than I'd predicted. Unrecognizable sounds erupted from my mouth. Deep and throaty, they made my eyes sting and chills run the length of my spine.

"My God. Help me."

I don't want to feel like this. I don't want this guilt. This pain. This anger. This anchor. God, help me, please. I prayed, silently.

I struggled with my phone, momentarily. Getting the screen unlocked through the tears was complicated. It didn't recognize my face and I barely had the strength to press the numbers. After a few tries, I was successful. I scanned my short list of contacts and placed a call to the woman who knew my heart better than anyone. She picked up on the very first ring as if she were privy to my pain before the call was made.

"Hi, babe," Art greeted me.

I attempted to spit out a few words, hoping my emotions wouldn't disable me completely.

"It's... It's... he..."

"Where are you?" Cutting to the chase, Art began asking questions. "What's the address?"

"Chemistry was ar-arrested."

With all my strength, I pushed out the words.

"Hang up, Egypt. Send me the address. I'm on my way."

Those four simple words were all I needed to hear. *I'm on my way.* Breathlessly, I ended the call and began texting the address. It was much easier than trying to speak clearly. Everything I was pushing out was nearly inaudible.

Droplets blurred the contents of the screen, but eventually, I managed to get the address sent. Feeling slightly accomplished, but still incredibly sensitive to the situation at hand, I curled into a ball on the floor next to the door. I was too afraid that if I left my post, Art would never get inside because I'd never get out of bed.

Visions of Chemistry cuffed replayed in my head over and over. The things he'd said. The way he looked. How my name sounded rolling off his tongue.

Hello, Egypt.

His baritone broke me and put me back together twelve hundred and fifty times on the floor. Even as he faced the uncertainty, his confidence never wavered. He looked me square in the eyes when he was ready. And never attempted to garner any sympathy. Still, even at his worst, Chemistry was at his best.

He was unbothered by the presence of the law. Over sixty officials combed through his massive home and it didn't faze him at all. He sat, patiently, in the backseat as they did what they'd come to do. He was cooperative, never showing resistance.

However, he established his position without

mumbling a word. He moved at his own pace, not theirs. And because his presence was so commanding, everyone had fallen in line unintentionally. They'd captured a legend. A myth of the sorts. They were honored to be in his presence and it showed.

It must've been a full hour before there was a knock. I'd long ago lost track of time, of anything but Chemistry's voice for that matter. It looped in my head, condemning me to a life of hell without his gentleness. His tenderness. His hands around my body. His head against my chest. His limbs clinging to me in bed. His lips on mine. His smile. His scent. His hugs. His care. His love.

I scrambled to my feet, slowly and completely void of balance. Nothing was as it should be. My equilibrium was rattled. My head was ringing. My heart was aching.

I unlocked the door and pulled it open to find my best friend with widened arms, a bouquet of flowers in one hand, and two bags of groceries in the other. She walked in, I stepped backward. And, once the door closed, I was engulfed in her love.

She smelled divine. A fragrance lover, she was never too far from a good bottle of something soft, feminine, and long-lasting. I inhaled, trying to stabilize my breathing as more tears erupted from the surface.

"I-I am *gutted*, Art."

My stomach sunk a bit deeper, proving to me it was possible. We both pulled away slowly. Art's eyes combed my frame before she wrapped her arms around me again.

"Awwww, baby. I'm here to talk if you want to talk. If

you want me to listen, I'm here for that, too. Should you choose to be quiet, then I will just hold this space with you. Whatever you need, Egypt. I've let my husband know I will not be home tonight. Until you're better, I'll be with you. For however long, babe. I'm by your side."

She released me.

"Thank you."

"It's still a bit early. Have you eaten anything?"

As the question left her mouth, my stomach announced its lack of contents.

"How about we get you to bed and I get a late lunch started?"

She headed for my bedroom.

"He took the bed."

Before I realized it, light chuckles were pouring from me. It almost felt incriminating to smile after the morning I'd had, but considering the things Chemistry did and the way he expressed himself was humorous. He'd taken my bed because he slept better in the queen-sized pillowtop than his custom bed.

"I don't know if I want to laugh or get a little more context." Art joined, sniggering. "Is there another bed here?"

It was her first time in the loft. I was quickly reminded.

"Up there." I tilted my head toward the banister.

"Then let's get to the loft area unless you prefer the couch."

"The bed."

How I'd get up the stairs was a mystery but I'd rather

be in solitude than on the couch expelling stale energy where Art was liable to catch strays. I gathered myself as best I could and began the short journey. I knew it would take time to get up to the loft area, but time was about all I had on my side right now. I'd lost everything else, it seemed.

THE GREY LIST

Numb.

Utterly and completely **numb**.

Aside from the pain of my heart, I felt little to nothing. My eyes, nose, and lips were swollen beyond recognition. The migraine promised to slit my head wide open at any second. My energy was depleted. I didn't even have enough to cry anymore.

Darkness sheeted the windows. So much time had passed and I hadn't budged. Lunch was hours ago and the plate was still sitting next to the bed on the small table. I'd taken two bites from the quesadilla Art prepared and finished the full glass of ice water. Yes, I was hungry, but the stress I was under wouldn't allow me to consume food.

"Heeeey."

Art nudged me. Though I wasn't sleeping, my body was pleading for rest. Because my brain wouldn't shut off and allow it to recharge with a nap or good night's sleep, I lie awake with my eyes closed.

"Egypt.

"It hasn't been a full day and I'm helpless without him. I keep wondering what level of misery I'd reached before he came into my life. Because I can't fathom going back to being so– so– Whatever I was without him."

"Maybe you won't have to," Art expressed.

She flipped the cover back and slid into bed behind me. With her arms wrapped around me, she sighed.

"I know this is farfetched, but maybe... just maybe when it all settles and he's had time to think about it, just maybe he'll make contact. You've made it clear he's a man of many resources. Give him time to clear his head. Maybe you'll look up and there's a piece of mail from him or even a phone call."

"This isn't a movie, Art. He doesn't want my love anymore. He wants my head. And, I can't quite determine whether he's justified or not. I almost feel as though he is."

"Hey, let's think positively."

"You don't know them. Believe me when I say I've never seen anything like it. They're something different. They're not remorseful. They're brave. They're confident. They're wealthy. They're elegant. Intelligent. Very smart. And zero tolerance."

"They?"

"Yes. His entire family. It was never just Chemistry. We've been after everyone in his operation. We thought it was a group of men."

"It's not?"

"No. All women. Everyone. And, they're his sisters."

"Oh, wow."

"Exactly. We have absolutely nothing on them. How they were able to get a number and location on Chem, I'll never know. We've been blind for two years. I lucked up, Art. I just wish he'd never taken me out of that club and let me go into that meeting."

"Why didn't he?" she wondered out loud.

She was cringing inside. I could see the change in her facial expression. It matched the contortion of my stomach.

"He hated the idea of anyone else... any other man having access to me."

"Sounds like any man I know with a love interest, girlfriend, or wife."

"He's not like any other man, Art."

"I can tell."

"He was obsessed."

"As a man should be, Egypt."

"His obsession ran deep. Really deep."

"Unfortunately, it cost him his freedom."

"I cost him his freedom."

"Don't blame yourself. You had a job to do and you did the best you could with the feelings that were already circulating before your discovery. You've made that clear. Don't beat yourself up about it. You did what you had to. If the team had been better at their jobs, they wouldn't have sent you in blind."

"I was a part of the team, Art."

"And willing to risk more than any of them. Big risk, big reward, babe. You deserved the love Chemistry bestowed upon you, despite everything else. And I will still hold hope it isn't the end of such a beautiful beginning."

"Please don't. Use that hope for something else. Something worthy. I've made my bed."

"You're worthy. Your heart is worthy. Your love is worthy. Your happiness is worthy."

A knock at the door startled me. I sprung from the bed in pursuit of my service weapon. I wasn't expecting anyone. If there was someone at the door, they weren't here for laughs and giggles. The thought of my best friend becoming a casualty of a war she wasn't directly involved in had my palms sweaty and my nerves rattled. I flushed with heat.

"Stay up here. Whatever you do, don't make a sound, and do not come downstairs. No matter what happens, no matter what you hear. Do not come downstairs. Tonight is not the night to be my hero, Art. Save yourself. Make it back home to your husband," I explained with my hands on both sides of her face. "Understand."

The knocking began again, this time louder and harder. I dashed from the bed, ready to put distance between Art and me.

"Egypt."

I hadn't gotten far from the bed when she called out to me. I whipped my body around, wondering if she was trying to make this her last night on earth.

"Art," I whispered, chastising her with my eyes. I placed my index finger on my lips, reminding her of the need for silence I'd explained seconds earlier.

"It's your mother."

She lifted her vibrating phone, showing me the face on her screen. My mother's smile quickly eased my thunderous heartbeat. She was the eye of the storm tearing through my body and making a mess of me.

"She shouldn't be here," I admitted.

As much comfort as she brought me, her safety was my top priority. Protecting one asset in my world was much easier than protecting two of them.

"You need her, Egypt."

"I do." Nodding, I agreed. "But not at this cost. Having you here wasn't the best decision, either. But, we've built an entirely new identity for you. To them, she's Ellen Johanson. No alias."

"I didn't consider– I apologize."

"It'll be okay."

"I can have her leave."

"Please. Please don't. I doubt she will, anyone. She's here now."

"She brought over dinner. She's not staying long."

The next few words from my mouth pained me but were necessary.

"When she leaves, Art, I think it's best if you do the same. For your safety and hers. Did valet take your car?"

"Yes."

"Good. Hopefully, they have hers as well. I don't want either of you walking alone or in a dark garage. I need you to walk together. I'll have your cars ready before you make it down. I'll make the call sooner so there won't be a wait."

"Are you sure?"

"My life is on the line, Art. Yes, I'm sure."

I moved to go down the stairs to open the door, but she grabbed my hands.

"When my time comes, it comes, babe. I'm not afraid of dying, especially on your behalf."

"I'm afraid of you not living, especially on my behalf. I'm going to get the door."

"I'll get it."

"I should, Art."

"I'll come down and set the table."

"Alright."

I descended the stairs and took a few seconds to retrieve my weapon from the kitchen counter where I'd forgotten I'd left it. When I pulled the door open, my mother's flustered face bandaged every wound the day had opened.

I wrapped her in my arms, pulling her forward and into the loft. It had been months since I'd had the chance to see her, touch her, or feel her presence. It was soft and gentle just like the woman I'd become the best of friends with.

"Egypt, honey, you're shaking."

My nerves were irreparable at this point. Having both her and Art in one place, a place they didn't belong had me on edge. The sooner I got them out of here, the better I'd be. I locked the door and made my way into the kitchen behind her.

"Hey, baby," she greeted Art, hugging her.

"Hey."

It was so good seeing my mother. I wished the circumstances were different. However, I was in a scope. I wasn't sure where it was or when it would fire, but keeping my two favorite people alive would remain my goal until I took my last breath.

Absentmindedly, I ventured over to the window and peered out into the evening crowd of downtown Clarke. Chem's overwhelming presence didn't greet me. The phone he'd given me didn't begin chiming in the distance. He wasn't on the other line demanding I lift my head and fix my face. Neither was his asking how he could fix whatever problem I had.

It's over.

The air in my lungs pushed through my body and out of my mouth, deflating my chest.

It's really over.

The vibration of a cellular device had me combing the room for it. Unsure of where the vibrations were coming from or who had the device, I stalked the room for the source. To my dismay, the phone I'd been issued by the agency was dancing on the hardwood countertop.

Whatever was waiting for me on the other end, whoever was waiting for me on the other end, I wasn't prepared for. The bit of solace Art and my mother offered hadn't yet performed its magic, but a little conversation, laughter, and reassurance would do the trick.

I needed more time with them. More time to process my thoughts. More time to face my reality. More time with my very small community.

I watched until the buzzing stopped. Almost instantly, it began ringing again. With flared nostrils and an inflated chest, I answered.

"Hello?"

"We're on our way up, Johanson."

Silently, I closed my eyes and began releasing an exhausted sigh. Instead of responding, I ended the call. I hadn't packed a single thing. I didn't have the strength. They'd hauled my lover off to a black site where he wasn't accessible to me or anyone else for that matter as he awaited a transfer. I'd never see him again a day in my life. I was still trying to comprehend the nature of the situation, yet they were here to haul me off to protective custody.

"Everything okay?" my mother asked, sensing my frustration.

"The team is here."

"Protective custody?"

"Yes, Mom, and I haven't put a single item in a bag. I need more time."

"Don't worry, Egypt. That's what Art and I are here for. We'll get started instead of sitting down for dinner. I've made your plate. Get something on your stomach."

"Thank you."

"No need to thank me, baby."

She scurried toward the bedroom where Art had already taken off to. The knock at my door left me with so many unresolved feelings. I slid my feet across the floor, hating how swiftly they'd made it to my door. I removed the latch, twisted the lock, and opened the door.

"Hello, Egypt."

Thunderous coughs followed the introduction. My body stilled, my bowels threatened to move, and my bladder began to release small droplets of urine in my underwear. Chemistry's father stood in front of me with Aden at his side.

"I... Uh... I... sor..."

The scrutiny was written all over his aging face. As if I had some sort of superpower, I heard the pinging of the elevator. Closing my eyes, I waited for my fate, but secretly prayed it was the team I'd let down for the man I loved rounding the corner.

My body ached, strangely yearning for the hot rounds to cut through my flesh. Death had to feel better than this. I'd rather my heart stopped than be in the amount of pain I was in.

Footsteps grew louder as they closed in. I could hear Bradford's baritone but couldn't make out what he was saying. The lack of urgency in his voice made me wonder if I'd reached his line of vision. Rooted in place, I tried silencing the hammering of my heart.

I'm sorry. My final thought ruptured my beating heart.

Sorry, Chemistry.

Sorry, Richie.

Sorry, Rhea.

Sorry, Roulette.

Sorry, Range.

Sorry, Roaman.
Sorry, Rugger.
Sorry, Royce.
Sorry, Rather.
Sorry, Rome.
Sorry, Aden.
Sorry, Mother.
Sorry, Art.
Sorry, Bradford.
Sorry, Macy.
Sorry, Jack.
Sorry… sorry, Dad.

"Johanson!" With glee, Bradford chanted. "You don't know how fucking proud we are of you, partner!"

Feeling his arms around me had me stumped. I opened my eyes, and it was his face I saw instead of the man responsible for Chemistry's presence on Earth. I scanned the hallway, eyes traveling in every direction possible. It wasn't until I followed Bradford's trail that I noticed the sleek, unbothered figure. With one hand in the air, his index and middle fingers pointed in my direction, and his thumb upright, he winked.

Fuck.

SEVENTEEN

Chemistry

Four months after the raid...

One hundred one.

One hundred two.

One hundred three.

One hundred four.

Footsteps crept toward my cell. Mine was the only one on the unit of the maximum security facility. It was made annoyingly clear they were headed in my direction. Interaction with the low lives who thrived on the small taste of authority made my balls itch. In their real lives, they were bitches.

Suckers.

Less than.

Replaceable.

Not too many would suffer when they came up missing because each and every one of them would with time. To keep from adding additional time to my pending sentence, I kept my hands to myself. But, it was a struggle.

Restrict his airways. Silence him once and for all.

Confinement sharpened the voices in my head. They were louder. Bolder. More demanding. The guard appeared, pulling at his collar with one hand and swiping his baton on the bars with the other. I looked up momentarily, eyes locking on his neck.

Snap it.

"Childers."

One hundred five.
One hundred six.
One hundred seven.
One hundred eight.

I continued my set. One hundred and fifty in the morning. One hundred and fifty at sunset. One hundred and fifty before bed. Pushing my body to its limits kept my thoughts in my head and the urge to act on them much more tolerable.

"Childers."

One hundred nine.
One hundred ten.
One hundred eleven.

One hundred twelve.

With my eyes trained on the wall of the small cell, I locked in to complete the last leg of this morning's set. The sound of cuffs caused my nostrils to flare. There were only one of three things that could be happening.

I was being transported.

I had a visitor.

A pig was here to talk to me.

I wasn't interested in either scenario. In my cell was where I wanted to remain until the sunset so I could hit the floor and get another set in.

"Time to cuff up."

One hundred twenty-five.

One hundred twenty-six.

One hundred twenty-seven.

One hundred twenty-eight.

"Childers."

Sever the spine.

"I'm easily provoked," I admitted.

I smiled, contemplating the acts I'd played out countless times in my head.

"I don't give a fuck. This is nothing like out there. Get your ass beat in here."

By you? I was closed to asking but understood it would be a waste of words.

"You're a sick fucker. Always laughing and talking to the fucking wall."

Punish him.

Lowly, I sniggered, listening to him go on and on about my *unusual* behavior. Truthfully, I minded my business and wished they'd all do the same because it could save their lives. Not this one though.

"Cuffs, man!"

One hundred forty-eight.

One hundred forty-nine.

One fifty.

Without haste, I stood on my feet and rotated my arms to keep my muscles from locking. I stretched my entire body, waiting until my back popped twice.

"Come on, Childers. I'm not waiting all day."

You're free to leave.

Don't let him leave.

Conversing inside was like nails on a chalkboard. Instead of entertaining the pointless human, I began redressing at a snail's pace. My shirt slid down my arms with ease. I pulled the freshly dried white socks over my bare feet. Without them on during my sets, I had more leverage and a better grip. After getting my shoes on, I brushed the wrinkles out of my sheets.

"This motherfucker," the CO hissed, kissing his yellowing teeth.

When there was nothing more to be done in my cell, I turned around, faced the back wall, and placed my hands in the slit designed for trays and cuffing inmates.

89203259128499.

I was no longer a person according to the government. I was a fucking number.

"Open!" he called out, taking his eyes off me for a few seconds too long.

Wrong move.

I stepped away from the bars with my wrists cuffed. The door opened eight inches exactly by the time my arms rotated, ending up in front of me. I reached out into the hallway, and brought Chubbs, the CO, into the cell, using my cuffs to apply pressure on his throat.

"Scream and I'll break it."

"Yo. Alright. Alright. Man. Please. I have a fucking kid, man. I have a daughter."

"Does she know her daddy is a bitch?" I asked, shoving him forward and back into the hallway where the cameras could see him.

Partially satisfied, I stepped into the hallway after him. Dramatically, he leaned forward, holding onto his neck.

Humorous. I laughed, finding him comical.

"You're a sick ba–"

"No, Chubbs. I am a killer. And I will kill, no matter the environment. Keep fucking around and you will find out."

Without another word, he continued down the hallway, leading me to what felt like doomsday.

Good.

The small, nearly empty room I entered was familiar. Three times before I'd been dragged inside. Each time, I was questioned by another official of some kind, from another branch, with hopes of cracking me. They wasted hours of their days because even with a lawyer present, I had nothing to say. If they had charges to bring against me, then I'd make them do their fucking jobs.

Giving them a case when theirs was barely intact was out of the question. With the evidence they had against me, the most time I'd see on the inside was four years. That could change, but for now, I wasn't too worried. They were very lucky they'd even gotten four months out of me. I was simply sitting so the attention would remain on the subject in custody and not be dispersed among my sisters.

I'd remain in custody as long as it meant them staying free. Keeping them busy building my case gave them very little time to build anything against my girls. Exasperated with the impromptu visits, I had a seat at the table and waited to be cuffed to it. To my surprise, I was released from the cuffs and left alone in the room. This could only mean I was getting a privileged visit.

Who the visit was from, I didn't have an idea. My lawyer wasn't scheduled to visit me for another three weeks. Because I refused to mumble another word to the staff I knew was on the other side of the door, I got comfortable and let the wait begin.

Six-hundred-and-fourteen seconds later, the door stretched. I didn't budge. Footsteps closed in, stopping in front of the empty chair across the table. It wasn't until my guest was seated that I recognized exactly who they were.

"Here to replace council this evening. We have quite a bit of business to discuss."

Priest sat a few inches away, disguised behind thick

glasses, a folder full of unnecessary documents, a brief-case, and a suit. My lips curled upward slightly as I leaned back in my seat.

"Shall we begin?"

"We should."

Because I couldn't get to The Triad of Ara, The Triad of Ara had come to me. He adjusted his glasses, taking a second to gather his thoughts. At the clearing of his throat, the pit of my stomach emptied. The hollow dwelling was where my heart rested. The dread on Priest's face was daunting. He cleared his throat a second time.

"My sisters?"

He shook his head.

"My brothers?"

I could feel the contortion of my face as I asked one question after the other.

He shook his head again.

"No."

I waited for him to continue.

"Your father," he revealed.

The oxygen in the room evaporated.

"He is no longer with us."

Comprehension was farfetched. I couldn't... I didn't understand what he was telling me.

"Come again."

"Richie is no longer with us."

My stomach flipped twelve hundred times in a matter of seconds. My heart struggled to continue beating, continue pumping. Half of it had been ripped from my chest.

"We are keeping his remains safe. They will not go underground until you touch soil."

I ached, awfully. And though I wanted to know the rest of the context of the meeting, I'd reached my capacity.

"I– I need to– to go get my head together."

"Business, Chemist. Business."

"You're telling me my fucking pops died and you want me to talk business? Nigga, are you hearing yourself right now?"

"Composed Chem. Where is he?"

"Fuck him and fuck business."

"This isn't The Triad of Ara business," Priest whispered. "This is Chemistry's business. I'm only here out of courtesy. Don't waste my time and I won't waste yours."

"Speak, nigga."

"Your father made arrangements before he left us."

"Arrangements?"

"A sacrifice."

My eyes grew as my heart shrunk, constricted and confused.

"A sacrifice?"

It was a commandment, but one that had never been utilized. It was one of the many we were aware of but hadn't exercised.

"Who?"

Rome. The name circled in my head. I prepared to

flip the fucking table if her name came from his lips. She was a baby. Though she was nineteen, she was still a baby and there wasn't a nigga in The Triad of Ara who deserved her or her innocence. I'd never forgive myself if she became a casualty of circumstances.

"Rather."

"Why not Roaman? Why not Range? Or Royce?"

"You know how this works, Chem. Youngest or the closest to her. They're both of age, but your father wasn't willing to give the youngest of your siblings away."

"Who will she– fuck."

"The youngest of our flock. In addition to the arranged nuptials, she will receive full protection."

"I understand."

I digested what he was telling me one word at a time. Though we'd kept the girls out of our dealings with The Triad of Ara, we were certain they'd cross paths one day. This wasn't how we'd expected the acquaintance to come to fruition, but we could only play the cards we were dealt at this point.

"They're good girls, Priest. Every one of them is just mixed up in this crazy world we created for them. Rather is special. Make sure your people treat her well."

"You have my word."

"They won't return until their freedom is solidified."

"We understand. Upon their return, introductions will be made and we will move forward."

"Is that all?"

I was ready to put an end to this meeting and take the rest of the day to decompress. So much was being dumped on me at once. There hadn't been a single piece of information I was happy to hear but Rather's protection order.

"It isn't."

"Fuck. I can't suffer through another round of bullshit."

"Tell me, Chem, how else will you get the information I have for you in this meeting."

"Talk," I huffed. His accuracy was disarming.

"Egypt Johanson."

He had my full attention. My spine straightened like a rod. My eyebrows hiked on my forehead. My thoughts immediately became fuzzy. There were so many unresolved feelings there that I still needed to work through. Today wouldn't be the day. Most likely, it wouldn't be tomorrow either.

"We had no idea what she knew. How much she knew. What she planned to do with the information she had access to. What she'd already said... did... She needed to be taken care o–"

My teeth grinded against each other. I bit into my bottom lip, extracting blood from two different places.

"If any-fucking-body touches a fucking hair on Egypt's head, when I touch soil, I will wage a war that will end every fucking lineage of The Triad of Ara. Bloodlines won't survive a week of my freedom. And that is on my fucking father and my mother. May they both rest peacefully in hell."

Taking a breath, I continued.

"She's proved the exact belief The Triad of Ara has

tried to dismantle from day one. Women are capable! Even with feelings involved, the job will still get done. I have eleven siblings, seven of which are women and offsprings of a founder. At least three of them are beyond capable. They have what it takes to sit at that table when and if I can't."

"Eden—"

"We don't have shit to talk about when it comes to her."

"Your anxiousness is off-putting. I've never known you to be a man of little patience."

"Stop blowing smoke up my ass."

At the mention of Egypt, I'd lost all my composure. It didn't exist. It never had with her. That lone fact angered me more than the Priest had with his statement. The thought of them having harmed her had me foaming at the mouth. The realization that I had yet to dismiss my feelings for her had me brimming with anger.

"You never let me finish," he told me.

"Then what are we waiting for?"

"She needed to be taken care of. We had every intention, but the hit was called off. We were forced to abort the mission."

"We don't abort missions," I reminded him. "Why was it called off?"

"Because she is in possession of something precious to The Triad of Ara. Something we are unable to interfere with, no matter what she's done."

"What does she have?"

"A possible heir."

My heart sank into my stomach.

T H E **G R E Y** L I S T

The meeting continued long after I'd been struck in the chest several times and had ended only minutes ago. With each step I took toward my cell, my heart broke a little more. Choosing peace over the violence I wanted to ensure, I entered my cell and drug my feet toward my bed.

In a matter of minutes, I'd been reduced to almost nothing. For the third time in my life, my heart broke. It broke loudly. Rapidly. Painfully.

First my mother.

Then, Eden… Egypt.

And my father.

I laid my back against the sheets and folded my hands in front of me, resting one on my chest where it hurt the most.

"Pops," I whispered.

My eyes pricked with saltiness. A single blink released the tears. Slowly, deliberately, they rolled down the sides of my face. They were a foreign concept to me. Since I'd been a teenager and received the news my mother had ended her life and Maurice's just seconds before, I hadn't shed a tear.

"Pops." Lowly, I wept.

It was as if I'd been injured, physically and emotionally. Something sharp, big, and heavy pierced my heart. Something ruthless. Something inexplicable.

"Mom."

Catherine.

Maurice.

My fear of being a parentless child, even in adulthood, had come to fruition. Losing my father was an overwhelming fear of mine and it had come to fruition.

Oh, Rhea.

The heartbreak she must've felt broke me some more. Tears flowed freely, unapologetically.

Roaman.

Covering my eyes, I began to weep into the sleeve of my shirt.

Rather.

Roulette.

Royce.

My chest caved as the oxygen fled my body.

Range.

Rugger.

She wasn't as invincible as she portrayed to be. Her heart was pure. She loved hard and the man who'd helped create her, she loved most. I used my fist to pat my chest, desperate for air.

"Rome."

Barely audible, I called the name of the person who worried me most. She'd reached twenty mere months ago. Fatherless was no way to begin the journey of adulthood.

Mercer.

Makai.

Malachi.

"Milo."

He was the youngest, the baby of the bunch when our mother committed the murder-suicide.

I wasn't there.

I'm not there.

The pain was crippling. Clarke had welcomed me as a permanent resident by the time everything went downhill. The system had welcomed me as an inmate this time, filling me with unprecedented amounts of regret.

I was in the middle of the ocean at a maximum security prison laying on a flat pillow and previously used sheets. At my fucking lowest, I'd been assured there was more depths to reach. I didn't have the privilege of holding my siblings in my arms as they cried into my chest. I didn't have the privilege to wipe the tears from their eyes, although it was only to make room for more. I didn't have the privilege of lying to them like everything would be okay.

Not this time and not the last time, either. That shit cut deep.

EIGHTEEN

Egypt

Nine months after the raid...

Please. What is it?

My vibrating phone quickly became a thorn in my side. I opened one eye, peeping at the digital clock beside the bed.

5:06 a.m.

The vibration stopped momentarily. Seconds later, it began again. I'd only been asleep for thirty minutes. I desperately needed more time, more rest. Whoever was calling desperately needed to speak to me. So, rather than letting their insistence keep me awake longer than necessary, I patted the bed in an attempt to locate my phone.

"Johanson!"

Bradford was vexed. I could hear it in his tone. Concerned, I flung the covers from my body and sat at the edge of the bed.

"Is everything okay?"

"Are you okay?"

"I'm fine, Bradford. What's going on?"

"Has no one contacted you this morning? Fuck!"

"No. What's going on? Talk. I don't understand."

"He's gone, Johanson."

"Who?"

The thought of Jack losing his life in the line of duty crossed my mind. My heart hurt at the thought of it.

"Jack?"

"No. No. Not Jack. Jack is on his way in."

"Then, wh–"

"The Chemist."

I held onto my chest. My lungs deflated along with it. The wind had been knocked right out of me.

"Bradfor—"

"He escaped, Johanson. During the 4:00 a.m. count, they discovered he was not in his cell. Guard charged in, searching for him and there was no sign of him. Neither was there any indication of how he'd escaped, when, or where to. It's a fucking island. It is the most secure facility in the country. There's no way he'll survive the sea even if he succeeds. No one can. That's why the prison was built there."

"Air or sea."

"Sea."

"*Sea?*"

"*I have arms and legs. I don't have wings.*"

The conversation I'd had with him not long after we'd met replayed in my head. It was a shame just how many layers of Chem the agency hadn't pulled back. There was so much more to the man they'd captured. They wouldn't begin to understand even if I wrote it all down for them to study.

He's a swimmer, Bradford. A damn good one.

"If they don't find him in the facility, then maybe one day his body will turn up in the water. It's deadly out there. To know he'd rather face that than be confined just blows my fucking mind. Essentially, he's suicidal. His mother comm—"

Don't. Don't bring her into his.

"Bradford, do you think he would attempt an escape if he didn't have a complete plan in place? Does that sound like the man we hunted for two years?"

He paused, taking a second to think.

"Do you need an officer to come sit outside your home?"

That's more logical.

"Johanson. Do you need us to have someone come out?"

"Save yourself, Bradford."

The hunters had become the hunted. The tables had turned. And unlike the agency, it wouldn't take two years to scratch the surface.

"I've made my bed, Bradford. I'm prepared for whatever Chemistry brings my way."

With my heart in shackles, I ended the call. The moment I'd been dreading had come. I wrapped my fingers around the handle of the drawer on the side of my bed. At the sight of an empty drawer, my brows furrowed on my forehead.

The unknown became clear. They were searching miles and miles away for a man who was so close I could feel the potency of his presence.

Oh shit.

I tightened my robe around my body and marched through the hallway. My footsteps sounded off like grenades in a field. Anxiously, I pushed open the door that was only two doors down from mine. The simple layout of the new home made the journey a swift one. Yet, it seemed to take forever to reach the knob.

Slowly, carefully, I stepped inside. Fear disabled me. Paralyzed me. Planted my feet and toyed with my feelings. Dressed in a tailored suit and resembling a man who hadn't spent a day behind bars, there Chemistry sat.

He wasn't empty-handed. Our child rested on his arms. On his lap was the gun I'd searched for along with another one. The initial shock subsided and my motherly instincts kicked into high gear. I lunged forward and was stopped in my tracks at the sound of muffled fire.

Pausing, I stood still with my eyes closed, waiting for the burn to birth unbearable pain all over my body. Upon realizing it wouldn't happen, I lowered my arms and opened my eyes. Behind me were two holes in the wall of the nursery.

"Che– Chemistry."

"Hello, Egypt."

My name rolled off his tongue so effortlessly.

"I..." Words didn't find me.

"Take another step and the next bullet will pierce your skull, not the wall. My aim is perfection, Egypt. I missed because I wanted to. I don't have much more restraint in me."

"I'm sorry."

"You are." He sighed, taking a look at the precious child in his arms. "She's beautiful."

The brown blanket I'd managed to confiscate from his home during the raid was wrapped snuggly around her body. I'd learned why it was so significant to him the evening of Roaman's dinner. Losing his father had him clinging to it a little more often.

"Chemistry Jru Childers," he whispered as he leaned down and kissed her forehead.

The son he wanted wasn't in God's plans. I'd birthed a baby girl four and a half weeks ago with my mother and Art at my side. It had only been a few days since my mother had gone home. Art stuck around for a week before she had to get back to her world. Still, we talked every day, just as we did whenever I wasn't on a case.

"For what it's worth, I– I had no idea who you were."

"It's not worth shit to me, Egypt."

"Chem. Please. I–"

"Did your fucking job."

He stood, forcing me backward. He tucked both

guns in his waistline. I watched as he lowered our daughter into her crib, gently.

Springing into action, I removed the one closest to me. Chem never flinched when he rose to find the gun pointing in his direction. Slowly, he took a step. Then, two. By the third step, his shirt was against the barrel.

"Handle your business, Egypt. Pull the trigger. End it all and prove to me I was wrong about you all along. Prove to me it was the voices convincing me what we have is unconditional. Prove to me everything we ever said was all bullshit. Prove to me, Choc. Prove to me my life means nothing to you. Prove to me you'd be happy and at ease without me in your world. Prove to me I'm not the nigga for you. Prove to me I'm in far over my head.

"Prove to me how foolish I was to tread those waters while thinking I'd rather die than not make it back to you. Prove to me you were never worthy of me. Prove to me you never loved me the same as I love you. Prove to me I belong with my mother and father. Prove to me loving you bad was all bad. Prove it to me, Choc. Right in the center. Hit me right in my heart. Prove it."

Tears spilled from my eyes as I held onto the weapon. Bricks weighed my heart down. The heaviness was unbearable. Sweat beads seeped through my skin, staining my forehead and underarms.

Forcefully, Chemistry smacked the gun from my hand and pushed me backward until my back slammed against the wall. My head bounced off the surface. The pain caused my mouth to part. His hand was around my neck. His eyes penetrated my skin, all three layers, in seek of my soul.

"Chemistry."

"I'm a man of my word." He choked. "When I said unconditional, I meant through whatever!"

The conviction in his tone gutted me.

"I have not come because of my hatred for you, Egypt. I have come because the love I harbor is bigger, wider, tougher. And it wouldn't let me get on that fucking plane and leave without you or our daughter. Fuck the choices you've made. Fuck the consequences. The choice you make right now is the only one that matters. You did your fucking job.

"I have seven sisters, all with very important responsibilities in my family's operation. The day one doesn't perform is the day everything goes to shit. Everyone matters. You were a piece to a much bigger puzzle, a much bigger plot. I will not fault you for abiding by the rules and honoring the oath you took. But, today, you have to make a choice."

"The choice was already made for me." I wept. "It's been you. It'll always be you."

His hands moved upward, cupping my chin and lifting my head simultaneously. His lips were on mine in an instant. His tongue was down my throat thereafter. Butterflies flocked in my stomach. Because, for the first time, I wasn't encountering Chem under a false identity.

I was no longer Eden. I'd become Egypt. Egypt Johanson. And despite the trail of flames Eden had left behind, Egypt still had a future with Chemistry.

He lifted me into his arms, holding onto me as if I'd vanish into thin air. I wouldn't. Not this time. I was his, forevermore.

"I'm indebted to you. I love you." I breathed against his lips.

Submission was most natural under Chem's watchful eye. The wind beneath me was followed by an easy entry.

"In this lifetime and the others."

His thrusts filled me continuously. I wrapped my arms around his neck and pulled him closer, deeper.

"Yesssssssss."

Everything is well. I promised myself. Though fearful I'd be giving up my enter life to begin one with Chemistry, regret eluded me.

The people I loved and cherished most understood the magnitude of his arrest and absence. Devastation nearly ended my life. But, the discovery of the tiny being growing inside of me gave me a reason to live. If I couldn't have Chemistry, having a piece of him would suffice.

"My God, I've missed you. Uhhhhh."

He fucked me with intention. With vengeance. With care. With love. And with grief for all we'd lost in the midst of our troubles. Passion rested on the tips of our roaming fingers. I familiarized myself with every reachable inch of his body, of my body. Because undoubtedly, Chem belonged to me and I to him.

In another lifetime, we'd been lovers. In this lifetime,

we'd remain lovers. In the next lifetime, we'd become lovers, again.

His strokes filled me with so many good things, so many good memories, and so much good energy. I closed my eyes as my orgasm mounted.

"Che—"

Silently, he continued plowing into me. With his right hand, he squeezed my left nipple between his fingers.

"Oh fuccccck."

"Don't wake my daughter, Choc," he warned, barely above a whisper.

His request was felt impossible as the moon and stars exploded in the darkness. My center began to contract, attempting to deplete Chemistry of his semen.

He ejected himself. "Shit."

His muscles tensed as he sunk his teeth into my shoulder. The worry that had begun to creep up my spine dissipated. I was a mere four and a half weeks postpartum. Until I fully embraced motherhood and truly experienced Chemistry in her essence, I wouldn't bring another child into this world.

"Thank you," I mumbled.

"Not until we're better, Choc."

I nodded, understanding his logic. It was parallel to mine.

"We should be going."

I nodded, again, suddenly feeling like I was walking on pins and needles. Chemistry's attention to detail didn't allow him to see past it.

"Don't do that, Egypt."

With raised brows, I questioned, "What, Chem?"

"We start anew. Today, we say fuck everything that happened before this moment. Right here. Right now. You won't walk around me moping with your head low and your heart heavy. I'm a grown-ass man, Choc. All has been forgiven."

"Every day I wondered if it would be the day you found out. In a way, I was hoping you did, so I could stop pretending."

Chuckling, he tossed his head back. "What kind of fool do you take me for, Choc? I'd be lying through my teeth if I told you I didn't know who you were."

"Ho– how?"

His confession was baffling. He took me by the hand and down the hall toward the bathroom. He twisted the knob to start the shower.

"I wasn't born yesterday, my love. And, for that particular day, I'd been preparing my entire adulthood. My addiction to water didn't form until I became a Chemist for people the law wouldn't approve of. I discovered the only facility that would house my level of ignorance and it was built in the middle of nowhere, surrounded by the blue shit I bathe my troubles in every chance I get.

"From that moment on, I began preparing. My body quickly adapted. I can reach depths other human can't. My arms don't grow tired for hours. I can hold my breath for minutes at a time. I embrace tides. Waves fuel me. You didn't push me off the ledge, Egypt. I jumped. I knew. My father knew. My driver... he knew as well."

"But, how?"

"The agency's payments on your lease," he explained. "They made me curious, but not enough to start digging. The call to your mother was the one. She never called you by name. Not once. She was protecting her daughter. I have seven sisters and four brothers.

"I've made a habit out of never saying their name at any point of any conversation, unless I'm alone with them. Then there was Adonis. He's mouthy. Vomited at the mouth from the second Aden put him in the truck until we dropped his pissy ass off at the airport where his car was waiting."

He began to undress. Stunned silent, I marveled at the enormous tattoo covering his entire back. I knew those eyes. Those ears. That face. It stared back at me daily. A beautiful, colorful mural mimicking the renowned image of the Virgin Mary holding her child inked his skin. I, too, was holding a child. Our child.

"Che– Chemistry."

With my finger, I began to trace the intricate details.

"After everything he'd said got back to me, I retraced your steps. The home you'd visited your old friend at wasn't just any home, Choc. There was a passageway that led to another home, two houses down the block. There, I found bits and pieces of the case that was being built against my family."

My head grew lighter. The room began spinning. At any second, I was bound to collapse. Both undressed, we climbed into the shower. I didn't know how long my legs would last. I didn't know how long I'd last.

"And then there was Art. She was the final evidence."

He stopped, momentarily, but continued almost immediately after.

"Even with all I knew, I found solace in the fact you had been most honest with me about everything else. You didn't feed me the bullshit profile they'd designed for your cover. You gave me you, Egypt.

"And, you included everyone you loved, putting them in harms way so you could sleep well knowing they'd had a glimpse of or even heard about the man in your world. Though it was against protocol, you exposed yourself to me. Without regret. That let me know just how deep you were in. How those three words you said to me over and over again weren't a lie.

"They were gems in my discovery. But, the house was the golden ticket. I waited patiently for you to do what needed to be done, but you were taking your precious time. To protect those girls, I was willing to do anything, even leak my cell number."

"It was you!"

"It was you, Choc. All I did was speed up the process because I was so fucking tired of waiting."

Bradford came to mine, immediately.

"*... when we entered, he was sitting at the table. Fully suited. Un-fucking-bother. I've never seen anything like that before and I've been on this fucking job for twenty years, Johanson. Our presence didn't disturb him, not one bit. I almost turned my ass around when I saw him. Some-*

thing about this man says he means business, man. Shit. He's been cooperative, dictating our moves without saying a fucking word. This shit is– I don't know. Just take the fucking protection."

"Why didn't you say anything?"

"What would it have changed?"

"You led them right to you."

"You led them right to me." He chuckled. "I made them reveal their hand."

"Chemistry."

His mind was such a complex place. His wisdom was far beyond his years.

"Yes, Choc."

"I thi– fain–"

THE GREYLIST

The low lights of the cabin brought me comfort. An hour ago, I'd stirred awake in unfamiliar airspace with the two people who meant the world to me nearby. I wasn't sure when we'd left my home or how Chem managed to get us both out and onto the plane. Completely over-whelmed with all that was happening, I'd collapsed in his arms.

A few feet away, Chem rocked our daughter, trying to get her to settle after a full, eventful feeding. Shit fit so perfectly in his arms. The view was nothing like I'd imagined. It was better. The fussing had finally subsided and she was resting peacefully in her father's arms.

"How much longer?" I yawned.

"Four hours."

"She'll be ready to eat in two."

"Then, go to sleep until then. I'll wake you when she's ready."

He was so good with her, so patient and so loving.

"Holding her will spoil her."

I snuggled up in the seat with a long blanket draped over me. The warning rolled off his shoulders.

"She won't be the first one I've spoiled. I have seven more."

The heaviness returned. Thinking of Chem's sisters filled me with gloom.

My brows pulled together as my thoughts surfaced. "They hate me."

Chem's lack of response was all the confirmation I needed.

"They're here, aren't they?"

"Where?"

"Where we're headed."

He nodded. "They are."

Nine months later we were finally on the plane headed to his sisters. This time, though, there was nothing festive about my mood. I'd just given birth to a child I'd carried for nine months. The newborn stage was a battle in itself. Breastfeeding was an entirely different beast. I didn't have the bandwidth to defend my honor or my choices against seven women with chips on their shoulders.

"It doesn't matter whether they hate you or not, Egypt. As long as they respect you, each and every one of them. Now, get some rest. The baby will be fine."

Trusting him, I closed my eyes and began drifting, again. I'd need the rest to face the mob of women waiting for our arrival.

I fell in and out of consciousness. Each time my eyes unglued themselves, I got a glimpse of Chemistry and her father sleeping peacefully beside me. My blessings were plentiful. A man whom I'd thought I'd lost for good had come back to me. The child we'd created didn't have to grow up fatherless. And I didn't have to spend the rest of my life alone, blaming myself for the downfall of an entire family.

I'd connected many of the dots the agency had failed to. I'd unknowingly seduced the head of the operation. And I'd fed my team intel in hopes it would lead to the closing of the case. But, even with all I'd done, Chem had the smoking gun.

The pain and anger he experienced weren't forgotten, although I'd been forgiven. It rested in his eyes. In his words. In his smile. Finding out I was an agent, at whatever point he'd made the discovery hurt him to the core.

I was awoken by a small, bright light above our seats. Chemistry's fingers patted my leg, stirring me from my sleep.

"Hmm?"

"We have arrived, Egypt."

"Hmmm? Where is the baby?"

Nervously, I searched for her seat, wondering where she was and why she was no longer in her father's arms.

"She's fine. She's sleeping in the bed, strapped down in her seat, and ready to go."

"We've landed?" I questioned, lifting the small window to take a peek.

"I've said that already, Choc."

"Sor– sorry. I didn't hear you."

I didn't hear anything after noticing the baby wasn't in his arms.

"I have something for you."

He held up a gold, dainty necklace with a diamond pendant. It had been unfastened and was ready to wear.

"Baby." I sighed.

How quickly I'd forgotten gift-giving was one of his love languages.

"Turn around."

I complied, turning in the chair, anticipating the moment my fingers would graze the beautiful diamond.

"Lift your hair, Choc."

The sound of his voice made my blood rush. My heart pumped loudly and dramatically. So much it hurt. I swept my hair up and placed a hand on my chest.

Still.

Closing my eyes, I waited for the gold to touch my skin. The cold metal never landed. It was a full minute before I came to the conclusion.

"Baby?"

His fingers traced the ink on the back of my neck. Right in the center, in bold, black letters, was a name. *His* name. The name I'd given to his daughter so I was reminded of the love I once shared with him. Reminded that he existed. Reminded I'd experienced something so precious. Reminded I'd lost it all.

CHEMISTRY.

Finally, the gold fell against my skin. I flattered it with my right hand imagining how beautiful it must've been around my neck. The jewelry Chem had collected for me over the time span of our relationship was the only thing I'd managed to bring with me from the loft.

Everything else, I'd left with my mother for safekeeping. The shoes. The purses. The clothes. Everything was waiting for my return. But, it was possible the day would never come. I'd chosen my future and it didn't include visits home.

"We should be going."

Time began to move uncomfortably fast after those words left Chem's mouth. We went from the plane to a truck. From the truck to a car. And from the car inside of a home that was surrounded by marksmen of every size and almost every color. The intense melanin was evidence they'd been in the sun for days on end.

Chem opened the door of a beautiful home and stepped aside so a breastfeeding Chemistry and I could enter. The massiveness was overwhelming. I held my daughter tighter while scanning the home for the unknown. I wasn't sure what I was looking for exactly, but when I found it, I'd know.

"Relax, Choc."

Chemistry's hands caressed me, settling me at once. I followed him down the hallway until we reached a set of doors. The chatter halted my stride. I clammed, immediately, recognizing each and every voice. The happiness that radiated behind those doors was medicinal. I'd been crying for nine months straight. However, I knew that joy wasn't a result of my presence.

"I can't."

Low and barely audible, I admitted to Chem.

"Yes, you can."

"I've wronged them all. Uprooted their lives. Took you away from them."

"You've loved their brother despite it all. You've kept your mouth shut about his extra-curricular activities that weren't pleasing to the law. I have an entire fucking body that never surfaced in the evidence they had against me. You've proven yourself to me time and time, again, risking everything to fix what was fucked up from the start.

"If it wasn't you, Choc, it would've been somebody else, and that's what you're failing to realize. You've made me a better person. You've made me a better man. You've given me every reason to love you, including the child you're holding in your hand. I don't give a fuck what anyone thinks about you, about us. All that matters is they respect you. I've made my choice. There's nothing to worry about.

"I give you my word. It's us, Choc, against everything and everybody. My sisters are not exempt. If they found something like we have, they'd be giving the same fucking speech. What I say would hardly even matter. That's how love works. No one understands it but you and the person you have the pleasure of loving every single day. Do you understand?"

A nod wouldn't suffice.

"I need words, Egypt."

"Yes."

"Good, then."

The doors swung open under the pressure of his hands. Instantly, the room grew silent with wonder. I could feel the daggers tossed in my direction as Chem led me to the very end of the table where we stood.

The scrutiny.

The anger.

The disgust.

The devastation.

The disbelief.

I felt it all, even though no one said a word. I fixed my eyes on the exit, straight ahead where we'd come from, in the event I needed to retrace my steps.

"It's been a while," Chemistry started.

"Far too long," Rhea chimed in.

"Hello, Chemistry." Roulette was the first of the sisters to speak up.

"Hello Roulette. Roaman. Royce. Rather. Range. Rugger. And *Rome*."

"Hello," they responded one after the other.

A titter fell from Chem's lips. "Rugger," he called out. "Are you not happy to see me? It's been nine long months."

"I am happy to see you, but I'd be dishonest if I told you I was happy to see the person standing beside you."

"I'm sorry Egypt's presence upset you, but I've made my choice. I bear no regrets. If there's anyone who feels slighted by the decision I've made, feel free to walk right out of that door. But, understand you're choosing a life without me.

"One day you'll all make choices of your own and they won't be based upon my preference, but those of your own. And I'll have no choice but to respect it. I expect that from each and every one of you. Even if you don't like her, respect her. And remember, you don't choose love. It chooses you."

I waited with bated breath for footsteps to sound in the silence. No one stood. No one moved.

"Then, all is well."

I placed my hand on Chemistry's arm, stopping him from continuing. This wasn't his battle alone. It was mine, too.

"I won't spend all of our time together apologizing for the harm I've done. But, right here, right now, I'm inclined to tell each and every one of you how sorry I truly am. Chemistry and I happened, and as much as I'd like to think it was, it wasn't on accident.

"Despite what I've done in the past, I love you brother dearly. Sometimes it feels like I love him more than my-myself. And as scary as that can be, I feel safe knowing I'm not alone. He, too, loves me more than life itself. We aren't perfect, neither of us.

"But, we work. We work well. We work so well I've decided to give up everything to join him. I don't know where we're headed or what we're doing, but I'm here for the ride... wherever it takes us. I've abandoned the small support system my daughter and I had to be surrounded by Chemistry's village.

"If not for me, please find it in your heart to forgive me for this child. Not only does she need you, but so do I. You're the closest thing to family I have, now."

Tears welled in my eyes. My lips quivered as I tried my hardest not to cry. One blink and the waterworks began. There was too much silence. Too much stillness. I wanted to run for the hills. Run to a faraway place, until three words landed right on top of me and wrapped me in tenderness and grace.

"We are family!" Rome yelled across the room.

"We're far from perfect, ourselves," Roaman added.

"We've done things we regret," Royce admitted.

"Made messes that felt too big, too clean," Range chimed in.

"It's life, Egypt." Rhea sighed. "Don't keep punishing yourself for it."

I shook my head, wiping the tears from my eyes with the hand I wasn't holding Chemistry in. "I won't."

"Good," she responded.

"Rugger," I whimpered. The pain resided in me without signs of fleeing.

She didn't respond, but her eyes were on me, assuring me I had her attention.

"Thank you."

If no one else in the room understood why she had given thanks, she and I did. The visit to my home when I was five months pregnant could've ended much differently. But, the sight of my belly didn't allow her to make good on her promise.

"My brother would never forgive me. His love is worth more to me than your life. Goodbye, Egypt."

I didn't sleep for a week after she'd left, afraid she'd have a change of heart and return to finish the job.

"All is forgiven, Egypt. Under one circumstance."

"Anything."

"I am the first to hold my niece."

Hell broke loose. The well-poised, collected family was in disarray at once. Everyone lost their composure, racing toward me with the idea of being the first to get their hands on Chemistry. But, for my heart's sake, I honored Rugger's request and handed Chemistry off to her once she was close enough.

My smile split the corners of my lips. This was the reunion I was too afraid to hope for. Its fruition doubled my tears and widened my heart eight times.

For Rhea.

For Rome.

For Range.

For Roulette.

For Royce.

For Roman.
For Rather.
For Rugger.
"And you're worried about me spoiling her." Chem chuckled, pulling me into his side.

Egypt

"Despite the circumstances, your father would be happy to have you. Happy to hold you in his arms. And, one day, I pray that's possible. In a perfect world, it would be." I sighed. "So ideal."

The video ended abruptly. Every emotion I felt in that moment resurfaced. But, Chemistry's hand on my knee gave me the reassurance I needed at that very moment, soothing the pain of his absence and my guilt during his incarceration. I swiped, starting another video from the collection I'd started to share with our daughter when she was older.

"No more, Egypt," Chemistry pleaded.

The bitterness and pain in his voice forced me to shut

the entire phone down. The videos were in an online album I'd been building and storing the documentary of my pregnancy. There were nearly two hundred videos and over five hundred photos.

Day by day, Chemistry and I were making our way through them. He was experiencing the pregnancy through my eyes. Even the birth was documented, but we hadn't gotten that far yet. We were still in the second trimester and cruising along slowly.

"A walk?" I proposed, placing my hand over his.

"I'd love that."

Twice a week, we promised time to each other. No CJ, no family, no disruptions. After so much transpired, we found it difficult to get back to us, back to our roots.

Having a newborn, a host of family members around, learning a new culture, growing comfortable with new territory, the mess we'd left in the States, the guilt, the absence, the grief, and so many other factors made the journey hard.

But, we quickly learned it was necessary to separate ourselves from it all to rebuild and restore. I looked forward to Wednesday and Friday nights. There was only silence and me and Chemistry and the love we shared.

Chemistry took me by the hand after finishing his drink. I sipped the last of my wine and joined him standing. The empty dinner plates and bowls would be handled. There was no need to worry about those, but I still found myself stacking plates to make the jobs of the staff easier. Chem had two Catanian women staffed inside our home and a flock of men keeping the land secure.

"Choc."

Butterflies swarmed. It was so hard keeping them at bay when that name surfaced. CJ had even adopted the name Baby Choc. Her complexion resembled mine. She had all my features and was truly a Momma's girl.

She and her father had the most adorable relationship. They napped together. Watched sports together. Swam together, because even at her young age he'd already taught her. She'd gotten in the water at only five weeks old. We hadn't settled in before Chemistry was tossing her into the deep end, promising me she'd survive because it was in her nature.

She'd just come out of the womb. I panicked. It took all seven of his sisters to pin me down and keep me from going in after her. As if she'd acquired her father's water tolerance, my five-week-old baby managed to land on and remain on her back until he swam to her from the other end. I kept silent and didn't speak to Chemistry for two days after the incident. Meanwhile, every chance he got, he was sneaking off with our daughter to get her more acquainted with the water. I hated it and loved it at the same time.

I was the most beneficial to Chemistry Jru Childers, which was the only reason she was a Momma's girl. I wasn't her pick of the litter though. That title was reserved for someone else. And, out of seven aunts, I think it was Rome she adored most. Roaman soothed her better than them all.

Rugger showed her no mercy. She was trying to teach her how to crawl before she was able to hold her head up. If it was left to her, the baby would be walking by her seventh month of life. Rather and Royce and Roulette and Range were all in love with their niece, but were still trying to clean the mess we'd left back home. Their time was divided. So was their attention.

"Sorry. It's a habit."

We began on the east of the water's edge. In a comfortable silence, we trekked at a slow, steady pace. I was still in disbelief at the beauty of the land, our story, and our future.

This is my life.

Chemistry's unconditional love had gotten us here and I knew it would take us so much further. My faith would keep us grounded and make sure we always believe our love can withstand the impossible. Because it could.

There was no person on earth I'd rather love. There was no place on earth I'd rather be. Chemistry was my destination. A long life with him was my goal.

"Is this what heaven feels like?"

Sand nestled between my toes as we walked along the beachside, hand in hand.

"I fear I'll never be able to confirm."

"A perfect world, at least?"

"This world is far from perfect, Choc. In a perfect world, I could pull up to my mother's crib and kiss her cheek any time I wanted. In a perfect world, my father would be on this island somewhere with his feet up. In a perfect world, I would be closer to my brothers. In a perfect world, you'd be my wife already. In a perfect world, I would've met you so many years ago."

His idea of perfection wasn't too farfetched. Though I couldn't give him everything he desired, there were a few I could make happen. And for the last three months on the island, I'd been using all my free time to do so.

I stared at the ring he'd placed on my finger after asking for my hand in marriage the night we'd made it to St. Catana, one of three islands he owned. It was one of two that were full of civilization.

"I can't bring your parents back," I began as we approached the path of seashells.

"Neither can I get you any closer to your brothers without raising any red flags."

The path widened to accommodate thirteen and a half people. Eight women stood on the left. Four men stood on the right. The island's spiritual leader stood between them all. The last guest held our daughter tightly, keeping her from catching so much of the night air.

Chemistry couldn't go any further at the sight of three men who shared almost all of his features, waiting for him down the aisle. He hadn't seen their faces in months. Each time he mentioned them, I witnessed the abyss their absence created grow bigger and bigger.

"Anna?" he whispered, turning to me for confirmation.

"She helped me pull it all together."

"Milo. Malachi? Makai." His nostrils flared, revealing the true nature of his emotions.

I learned Mercer was serving time the week we'd visited Berkeley. If I had a crystal ball that granted my wishes, he'd be standing beside the others. But, I didn't and he wasn't.

"I never doubted it. Not even once. I never doubted you. I never doubted us. I never doubted the love we shared, no matter how fucking complicated it was. I'm a giver, Choc. I give and I give and I give and I give.

"That's my job. That's what I was born to do. That's what makes me feel good in here," he exclaimed, pointing to his chest. "When something is given to a giver, you don't know what that shit means. What it does. Nobody has ever given me a fucking thing. I wouldn't let them. But you have been giving and giving since the night I met you, Choc.

"You've given me life. You've given me your heart. You've given me your body. You've given me your time and attention. You've given me your trust. You've given me your career. You've given me your future. You've given me your hand.

"You've given me the greatest gift a man could ever ask for. A child. A daughter, nonetheless. And I thought that was the end of the giving, but you... you just had to give me a little more, huh?"

Smiling, I lifted a hand to swipe the tear that had yet to fall. "And I won't stop giving until I take my last breath. No one deserves it more than you, Mister."

Chem leaned down, taking my lips into my mouth as he gripped my butt through the linen dress I wore. I melted against him, fitting perfectly in his contours. Our puzzle was far from finished, but it was coming along nicely and I was enjoying the process.

"Hey! It's not that time yet. You have to actually get married before you can kiss the bride."

Chuckling, we pulled ourselves apart and ran toward the others. I grabbed the beautiful bouquet Rhea had spent two days making and took my place in front of the man I loved. Peering in those dark eyes, I prayed I never spent another day without him.

The end

NEXT...

The hunted become the hunters...

I twirled the massive diamond around my finger, watching as dirt was dumped onto Richie's casket. Every face was dry, void of emotion. His children had all come to terms with his death. Burying him was the finality they needed to properly grieve. It had taken months for them to get to this point, but it was painful progress that was necessary.

His casket was beautiful. It was black with a glossy coat and precious finishings. They'd spared no expense laying him to rest.

The magnitude of his absence left me wishing I would've known him longer, better. The way he was remembered left a smile on my face each time he was the topic of conversation. Chemistry would never meet her grandfather. That toyed with her father's emotions.

Without a doubt, he would've loved her just as much

475

as he loved the others. According to Chem, he'd tried for years to have a second son but failed miserably. It seemed as though his son was on the same path.

With any luck, when we decided to have another child, his duty would be fulfilled. Until then, we were crossing our fingers and hoping it didn't take seven pregnancies to determine he was ineligible.

"Egypt." Chem's voice startled me. Wrapped up in my own head, I was unaware everyone had begun to disperse.

"Where's Chemistry?" I asked, unable to see where she'd gone.

"With Rhea, they're going to head back to the house."

On the compound, everyone had a home of their own. Rhea frequented ours as she was Chemistry's primary caretaker. She relieved her father and I at eight every morning and didn't relinquish control until after dinner.

She'd spoiled our girl rotten and I loved watching every bit of it. Rhea was her favorite person. She was Rhea's favorite girl. She saved her from the darkness the death of Richie had left at her doorstep. She gave her something to do so grief wouldn't swallow her whole.

We piled into the truck with Aden at the wheel. After a few weeks, he'd made it safely and had been our driver ever since. Familiar faces made the experience less daunting and much more comfortable. St. Catana was incredible. I didn't have a complaint.

"Then, where are we headed?" I asked, noticing we were not headed in the direction of our home.

Richie was buried within the walls of the compound, at the very end where Rhea would also be laid to rest when her time came.

"To see Rather."

"It's not Thursday."

Chem was committed to his treatment. After revealing his condition, I made sure of it. He didn't skip a session. And instead of once a month, as he'd gone back to the States. He was at her home for weekly visits, keeping his mind sharp and his thoughts in order.

"It's not me that's going to see Rather, Egypt. It's you. And not for a therapy session."

A lump lodged itself in my throat. The truck stopped and the door swung open. Though things were moving relatively slowly, I felt like I'd been ambushed. My stomach knotted. It coiled. It curled. It flipped. Over and over and over.

I grabbed hold of Chem's hand as we reached her front door. I'd heard of the things Rather had done and the limits she'd go to extract every bit of information her clients were holding onto. I'd known for a while this day was coming, but I still hadn't accepted my fate. Even with it staring in my face, I wasn't ready.

"Chem—wait."

He paused, turning around until we were face to face. I rested my palms against his cheeks, hoping to regulate my breathing and steady my heartbeat. He was the calm to my storm but not even he could calm me.

"Egypt, I love you with every fiber in my being. But, beyond this point, I cannot save you. You have to save yourself. What happens to you after I leave is solely up to you. You have information. We need that information. There's only one person who's qualified for this job. Don't fuck her over and this will be a breeze. But, if you're withholding anything, she'll know. And things will get ugly for us all. I'll be waiting to nurse you back to health, but I cannot dictate how Rather handles her business."

As he concluded, the front door opened. Rather, still dressed in black, stood behind it without as much as a grin on her face. She tilted her head, requesting my presence at once.

"Goodbye, Chem."

Seeing The Therapist under these circumstances jogged my memory, rapidly. Before I stepped foot inside her home, I began to vomit at the mouth. Her chambers were a place I never wanted to visit. If intel is what would save me, then it was intel they'd receive.

"The supervising agent on the case is named Jack..."

The Therapist... **Summer 2024**

HUFFINGTON NEWS

Join over 11,000 honorary Huffington residents for monthly broadcasts delivered right to their preferred devices.

Broadcasts include but aren't limited to:

- A beautiful monthly newsletter detailing everything happening in Huffington
- Extensive snippets of upcoming projects (sneak peeks)
- Release day reminders that include links (to remove the guest work from searching for books on Amazon/Ghuffington.com)
- First to hear about surprise releases
- Exclusive discounts + offers for Huffington residents
- A monthly wrap-up detailing everything that has happened in Huffington since the release of the Huffington Newsletter

Ready to become a resident?

MORE FROM GREY HUFFINGTON

Find the entire collection of Grey Huffington titles below. Titles in the catalog are available in eBook (amazon.com, + ghuffington.com), paperback (ghuffington.com), or audiobook (audible + ghuffington.com) formats.

Syx + the City
Syx + the City 2
Syx Thirty Seven
Syxth Giving
Syx Whole Weeks

Wilde + Reckless
Wilde + Relentless
Wilde + Restless

Mr. Intentional
Unearth Me

The Sweetest Revenge
The Sweetest Redemption

Half + Half
The Emancipation of Emoree

Sleigh
Sleigh Squared

The Gifted
Memo
Give her Love. Give her Flowers.

Unbreak Me
Uncover Me

As we Learn
As we Love

Just Wanna Mean the Most to You
Sensitivity
10,000 Hours
Darke Hearts
muse.

Softly
Peace + Quiet
Press Rewind
Jagged Edges
My Person

The Realm of Riot Thimble
Whose Love Story is it Anyway?
Unhand Me

Home*
Blues*
31st*
Now That We're Here.*

Then Let's Fuck About It*
Giving Thanks

A Month of Sundays Ep 1
A Month of Sundays Ep 2
A Month of Sundays Ep 3
Dinner at Ever + Luca's
Saylah
The Mayor's Ball
Elm

THE EINSENBERG EFFECT
Luca
Lyric
Ever*
Laike
Baisleigh*
Liam

THE DOMINO EFFECT
Ledge

Halo*
Lawe
Kleuless*

BERKELEY BRED
Malachi
Anna*
Milo
Makai
Glacier*
Mercer
Vallei*

THE GREY LIST
Chemistry
"The Chemist"
Egypt
Rather
"The Therapist"
Priest
Rugger
"The Huntress"
Psalms
Roulette
"The Madam"
Israel
Rome
"The Ballerina"
Saint

—

* signifies the publication is available EXCLUSIVELY on ghuffington.com.

—

Prefer Audiobooks?

Did you know **there's a library FULL of audiobooks on ghuffington.com** for the lovers who listen?

Audiobooks Available (**exclusively on GHuffington.com**)

Egypt
Ever
Baisleigh
Halo
Kleuless
Anna
Glacier
Vallei
Elm.
And more